FROM THE EARTH TO THE MOON
AROUND THE MOON

FROM THE EARTH TO THE MOON
AROUND THE MOON

Jules Verne

with an introduction and notes
by R. G. A. Dolby

WORDSWORTH EDITIONS

For my husband
Anthony John Ranson
with love from your wife, the publisher
Eternally grateful for your unconditional love, not just for me but for our children Simon, Andrew and Nichola Trayler

1

Readers interested in other titles from Wordsworth Editions are invited to visit our website at www.wordsworth-editions.com

For our latest list and a full mail-order service contact
Bibliophile Books, Unit 5 Datapoint,
South Crescent, London E16 4TL
Tel: +44 020 74 74 24 74
Fax: +44 020 74 74 85 89
orders@bibliophilebooks.com
www.bibliophilebooks.com

This edition published 2011 by
Wordsworth Editions Limited
8B East Street, Ware,
Hertfordshire SG12 9HJ

ISBN 978 1 84022 670 6

Typeset in Great Britain by Roperford Editorial
Printed by Clays Ltd, St Ives plc

CONTENTS

INTRODUCTION

Jules Verne's anticipation of mankind's first venture into space in the two novels, *From the Earth to the Moon* (*FETM*) and *Around the Moon* (*AM*), transformed the entire culture of space travel, turning an impossible dream into a believable technological adventure and changing space fiction from marginal literary whimsy into a growing enthusiasm in popular culture. After Verne, stories, pictures and films could plausibly be set in space, while a handful of scientifically skilled Verne enthusiasts worked at turning the dream into reality.

It is only natural to suppose that since it was *his* story which triggered this major cultural change, Verne, too, must have believed in the achievability of space travel, and that it was his *own* dream that he was working out and popularising. However, Verne did *not* actually think that men could be fired from a cannon all the way to the moon. He was playing a literary trick. He had learned from Edgar Allan Poe how to make the fantastic seem believable, and used Poe's techniques to fool his readers into thinking that in the modern technological age, such a voyage was at last possible. His literary conjuring tricks of misdirection made it difficult for readers to notice crucial weaknesses. Many of them bought into the dream of space travel and looked forward to man landing on the moon and the planets in the coming space age.

Verne spelled out the scientific knowledge that would bring about this dream. More technically informed readers soon realised that there were weaknesses in Verne's story. But having been ensnared by the possibility of space travel, rather than turn away from it, they looked for ways to overcome the difficulties. One early idea was to make the cannon with a very much longer barrel, so that the crushing force of firing did not kill the astronauts. Eventually, Verne enthusiasts found the key to a more practical solution – to replace his giant cannon by rockets. A century after Verne's stories were first published, human beings actually reached the moon.

Jules Verne

Born into a provincial bourgeois family, Jules Gabriel Verne (1828–1905) spent the first three decades of his life ineffectually trying to escape his cultural roots, until, successful at last as a novelist, he finally returned to them. He had found a way in which copious research, careful planning and industrious writing habits could support an affluent middle-class life style.

The son of a successful lawyer in Nantes, Jules attempted to run away to sea aged twelve, but his father managed to retrieve him just after the ship had left the harbour. Later, he dutifully trained as a lawyer in Paris, but on qualifying, immediately switched to writing plays and helping run a theatre, though with limited success. He made friendships in literary and scientific circles. As his hopes of a lasting career in the theatre faded, he wrote short stories, some of them about balloons. At the end of 1856, he married Honorine de Viane, a moderately well-off widow with two children. Around the same time, with his father's help, he took up stock-broking, with minimal success in the short period he worked at it.

His literary projects continued. They included a draft novel of the future, *Paris in the Twentieth Century*, the later 1863 version of which was rejected by his publisher and published only in 1994. Then, in 1862, he approached the publisher Jules Hetzel, offering him one of his balloon stories, partly inspired by Poe's 'The Balloon Hoax'. Hetzel rejected it, but suggested to Verne how it might be rewritten. The full-length novel, *Five Weeks in a Balloon*, was published in 1863, and Verne signed a contract to write more such stories at the rate of three (later two) a year. Verne, who had been struggling for so long to consolidate a writing career, put all his effort into fulfilling the contract with Hetzel. Success and financial security came quite quickly. *Journey to the Centre of the Earth* (1864) and *From the Earth to the Moon* (1865) continued the long series of novels that came to be known as *Les Voyages Extraordinaires.* With Hetzel's editorial guidance, he developed a writing formula based on the early novels. His skill was to turn the escapist dreams of his youthful readers into believable travel adventures in which heroes used their scientific and technological knowledge to make careful preparations when they could, and to show great resourcefulness when they could not. Verne's technique also included packing the stories with scientific and technical information about the unusual modes of travel used and about the regions through which the characters travelled.

Verne moved from Paris to Amiens in 1872. He became wealthy with the sustained success of the stage play adaptation of *Around the World in Eighty Days* (book 1873; play 1874), and spent some of his money on larger houses and more luxurious yachts. One crisis in the bourgeois lifestyle of his mature years came in 1886 when his mentally disturbed nephew, Gaston, asked him for money, and, when refused, shot and lamed him.

The believability of space travel stories before Verne

Before Verne, modern science had revealed that although the moon and the planets were comparable in size to the Earth,[1] and therefore potentially habitable, they were also immense distances away and therefore inaccessible. The whimsy of imagining a meeting with inhabitants of the moon (Verne called them Selenites)[2] or more distant planets could only be told as unbelievable fantasy. In Chapter 2 of *FETM*, Verne used Barbicane's speech to sketch a history of earlier stories of travel to the moon. The history ends with an account of Edgar Allan Poe's 'The Unparalleled Adventure of One Hans Pfaall' (1835). Poe's writing, including this story, was an important resource for Verne. Verne's own moon voyage was partly modelled on the way Poe turned an outrageous tale into a plausible lie.

Poe's story is narrated by Hans Pfaall, an improvident Dutch bellows maker who decides to escape his creditors by flying up to the moon in a specially designed balloon. The story mixes black humour with science and scholarship. Pfaall's departure and initial ascent accidentally causes the death of his creditors and then of his animals, several times also putting his own life in danger. Along with extreme adventure, Pfaall's narrative is full of arguments and evidence to show why his balloon trip should succeed. He refers to learned astronomers in support of his claim that although the atmosphere gets less dense as we go higher, there is air as high as the moon and beyond. His balloon is filled with a newly made ultra-light gas enabling it to float in the thinnest air. Pfaall has also developed a powerful bellows system to compress the thin air into a breathable supply (except, of course, when he is asleep). The story is also packed with detailed calculations, descriptions of what the Earth looks like from great heights, and accounts of frightening events such as passing meteorites. The story breaks off when Pfaall reaches the moon.

How Verne tricked his readers into finding space travel believable

FETM is also full of black humour, this time centred on the exaggerated characters of a group of American warmongers who are dedicated to developing ever larger and more destructive cannons. J. T. Maston, for example, is introduced in chapter 1 of *FETM* as the inventor of a formidable mortar, a single shot of which killed a record-breaking 337 people. Admittedly that was when it burst, on its trial shot! These men want to accomplish even more, even though the American Civil War has just ended. Verne, like Poe, used such comic effects to draw readers into the story and such dramatic events to sustain interest.

Verne, again like Poe, packed the story with scientific information and calculations – far more than is customary in adventure stories. The main difference between the two authors is that (except in poor translations which mix up measurement scales) Verne's figures were generally in accord with the science of his day. It seems that while Poe's story is not scientifically feasible, Verne's story is. Well, no, it isn't, and never was, not even in terms of the science of Verne's day. By applying and improving on Poe's tricks to make the fantastic believable, Verne displayed his skill as a literary illusionist.

Verne's first illusory technique was a form of 'blinding them with science'. He provided careful descriptions of how the over-sized machines were made and calculations showing how they worked in order to persuade the reader that the events of the story are possible. Readers of Verne's story, no matter how much, or how little, they knew about such matters previously, would find that as they ploughed through the vast quantities of information and argument provided, their critical faculties were, at some point, overwhelmed and they were persuaded to take the rest of the claims on trust. In addition, where Poe had added a few scholarly references to his story, as if they would help the reader make a start in checking out the text, Verne included many real scientific authorities, blending their accomplishments with those of his fictional characters.

After talking his moon story through with his scientific friends, Verne may well have convinced himself that a projectile fired from a powerful enough cannon could indeed reach the moon. But that was not why he spelled out the underlying science. The descriptions and calculations are quite tedious, at least for someone wanting to read an adventure story. His literary conjuring trick was to ensure that his readers had ceased checking long before the weak spots became apparent.

A second misdirection by Verne is to draw our attention away from the fact that while the initial calculations consider an unmanned projectile, the project is later modified to carry passengers, as if that makes no significant difference. But, of course, it does. The shock of being fired out of a giant cannon should be survivable. In fact, the astronauts would be crushed to death by the momentary force of acceleration as the cannon fired. There would be a similar unsurvivable deceleration if the capsule had impacted at full speed into the moon or, as it turns out in *AM*, when crash landing on Earth. In chapters 21 and 23 of *FETM*, we read how Barbicane develops a way to reduce the shock of firing, in which the interior of the projectile sits on a disk suspended over three feet of water. As the cannon fires, the inner cabin presses down and squeezes water out of the projectile, so reducing the shock for the occupants. This, too is misdirection, for no hint is given to the reader that the water cushion is quite incapable of reducing the shock sufficiently.

Another misdirection surrounds the character, Captain Nicholl, who opposes the whole idea of firing a cannon at the moon. He offers criticisms, some of which are ridiculed. The reader naturally sees Nicholl as one of several comically exaggerated characters and initially he seems full of wrong-headed obsessions. Our attention is directed away from the possibility that he might have effective objections along with his sillier ones. For example, an aluminium-encased projectile if fired at 12,000 yards per second (and lacking the ceramic shielding that enables modern real-life space capsules to survive re-entry), would indeed overheat, perhaps as it reached the mouth of the cannon, and certainly long before it had risen through the Earth's dense lower atmosphere.

By his development of Poe's literary techniques, and by his skill at directing readers' attention away from scientific weaknesses in the story, then, Verne successfully persuaded his original readers that a horrific military marvel of the industrial age could be turned into a mode of travel to the moon.

Verne's use of Poe's 'Hans Pfaall' as a literary model continued in the second novel, *AM*. Poe and Verne both used scientific detail and technical descriptions of unprecedented dramatic incidents to maximise believability. Verne's protagonists draw upon their scientific skills and a vast range of packed supplies to manage the predictable difficulties (such as regulating their oxygen supply) and unexpected crises (such as the nearby explosion of fiery meteors) of surviving in deep space. When worried that their space capsule will miss its target, they attempt to redirect it by using rockets, to little effect; eventually it falls back to Earth. As they orbit the moon, they observe it more closely than any observer on Earth. What they see is not Verne's imaginative invention but a detailed description carefully tied into the recent history of moon observations from the Earth.[3] The Earth is in darkness when Verne's travellers look back at it, and the far side of the moon is also in darkness as they pass around. The lack of information about these famously unknown views, oddly, makes the story more plausible. In a real voyage you can't expect to see everything.

Verne kick-started the popular market for space fiction, which grew into an endless succession of technologically plausible adventures. However, as I argue in the next section, few subsequent authors felt the need to return to such detailed scientific exposition as Verne's in their own tales.

After Verne, space travel became a story form in which believability was taken for granted

Within a few years of publication, new readers of *FETM* and *AM* no longer experienced the initial shock of the fantastic being made believable. They belonged to a world already persuaded that space travel was possible in our industrial age and that it would eventually happen. When Schiaparelli reported seeing straight channels (mistranslated as 'canals') on Mars when it was exceptionally close to the Earth in 1877, speculation grew that this might be evidence of intelligent alien canal-building life. Stories of space travel took off in an explosion of popular enthusiasm. Verne could not join in without breaking his own story conventions. His requirement of scientific believability had not even allowed him to land his astronauts on the moon. He did not have a realistic mechanism for a soft moon landing, or a plausible way to send a useful message back to Earth.

Verne's 'scientific' demonstration of the feasibility of space travel was taken for granted in the stories of later authors. The change is illustrated by a brief comparison of Verne's moon story with two of H. G. Wells's scientific romances, *War of the Worlds* (1898) and *First Men in the Moon* (1901).

When, in *War of the Worlds*, Wells fantasised that the more highly evolved and more technologically advanced Martians, who built Schiaparelli's canals, might wish to leave their dying planet and colonise the Earth, he had them employ Verne's scientifically plausible form of interplanetary space travel: the invading capsules were fired from Mars by a giant cannon. But as the narrator can only witness their departure from the Earth, Wells had no need to spell out the details.

In *First Men in the Moon*, as in his other scientific romances, Wells treated believability in a different way from Verne. He had already developed a technique of permitting himself one fantastic 'what-if?' postulate, and then working out its consequences as realistically as possible. As Wells later explained, although anyone can have outlandish fantasies, nothing remains interesting if anything may happen. 'The thing which makes such imaginations interesting is their translation into commonplace terms and the rigid exclusion of other marvels from the story.'[4] In Wells's moon story, he postulates, *what if* there is intelligent life on the moon and a pair of humans discover a way of getting there? (This is the only 'what-if?' conjecture of *First Men in the Moon*.) Wells adopted the far-fetched idea of space travel using anti-gravity, already a feature of the Mars stories of some of his contemporaries. Wells explained it in terms of the gravity-screening material, Cavorite.[5] This was part of the initial fantastic conjecture. The challenge for Wells, as he saw it, was to make the *consequences* of that fantastic supposition believable. His characters are able to arrive on the moon without too many difficulties and get down to the core adventure of making contact with Selenites. Nevertheless, to be realistic and believable, Wells's characters had to face similar problems to those of Verne when travelling through the vacuum of space. The narrator, Bedford, mentions Verne's story to his associate, the scientist, Cavor, as they discuss how it is to be done. But, we learn, 'Cavor was not a reader of fiction.'[6]

Wells later referred to his literary relationship to Verne. 'His work dealt almost always with actual possibilities of invention and discovery, and he made some remarkable forecasts. Many of his inventions have "come true". But these stories of mine collected here do not pretend to deal with possible things: they are exercises of the imagination in a quite different field.'[7]

In old age, Verne commented on the contrast between his own novel and Wells's: 'I do not see the possibility of comparison between his work and mine. . . . I make use of physics. He invents. I go to the moon in a cannon-ball, discharged from a cannon. There is no invention. He goes to Mars (sic) in an airship, which he constructs of a metal which does away with the law of gravitation. That is all very well, but show me this metal. Let him produce it.'[8]

Although Verne had not been writing about the future, that is very soon what his fans remembered him doing. Verne carefully constructed most of his novels as documented reports of what had just happened – for that would be the most believable. Stories set in the future had been common enough since the mid-eighteenth century, but they were regarded as mere speculation. Verne did not know how to make stories of the future believable, for who knows what will happen next? It was his readers who very quickly took to saying that Verne was writing about the future, supposing that technology, at least, will develop in a predictable way.

Wells succeeded in domesticating the future, after a fashion, by fantasising a machine that could travel through time in a controlled way with *The Time Machine* (1895). After Wells, science fiction writers quickly built up a collective vision of future history within which to set their stories. This science fictional future was, within the genre, accepted as believable.

My analysis, in summary, is that Jules Verne is important in the rise of space fiction (and other science fiction), not simply because he pioneered such stories, but much more because by making such stories believable, he created cultural enthusiasms which other writers could exploit. The believability of the later stories did not have to come from internal evidence and arguments, for it was in the common context, created in part by Verne.

Verne and the imagery of space travel in popular culture

Once Verne had made space travel believable, the notion could spread easily through popular culture, far beyond new books and short stories. People wanted images of space travel to carry in their minds. One early source was the first illustrated edition of *FETM* (1872), which gave visual form to Verne's story, and whose iconic images have been reproduced in this volume. Although the 1872 illustrations are faithful to Verne's text, one of them illustrates a motivating but unscientific speech by Michel Ardan in which he speaks of a future with 'trains of projectiles . . . in which the journey from the earth to the moon may be comfortably made' (see page 135). The accompanying engraving of a space train (presumably authorised by Verne) is an impossible technological fantasy: the lead projectile of the train has a smoking chimney, there is a coal bunker wagon and flags stream from the last carriage. But as people forgot the joke, they continued to enjoy the symbolism of the picture. It has become one of the most widely used early images of space travel.

Jacques Offenbach initiated and wrote the music for an operetta 'Le voyage dans la lune' (1875), loosely inspired by Verne's novel. The moon capsule is fired from a cannon and looks like a railway car. Among early films, *Le voyage dans la lune* by Georges Méliès (1902) used film trickery to enhance a story very similar to the earlier operetta. Because these visualisations had no interest in returning to the issue of believability, they were able to show the projectile landing on the moon and meeting the showgirls and (in the film) exploding Selenites who live there, before triumphally returning.

After Méliès, Verne's space travel story appeared frequently in movies (the best known were in Byron Haskin, *From the Earth to the Moon* 1958 and Don Sharp, *Jules Verne's Rocket to the Moon* 1967). Believability, or even internal consistency, has not been an issue in such films, perhaps because Verne's story was reduced to entertainment for young children.

Verne, the rise of rocketry and the conquest of space

Verne's *AM* uses rockets as a means of propulsion while in deep space. However, Verne thought that rockets could, at best, only produce minor changes in his space projectile's speed and direction. Priority in thinking through the possibilities of space rocketry goes to the Russian, Konstantin Tsiolkovsky (1857-1935). He was a deaf and somewhat eccentric school mathematics teacher who had been exposed to the religious cosmology of his teacher Nikolai Fedorov. (Fedorov wanted mankind to populate the planets.) Tsiolkovsky had read Verne in the 1870s, and was inspired by *FETM* and *AM*. Realising that the acceleration of firing a space projectile from a giant cannon would kill the passengers, he dreamed and schemed how to overcome such problems. His designs for space rockets led to fragmentary publications in the early twentieth century, followed by learned papers and science fiction stories, which became internationally known around 1920. Tsiolkovsky's vision of the conquest of space caught on. The best option for getting into space, he argued, would be to use multi-stage liquid-fuelled rockets. Once in orbit, we could construct an Earth-orbiting space station, then moving on to visit the moon and asteroids. Tsiolkovsky made the use of rockets in space travel believable. Unlike Verne's, most of his ideas can be, and have been, put into practice. His work is honoured by modern space scientists, especially in Russia. A large and especially obvious dark-floored crater on the far side of the moon now has his name. It is not far from Verne Crater.

The believability of Verne's space fiction and the modern reader

Edgar Allan Poe sought to intensify the impact of his stories by fooling the reader into thinking they were *actually* true. For Poe, a believable story could work as a hoax. Jules Verne, under Hetzel's guidance, sought to make his extraordinary voyages believable by persuading the reader that his stories *could be* true. H. G. Wells sought believability in his scientific romances by treating realistically a fantastic hypothesis: 'What if it *were* true?' Twentieth-century science fiction stories explore internally coherent realities in which numerous speculative ideas are all *assumed* to be true, taking advantage of the reader's familiarity with earlier stories of the same type, including those of Poe, Verne and Wells.

In the twenty-first century, we have become so accustomed to fantasy, especially in films, that believability is irrelevant to many (but not all) story types. Who would criticise a James Bond movie for being unbelievable? When modern readers pick up Verne's moon voyage novels, they have to come to terms with the vast amount of scientific and technical information. It looks like padding, when a pithy phrase of technobabble might have been enough. Just as Verne intended, the eyes of modern readers glaze over on reading yet more calculations or working through long descriptions of lunar terrain. However, modern readers are more likely to complain. We are easily bored. Furthermore, a century and a half after it was written, some of the science of Verne's day is now judged erroneous, no longer aiding believability.

We still read genres which strive for realism, cultivating believability. It would not do at all if, in a historical novel, full of inconsistency and implausibility, no resolution is offered until, at the very end, the main character wakes up, declaring 'That was all a dream . . . or was it?'

If *modern* readers wish to decide whether Verne's moon novels are believable, they might apply the following four criteria, involving the plot, the characters, descriptions, and way the story is linked to the known external world. Firstly, a believable story should allow the reader to work through any ambiguities and apparent contradictions to reconstruct a coherent view of what might 'really' have happened. Secondly, we prefer plausible characters whose actions come to make sense. Thirdly, we like descriptions of scenes and events in the story to be realistic, in the manner of informative and insightful reporting in the non-fictional world. And fourthly, we expect to be able to recognise connections between a realistic story and the world as we know it, even though the reading experience may lead us to rethink some of our previous attitudes and assumptions.

Plot: Verne's moon voyage is, like his stories generally, well paced and plotted. It tells of the realistic fulfilment of a wish in a way that overcomes challenges and brings triumphs. Many of us still dream of space travel and even though we can no longer be the first to reach the moon, we appreciate that Verne worked out how this might be done using the knowledge and resources of his own time. The plot develops Michel Ardan's insight that by joining the Baltimore Gun Club's project of firing a cannon at the moon, he can fulfil such a dream. Without his arrival on the scene, the projectile would have been unmanned. The combination of the ideas of Ardan and Barbicane drives the plot, which hangs together for the modern reader, just as it did in Victorian times.

Characters: It was probably not particularly important to Verne that his characters be fully believable, and little has changed since. Verne had, after all, set up *FETM* as a satirical black comedy. In his writing, he frequently used characters based on national and class stereotypes and he did that here. (That is why Verne often used English and American heroes – it is easier to recognise national stereotypes if they are of countries other than one's own.) With his background in comedy theatre, he wanted his characters to be instantly recognisable and capable of getting the story going without delay. When his plot needed conflict, he made Barbicane and Nicholl argue, quarrelling so violently that they challenge one another to a duel. When his plot needed the same pair to become part of a harmonious team of astronauts, Ardan is able, instantaneously, to persuade them to set aside their disagreements and join him in a 'no-return' expedition, with no expectation that any discoveries made on the voyage could be passed on to others. Adventure stories, then and now, don't have time to develop deep and complex characters, especially not in comedy adventures like *FETM*. In *AM* the three men settle into a new but harmonious relationship in which Ardan is well intentioned but often clumsy, asking endless questions to which Barbicane supplies well informed answers. Barbicane has changed from the timber merchant who became a cannon builder into an expert space navigator, with Nicholl now as his assistant. The five year gap between the publication of the two books made it easier for readers to tolerate the abrupt change in the relationship of the characters. So, although Verne was striving for believability, that quest did not extend to his characters.

Modern readers, noticing that these two novels have no women characters, sometimes wonder if this is a limitation in Verne. But in Verne's day, the male and female cultural domains overlapped less than they do now. It would have been inappropriate to have women in a club such as the Gun Club, or participating in an adventure as dangerous as being fired out of a cannon to the moon.

Descriptions: Verne's authentic and richly detailed descriptions still stimulate the imaginations of readers, enabling them to construct enjoyable and convincing mental pictures of what is happening. In this respect, his stories are as believable as they ever were. His ability to stimulate visualisation even works well in translation; only in weaker translations does his writing appear flat and laboured.[9]

When modern stories replace real science by technically nonsensical technobabble, it is crucial never to look at detailed descriptions too closely or the illusion of believability will be lost. That rarely happens with Verne's imagery, even for the modern reader.

Connections to the wider context: I have already argued that Verne did all he could to make the story more believable by using book knowledge to tie it into the wider cultural context of his readers, drawing copiously upon the learned works of science, history and geography that they might know or be able to consult. His richly allusive style made his better educated readers feel, with enjoyment, that they were reading about things they already knew – that these were new developments within the cultural milieu of familiar scholarship. (His style may also have motivated his younger readers to acquire greater learning which they could put to use in adventures like these.) But does the allusive technique spoil a text for later readers? There may be pleasure in the sudden recognition of contextual details you happen to know, but you cannot so easily build up a sense of solidarity with the author if you have to go to other books or to the internet to identify allusions to obscure details of a long-lost past.

The modern reader brings a century and a half of additional cultural baggage to reading Verne. His errors and weaknesses have become more obvious and his successes have been trivialised by our over-familiarity with his imitators. Although this shapes our expectations and attitudes, we should not judge his work by later developments that he could not have anticipated.

One widely known item of modern contextual knowledge really *must* be set aside before reading Verne. Many of us know a little about g-forces, and how they make a total nonsense of Verne's story. When the space shuttle carries astronauts into outer space, they feel the sustained acceleration as if they had trebled in weight (a g-force of 3). If the g-force were substantially greater, they would black out or even die. To gain enough speed to reach space when being fired from Verne's cannon, the required acceleration would be concentrated into a fraction of a second. The astronauts would momentarily be more than 20,000 times their normal weight!

In present-day popular culture, our imaginative and emotional involvement usually has a higher priority than believability. We are accustomed to having our emotions intensified by loud music in horror films, even though orchestras rarely turn out in support of mass murderers in real life. (Or is the noisy music from next door drowning out the cries from a wife-beating?) The scientific novelties in modern science fiction are rarely understood by the reader. They have become powerful and potentially dangerous technological magic. In spite of these cultural changes, Verne's tactic of overwhelming readers' critical faculties with a surfeit of science should be as effective as ever. For example, in chapter 4 of *AM*, he includes several of the equations with which Barbicane works out the path of the projectile. Most modern readers will react as Michel Ardan does, with total incomprehension.

But some modern readers, those who know more science, may find themselves facing added challenges. In Verne's day, it seemed safe to pack his stories with science because it was seen as a growing and well-consolidated pile of established knowledge. Since then, however, modern culture has undergone a series of scientific revolutions. What was once accepted as scientifically established has been reworked and some of it is later seen to be clearly false. The effects of scientific revolutions trickle down even to apparently theory-free observations.

For Verne, for example, it seemed trivially obvious that the astronauts would see a moon covered with volcanoes, most or all of them extinct. Verne did not know, indeed, could not know, that the moon's surface carries the scars of billions of years of meteor impacts. In chapter 12 of *AM*, Barbicane tells his companions the mystifying fact that the interior floors of moon craters, unlike volcanic craters on Earth, are generally lower than the land outside. He could not appreciate how simply this can be explained if moon craters are rings of rock splashed out from the holes made by giant meteor impacts. Similar meteor craters must have scarred the Earth as well, but were not obvious on our planet until we learned how to look for them because so many have been eroded away by weathering. In Verne's day, the Earth and the solar system were thought to be a few million years old, at most, leaving too little time for Earth's craters to disappear.

Similarly, modern scientifically literate readers will immediately notice that Verne was badly mistaken in *AM* about how gravity affects the projectile's occupants as it falls away from the Earth and around the moon. The way gravity is experienced in free-fall became obvious only after another scientific revolution, later backed up by the documented experiences of real-life astronauts. Verne had supposed that the projectile's occupants would experience a gradually diminishing pull of the Earth's gravity keeping them firmly on the floor of their spacecraft, until they approached the moon closely enough for its gravity to be the stronger. They would be weightless only at the transition point. At the beginning of the twentieth century, Einstein thought systematically about the experience of weight in a freely falling manned projectile and worked out the modern view in his theories of relativity. It is pleasing to speculate that Einstein might have read and puzzled over *AM* as a child, later realising that something was wrong with it.

For those who have some knowledge of modern science, judging the believability of Verne's science is not just a matter of recognising the science which has changed since his day, but also of identifying where he got the science of his own day wrong. For example, his spacemen open a small hatch from time to time to throw out rubbish (including the dead dog), losing more air than Verne supposes. As Verne explains, they can replace the oxygen but not the nitrogen, so the astronauts would end up breathing, and the gas lights would be burning, nearly pure oxygen. (Verne later describes the effects of this, from a different cause.)

Other parts of the science (such as the crushing forces of takeoff and landing and the over-heating of the aluminium projectile as it leaves the cannon) appear to be wrong because they were weak points in Verne's plot, of which he was well aware and needed to disguise. Working out systematically, however, whether Verne could have known that any particular part of his science was wrong is a game for scholars, and it is inappropriate to play at it any longer in an introduction to a popular edition.

The development of astronomy and space science, and especially the successful American moon landings, have added to the contextual believability of Verne's *FETM*. New, more powerful, telescopes were constructed in high regions in the Rockies, long after Verne had settled on Longs Peak as his favoured location for a new observatory. In chapter 11 of *FETM*, Verne discussed the relative merits of Texas and Florida as the place to build the giant cannon, deciding on the latter. NASA's main rocket firing site was indeed sited in Florida. When Verne described building the giant cannon, in chapters 13 to 16, he spelled out the industrial pollution, the despoliation of the countryside, the effect of the large-scale influx of workers and sightseers, and so on. His account has become even more believable because it plausibly anticipated the impact of setting up the NASA rocket firing site. In this respect, Verne's persuasive power has *increased* for modern readers. All this is echoed in the historical sensibility of popular culture. The images of Jules Verne, rockets, space travel and the moon landings were pulled together in earlier versions of the Space Mountain roller-coaster rides of Disneyland.

Conclusion

The central message of Jules Verne's *Voyages Extraordinaires* was that although the modern industrial world is not always pleasant, it has opened up new possibilities of escape. Empowered by scientific and technical knowledge, we can more easily move away from intractable local problems to new adventures in distant parts of the world – on a desert island, deep underground, or under the sea. And in *FETM* and *AM* we are told how we might reach new worlds beyond the Earth. In applying his central message to space travel, Jules Verne changed our world. His accomplishment was not to write a literary masterpiece but to force a new idea into popular consciousness. Inspired by Poe's literary hoaxes, Verne fooled the world into believing that travel to the moon and beyond is not an impossible dream but a practical possibility. Inspired by Verne, a myriad of writers took up variants of the idea, and space travel became a new myth for the industrial age. Within a century, the dream had been turned into reality. Its inspirational power then faded, as it began to look like a needless extravagance. But it hasn't gone away. One day, if we survive long enough, mankind will indeed live among the stars.

R. G. A. DOLBY

NOTES TO THE INTRODUCTION

1 Should it be 'earth' and 'moon' or 'Earth' and 'Moon'? Traditionally neither is capitalised, as is usually the case in the present translation of Verne's book. The convention in astronomy, however, is that 'Earth' is capitalised, signalling that it is the name of a planet like Mercury, Venus, Mars and so on (the present translation *also* capitalises Earth in a listing of the planets), and the Earth's unique moon is named 'the Moon'. In this introduction, only 'Earth' is capitalised.

2 According to the *Oxford English Dictionary*, the term 'Selenite' has been used since the seventeenth century to label the moon's possible inhabitants. Jules Verne and H. G. Wells brought it into wider use in early science fiction, but as the moon is now known not to have intelligent native inhabitants, it is once again rare.

3 I spent several happy minutes while preparing this introduction by following Verne's detailed observations of the moon with the 'Moon Globe HD' app on an Apple iPad. The experience of floating over the 'seas', mountains and craters named and described by Verne, seeing them in rather more detail than was possible for his favourite lunar map, increased the believability of his story immensely, even though it slowed its pace. You might like to try something similar.

4 From the H. G. Wells 'Preface' to the 1933 edition of his collected scientific romances.

5 When Cavorite panels shield the vessel from the gravitational pull of the Earth and the sun, it falls upwards towards the moon.

6 H. G. Wells, *First Men in the Moon*, (originally 1901), chapter 3.

7 From the H. G. Wells 'Preface' to the 1933 edition of his collected scientific romances.

8 Reported by R. H. Sherard, in 'Jules Verne Re-visited' *T.P.'s Weekly*, October 9, 1903.

9 The 1877 translation by T. H. Linklater, reproduced in the volume you are now reading, is widely regarded as the best from the Victorian period. It is full, fair and scientifically accurate.

FROM THE EARTH TO THE MOON

DE LA TERRE A LA

CONTENTS

CHAPTER ONE

The Gun Club

During the American War of Secession[1] a new and very influential club was formed in the city of Baltimore, Maryland. We all know with what rapidity the military instinct developed itself in this people of shipowners, merchants, and mechanics. Simple shopkeepers stepped over their counters transformed into captains, colonels, and generals, without having passed through the School of Application at West Point; nevertheless, they were soon equal in the art of war to their colleagues of the Old World, and, like them, obtained their victories at the cost of an immense expenditure of bullets, money, and men.

The main point in which the Americans were so much superior to the Europeans was the science of gunnery; not that their arms had attained a greater degree of perfection, but they were of unusual dimensions, and consequently reached distances until then unknown. As regards grazing, plunging, point-blank, or enfilading and side-firing, the English, French, and Prussians have nothing to learn; but their cannons, howitzers, and mortars are but pocket-pistols compared with the formidable engines of the American artillery.

Nor is this matter for surprise. The Yankees, the first mechanics in the world, are born engineers, as Italians are born musicians, and Germans metaphysicians. What is therefore more natural than to see them bring their audacious ingenuity to bear upon the science of gunnery? Hence these gigantic cannons, less useful than sewing-machines, but just as astonishing and yet more admired. We have seen in this respect the marvels of Parrot, of Dahlgren, and Rodman; Armstrong, Palliser, and Treuille de Beaulieu must bow before their transatlantic rivals.

Thus, in the terrible struggle between the North and South, the artillery played the great part. Each new invention was celebrated with enthusiasm by the newspapers of the Union, and, down to the smallest storekeeper, every American citizen devoted his time to the calculation of extraordinary trajectories.

When an American has an idea he looks out for a second American to share it. If there are three of them they elect a chairman and two secretaries. If four, they appoint a recorder, and the committee is in working order. If five, they convene a general meeting, and a club is formed. This is what happened in Baltimore. The first who invented a new cannon allied himself with the second, who cast it, and the third, who bored it. This was the nucleus of the Gun Club.[2] One month after its formation it counted 1,833 effective members, and 30,575 corresponding members.

One condition, *sine quâ non*, was required of each person desirous of joining the association; this condition was to have invented, or at least perfected, a cannon; if not a cannon, at any rate some sort of firearm. However, inventors of fifteen-shooters, revolving rifles, or sword-pistols, were not much thought of. Artillerists took precedence of such on every occasion.

'The amount of esteem which each obtains,' said, one day, one of the most learned orators of the Gun Club, 'is proportionate to the weight of his gun, and in direct ratio of the square of the ranges attained by his projectiles.' A social application, so to speak, of Newton's law of universal gravitation.

So soon as the Gun Club was established, it is easy to imagine what the inventive genius of the Americans would produce. Engines of war attained colossal proportions, and projectiles flew beyond their proper limits, much to the detriment of inoffensive spectators. All these inventions far surpassed the timid instruments of European artillery. Witness the following figures –

Formerly (in the good old time) the shot from a 36-pounder, at a distance of 300 feet, cut through 36 horses standing flank to flank and 68 men. This was but the infancy of science. Since that time projectiles have improved. Rodman's cannon, which sent a shot weighing half a ton to a distance of seven miles, would easily have cut through 150 horses and 300 men. At one time there was a question of making a solemn trial at the Gun Club. But even had the horses consented to the experiment, the men unfortunately could not be found.

Joking apart, the effect of these cannons was tremendous, and at each discharge the combatants fell like blades of grass before the scythe. Of what account beside such projectiles was the famous cannon-ball which, in 1587, at Coutras, put 25 men *hors de combat*, and that other which, in 1758, at Zorndorff, is reported to have killed 40 foot soldiers? Or, again, the Austrian cannon of Kesselsdorf, in 1742, each shot of which took the lives of 70 enemies? What was the extraordinary cannonading of Jena or Austerlitz which decided the fate of the battle? Something very different was seen during the War of Secession. At the battle of Gettysburg a conic projectile, fired from a rifled cannon, brought to the ground 173 Confederates; and at the passage of the Potomac a shot from Rodman's gun sent 215 southerners into a better world. Nor must we forget a formidable mortar invented by J. T. Maston, a distinguished member and perpetual secretary of the Gun Club, which attained yet more murderous results, for at its trial shot it killed 337 persons – by bursting.

What can be added to these figures, so eloquent in themselves? Nothing. So we must admit without contestation the following calculation by the statistician Pitcairn: dividing the sum total of the victims by the number of the members of the Gun Club, it was found that each of the latter had killed for his own account an average of 2,375 men and a fraction.

In presence of such results it is evident that the sole preoccupation of this learned society was the destruction of humanity from motives of philanthropy, and the perfecting of firearms considered as instruments of civilisation: an assembly of exterminating angels, otherwise the best fellows in the world.

It is but just to add that these Yankees, brave beyond a doubt, did not confine themselves to mere formulae, but risked their persons without hesitation. They counted amongst them officers of every grade, from lieutenants to generals, military men of all ages – those who were making their *débuts* in the career of arms, and those who had grown old in the service. Many remained upon the field of battle whose names figure in the book of honour of the Gun Club, and, of those who returned, many bore marks of their undaunted intrepidity. Crutches, wooden legs, cork arms, hooks instead of hands, india-rubber jaws, silver skulls, platinum noses – nothing was wanting to the collection; and the above-mentioned Pitcairn calculated that in the Gun Club there was not quite one arm to four persons, and only two legs to six.

But those valiant artillerists were not very particular on such points, and they were justly proud when despatches from the field of battle showed a number of victims ten times in excess of the number of projectiles used.

One day, however – sad and lamentable day! – peace was signed by the survivors of the war. The firing gradually ceased, mortars were silent, muzzled howitzers and cannons returned to their arsenals, shot and shell were piled up in the parks, bloody remembrances were wiped out, cotton trees flourished luxuriantly in the well-manured fields, and the garments of woe were laid aside with the griefs of their wearers, and the Gun Club relapsed into a state of profound inactivity.

Certain of the members, hard-working fellows, still applied themselves to abstruse calculations in the science of gunnery. They still dreamt of gigantic shells and incomparable shot. But without practical application theory soon loses its charm. So the club was deserted, the servants slept in the ante-rooms, the newspapers mildewed on the table, snores were heard to issue from the darker corners of the rooms, and the members of the Gun Club, formerly so noisy, but now reduced to silence by disastrous peace, resigned themselves to visions of Platonic artillery.

'This is dreadful,' said, one evening, bold Tom Hunter, carbonising his wooden legs in the smoking-room grate. 'Nothing to do! Nothing to hope for! What a dreadful existence! Where is the time when the cannon awoke us each morning with its welcome boom?'

'That time is no more,' said the sprightly Bilsby, stretching what remained of his arms. 'There was some fun to be had then! One could invent a howitzer, and, as soon as it was cast, run off and try it on the enemy, and return to the camp with a word of encouragement from Sherman, or a clasp of the hand from MacClellan. But now the generals have gone back to their stores, and, instead of cannon-balls, send off inoffensive bales of cotton. Alas! artillery is of no further account in America.'

'Yes, Bilsby,' said Colonel Blomsberry, 'these are cruel disappointments! We leave our accustomed habits, we learn the use of arms, we leave Baltimore for the fields of battle, we fight like heroes, and two or three years later we lose the fruit of so many fatigues, relapse into hateful inactivity, and may keep our hands in our pockets.'

Notwithstanding which statement, the valiant colonel would have found great difficulty in giving this latter proof of his inactivity; not from want of pockets, however.

'And no prospect of war,' said the famous J. T. Maston, scratching his gutta-percha skull with his iron hook, 'not a cloud in the horizon, and so much still to be done in the science of artillery! For instance, this very morning I completed the drawings, with plan, section, and elevation, of a mortar which will alter the whole theory of war.'

'You don't mean to say so!' said Tom Hunter, involuntarily thinking of the Hon. J. T. Maston's last attempt.

'It is quite true,' said the latter. 'But to what purpose all these studies, these difficulties overcome? I am working in pure waste, for the people of the New World seem to have made up their minds to live in peace, and our warlike *Tribune* is already prophesying a catastrophe from the scandalous increase of population.'

'Nevertheless, Maston,' replied Colonel Blomsberry, 'there is still fighting in Europe to maintain the principle of nationalities.'

'What then?'

'Why, we might be able to do something there, and if they would accept our services – '

'What are you thinking of?' cried Bilsby. 'Give foreigners the benefit of our science!'

'That would be better than doing nothing,' replied the colonel.

'No doubt,' said J. T. Maston, 'but unfortunately that expedient is not to be thought of.'

'Why not?' asked the colonel.

'Because in the Old World they have ideas about promotion quite contrary to our American notions. People do not believe it possible for a man to become a general until he has served as a sub-lieutenant, which is almost tantamount to asserting that one cannot be a good marksman without serving one's time in a cannon foundry, which is simply – '

'Bosh,' said Tom Hunter, whittling the arm of his chair with a large bowie-knife. 'And since matters have gone so far, it only remains for us to plant tobacco or refine spermaceti.'

'What!' cried J. T. Maston, in a stentorian voice, 'are we not to employ the last years of our existence in improving firearms? Are we to have no new opportunity of testing the range of our projectiles? Are we never again to light up the air with the flash of our cannon? Will no international difficulty arise, that we may declare war against some transatlantic power? Won't the French run down a single one of our steamers? Won't the English hang a few of our compatriots, in defiance of international law?'

'No, Maston,' replied Colonel Blomsberry. 'No such luck! None of those opportunities will arise, and if one did, we should not take advantage of it. American susceptibility is daily decreasing; we are degenerating into old women.'

'We are eating humble-pie,' said Bilsby.

'We are daily subjected to humiliations,' said Tom Hunter.

'It is but too true,' replied J. T. Maston, with renewed vehemence. 'We have a thousand reasons for fighting, yet we don't fight! We economise arms and legs for people who don't know what to do with them. Why, look here! Without seeking farther for a *casus belli*, did not North America formerly belong to the English?'

'Doubtless,' replied Tom Hunter, poking the fire savagely with the end of his crutch.

'Then,' continued J. T. Maston, 'why should not England, in its turn, belong to the Americans?'

'It would only be fair,' replied Colonel Blomsberry.

'Go and propose it to the President of the United States,' cried J. T. Maston, 'and see how he'll receive you.'

'He'd receive us badly enough,' grumbled Bilsby, through the four molars which the wars had left him.

'Bedad!' cried J. T. Maston, 'he need not count on my vote at the next election.'

'Nor on ours,' cried the warlike invalids with one voice.

'Meanwhile,' continued J. T. Maston, 'and to conclude, if I am not given an opportunity of trying my new mortar on a real battle-field, I shall send in my resignation to the Gun Club, and withdraw to the plains of the Arkansas.'

'We'll all follow you,' replied the interlocutors of the audacious J. T. Maston.

Such was the state of affairs. The feeling of discontent was becoming more and more general, and the club was threatened with early dissolution, but this catastrophe was averted by an unexpected event.

The very day following the above conversation, each member of the club received a circular to this effect.

> Baltimore, 3rd October
> The President of the Gun Club has the honour to inform his colleagues that he proposes to make a communication of great interest at the meeting of the 5th instant; he therefore begs that members will make a point of attending the said meeting, in answer to the present invitation.
>
> And remains, very cordially,
>
> IMPEY BARBICANE, P.G.C.

CHAPTER TWO

President Barbicane's communication

On the 5th of October, at eight o'clock in the evening, a compact crowd filled the rooms of the Gun Club, at 21, Union Square. All the members of the club living in Baltimore were present in compliance with their president's invitation. As for the corresponding members, special trains brought them by hundreds to the town, and notwithstanding the size of the great hall, was insufficient to contain this crowd of *savants* which filled up the adjoining rooms and passages, and even half the exterior courtyards. They were met by masses of the public pressing in through the gates, each trying to force his way to a front rank; all anxious to hear President Barbicane's important communication, pushing, shoving, and crushing each other with that liberty of action peculiar to crowds educated in ideas of self-government.

On that evening no stranger in Baltimore would have been able for any sum of money to penetrate into the great hall, which was specially reserved for resident and corresponding members. None others were admitted, and the notabilities, the magistrates and magnates of the city, had to mix with the crowd of citizens, eager to catch, if possible, some item of news from the great hall.

The immense hall presented a curious spectacle. The vast space was marvellously well suited to its purpose: high columns formed by cannons, superposed with mortars for their base, supported the elegant framework of the dome, itself a real lacework of wrought iron. Trophies of blunderbusses, matchlocks, arquebuses, rifles, and all kinds of ancient and modern firearms spread over the wall in picturesque arrangement. Flames of gas issued from a thousand revolvers grouped as lustres, while girandoles of pistols, and chandeliers of stands of guns, completed the splendid illumination. Models of cannons, specimens of bronze, targets riddled with bullets, plates of metal broken by the shot of the Gun Club, rammers and sponges, chaplets of shell, collars and projectiles, garlands of grapeshot – in a word all the weapons of the artillerists, surprised the eye by the tastefulness of their arrangement, and led one to believe that their destination was rather decorative than murderous.

In the place of honour, under a splendid glass case, might be seen a piece of the breach of a cannon, broken and twisted by the force of an explosion. This was the precious relic of J. T. Maston's gun.

At the extremity of the hall, the president and his four secretaries occupied a large daïs. A seat raised upon a sculptured base, represented a thirty-two-inch mortar, pointed at an angle of 90°, and suspended by the trunnions, so that the president could give it a backward and forward motion like a rocking-chair, which was most agreeable in the great heats. On the bureau, formed by an immense sheet of iron, supported by six carronades, lay an ink-bottle of most exquisite taste, made from a delicately-chiselled cannon-ball, and a detonating handbell, which went off when required with a report like a revolver. During vehement discussions, this new kind of bell could hardly make itself heard above the roars of this legion of excited artillerists.

In front of the bureau, benches placed in zigzag, like the circumvallations of an intrenchment, formed a succession of bastions and curtains where the members of the Gun Club were seated; and on this evening it might truly be said that the ramparts were fully manned. They knew the president too well to think that he would have assembled his colleagues without motives of the highest gravity.

Impey Barbicane[3] was a man of about forty; calm, cold, austere; of a character eminently serious and concentrated; as exact as a chronometer, of a temperament above proof, of immovable force of mind; not romantic, although adventuresome, but bringing practical ideas to bear upon the wildest undertakings; a true son of New England, a colonising northerner, a descendant of those

Roundheads who proved so fatal to the Stuarts, an implacable enemy to the southern gentlemen, those ancient cavaliers of the mother-country. In a word, a Yankee all over.

Barbicane had made a great fortune in the timber trade. Appointed Director of Artillery during the war, he had shown himself fertile in inventions. By the audacity of his conceptions, he contributed powerfully to the progress of that arm, and gave incomparable impulse to experimental researches.

He was a personage of middle height, possessing, by a rare exception in the Gun Club, all his members intact; his marked features seemed traced by the rule and square; and if it be true that a man's instincts are shown by his profile, Barbicane, in this respect, afforded the most perfect indications of energy, audacity, and self-possession.

At that moment he was seated immovable on his chair, mute, absorbed, with a preoccupied look beneath his tall hat – one of those black silk cylinders which seem screwed on to American heads.

His colleagues were talking noisily around him without attracting his attention; they asked each other questions; they made suppositions; they examined their president; and sought, but in vain, to work out the unknown quantity from his imperturbable countenance.

When eight o'clock had struck from the fulminating clock of the great hall, Barbicane rose suddenly, as though moved by a spring, and there was a general silence, while the speaker, in somewhat emphatic tones, began as follows: 'Worthy colleagues, for some time past a disastrous peace has plunged the members of the Gun Club in a state of deplorable inaction. After a few eventful happy years, we have been obliged to renounce our labours, and to come to a sudden halt in the path of progress. I do not fear to proclaim loudly that any war which would put arms into our hands would be welcome.'

'War for ever!' cried the impetuous J. T. Maston.

'Hear, hear!' echoed from all sides.

'But,' said Barbicane, 'war is impossible under present circumstances, and, notwithstanding the hopes of my honourable interrupter, long years will pass ere the thunder of our cannons will be again heard on the field of battle. We must make up our minds to this, and seek elsewhere food for our all-devouring energies.'

The meeting felt that the president was nearing the delicate point, and attention was redoubled.

'For some months, my worthy colleagues,' continued Barbicane, 'I have put the question to myself whether, whilst remaining within the limits of our speciality, we could not undertake some great experiment worthy of the nineteenth century, and whether the progress we have made in the art of gunnery would not enable us to carry such an experiment to a successful issue. I have studied deeply, worked and calculated, and from my studies the conviction has arisen that we ought to succeed in an undertaking which would appear impracticable in any other country. This project, carefully worked out, will form the subject of my communication. It is worthy of you, worthy of the reputation of the Gun Club, and cannot fail to make a stir in the world.'

'A great stir?' asked an enthusiastic artillerist.

'A great stir, in the true acceptation of the word,' replied Barbicane.

'Don't interrupt,' cried several voices.

'I therefore beg, worthy colleagues,' continued the president, 'that you will give me all your attention.'

A thrill of impatience ran through the assembly, and Barbicane, having rapidly pressed down his hat over his forehead, continued his speech in a calm voice.

'There is no one amongst you, worthy colleagues, who has not seen the moon, or, at least, heard about her; so you will not be astonished if I speak to you about the orb of night. It is, perhaps, reserved for us to be the discoverers of a new world. Follow me, assist me with all your power, and I will lead you to her conquest, and her name shall be added to the other thirty-six[4] states which form this great country of the Union.'

'Hurrah for the moon!' shouted the Gun Club, with one voice.

'The moon has been the subject of much study,' continued Barbicane. 'Her mass, her density, her weight, her volume, her constitution, her movements, her distance, the part she plays in the solar system, are all perfectly well defined; selenographic maps[5] have been prepared with equal, if not greater, minuteness than the terrestrial maps; photography has given us proofs of our satellite, of an incomparable beauty – in a word we know all about the moon that the mathematical sciences, astronomy, geology, and optics can teach us; but, up to the present time, no direct communication has ever been established with the luminary.'

This statement occasioned a general movement of interest and surprise amongst the audience.

'Allow me,' continued the speaker, 'to recall, in a few words, how certain enterprising minds – thanks to their vivid imagination! – claimed at various times to have penetrated the secrets of our satellite. In the seventeenth century a certain David Fabricius boasted that he had seen inhabitants in the moon. In 1649 a Frenchman, named Jean Baudouin, published a *Journey from the World to the Moon*, by Domingo Gonzalez, a Spanish adventurer. About the same time, Cyrano de Bergerac instituted that celebrated expedition which had so much success in France. Later on, another Frenchman (those people seem to take a great interest in the moon!), a certain Fontenelle, wrote the *Plurality of Worlds*, a masterpiece for his time; but the advance of science crushes even masterpieces! Towards 1835, a small work, translated from *The New York American*, related how Sir John Herschel – sent to the Cape of Good Hope to make certain astronomical observations – had, by means of a telescope perfected with an interior light, brought the moon to a distance of eighty yards. He then is stated to have seen distinctly caverns, in which dwelt hippopotami, green mountains fringed with golden lace, sheep with ivory horns, white deer, and men and women with membraned wings like bats. This book, written by an American named Locke, met with great success at first, but was soon discovered to be a scientific hoax, and the French were the first to laugh at it.'

'Laugh at an American?' cried J. T. Maston; 'that is a *casus belli*!'

'Do not alarm yourself, worthy friend! The French, before laughing, had been thoroughly duped by our countryman. To close this rapid sketch, I may add that a certain Hans Pfaall, of Rotterdam, travelling in a balloon, filled with an oxygen gas thirty-seven times lighter than hydrogen, reached the moon after a nineteen-days' journey. This journey, like the other attempts, was merely imaginary, being the work of a popular writer in America, a strange, contemplative genius. I refer to Poe.'[6]

'Hurrah for Edgar Poe!' cried the electrified assembly.

'I have done,' continued Barbicane, 'with these attempts, which I may call purely literary, and quite insufficient to establish any real communication with the Queen of the Night. However, I must add that some practical minds have endeavoured to establish such communication. A few years ago, a German mathematician proposed to send a commission of scientists into the steppes of Siberia. There, on the vast plains, immense geometrical figures were to be described by means of luminous reflectors; amongst others, the problem of the square of the hypothenuse, called by Frenchmen, the *pons asinorum*. "Every intelligent person must understand the scientific value of this figure. If there are any inhabitants in the moon they will reply by a similar figure; and, communication once established, it will be easy to create an alphabet, which will allow of intercourse with the inhabitants of the moon." Thus reasoned the German mathematician; but his project was not put into execution, and, up to the present time, no direct means of communication exists between the earth and its satellite. It is reserved for the practical genius of Americans to place themselves in communication with the sidereal world. The way to arrive at this is simple, easy, and certain, and will form the subject of my communication.'

A very tempest of exclamation here burst from the assembly; not one of the audience but was dominated and carried away by the words of the orator.

'Hear, hear! Silence!' was cried from every side.

When the agitation had subsided, Barbicane, in a grave tone of voice, continued his interrupted speech.

'You know,' said he, 'what progress the science of gunnery has made in the last few years, and to what degree of perfection firearms would have reached if the war had but continued. You are aware, also, that in a general way, the resisting power of cannon and the expansive power of gunpowder are unlimited. Acting upon this principle, I have asked myself whether, by means of a sufficient apparatus, manufactured under given conditions of resistance, it would not be possible to send a shot to the moon.'

At these words a cry of stupefaction burst from a thousand excited breasts, followed by a moment of silence like the calm before a storm. Then came a roll of thunder; but it was the thunder of applause, shouts, and clamours, which shook the hall to its foundations. The president tried to speak, but could not. For ten minutes, at least, he was unable to make himself heard.

'Let me finish,' said he calmly. 'I have examined the question in all its phases, and the result of my calculations is, that any projectile having an initial velocity of 12,000 yards per second, and fired in the direction of the moon, must necessarily reach her. I have, therefore, the honour to propose to you, worthy colleagues, to try this little experiment.'

CHAPTER THREE

Effect of Barbicane's communication

It is impossible to describe the effect produced by the hon. president's last words. The cries, the vociferations, the succession of cheers, Hip, hip, hurrahs! and other onomatopoeia in which the American language is so rich. The scene of disorder was utterly indescribable. Shouts were raised, hands clapped, and the very foundations were shaken by the stamping of many feet. Had all the firearms in the Museum of Artillery exploded at once, they would not have produced a greater volume of sound. Nor is this to be wondered at, for some cannoniers are almost as noisy as their cannons.

Barbicane remained calm in the midst of this enthusiastic clamour. Perhaps he wished to address some further words to his colleagues, for his gesticulations seemed to ask for silence, and his detonating hand-bell fired a perfect volley of shots, but was not even heard; and soon the president was snatched from his seat, carried in triumph, and passed from the shoulders of his faithful comrades into the arms of the not less excited crowd outside.

Nothing surprises an American. It has often been repeated that the word 'impossible' was not French, but this last word is evidently a *lapsus linguae*. In America all is easy, all is simple; and as regards mechanical difficulties, they are conquered before they arise. Between Barbicane's project and its realisation, no true Yankee would have allowed himself to admit the appearance of a difficulty. A thing was carried out as soon as decided upon.

The president's triumphal progress lasted till evening, when it became a real torch-light procession. Irishmen, Germans, Frenchmen, and Scotchmen – in fact all that heterogeneous assemblage which composes the population of Maryland – cheered in their mother-tongues, and their shouts and bravoes combined in an inexpressible burst of acclamation.

At that moment, as if fully understanding that the question was of her, the moon shone forth with serene magnificence, and eclipsed with her intense brilliancy all the surrounding illumination. All eyes were turned towards her lambent disc; some waved their hands to her, others called her by the most endearing names, some tried to measure her with the eye, whilst others shook their fists at her. From eight o'clock to midnight, an optician in Jones' Falls Street made his fortune by the sale of telescopes. The Queen of the Night was the object of as much attention as any fine lady. The Americans treated her as if she were their property. It seemed as though fair-haired Phoebe belonged to these audacious conquerors, and already formed part of the territory of the Union; and yet they were only proposing to take a shot at her, which was certainly a rather brutal way of entering into communication, even with a satellite, though greatly in vogue amongst civilised nations.

Midnight had struck, but the enthusiasm had not calmed down. It was equally shared by all classes of the population: the magistrate, the man of science, the merchant, the shopkeeper, the porter, intelligent men as well as fools, were subject to the same excitement. It was a question of a national undertaking: so the upper and lower parts of the town, the quays bathed by the waters of the Patapsco, and the ships floating in the docks, were crowded with men and women intoxicated with pleasure, gin, and whisky. Everyone was talking, speechifying, discussing, disputing, approving, applauding, from the gentleman reclining easily on the sofa of the bar-room before his glass of sherry-cobbler, to the waterman getting drunk upon knock-me-down[7] in the dark taverns of the Fells.

However, about two o'clock in the morning the agitation subsided. President Barbicane succeeded in reaching his home, literally dead with fatigue. Hercules could not have borne so much enthusiasm. The crowd gradually withdrew from the squares and the streets. The four lines of railway to Ohio, Susquehanna, Philadelphia, and Washington, which meet in Baltimore, carried back the visitors to the four corners of the United States, and the town relapsed into comparative tranquillity.

It would, however, be erroneous to think that during this memorable evening Baltimore alone was a prey to this agitation. The great towns of the Union – New York, Boston, Albany, Washington, Richmond, New Orleans, Charlestown, and Mobile – from Texas to Massachusetts, from Michigan to Florida – all had their share in the delirium. In fact, the 30,000 correspondents of the Gun Club were acquainted with the letter of the president, and were awaiting, with equal impatience, the famous communication of the 5th of October. So that, that very evening, in proportion as the words left the lips of the speaker, they were transmitted by the telegraph through all the States of the Union with a rapidity of 248,447 miles per second.[8] We may therefore say, with absolute certainty, that at the same instant the United States of America, ten times as large as France,[9] sent up one great shout, and that twenty-five millions of hearts inflated with pride, beat with the same pulsation.

The next day 1,500 papers – daily, weekly, fortnightly, and monthly – took up the question and examined it in its different bearings – physical, meteorological, economical, and moral – as well as in its relation to political preponderance and to civilisation. They discussed the question whether the moon was a completed world, and whether it would not undergo some further transformation. Was it like the earth at the time when the atmosphere did not exist? Of what nature and formation was the face invisible to the terrestrial spheroid?

Although it was as yet only a question of firing a shot at the Queen of the Night, all saw therein the commencement of a series of experiments, all hoped that one day America would penetrate the last secrets of this mysterious disc, and some were even afraid that its conquest might seriously disturb European equilibrium. Whilst discussing the project, not a single paper doubted its realisation.

The reviews, the pamphlets, the magazines, published by learned societies, literary or religious, pointed out its advantages; and the Society of Natural History of Boston, the American Society of Arts and Sciences of Albany, the Geographical and Statistical Society of New York, the American Philosophical Society of Philadelphia, the Smithsonian Institution of Washington – all sent a thousand letters of congratulation to the Gun Club, with immediate offers of service and of money.

We may therefore say that no proposal ever met with so large a number of admirers. There was no question whatever of hesitation, doubts, or uncertainties. As regards jokes, caricatures, or songs, which in Europe – especially in France – would have ridiculed the idea of sending a projectile to the moon, they would have done bad service to their authors: all the life-preservers in the world would have been powerless to protect them from general indignation. There are some things at which one dare not laugh in the New World.

So Impey Barbicane became, from that day, one of the greatest citizens of the United States, something like a Washington of science. And one very characteristic fact, amongst many others, shows to what pitch the respect of a nation for one man can be carried.

Some days after the famous meeting of the Gun Club, the manager of an English troupe advertised the play of *Much Ado about Nothing*, at the theatre of Baltimore; but the population of the town, who saw in this title an allusion to the projects of President Barbicane, broke into the theatre, tore up the seats, and obliged the unfortunate manager to alter his programme. He, like a sensible fellow, complied with the public wish, and replaced the above popular comedy by *As You Like It*; and during several weeks his receipts were phenomenal.

CHAPTER FOUR

Reply from the Cambridge Observatory

Meanwhile Barbicane did not lose a minute in the midst of these ovations. His first care was to assemble his colleagues in the committee-room of the Gun Club, where, after long discussion, it was resolved to consult the most learned astronomers upon the astronomical part of the undertaking, and when their reply was known, to discuss the mechanical means, so that nothing should be neglected to ensure the success of this great experiment.

A very precise note, containing special questions, was drawn up and addressed to the Observatory of Cambridge, Massachusetts. This town, which contains the first university of the United States, is justly celebrated for its astronomical college. There are collected *savants* of the highest merit. There is to be found the powerful telescope which enabled Bond to resolve the nebulae of Andromeda, and Clark to discover the satellite of Syrius.[10] This celebrated establishment fully justified in all respects the confidence of the Gun Club, and two days later the reply, so impatiently expected, reached the hands of President Barbicane.

It was couched in the following terms –

From the Director of the Cambridge University to
the President of the Gun Club at Baltimore

Cambridge, 7th October

Upon receipt of your favour of the 6th instant, addressed to the Cambridge Observatory in the name of the members of the Gun Club of Baltimore, our committee immediately met and resolved to reply as follows.

The questions asked are these:

(1st) Is it possible to send a projectile to the moon?

(2nd) What is the exact distance which separates the earth from its satellite?

(3rd) What would be the duration of the passage of a projectile to which a sufficient velocity had been imparted, and consequently at what moment ought the same to be despatched to reach the moon at a fixed spot?

(4th) At what precise moment will the moon be in the most favourable position to be reached by the projectile?

(5th) At what point of the sky must the cannon be aimed which is to despatch the projectile?

(6th) What position will the moon occupy in the sky at the moment the projectile is despatched?

As regards the first question – Is it possible to send a projectile to the moon?

Yes. It is possible to send a projectile to the moon, if you are able to endow the projectile with an initial velocity of 12,000 yards per second.

Calculations prove that this velocity is sufficient. As it leaves the earth the action of gravitation diminishes in inverse ratio of the square of the distances – that is to say, for a distance three times greater the action is nine times less. Consequently the weight of the projectile will decrease rapidly, until it becomes completely null at the moment when the attraction of the moon equals that of the earth, that is to say, at 47/52nds of the distance. The projectile will then have no further weight, and if it passes this point it will reach the moon by the mere effect of lunary attraction. The theoretical possibility of the experiment is thus absolutely proved. As regards its success, that will depend solely upon the power of the gun employed.

As regards the second question – What is the exact distance which separates the earth from its satellite?

The moon does not describe around the earth a circle, but an ellipse, of which our globe occupies one of the foci; hence the moon is sometimes nearer and sometimes farther from the earth, or, in astronomical terms, sometimes in her apogee and sometimes in her perigee.[11] The difference between her greatest and smallest distances is sufficiently

important not to be neglected in the present instance. When in her apogee the moon is 247,552 miles, and in her perigee only 218,657 miles distant, which makes a difference of 28,895 miles, or more than a ninth part of the whole distance. Consequently it is the distance of the moon when in her perigee which must serve as a basis of our calculations.

As regards the third question – What will be the duration of the passage of a projectile to which a sufficient initial velocity has been imparted, and, consequently, at what moment must it be despatched to reach the moon at a given point?

If the projectile retained indefinitely the initial velocity of 12,000 yards per second, with which it was endowed at its departure, it would only take about nine hours to reach its destination; but as this initial velocity will continually decrease, it results from calculations made that the projectile will take 300,000 seconds, or 83 hours and 20 minutes, to reach the point where the terrestrial and lunary attractions are equal, and from this point it will reach the moon in 50,000 seconds, or 13 hours, 53 minutes, and 20 seconds. It will therefore be necessary to despatch the projectile 97 hours, 13 minutes, and 20 seconds before the arrival of the moon at the point aimed at.

As to the fourth question – At what precise moment will the moon be in the most favourable position to be reached by the projectile?

It results from what has been above stated that you must choose not only the moment when the moon is in her perigee, but also the moment when she crosses the zenith,[12] which will again diminish the distance by a length equal to the radius of the earth, or 3,919 miles, so that the whole distance will be 214,976 miles. But although the moon reaches her perigee each month, she does not always at the same moment cross the zenith; she only unites these two conditions at long intervals. You must therefore wait for the coincidence of the passage to the perigee with that of the zenith. By a fortunate circumstance, on the 4th of December of next year the moon will unite these two conditions. At midnight she will be in perigee, that is at the shortest distance from the earth, and she will cross the zenith at the same time.

As regards the fifth question – At what point of the sky must we aim the cannon which is to discharge the projectile?

The preceding observations being admitted, the cannon must be aimed at the zenith of the spot so that its line of fire will be perpendicular to the plane of the horizon, and the projectile will escape more rapidly from the effects of gravitation. But in order that the moon should reach the zenith of a certain spot, it is necessary that that spot should not be situated in a higher latitude than the declination of the satellite – that is to say, it must be situated between 0° and 28° north or south. In any other spot the line of fire must necessarily be oblique, which would impair the success of the experiment.

To the sixth question – What place in the sky will the moon occupy at the moment the projectile is despatched?

At the moment the projectile is despatched into space, the moon, which advances each day 13° 10' 35'', must be distant from the point of the zenith four times that number, or say, 52° 42' 20'', which distance corresponds with the distance she will travel during the flight of the projectile. But as we must also take into account the deviation caused to the projectile by the rotatory movement of the earth, and as the projectile will only reach the moon after having deviated a distance equal to 16 radii of the earth – which, computed upon the orbit of the moon, make about 11° – we must add these 11° to those which represent the delay of the moon already mentioned, making, in round numbers, 64°. Thus, at the moment of firing, the line of sight drawn direct to the moon will form, with a perpendicular erected on the spot, an angle of 64°.

Such are the replies to the questions proposed to the Cambridge Observatory by the members of the Gun Club.

To recapitulate: –

(1st) The cannon must be established in a country within 0° and 28° of latitude north or south.

(2nd) It must be pointed at the zenith of the spot.

(3rd) The projectile must be endowed with an initial velocity of 12,000 yards per second.

(4th) It must be discharged on the 1st of December of next year, at 13 minutes and 20 seconds to 11 p.m.

(5th) It will reach the moon four days after its departure, on the 4th of December at midnight, at the moment when the moon crosses the zenith.

The members of the Gun Club should therefore lose no time in commencing the works necessary for such an undertaking, and should be ready to operate at the moment fixed; for if they allow the date of the 4th of December to pass, they will not again find the moon in the same conditions as to perigee and zenith for 18 years and 11 days.

The committee of the Cambridge Observatory place themselves entirely at the disposal of the Gun Club upon all questions of theoretical astronomy, and they beg to add herewith their congratulations to those of the whole of America.

For the Committee,

J. M. BELFAST
Director of the Cambridge Observatory

CHAPTER FIVE

The romance of the moon

An observer gifted with an infinitely penetrating sight, and placed at that unknown centre around which the world revolves, would have seen, at the chaotic period of the universe, myriads of atoms floating in space. But gradually, with the centuries, a change was produced: a law of attraction manifested itself which the floating atoms obeyed. These atoms chemically combined according to their affinities, became molecules, and formed the nebulous masses which are scattered over the depths of the sky.

Then these masses were animated by a movement of rotation around their central point. This centre, formed by inchoate molecules, revolved upon itself and became progressively condensed. According to the immutable law of mechanics, in proportion as its volume diminished by condensation its rotatory movement increased, and both these effects continuing there resulted one principal star, the centre of the nebulous agglomeration.

By careful attention, an observer would have perceived other molecules from the masses follow the example of the central star, condense in the same way – by a rotatory movement progressively increased – and gravitate round the same in the form of innumerable stars.

Thus were the nebulae formed, of which astronomy counts nearly 5,000.

Among these 5,000 nebulae there is one called the Milky Way, containing millions of stars, of which each has become the centre of a solar system.

Had the observer then specially examined, amongst these 18 millions of stars, one of the most modest and the least brilliant, a star of the fourth order, which is proudly called the Sun, all the phenomena to which the formation of the universe is due would have been successively accomplished before his eyes.

That sun, still in a gaseous state, and composed of floating molecules, might have been seen revolving on its axis to complete its work of concentration. This movement, true to the laws of mechanics, would have increased with the diminution of volume; and at a certain moment the centrifugal force would have conquered the centripetal force, which latter attracts molecules towards the centre.

Then another phenomenon would have happened before the observer's eyes, and the molecules situated on the plane of the equator, escaping like a stone from a broken sling, would have formed round the sun several concentric rings, like that of Saturn. In their turn these rings of cosmical matter, gaining a rotatory movement around the central mass, would have been broken up and decomposed into secondary nebulosities – that is to say, into planets.

If the observer had then concentrated his attention upon these planets, he would have seen them act in the same manner as the sun, and each give birth to one or more cosmical rings, which are the origin of those stars of inferior order which are called satellites.

Thus, in tracing back from the atom to the molecule, from the molecule to the nebulous agglomeration, from the nebulous agglomeration to the nebulae, from the nebulae to the principal star, from the principal star to the sun, from the sun to the planet, from the planet to the satellite, we have the whole series of transformations undergone by the celestial bodies since the first days of the world.

The sun seems lost in the immensity of the starry world, and yet it is connected by the present theories of science with the nebulae of the Milky Way. It is the centre of the world, and however diminutive it may appear in the midst of the ethereal regions, it is nevertheless enormous, for its size is 1,400,000 times that of the earth. Around it gravitate eight planets, which were drawn from its very entrails during the first epoch of creation. These are – to commence with the nearest – Mercury, Venus, the Earth, Mars, Jupiter, Saturn, Uranus, and Neptune. Farther, between Mars and Jupiter, there are other bodies of less size, the floating remnants, perhaps, of some star shattered into a thousand pieces, and of which the telescope has hitherto revealed ninety-seven. Some of these attendant bodies, which the sun maintains in their elliptical orbit by the universal law of gravitation, have satellites in their turn. Uranus has eight; Jupiter four; Neptune three, perhaps; and the Earth one.[13]

The latter is one of the most important in the solar system, and is called the Moon, which the audacious genius of the Americans aimed to conquer.

The Queen of the Night, by her comparative proximity and the frequently-renewed spectacle of her several phases, was the first to divide with the sun the attention of the inhabitants of the earth. But the sun is fatiguing to the glance, and the splendour of its light dazzles the eyes of its observers.

Fair-haired Phoebe, on the contrary, complacently shows herself, robed in her modest graces; she is soft to the eye and not ambitious, although she sometimes takes upon herself to eclipse her radiant brother Apollo, and is never eclipsed by him. The Mahomedans understood the gratitude which they owed to this faithful friend of the earth, and have regulated their months by her revolutions.

This chaste goddess was the object of particular adoration by the first inhabitants of the earth. The Egyptians called her Isis; the Phoenicians, Astarte; the Greeks adored her under the name of Phoebe, daughter of Latona and Jupiter, and they explained her eclipses by the mysterious visits of Diana to the beautiful Endymion. If we are to believe the legends of mythology, the Nemean lion ranged over the countries of the moon before his appearance upon earth; and the poet Agesianax, cited by Plutarch, celebrated in his verses the soft eyes, the charming nose and adorable mouth formed by the luminous parts of the beauteous Selene.

However the ancients may have understood the character and temperament, in a word the moral qualities of the moon from a mythological point of view, the most learned amongst them were very ignorant of selenography.

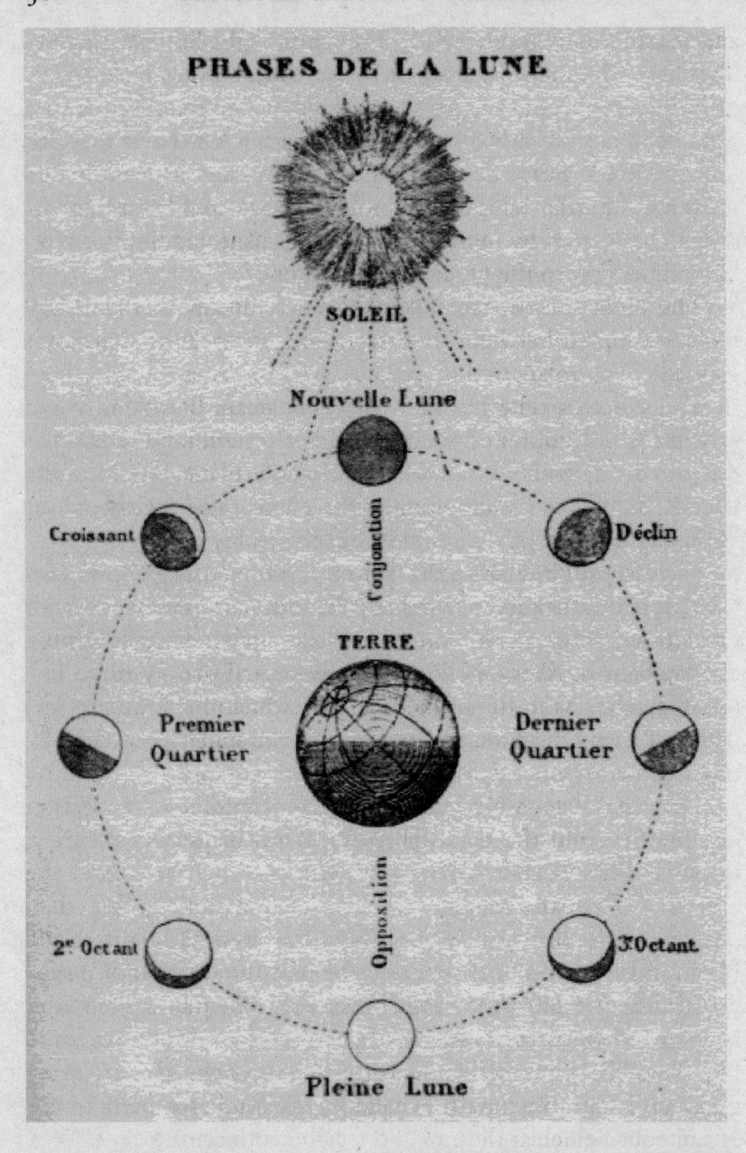

Many astronomers in earlier times discovered, it is true, certain particulars which science confirms today, although the Arcadians pretended that they had inhabited the earth at a time when the moon did not yet exist. Simplicius thought her immovable, and fixed to a dome of crystal; Tacitus thought her a fragment detached from the solar disc; and Clearchus, a disciple of Aristotle, called her a polished mirror in which the images of the ocean were reflected. Whilst others only saw in her a mass of vapour exhaled by the earth, or a globe half fire and half ice, revolving upon its own axis, some learned men, by sagacious observation, though unassisted by optical instruments, suspected most of the laws which govern the Queen of the Night.

Thus Thales of Miletus, 460 B.C., gave as his opinion that the moon borrowed her light from the sun. Aristarchus, of Samos, gave the true explanation of her phases. Cleomedes thought that she shone with a reflected light. The Chaldean, Berose, discovered that the duration of her movement of rotation was equal to that of her movement of revolution; and he explained in this way the fact that the moon always presents the same face. Lastly, Hipparchus, 200 B.C., discovered some inequality in the apparent movements of the earth's satellite.

These several observations were confirmed later, and were useful to new astronomers. Ptolemaeus, in the second century, and the Arab, Aboul Wefa, in the tenth, completed the observations of Hipparchus as to the inequalities which the moon undergoes when following the undulated line of her orbit under the action of the sun; then Copernicus, in the fifteenth century, and Tycho Brahe, in the sixteenth century, completely unfolded the system of the world and the part which the moon plays amongst the celestial bodies.

At this epoch the movements of the moon were pretty well determined, but little was known about her physical constitution. It was then that Galileo explained the phenomena of light produced in certain phases by the existence of mountains, to which he assigned an average height of 4,400 fathoms. Subsequently Hevelius, an astronomer from Dantzic, reduced the greatest altitudes to 2,600 fathoms; but his colleague, Riccioli, set them down at 7,000. Herschel, at the end of the eighteenth century, with the aid of a powerful telescope, reduced the above measures considerably. He fixed the highest mountains at 1,900 fathoms, and reduced the average of different altitudes to only 400 fathoms. But Herschel was still wrong, and it required the observations of

Schroeter, Louville, Halley, Nasmyth, Bianchini, Pastorf, Lohrman, Gruithuisen, and especially the patient studies of Messrs Beer and Moedler, to solve the question definitively. Thanks to these learned men, the altitude of the mountains of the moon is thoroughly well known today. Messrs Beer and Moedler have measured 1,905 summits, six of which are above 2,600 fathoms, and twenty-two above 2,400. Their highest summit rises to a height of 3,801 fathoms above the surface of the lunar disc.

At the same time the examination of the moon was completed; this luminary appeared covered with craters, and its essentially volcanic nature was confirmed by each successive observation.[14]

From the absence of refraction in the rays of the planet occulted by the moon, it was concluded that the latter could have no atmosphere. This absence of air necessitated absence of water. It was thus manifest that the Selenites,[15] to be able to live under these conditions, must be endowed with a special organisation and be very different from the inhabitants of the earth. At last, thanks to new inventions, more perfect instruments examined the moon without ceasing, and left not a single spot of her surface unexplored. Her diameter measures 2,500 miles; her surface is 1/13th part of the surface of the globe; her volume 1/49th part of the volume of the terrestrial spheroid; yet none of her secrets could escape the eyes of astronomers, and these clever *savants* carried their prodigious observations farther still.

Thus they observed that during the full moon the disc appeared in certain parts marked with white lines, and during the phases with black lines. By examining with yet greater precision they succeeded in discovering the exact nature of these lines. They are long and narrow furrows dug between parallel lines, generally terminating at the edge of the craters; they are from about 10 to 100 miles long, and 800 fathoms wide. Astronomers call them rifts, but are only able to give them a name. As to knowing whether these rifts are dry, the beds of ancient rivers or not, they could come to no satisfactory conclusion. The Americans hope one day or other to decide this question. They also hoped to reconnoitre that series of parallel ramparts discovered on the surface of the moon by Gruithuisen, the learned professor of Munich, who thought them a system of fortifications thrown up by Selenite engineers. These two points, still obscure, and many others no doubt, could only be definitively settled when direct communication had been established with the moon.

As to the intensity of her light, there was nothing further to learn on that head; it was known to be 3,000 times weaker than that of the sun, and that its heat has no appreciable action on the thermometer. As to the phenomenon known as the ash light, it is naturally explained by the effect of the rays of the sun reflected from the earth to the moon, which seem to complete the lunar disc when the latter presents itself under the form of a crescent in its first and last phases.

Such was the state of knowledge acquired with reference to the earth's satellite which the Gun Club proposed to complete in all respects, whether cosmographical, geological, political, or moral.

CHAPTER SIX

Things that all must know, and things that none are allowed to believe, in the United States

The immediate result of Barbicane's proposal was to draw attention to all astronomical facts relating to the Queen of the Night. Everyone gave himself up to the study of the matter. It was as though Luna had just made her first appearance above the horizon and no one had yet perceived her in the heavens. She became quite the fashion; she was the lion of the day without appearing the less modest on that account, and she took her place amongst the 'stars' without any signs of pride. The papers revived all the old anecdotes about the 'Sun of the Wolves'; they remembered the various influences which were attributed to her by the ignorance of former ages; she was the universal topic of conversation; they nearly went to the extent of retailing her latest witticisms; the whole of America was struck with selenomania.

The various scientific reviews published treatises upon questions relating to the undertaking of the Gun Club, and the letter from the Cambridge Observatory was published, commented on, and unreservedly approved.

In short, it was impossible for the most illiterate Yankee to ignore a single fact relating to his satellite, nor was it possible for the most bigoted old woman to entertain any superstitious terror on the subject. Science reached them in every shape; it penetrated by the eyes and by the ears; it was quite impossible to be an ass – in astronomy.

Until this time many people had been unaware by what means it was possible to calculate the distance between the moon and the earth. They were now informed that this distance was obtained by measuring the parallax of the moon. If the word parallax was unfamiliar to them, it was explained to be the angle formed by two straight lines drawn from each extremity of the eye's radius to the moon. If they had any doubt as to the exactness of this method, it was immediately proved to them that not only the average distance was in reality 234,347 miles, but that astronomers could not possibly be more than seventy miles out in their calculations.

To such as were not familiar with the movements of the moon, the daily papers showed that she possesses two distinct movements, the first known as rotation upon her axis, the second, revolution around the earth, both being executed in the same time, say 27 days and one-third.

The movement of rotation is that which causes day and night on the surface of the moon, only there is but one day and one night in each lunar month, and each of these lasts 354 hours and one-third. Fortunately for the moon, the face turned towards the terrestrial globe is illuminated by the latter with an intensity equal to the light of fourteen moons. As regards the other face, which is always invisible, it has, naturally, 354 hours of absolute night, only tempered by that pale glimmer which falls from the stars. This phenomenon is solely due to the particular circumstance that the movements of rotation and revolution are each completed in exactly the same time. Cassini and Herschel declare that this phenomenon is observable in the satellites of Jupiter, and very probably in all other satellites.

Some well-intentioned people were inclined to cavil, and did not at first understand how, if the moon invariably shows the same face to the earth during her revolution, she could possibly in the same lapse of time rotate upon her axis. To such as these the following explanation was given: 'Go into your dining-room and walk round your table, always keeping your eye on the centre. When your circular walk is completed you will find that you have made one turn upon your axis, for your eye will have successively glanced over all the parts of the room. There you have it – the room is the sky, the table is the earth, and you are the moon.' And they went away delighted with the comparison.

Thus the moon turns continually the same face towards the earth; however, to be exact, we must add that on account of a certain oscillation from north to south, and to the west, which is called libration, she shows rather more than half of her disc, in all about 57/100ths.

So soon as the most ignorant were as well informed as the Director of the Cambridge Observatory with regard to the rotation of the moon, they at once took a great interest in her movement of revolution around the earth, and twenty scientific reviews immediately undertook to instruct them. They learned that the firmament, with its infinity of stars, may be compared to an immense dial, round which the moon travels, marking the exact time to all the inhabitants of the earth. During this movement the Queen of the Night presents her various phases. The moon is full when she is in opposition with the sun, that is, when the three orbs are in the same line, the earth being the centre; the moon is new when she is in conjunction with the sun, that is, when she stands between the earth and it; lastly, she is in her first or last quarter when she forms with the sun and earth a right angle, of which she is the apex.

Certain perspicacious Yankees arrived at the conclusion that eclipses could only occur at times of conjunction or opposition, and their reasoning was correct. When in conjunction the moon can eclipse the sun, whereas, in opposition the earth eclipses it in its turn, and if these eclipses do not happen twice in each revolution it is because the plane on which the moon moves is elliptically inclined, like the plane on which the earth moves.

The letter from the Cambridge Observatory had said all that was requisite with reference to the height which the orb of night can attain above the horizon. Everyone knew that this height varies according to the latitude of the spot from which the moon is observed. But the only zones of the globe in which the moon attains the zenith – that is to say, places herself directly above the heads of the observers – are necessarily comprised between the equator and the twenty-eighth parallel. Hence the important recommendation to make the experiment upon some spot in this portion of the globe, so that the projectile might be discharged perpendicularly, and thus escape sooner from the action of gravitation. This was a condition essential to the success of the undertaking and greatly preoccupied public opinion.

The Cambridge Observatory had sufficiently taught even the most ignorant in the country that the line followed by the moon in her revolution around the earth is not a circle but an ellipse, of which the earth forms one of the foci. These elliptic orbits are common to all the planets as well as to all the satellites, and the laws of mechanics prove that things could not be otherwise. It is well understood that the moon in her apogee is farthest removed from the earth, and nearest to it in her perigee.

Every American learnt the above, whether he would or not, and indeed no one could decently be ignorant upon such matters. But if true principles spread rapidly, many errors and illusory fears were not the less difficult to uproot.

Thus, for instance, some well-meaning people maintained that the moon was nothing but an old comet which, travelling on its long orbit around the sun, had come so near to the earth as to be retained within its circle of attraction. These drawing-room astronomers tried to explain in this way the burnt appearance of the moon, which irreparable misfortune they attributed to the solar rays. But when it was pointed out to them that comets have an atmosphere, and the moon has little or none, they were somewhat at a loss for a reply.

Others, of more timid nature, entertained certain fears concerning the moon. They had heard that, since the observations taken in the time of the Khalifs, its movement of rotation had increased in a certain proportion, whence they deduced, and with a certain amount of reason, that as an increase of velocity must entail a diminution in the distance separating the two orbs, the moon would one day come into collision with the earth. However, they were reassured, and their fears on behalf of future generations were dissipated, when they learned that, according to the calculation of Laplace, a well-known French mathematician, this increase of movement was restrained within very narrow limits, and will soon be succeeded by a proportionate diminution. Thus the equilibrium of the solar system will not be disturbed in future ages.

Lastly, there remained the superstitious class of ignoramuses. These people are not only ignorant, but they know what does not exist, and in this manner their knowledge of the moon was inexhaustible. Some considered its disc merely as a polished mirror in which they could see themselves from various points of the earth, and communicate their thoughts to each other. Others declared that out of a thousand new moons which had been observed, nine hundred and fifty had brought about most notable changes, such as cataclysms, revolutions, earthquakes, deluges, &c.; they therefore believed in some mystical influence of the orb of night upon human destinies. They looked upon it as the real counterbalance of existence: they thought that each Selenite was attached by some sympathetic bond to each inhabitant of the earth; they joined with Dr Mead in maintaining that the vital system is completely under lunar influence, that boys especially are born during the new moon, and girls during the last quarter, &c. However, these vulgar errors had to be given up and the real facts recognised; and if the moon, thus shorn of her influence, lost ground in the opinion of some, the immense majority pronounced in her favour. As to the Yankees, they had but one other ambition, which was to take possession of this new continent, and plant on its highest summit the stars and stripes of the United States of America.

CHAPTER SEVEN

The song of the shot

In their memorable letter of the 7th of October, the Cambridge Observatory had treated the question in its astronomical aspect; it now became necessary to resolve it by mechanics. The practical difficulties which this offered would have appeared insurmountable in any other country, but in America they were only matter for amusement.

President Barbicane had lost no time in appointing an acting committee in the Gun Club. This committee was to elucidate, in three sittings, the three great questions of the cannon, the projectile, and the powder. It was composed of four members learned in these matters: Barbicane (with a casting vote in case of equality), General Morgan, Major Elphiston, and lastly the irrepressible J. T. Maston, who acted as secretary to the committee.

On the 8th of October the committee held their first meeting at President Barbicane's, 3, Republican Street. As it was desirable that the wants of the stomach should not interrupt so important a discussion, the four members of the Gun Club took their seats at a table spread with sandwiches and teapots. J. T. Maston screwed his pen on his iron hook, and the meeting was declared opened. Barbicane spoke first.

'My dear colleagues,' he said, 'we have to resolve one of the most important problems in the science of gunnery, that noble science which treats of the movement of projectiles, *i.e.*, bodies thrown into space by some force of impulsion and then left to themselves.'

'Gunnery for ever!' cried J. T. Maston, already somewhat excited.

'Perhaps it would have been somewhat more consistent,' continued Barbicane, 'to discuss at this first meeting the apparatus.'

'It would indeed,' said General Morgan.

'However,' continued Barbicane, 'after much reflection, it does appear to me that the question of the projectile should have precedence of the cannon, and that the dimensions of the latter should depend upon the dimensions of the former.'

'Let me speak,' said J. T. Maston.

Permission was granted to him with a readiness justified by his splendid antecedents.

'My good friends,' said he in inspired tones, 'our president is right in giving the question of the projectile precedence over all others. This shot, which we are going to fire at the moon, is our messenger – our ambassador – and I ask permission to consider it in its purely moral aspect.'

This new mode of considering a projectile raised the curiosity of all the members of the committee, and they listened with deep attention to J. T. Maston's words.

'My dear colleagues,' continued the latter, 'I will be brief. I will leave on one side the physical shot – the shot that kills – and only consider the mathematical or moral shot. A shot, to my mind, is the most startling manifestation of human power, which it sums up in its entirety.'

'Bravo!' said Major Elphiston.

'God,' said the orator, 'has made the stars and planets; man has produced the cannon-ball, which is the great criterion of terrestrial velocity – a reproduction of wandering stars, which after all are only projectiles. Leave to the Deity the swiftness of electricity, the swiftness of light, the swiftness of stars, the swiftness of comets, the swiftness of satellites, the swiftness of planets, the swiftness of sound, the swiftness of wind; we have the swiftness of the cannon-ball – one hundred times greater than the swiftness of the most rapid trains and horses.'

J. T. Marston was carried away by his enthusiasm; his voice assumed lyrical accents, as he sang this sacred song of the shot.

'Would you have figures,' continued he, 'these are truly eloquent. Take, for instance, the ball of a 24-pounder. If it travels 800,000 times slower than electricity, 640,000 times slower than light, 76 times slower than the earth in its movement around the sun, at least, when it issues from the cannon's mouth, it exceeds the rapidity of sound; it travels 200 fathoms in a second, 2,000 fathoms in ten seconds, 14 miles in a minute, 840 miles in an hour, 20,100 miles per day; which is equal to the rapidity of the points of the equator in the rotatory movement of the globe, or 7,336,500 miles per annum. It would therefore take eleven days

to reach the moon, twelve years to reach the sun, and 360 years to reach Neptune on the limits of the solar system. See what a small cannon-ball is capable of! What would it be when its velocity is increased twenty-fold, and the shot is discharged with a rapidity of seven miles to the second? Superb shot! Splendid projectile! Doubtless it would be received above with the honours due to a terrestrial ambassador.'

This high-flown speech was received with cheers; and J. T. Maston, overcome by his feelings, seated himself amidst the congratulations of his colleagues.

'Now,' said Barbicane, 'having devoted so much time to poetry, let us commence the practical discussion of the question.'

'We are ready,' said the members of the committee as each bolted half-a-dozen sandwiches.

'You know the problem we have to resolve,' continued the president; 'it is necessary to endow a projectile with a velocity of 12,000 yards per second. I believe we shall succeed. But, let us commence by examining the velocities obtained up to the present time; General Morgan can give us information on this point.'

'The more easily,' replied the general, 'that during the war I was a member of the committee of experiments. I may tell you that the Dahlgren 100-pounders, carrying to a distance of 2,500 fathoms, despatched their projectiles with an initial velocity of 500 yards per second.'

'What about Rodman's columbiad?' asked the president.

'Rodman's columbiad, tested at Fort Hamilton, near New York, threw a shot weighing half a ton to a distance of six miles with a velocity of 800 yards per second, which result has never been attained by either Armstrong or Palliser in England.'

'Pooh! Englishmen!' said J. T. Maston, jerking his formidable hook towards the eastern horizon.

'It appears, then,' said Barbicane, 'that 800 yards represent the maximum velocity hitherto obtained.'

'Yes,' replied Morgan.

'I wish to say,' interrupted J. T. Maston, 'that if my mortar had not burst – '

'Yes, but it did burst,' said Barbicane with a good-natured smile. 'We can therefore only take into consideration this velocity of 800 yards. It must be increased twenty-fold. But setting aside for the moment the means for obtaining this velocity, I wish to call your attention, dear colleagues, to the dimensions which it would be necessary to give to the projectile. Of course you quite understand that there can be no question here of projectiles weighing half a ton.'

'Why not?' asked the major.

'Because the shot,' said J. T. Maston, 'must be large enough to attract the attention of the inhabitants of the moon if there are any.'

'Yes,' said Barbicane, 'and for another reason still more important.'

'What is that, Barbicane?' asked the major.

'I mean that it is not sufficient to send off a projectile, and then take no more interest in it; we must follow it during its passage, until the very moment when it reaches its goal.'

'What!' said the general and the major, somewhat surprised at the proposal.

'Doubtless,' continued Barbicane, with a confident mien; 'doubtless, or our experiment will produce no result.'

'But in that case,' said the major, 'the dimensions of the projectile must be enormous.'

'No, be good enough to listen. You know that optical instruments have attained a great pitch of perfection. With certain telescopes we are able to enlarge an object 6,000 times, and to bring the moon to within about forty miles. At this distance, objects sixty feet long are easily visible. The penetrating power of telescopes would have been carried farther still but for the fact that this power can only be exercised to the detriment of clearness, and the moon, which is after all but a reflecting mirror, does not emit sufficient light to allow of enlargements beyond this limit.'

'What will you do, then?' asked the general. 'Will your projectile have a diameter of sixty feet?'

'Certainly not.'

'Would you render the moon more luminous?'

'I would.'

'That's a little too strong,' cried J. T. Maston.

'Yet it is very simple,' said Barbicane. 'I have only to diminish the density of the atmosphere traversed by the rays of the moon; that will make the light more intense.'

'Quite so.'

'Well, to obtain this result, it is only necessary to erect a telescope on some very high mountains. We can surely do that.'

'I give in,' said the major; 'you have such a way of simplifying things. And what enlargement do you hope to obtain in this way?'

'Forty-eight thousand times, which would bring the moon to within five miles, when objects having nine feet in diameter will be easily visible.'

'Bravo!' cried J. T. Maston; 'our projectile will therefore be nine feet in diameter.'

'Precisely so.'

'Allow me to remark, however,' said Major Elphiston, 'that the weight will still be so great – '

'Oh, major,' said Barbicane, 'before discussing the weight let me tell you that our ancestors did wonders in that way. I should be the last to assert that the science of gunnery has made no progress, but we must not forget that the middle ages obtained astonishing results, I might say more astonishing than we.'

'How so?' said Morgan.

'Prove your words,' said J. T. Maston.

'Nothing is more easy,' replied Barbicane. 'I can bring examples to prove my assertions. During the siege of Constantinople by Mahomet II in 1543, stone shots were fired weighing 1,900 pounds. They must have been large enough!'

'One thousand nine hundred pounds!' said the major, 'that's a very big figure.'

'At Malta, when the knights had possession of the island, one of the cannons from Fort St Elme fired projectiles weighing 2,500 pounds.'

'You don't mean to say so!'

'According to a French historian, in Louis XI's time a mortar threw a shell weighing only 500 pounds; but this shell, fired from the Bastille, where fools imprisoned wise men, fell into Charenton, a place where wise men lock up fools.'

'Hear! hear!' said J. T. Maston.

'Since then what have we seen? Armstrong guns throwing shot weighing 500 pounds, and Rodman's columbiad projectiles weighing half a ton. It would seem, then, that projectiles have gained in range and lost in weight. But if we give our attention to this side of the question we ought to be able, with our advanced science, to manage ten times the weight of the shot used by Mahomet II and the Knights of Malta.'

'That is clear,' said the major, 'but what metal will you use for your projectile?'

'Merely cast-iron,' said General Morgan.

'Cast-iron!' said J. T. Maston with great disdain, 'that's a very common sort of metal for a shot intended for the moon.'

'Don't let us be extravagant, my good friend,' replied Morgan, 'cast-iron is quite sufficient.'

'Well, then,' said Major Elphiston, 'as the weight of the shot is proportionate to its volume, a cast-iron shot of nine feet in diameter will still be a tremendous weight.'

'Yes, if it is massive, but not if it is hollow,' said Barbicane.

'Hollow? That will be a shell.'

'We might put despatches into it,' said J. T. Maston, 'and samples of our terrestrial products.'

'It must be a shell. A massive shot of 108 inches would weigh more than 200,000 pounds – that would clearly be too heavy; however, as this projectile must have a certain strength of resistance, I propose that it shall weigh 20,000 pounds.'

'What would be the thickness of the sides?' asked the major.

'If we follow out the regular proportions,' said Morgan, 'a diameter of 108 inches would require a thickness of at least two feet.'

'That would be too much,' said Barbicane. 'You see we are not making a shot for piercing iron plates; it will only require sufficient thickness to withstand the pressure of the powder gas. This is the problem: What would be the thickness of a cast-iron shell only weighing 20,000 pounds? Mr Maston will tell us at once.'

'Nothing can be easier,' replied the hon. secretary; whereupon he traced some rapid algebraic formulae on the paper: x, y, and z followed each other in quick succession. He appeared to extract a certain cubic root, and said: 'The sides will only be two inches thick.'

'Will that be sufficient?' asked the major, doubtfully.

'No,' replied President Barbicane, 'evidently not.'

'Well, what's to be done?' said Elphiston, looking somewhat embarrassed.

'We must use another metal.'

'Copper?' said Morgan.

'No; that's too heavy. I have something better to propose.'

'What is it?' said the major.

'Aluminum,' answered Barbicane.[16]

'Aluminum?' cried the president's three colleagues.

'Certainly, my friends. You are aware that an illustrious French chemist, Henri St Clair-Deville, succeeded in 1854 in producing aluminum in large masses. This precious metal is as white as silver, as inalterable as gold, as tenacious as iron, as fusible as copper, and as light as glass; it is easily worked, easily found, as alumina forms the basis of most rocks; it is three times as light as iron, and would seem to have been specially created to supply the material for our projectile.'

'Three cheers for aluminum!' cried the secretary of the committee, always very noisy in his moments of enthusiasm.

'But, my dear president,' said the major, 'is not aluminum very expensive?'

'It was,' replied Barbicane; 'a short time after its discovery a pound of aluminum cost from 260 to 280 dollars; later on it fell to 27 dollars, and today it costs only 9 dollars a pound.'

'But nine dollars a pound,' replied the major, who was not easily beaten off, 'will make a tremendous sum.'

'No doubt, my dear major, but not an impossible one.'

'What will the projectile weigh?' asked Morgan.

'Here are my calculations,' replied Barbicane: 'a shot 108 inches in diameter and 12 inches thick, would weigh, in cast-iron, 67,440 pounds; in aluminum its weight would be reduced to 19,250 pounds.'

'Hear, hear!' said Maston; 'that comes within our programme.'

'Hear, hear!' replied the major; 'but don't you know that at nine dollars a pound this projectile will cost – '

'One hundred and seventy-three thousand two hundred and fifty dollars. I am well aware of it; but fear nothing, my friends, money will not be wanting for our undertaking. I'll answer for that.'

'We shall get more than we want,' replied J. T. Maston.

'Well, what do you think of aluminum?' asked the president.

'Accepted!' replied the three members of the committee.

'As to the shape of the projectile,' continued Barbicane, 'that is of little importance, for once the atmosphere is passed the projectile will be in vacuum. I should propose, therefore, a round shot which can turn upon its own axis, or otherwise behave as it thinks proper.'

So terminated the first meeting of the committee. The question of the projectile was definitively resolved, and J. T. Maston was delighted at the idea of sending an aluminum cannon-ball to the Selenites, 'which would give them a great idea of the inhabitants of the earth.'

CHAPTER EIGHT

The history of the cannon

The resolutions taken at this meeting produced a great effect on the outside world. Some timid persons were rather afraid at the idea of a shot weighing 20,000 pounds travelling through space. It was a question whether a cannon could ever endow such a mass with a sufficient initial velocity. The minutes of the second meeting of the committee fully answered all these questions.

On the evening of the next day the four members of the Gun Club seated themselves before new mountains of sandwiches, on the brink of a very ocean of tea. The discussion was continued, but this time without any preamble.

'Worthy colleagues,' said Barbicane, 'we are going to discuss the apparatus and its construction, its length, its weight, its form and composition. It is probable we may have to make it of gigantic dimensions; but, however great the difficulties, our mechanical genius will overcome them. Listen, then, and don't spare your objections; I do not fear them.'

This declaration was met by a murmur of approval.

'Do not let us forget,' continued Barbicane, 'the point at which our discussion finished yesterday. This is the present form of the problem: how to impart an initial velocity of 12,000 yards per second to a shell 108 inches in diameter, weighing 20,000 pounds?'

'That is the question,' said Major Elphiston.

'Let me continue,' said Barbicane. 'When a projectile is discharged into space, what happens? It is subjected to three separate independent forces: the resistance of the atmosphere, the attraction of the earth, and the force of impulsion given to it. Let us examine these three forces. The resistance of the atmosphere is not very important, as the terrestrial atmosphere only extends for forty miles.[17] Possessing a velocity of 12,000 yards per second, the projectile will have passed through it in five seconds, which is so short a space of time that the resistance of the atmosphere may be considered as insignificant.[18] Let us pass to the attraction of the earth *i.e.*, the weight of the shell. We know that this weight will diminish in the inverse ratio of the square of the distance. The laws of physics teach us that when any substance is left to itself, and falls to the surface of the earth, it travels fifteen feet in the first second; and if this same substance be carried to a height of 257,542 miles, which is the distance from the moon to the earth, its fall would be reduced to about half the width of a line in the first second, or almost immobility. It is necessary to conquer progressively this action of gravitation. How is it to be done? By the force of impulsion.'

'Therein lies the difficulty,' said the major.

'You are quite right,' said the president; 'but we will conquer it, for this force of impulsion which we require is the result of the length of the gun and the quantity of powder used; the latter being only limited by the resistance of the former. Let us take into consideration today the dimensions to be given to the cannon. It is well understood that we can construct it to resist almost any possible pressure, for it will not have to be moved about.'

'Very good,' said the general.

'Until now,' said Barbicane, 'our longest cannons – our enormous columbiads – have not exceeded twenty-five feet in length. Many people will be astonished at the dimensions which we shall now be forced to adopt.'

'For my part,' said J. T. Maston, 'I vote for a cannon half a mile long at least.'

'Half a mile!' cried the major and general.

'Yes, half a mile; and that will be too short by half.'

'Maston,' said Morgan, 'you are exaggerating.'

'No, I am not,' said the irrepressible secretary; 'I do not know why you should accuse me of exaggeration.'

'Because you are going too far.'

'Learn, sir,' said J. T. Maston with his grand air, 'learn that an artillerist is like a cannon-ball – he can never go too far.'

As the discussion was taking a personal turn the president interfered.

'Don't excite yourselves, my friends, but let us examine the question. The cannon must evidently be a long one, for the length of the gun will increase the detention of gas behind the projectile; but it is useless to exceed certain limits.'

'Quite so,' said the major.

'What are the usual rules in such cases? Generally the length of a cannon is from 20 to 25 times the diameter of the shot, and weighs from 235 to 240 times the weight of the latter.'

'That is not sufficient,' cried J. T. Maston.

'I agree with you, my worthy friend. According to these proportions the gun for a projectile nine feet broad, weighing 30,000 pounds, would only be 225 feet long, and would only weigh 7,200,000 pounds.'

'That is ridiculous,' said J. T. Maston. 'Why not take a pocket-pistol.'

'I am of the same opinion,' replied Barbicane; 'so I propose to quadruple that length and construct a cannon 900 feet long.'

The general and the major offered some objections, but nevertheless the proposal, seconded by the secretary of the Gun Club, was definitively adopted.

'Now,' said Elphiston, 'what is to be the thickness of the tube?'

'Six feet,' said Barbicane.

'You'll never be able to put such a mass on to a carriage,' said the major.

'It would look magnificent,' said J. T. Maston.

'But impracticable,' replied Barbicane. 'No, I am going to cast the gun in the earth, fit it with rings of forged iron, and surround it with a mass of stone masonry, so that it shall have the advantage of the resistance of the surrounding ground. So soon as the gun is cast, it shall be carefully bored and polished so as to avoid any possible windage; thus there will be no loss of gas, and all the expansive force of the powder will be applied to the impulsion.'

'Hear, hear,' said J. T. Maston, 'there we have our cannon.'

'Not yet,' replied Barbicane, motioning his impatient friend to be still.

'Why not?'

'Because we have not yet discussed its form. Is it to be a cannon, a howitzer, or a mortar?'

'A cannon,' replied Morgan.

'A howitzer,' said the major.

'A mortar,' cried J. T. Maston.

A new discussion was on the point of commencing, each one supporting his favourite arm; but the president stopped it short.

'My friends,' said he, 'you shall all be satisfied. Our columbiad shall have something of all three. It shall be a cannon, for its powder chamber shall have the same diameter as the bore; it shall be a howitzer, for it will fire a shell; lastly, it shall be a mortar, for it will be fixed at an angle of 90° without any possibility of recoil so as to transmit all its accumulated power of impulsion to the projectile.'

'Hear, hear,' said the members of the committee.

'I wish to ask one question,' said Elphiston; 'will the gun be rifled?'

'No,' answered Barbicane, 'it will not. We require an enormous initial velocity, and you are aware that the shot leaves a rifled cannon much less rapidly than a smooth-bore.'

'That is true.'

'We have got it this time,' repeated J. T. Maston.

'Not quite,' replied the president.

'Why not?'

'Because we have not yet decided what metal shall be used.'

'Let us decide at once.'

'I was going to make a proposal.'

The four members of the committee swallowed a dozen sandwiches, washed down by a dish of tea, and the discussion recommenced.

'My worthy colleagues,' said Barbicane, 'our cannon must be of great tenacity, of great hardness, unfusible by heat, and proof against the corrosive action of acids.'

'There can be no doubt about that,' said the major, 'and as we shall want an immense quantity of metal we have not much choice in the matter.'

'I propose,' said Maston, 'to employ the best alloy known. That is, one hundred parts of copper, twelve parts of tin, and six parts of brass.'

'My friends,' replied the president, 'I admit that this composition has given excellent results, but in the present instance it would cost too much, and would be difficult to employ. So I think we must adopt something good but cheap, such as cast-iron. What do you think, major?'

'I think the same,' said Elphiston.

'Cast-iron,' said Barbicane, 'costs ten times less than bronze, is easily melted, can be run into a sand mould, and is easily manipulated. It therefore offers an economy of money and of time. Besides, it is an excellent substance, and I remember that during the war, at the siege of Atlanta, some cast-iron guns fired 1,000 shots each, at intervals of twenty minutes, without being any the worse.'

'Cast-iron is very brittle,' said Morgan.

'Yes, but very resisting too; besides, I answer for it we shall not burst.'

'One may burst, and yet remain honest,' said J. T. Maston, sententiously.

'No doubt,' replied Barbicane. 'I am going to beg our worthy secretary to calculate the weight of a cast-iron gun 900 feet long, having an interior diameter of nine feet, and a tube six feet thick.'

'In a minute,' replied Maston.

And, as on the previous evening, he arranged his formulae with marvellous facility, and said, at the end of a minute: 'The cannon will weigh 68,040 tons; which will cost, at two cents the pound, 2,510,701 dollars.'

J. T. Maston, the major, and the general looked at Barbicane with some alarm.

'Gentlemen,' said the president, 'I beg to repeat what I said yesterday: Be without fear – the millions will be forthcoming.'

With this assurance the committee adjourned until the following evening.

CHAPTER NINE

The powder question

The powder question remained to be discussed, and the public awaited the decision with great anxiety. Given the thickness of the projectile and the length of the gun, what would be the quantity of powder necessary to produce the impulsion? The terrible agent, which man has been able to subdue, was to be called upon to play its part in unusual proportions.

It is very generally considered that gunpowder was invented in the fourteenth century, by a monk named Schwartz, who paid for his invention with his life; but it is proved now that this story is only a legend of the middle ages. No one invented gunpowder; it is directly derived from Greek fire, which, like it, was composed of sulphur and saltpetre, with this difference, that the one is only a slow-burning mixture, and the other a detonating mixture.

Although many learned men are well acquainted with the false history of gunpowder, very few know anything about its mechanical power. Yet it is necessary to understand this point, in order to comprehend the importance of the question submitted to the committee.

A litre of gunpowder weighs about two pounds, and produces by combustion 400 litres of gas; this liberated gas, under the action of a temperature raised to 2,400°, fills a space of 4,000 litres. Thus the volume of powder is, to the volume of gas produced by its combustion, as 1 is to 4,000. Judge from this the frightful propelling power of this gas when compressed in a space 4,000 times too small.

This was well known to the members of the committee when, next day, they opened their meeting. Barbicane called upon

Major Elphiston to speak, he having been Director of Powder Magazines during the war.

'My dear comrade,' said this distinguished chemist, 'I will commence by referring to the irrefutable figures which will form the basis of our discussion. The shot of the 24-pounder, mentioned the day before yesterday by the Hon. J. T. Maston in such poetic language, is discharged from the gun by sixteen pounds of powder only.'

'Are you certain of the figures?' asked Barbicane.

'Absolutely certain,' replied the major. 'Armstrong's gun employs seventy-five pounds of powder for a projectile weighing 800 pounds, and Rodman's columbiad takes 160 pounds of powder to throw a shot weighing half a ton a distance of six miles. These facts are beyond all doubt, for I extracted them myself from the minutes of the Committee of Artillery.'

'Very well,' said the general.

'The conclusion I draw from these figures,' continued the major, 'is that the quantity of powder does not increase with the weight of the shot. If it requires sixteen pounds of powder for the shot of a 24-pounder – in other terms, if, in ordinary cannons, the amount of powder used is two-thirds the weight of the projectile, the proportions are not maintained elsewhere. Make your calculations, and you will see that for a shot weighing half a ton the amount of powder has been reduced from 333 pounds to 160 pounds.'

'What do you conclude?' said the president.

'That if you carry your theory to its extreme limit, my dear major,' said J. T. Maston, 'you will arrive at the conclusion that when the shot attains a sufficient weight no more powder will be required at all.'

'Our friend Maston must have his joke,' said the major; 'but he need be under no apprehension. I intend to propose a quantity of powder which will satisfy even his *amour propre*. Only I wish to remark that during the war the weight of the powder for the largest cannons was reduced, after experiment, to one-tenth the weight of the shot.'

'Nothing could be more exact,' said Morgan; 'but, before we decide on the quantity of powder necessary, I think we had better decide as to its quality.'

'We will employ large-grained powder; its combustion is more rapid than that of smaller grains.'

'Doubtless,' replied Morgan; 'but it is very damaging and ends by destroying the bore of the gun.'

'That may be an objection if the cannon is to undergo a long service, but it cannot apply to our columbiad. We don't run any risk of bursting, and the combustion of our powder must be instantaneous, so that its mechanical effect may be complete.'

'We may,' said J. T. Maston, 'make several touch-holes, so as to ignite the powder in different parts at the same time.'

'No doubt,' replied Elphiston, 'but that would be creating difficulties. I prefer to adopt the coarse-grained powder at once.'

'Very well,' said the general.

'Rodman,' continued the major, 'used for his columbiad powder with grains as large as chestnuts, made from willow charcoal, carbonised in cast-iron vessels. This powder was hard and glossy, left no mark on the hand, contained a large proportion of hydrogen and oxygen, ignited instantaneously, and, though very powerful, did not damage the bore to any great extent.'

'It appears to me,' said J. T. Maston, 'that we ought not to hesitate one moment.'

'Unless you prefer tooth-powder,' replied the major, laughing at his susceptible friend, who shook his hook at him threateningly.

Up to this time Barbicane had abstained from the discussion; he let them speak and merely listened; he evidently had formed his opinion, and asked: 'Now, my friends, what quantity of powder do you propose?'

The three members of the Gun Club looked at each other.

'Two hundred thousand pounds,' said Morgan.

'Five hundred thousand pounds,' said the major.

'Eight hundred thousand pounds,' cried J. T. Maston.

This time Elphiston could not accuse his colleague of exaggeration. It was a question of sending to the moon a projectile weighing 20,000 pounds, and of giving it an initial velocity of 12,000 yards per second. A moment of silence followed the triple proposal made by the three colleagues.

Silence was broken by President Barbicane.

'My worthy comrades,' said he, quietly, 'I start from the principle that the resistance of our cannon, properly constructed, is unlimited; I shall therefore astonish the Hon. J. T. Maston by telling him that he has been too timid in his calculation, and I shall propose to double his 800,000 pounds of powder.'

'One million six hundred thousand pounds?' said J. T. Maston, excitedly.

'At least.'

'Then we shall require my cannon half a mile long?'

'That is evident,' said the major.

'One million six hundred thousand pounds of powder,' continued the secretary of the committee, 'will fill a space of 22,000 cubic feet, or thereabouts. Now, as your cannon has only a total capacity of 54,000 cubic feet, it will be half filled, and the bore will not be long enough to allow the expansion of gas to give a sufficient impulsion to the projectile.'

There was nothing to reply to this; J. T. Maston was right; all looked towards Barbicane.

'Nevertheless,' continued the president, 'I shall require that quantity of powder. One million six hundred thousand pounds of powder will create six milliards[19] of litres of gas. Six milliards! You understand?'

'What is to be done, then?' asked the general.

'It is very simple: we must reduce this enormous quantity of powder whilst retaining its mechanical power.'

'How is that to be done?'

'I will tell you,' said Barbicane. His interlocutors were all attention. 'Nothing is easier,' he continued, 'than to reduce this mass of powder to a volume four times less. You are all acquainted with that curious substance which forms the elementary tissues of vegetable matter, and is called cellulose.'

'Ah!' said the major. 'I can see what you mean, my dear Barbicane.'

'This substance is found in a state of perfect purity in cotton, which latter is nothing but the fibre from the seeds of the cotton tree. Cotton, combined in a cold state with azotic acid, forms a substance eminently insoluble, eminently combustible, and eminently explosive. Some years ago (in 1832) a French chemist, named Bracconot, discovered this substance, and called it xyloidine. In 1838 another Frenchman, Pelouze, made a study of its several properties; and lastly, in 1846, Schönbein, a professor of chemistry at Basle, proposed its adoption for purposes of war. This powder is azotic cotton.'

'Or pyroxyle,' replied Elphiston.

'Or gun-cotton,' said Morgan.[20]

'Is there no American name connected with this discovery?' cried J. T. Maston, whose sentiments of national *amour propre* were very highly developed.

'Not one, unfortunately,' cried the major.

'However, to satisfy Maston,' continued the president, 'I may tell him that the labours of one of our fellow-countrymen are connected with the study of cellulose, for collodium, which is one of the principal agents in photography, is merely pyroxyle dissolved in alcoholic ether, and was discovered by Maynard, when medical student in Boston.'

'Three cheers, then, for Maynard and gun-cotton!' cried the noisy secretary of the Gun Club.

'To return to pyroxyle,' continued Barbicane. 'You know its properties, which will make it so precious to us. It is prepared with the greatest facility. Some cotton is plunged into smoking azotic acid, left there for fifteen minutes, then washed in water and dried.'

'Nothing can be more simple,' said Morgan.

'Further, gun-cotton does not suffer from damp, which is an important quality in our eyes, as we shall require several days to load the cannon; it ignites at 170° instead of 240°, and its deflagration is so sudden that you can light it upon ordinary gunpowder without the latter having time to take fire.'

'Nothing could be better,' said the major, 'only it is more expensive.'

'What does that matter?' said J. T. Maston.

'Further, it transmits to projectiles a velocity four times superior to that of gunpowder. I may add that if it is mixed with eight-tenths of its own weight of nitrate of potash its expansive power is greatly increased.'

'Is that necessary?' asked the major.

'I do not think so,' replied Barbicane. 'Thus, instead of 1,600,000 pounds of gunpowder, we shall only require 400,000 pounds of gun-cotton; and as 500 pounds of cotton can, without danger, be compressed into twenty-seven cubic feet, this substance will only occupy a height of thirty fathoms in the columbiad. In this way the shot will have more than 700 feet of bore to travel under pressure of six milliards of litres of gas before taking its flight towards the Queen of the Night.'

At this period J. T. Maston could not contain his emotion. He flung himself into the arms of his friend with the force of a projectile, and would certainly have gone through him had not Barbicane, fortunately, been bomb-proof.

This incident closed the third meeting of the committee. Barbicane and his audacious colleagues, to whom nothing seemed impossible, had resolved the complex question of the projectile, the cannon, and the powder. Their plan was complete, and only required to be put into execution.

'Which is a mere detail, a bagatelle,' said J. T. Maston.

CHAPTER TEN

One enemy amongst twenty-five millions of friends

The American public took an immense interest in the minutest details connected with the undertaking of the Gun Club. They followed, day by day, the discussions of the committee, and got quite excited over the most simple preparation for this great experiment, and the question of figures which it raised, and the mechanical difficulties to be overcome.

More than one year would elapse between the commencement of the works and their completion; but this lapse of time would not be absolutely void of emotions; the place had to be chosen for the boring, for the construction of the mould, for the casting of the columbiad, and its dangerous loading.

This was more than was necessary to excite public curiosity. Once the projectile was despatched it would escape from their sight in some tenths of a second, and only a small number of privileged persons would be able to see what became of it, how it acted in space, and how it reached the moon. Thus the real interest in the matter was concentrated upon the preparations for the experiment and the precise details of its execution.

However, the purely scientific attraction was suddenly increased by an incident.

We know what legions of admirers and friends Barbicane's project had gained for its author; nevertheless, however honourable, however extraordinary it might be, this majority did not make unanimity. One man, one only, in all the states of the Union, protested against the attempt of the Gun Club. He attacked it with violence on every occasion; and human nature is so constituted that Barbicane was more sensitive to the opposition of this one man than to the applause of all the others.

However, he knew the motive of this antipathy, and whence this solitary enmity arose; he knew that it was personal and of ancient date, and he knew what had given rise to this rivalry of *amour propre*. The president of the Gun Club had never seen his persevering enemy, and this was fortunate; for a meeting of these two men would certainly have led to disastrous consequences. His rival was a scientist, like Barbicane – a proud, audacious, self-sufficient, violent man – in a word a pure Yankee. His name was Captain Nicholl, and he dwelt in Philadelphia.

Everyone is acquainted with the interesting struggle which was carried on during the American war between projectiles and the armour-plating of ironclads – the former intended to pierce, the latter firmly determined not to be pierced. Hence a radical transformation of the navies of the two continents. Shot and iron plate fought with unexampled persistence, the one increasing in size, the other thickening in the same proportion. Vessels armed with formidable guns went boldly into fire under shelter of their invulnerable armour-plates. The *Merrimac*, the *Monitor*, the ram *Tennessee*, and the *Weckhausen* discharged enormous projectiles, and were themselves plated to withstand the projectiles of others. They did unto others as they would should not be done unto them, upon which immoral principle the whole art of war reposes.

If Barbicane was a great shot-founder, Nicholl was a great manufacturer of iron-plates. The one worked day and night at Baltimore, the other worked day and night at Philadelphia. Each one followed a train of ideas essentially opposed to the other.

So, when Barbicane invented a new shot, Nicholl invented a new armour-plate. The president of the Gun Club passed his life in piercing holes, and the captain in endeavouring to stop him. Hence a continual rivalry which became personal. Nicholl appeared to Barbicane in his dreams in the form of an impenetrable armour-plate, against which he was shattered into pieces, and Barbicane in the visions of Nicholl became a projectile which pierced him through and through.

Although these two scientists followed diverging lines they would have finished by meeting, despite all the axioms of geometry; but then they would have met in duel. Happily for these citizens, so useful to their country, a distance of fifty or sixty miles divided them from each other, and their friends threw so many obstacles in the way that they never met.

It was very uncertain which of the two inventors had the best of it, for the results obtained made it difficult to form an exact opinion. All things considered, it would appear that the armour-plate must ultimately give way to the cannon-ball, yet competent men were undecided. At the latest experiments Barbicane's cylindro-conic projectiles stuck like pins in Nicholl's armour-plates. On that day the Philadelphian iron-founder considered himself victorious, and entertained the utmost contempt for his rival. But when the latter, a short time afterwards, substituted shells weighing 600 pounds for the conic projectiles, the captain had to lower his flag; for these projectiles, though discharged with moderate velocity, broke through, and smashed into a thousand pieces, the armour-plates of the best metal.

When things were at this point, and victory seemed to remain with the shot, the war ceased on the very same day that Nicholl had completed a new armour-plate of wrought-steel. It was a masterpiece of its kind, and defied all the projectiles of the world. The captain had it carried to the Polygon at Washington, and defied the president of the Gun Club to break it. As the peace had been signed, Barbicane declined to try the experiment.

In a great state of fury Nicholl offered to expose his armour-plate to any imaginable kind of shot – massive, hollow, round, or conical; but the president refused, not caring to endanger his last success.

Nicholl, angered beyond all bounds by Barbicane's obstinacy, endeavoured to tempt him by leaving him all the chances of success. He proposed to set up his plates 200 yards from the cannon. Barbicane still refused. 'At 100 yards?' 'Not even at 75.' 'At 50, then!' cried the captain through the organ of the press. 'I'll put it at 25 yards, and get behind it myself.'

Barbicane replied that even if Captain Nicholl were to get in front of it he would not fire.

At this reply Nicholl could contain himself no longer. He became personal; insinuated that cowardice was indivisible; that the man who refused to fire a cannon was very near being afraid of it; that in reality artillerists who now fight at a distance of six miles have prudently replaced individual courage by mathematical formulae; and, further, that there is as much bravery in quietly awaiting a shot behind an armour-plate as in firing off the projectile according to all the rules of science.

To these insinuations Barbicane did not reply. Perhaps, even, he did not know of them, for at that time he was completely absorbed by his calculations for the great undertaking.

When he made his famous communication to the Gun Club, Captain Nicholl's anger reached its paroxysm. It was mixed with an intense jealousy and a feeling of absolute powerlessness. How could he invent anything better than this 900-feet columbiad? What armour-plate could ever withstand a projectile weighing 30,000 pounds? At first Nicholl was overwhelmed and annihilated by this monstrous cannon, but he soon recovered himself, and resolved to crush the proposition by the weight of his arguments.

He violently attacked the works of the Gun Club; he published a number of letters which the papers were delighted to insert; he tried to pick Barbicane's work to pieces – scientifically. Once the war was commenced, any kind of argument served its purpose; and, in truth, they were often specious and illogical.

In the first place Barbicane's figures were attacked. Nicholl tried to prove by *a + b* that his formulae were incorrect, and that he was ignorant of the very rudiments of gunnery. Amongst other errors, according to Nicholl's calculations, it was utterly impossible to transmit to any object whatever a velocity of 12,000 yards per second. He maintained – algebra in hand – that even with this velocity no projectile, however heavy, could possibly pass the limits of the terrestrial atmosphere; it would not even go a distance of eight leagues. Better still: admitting the velocity, and admitting that it was sufficient, the shell would never resist the pressure of the gas developed by the combustion of 1,600,000 pounds of gunpowder, and, if it did resist this pressure, at least it could not support the temperature, but would melt as it issued from the columbiad, and fall back in boiling rain on the heads of the imprudent spectators.[21]

Barbicane met these attacks without wincing, and continued his work.

Nicholl then considered the question in its other aspects. Without speaking of its general uselessness, he considered the experiment exceedingly dangerous, both for the citizens who countenanced such a spectacle by their presence and for the towns in the neighbourhood of the deplorable cannon. He also remarked that if the projectile did not reach its goal, which it could not possibly do, it would naturally fall back upon the earth, and the fall of such a mass, multiplied by the square of its velocity, would create great damage in some part of the globe. Under such circumstances, without wishing to infringe the rights of free citizens, this was certainly a case in which the intervention of the Government became necessary, for the safety of all could not be endangered for the pleasure of one man.

It was plain that Captain Nicholl was addicted to exaggeration. He was alone of his opinion, and no one paid the slightest attention to his prophecies. He was allowed to say what he pleased and write what he pleased; he was defending a cause which was lost beforehand. He was heard, but not listened to; and he did not gain over one of the president's admirers. The latter did not even take the trouble of refuting his rival's arguments.

Nicholl, driven into his last intrenchments, determined to risk his money, as he could not risk his person, and he proposed, through the columns of the *Richmond Inquirer*, the following series of wagers. He offered to bet: –

(1st) That the funds necessary for the undertaking of the Gun Club would not be forthcoming – 1,000 dollars.

(2nd) That the operation of casting a cannon 900 feet long was impracticable, and would not succeed – 2,000 dollars.

(3rd) That it would be impossible to load the columbiad, and that the gun-cotton would ignite under the pressure of the projectile – 3,000 dollars.

(4th) That the columbiad would burst at the first shot – 4,000 dollars.

(5th) That the projectile would not travel even six miles, but would fall back to earth a few seconds after the discharge – 5,000 dollars.

Thus the captain's stubbornness induced him to risk a considerable sum, for the total of the bets amounted to no less than 15,000 dollars. Notwithstanding which, on the 19th of October he received this note of Spartan brevity –

Baltimore, 18th October

Done.

BARBICANE

CHAPTER ELEVEN

Florida and Texas

One question yet remained to be decided; it was necessary to choose the most favourable spot for the experiment. According to the recommendation of the Cambridge Observatory, a shot was to be fired perpendicularly to the plane of the horizon, *i.e.*, towards the zenith; but the moon only crosses the zenith in places situated between 0° and 28° of latitude; in other words, its declination is only 28°. It was therefore necessary to determine exactly the point of the globe where the enormous columbiad was to be cast.

On the 28th of October, at a general meeting of the Gun Club, Barbicane produced an immense map of the United States, by L. Belltropp. But before he had time to open it, J. T. Maston, with his usual vehemence, had claimed permission to speak, and commenced in the following terms.

'Honorable colleagues, the question to be discussed today has a truly national importance, and will give us an opportunity of showing a great deal of patriotism.'

The members of the Gun Club looked at each other without understanding what the speaker was coming to.

'No one amongst you,' continued he, 'would harbour the thought of diminishing this country's glory; and if the Union can claim one right above all others, it is to receive in its bosom the formidable cannon of the Gun Club. Under present circumstances – '

'Worthy Maston – ' said the president.

'Don't interrupt,' said the speaker. 'Under present circumstances we are obliged to choose a spot sufficiently near the equator, that the experiment may be made under favourable conditions – '

'If you will allow me – ' said Barbicane.

'I claim the freedom of discussion,' replied the choleric J. T. Maston; 'and I maintain that the ground from which our glorious projectile will be discharged should belong to the Union.'

'Quite right,' said several members.

'Well! As our frontiers are not sufficiently wide; as the ocean forms an impassable barrier to the south; as the 28th parallel must be sought in a neighbouring country beyond the United States – that, I say, constitutes a legitimate *casus belli*, and I demand that war be declared against Mexico.'

'No, no, no,' was echoed from every side.

'No?' replied J. T. Maston. 'I am astonished to hear such sentiments in this place.'

'But listen.'

'Never,' cried the impetuous orator. 'Sooner or later this war must occur, and I demand that it should commence at once.'

'Maston,' said Barbicane, firing a volley from his handbell, 'I must ask you to be silent.'

Maston wished to reply, but several of his colleagues succeeded in restraining him.

'I admit,' said Barbicane, 'that the experiment cannot and ought not to be tried elsewhere than on American soil; but, if our impatient friend had allowed me to speak, if he had only cast a glance at a map, he would have seen that it is quite unnecessary to declare war against our neighbours, inasmuch as certain frontiers of the United States extend beyond the 28th parallel. Look here! We have at our disposal all the southern portions of Texas and Florida.'

The incident then dropped, though J. T. Maston was not convinced without difficulty. It was decided that the columbiad should be cast either in Texas or Florida. But this decision created much rivalry between the towns of these two states.

The 28th parallel, on meeting the American coast, traverses the peninsula of Florida, which it cuts into two almost equal parts. Then passing through the Gulf of Mexico, to the south of Georgia, Alabama, and Louisiana, it reaches Texas, of which it cuts off a corner, stretches through Mexico, passes the Sonora, cuts through Old California, and is lost in the Pacific Ocean.

Thus only those portions of Florida and Texas which lie below this parallel presented the conditions as to latitude recommended by the Cambridge Observatory.

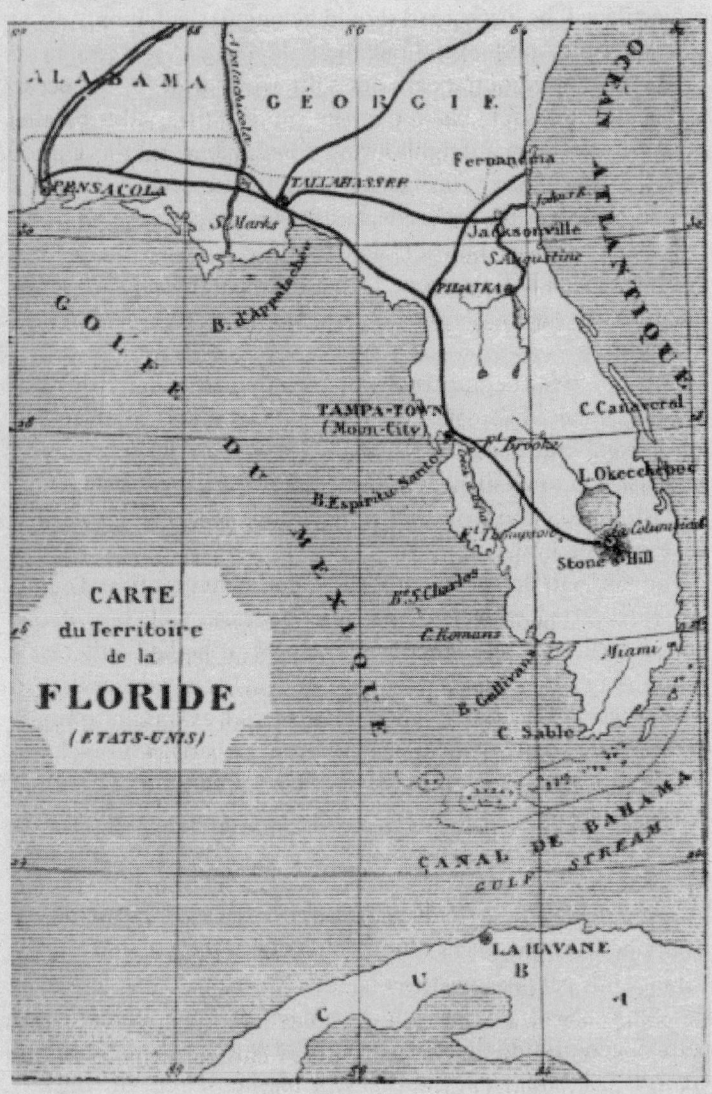

Florida, in its southern parts, has no important towns, but only a few forts constructed to keep the wandering Indians in check.

Tampa Town was the only city which could have any claim in regard to its situation.

In Texas, on the other hand, the towns are more numerous and more important. Corpus Christi in Nuace's County, and all the towns situated on the Rio Bravo; Laredo; Comalites; San Ignacio on the Webb; Roma and Rio Grande city on the Starr; Edinburg on the Hidalgo; and Santa Rita, Elpanda, and Brownsville, on the Cameron, formed an imposing league against the pretensions of Florida.

The decision was hardly known when Texan and Floridan deputies reached Baltimore by express train. From that moment President Barbicane, and the more influential members of the Gun Club, were besieged day and night by these formidable claimants. Seven towns of Greece disputed the honour of Homer's birthplace, but two states of America were ready to annihilate each other merely on account of a cannon.

These 'ferocious brothers' carried arms in the streets of the town. At each meeting some conflict was feared entailing disastrous consequences, but happily the danger was averted by President Barbicane's prudence and address. Personal animosities found an outlet in the papers of the different states. Thus the *New York Herald* and the *Tribune* supported Texas, whereas the *Times* and the *American Review* advocated the cause of the Floridan deputies. The Gun Club was unable to decide between the two.

Texas bravely brought its twenty-six counties into line of battle; but Florida replied that twelve counties were worth more than twenty-six in a country six times smaller.

Texas laid great stress on its 330,000 natives, but Florida, though not so large, maintained that it was more densely populated with 56,000. Further, it accused Texas of having a speciality of paludal fevers which carried off, on an average, several thousand inhabitants each year; and Florida was right.

In its turn Texas replied that as regards fevers Florida had enough of her own, and that it was at least imprudent to call other countries unhealthy when she suffered chronically from *vomito negro*;[22] and herein Texas was not wrong.

Further, the Texans maintained, in the columns of the *New York Herald*, that every consideration is due to a state which grows the finest cotton in America and the best oak for ship-building; a state which contains excellent coal and iron-ore yielding fifty per cent. of pure metal.

To this the *American Review* replied that the soil of Florida, without being so rich, offered greater advantages for casting the columbiad, as it was composed of sand and clay.

'But,' said the Texans, 'before casting anything in a country, you have to get there, and communication with Florida is difficult; whereas the Texan coast contains the bay of Galveston, which is fourteen leagues round, and might contain the united fleets of the whole world.'

'Very well,' replied the papers in the Floridan interest, 'but what is the good of your bay of Galveston situated above the 29th parallel? Have we not the bay of Espiritu Santo situated precisely on the 28th degree of latitude, and by which ships may reach Tampa Town?'

'A nice bay, indeed,' replied Texas, 'it's half full of sand.'

'Full of sand yourselves,' cried Florida; 'why don't you say at once that we're a country of savages?'

'I really don't know; there are still some Seminoles to be found in your prairies.'

'Well, and how about your Apaches and your Comanches – are they civilised?'

Thus the war had been waged for several days when Florida tried a change of tactics, and one morning the *Times* insinuated that the undertaking, being essentially American, could only be tried upon essentially American territory.

'American!' cried Texas; 'are we not as American as you? Were not Texas and Florida both incorporated in the Union in 1844?'

'No doubt,' replied the *Times*, 'but we belonged to the Americans since 1820.'

'I should think so,' sneered the *Tribune*, 'after having been Spanish or English during 200 years, you were sold to the United States for 5,000,000 dollars.'

'What does that matter?' replied the Floridans. 'Are we to be ashamed of it? Was not Louisiana purchased from Napoleon for 16,000,000 dollars in 1803?'

'It is a shame,' cried the Texan deputies, 'for a miserable slip of land like Florida to dare to compare itself with Texas, which, instead of being sold, achieved its own independence, drove out the Mexicans on the 2nd of March, 1836, and declared itself a federative republic after the victory gained by Samuel Houston, on the banks of the San Jacinto, over the troops of Santa Anna.

A country, in fact, which voluntarily joined the United States of America.'

'Because it was afraid of the Mexicans,' replied Florida.

'Afraid!' From the day this unparliamentary word was pronounced the situation became intolerable. A massacre of the two parties was daily expected in the streets of Baltimore. The authorities had to keep the deputies under constant supervision.

President Barbicane was at his wits' end. Notes, documents, and threatening letters literally poured into his house. What was he to do? As regards soils, facility of communication, and rapidity of transports, the rights of the two states were equal. As to political personalities, they had nothing to do with the question.

This hesitation and embarrassment had lasted for some time when Barbicane resolved to put an end to it, so he called his colleagues together, and proposed the following wise resolutions.

'When we consider,' said he, 'what has just taken place between Florida and Texas, it is evident that the same difficulties will arise between the towns of the favoured state. The rivalry will descend from the genus to the species, from the state to the city, and that is all we shall gain. Now Texas possesses eleven towns in the required conditions, which will each claim the honour of the undertaking and cause us an infinity of bother; whereas Florida has only one. I vote, therefore, for Florida and Tampa Town.'[23]

When this decision was made public, the Texan deputies were astounded. Their fury knew no bounds, and they sent personal challenges to the several members of the Gun Club. The Baltimore magistrates had but one course open, which they took; a special train was prepared, and the Texan deputies were hurried from the town, *nolens volens*, at a rate of thirty miles an hour.

Notwithstanding the speed of their departure they found time to discharge a last threatening sarcasm at their adversaries. Alluding to the narrowness of Florida – which is merely a peninsula sandwiched between two seas – they maintained that she would not resist the shock of the discharge, but would blow up at the first fire.

'Well, let her blow up,' replied the Floridans, with a brevity worthy of ancient times.

CHAPTER TWELVE

'Urbi et Orbi'[24]

The astronomical, mechanical, and topographical difficulties having been settled, there arose the question of money. It was necessary to procure an enormous sum for the execution of the project; and no individual, nor any single state even, would have been able to supply the required millions.

President Barbicane therefore decided that, although the undertaking was American, it should be made a matter of universal interest, to which the financial co-operation of every nation might be invited. It was at once the right and the duty of all the earth to take a share in the affairs of its satellite. The subscription opened for this purpose extended from Baltimore to the entire world, *urbi et orbi*.

The subscription succeeded beyond all expectation, although the money was to be given and not lent. The operation was purely disinterested, in the literal sense of the word, and held out no hopes of profit.

The effect of Barbicane's communication had not been confined within the frontiers of the United States; it had crossed the Atlantic and the Pacific, and invaded at once Europe, Asia, Africa, and Oceania. The observatories of the Union placed themselves in communication with the observatories of foreign countries. Those of Paris, St Petersburg, the Cape, Berlin, Altona, Stockholm, Warsaw, Hamburg, Breda, Bologna, Malta, Lisbon, Benares, Madras, and Pekin sent their compliments to the Gun Club; others maintained a prudent reserve.

As to the Greenwich Observatory, backed up by the twenty-two other astronomical establishments of Great Britain, it was very concise: it denied all possibility of success, and adopted the theories of Captain Nicholl.

When the different learned societies promised to send delegates to Tampa Town, the Greenwich committee declined to entertain Barbicane's proposal; but this was merely English jealousy, and nothing else.

As a general rule the effect upon the scientific world was excellent, and from thence it was disseminated amongst the masses who took a great interest in the question. This was a matter of great importance, as these masses were about to be called upon to subscribe an immense sum.

On the 8th of October, President Barbicane had issued a manifesto, couched in enthusiastic language, appealing to 'All Men of Good Will upon Earth'. This document was translated into all languages, and met with great success.

Subscriptions were opened in the Union to the credit of the Bank of Baltimore, 9, Baltimore Street, and in the different countries of the two continents:

In Vienna, at S. M. de Rothschild's.
In St Petersburg, at Stieglitz & Co.'s.
In Paris, at the Crédit Mobilier.
In Stockholm, at Tottie and Arfuredson's.
In London, at N. M. de Rothschild & Son's.
In Turin, at Ardouin & Co.'s.
In Berlin, at Mendelssohn's.
In Geneva, at Lombard, Odie, & Co.'s.
In Constantinople, at the Ottoman Bank.
In Brussels, at S. Lambert's.
In Madrid, at Daniel Weisweller's.
In Amsterdam, at the Credit Neerlandais.
In Rome, at Torlonia & Co.'s.
In Lisbon, at Lecesne's.
In Copenhagen, at the Private Bank.
In Buenos Ayres, at Maua's Bank.
In Rio de Janeiro, at Maua's Bank.
In Montevideo, at Maua's Bank.
In Valparaiso, at Thomas La Chambre & Co.'s.
In Mexico, at Martin Daran & Co.'s.
In Lima, at Thomas La Chambre & Co.'s.

Three days after President Barbicane's manifesto, four millions of dollars had been paid in at the different towns of the Union. With such an amount in hand the Gun Club could commence operations.

Some days later, telegrams to America brought news that the foreign subscriptions were yielding largely. Some countries distinguished themselves by their generosity, others were more penurious. It was a mere question of temperament. However, figures are more eloquent than words, and the following is an official statement of the sums credited to the Gun Club at the close of the subscription.

Russia subscribed for its share the enormous sum of 368,733 roubles. Those who are astonished at this evidently misunderstand the Russian taste for science and the impulse which they have given to astronomical studies by means of their numerous observatories, the chief of which cost two million roubles.

France began by laughing at the American pretensions. The moon served as a pretext for a thousand stale jokes, and twenty or thirty vaudevilles equally remarkable for ignorance and bad taste; but as the French formerly paid for singing they now paid for laughing, and subscribed a sum of 1,253,930 francs, at which price they certainly had the right to be jovial if they liked.

Austria was generous in the midst of her financial embarrassments. Her share in the public subscription reached 216,000 florins, which were well received.

Fifty-two thousand rix-dollars were subscribed by Sweden and Norway. This figure is comparatively high for the country, but it would certainly have been higher had the subscription been opened at Christiania as well as at Stockholm. For some reason or other, Norwegians do not like sending their money to Sweden.

Prussia showed its approval of the enterprise by sending 250,000 thalers. The different observatories readily contributed a large amount, and were amongst the warmest of President Barbicane's encouragers.

Turkey acted generously. It is true she had a personal interest in the matter, as the moon regulates the course of her years and her fast of the Ramadân. She could not give less than 1,372,640 piastres, but she gave them in a manner which indicated a certain pressure on the part of the Government of the Porte.

Belgium distinguished herself amongst secondary states by giving 513,000 francs, or about twelve centimes per head of her inhabitants.

Holland and her colonies took an interest in the operation to the extent of 110,000 florins, but they claimed five per cent. discount for paying cash.

Denmark, notwithstanding the diminutive size of its territory, subscribed 9,000 ducats, which proves the love of the Danes for scientific expeditions.

The Germanic Confederation undertook to subscribe 34,285 florins. More could not have been expected. At any rate no more would have been given.

Although very hard up, Italy found 200,000 lire in the pockets of her children, after much searching. If she had had Venice she would have done more; but then she had not got Venice.

The States of the Church did not think it necessary to send more than 7,040 Roman crowns, and Portugal went so far in its devotion to science as to subscribe 30,000 crusados.

As regards Mexico, it was the widow's mite – eighty-six piastres. But then, empires in course of formation are always in monetary difficulties.

Two hundred and fifty-seven francs was the modest subscription of the Swiss to the American undertaking. The fact is, Switzerland could not see the practical side of the operation. She could not understand how the mere fact of sending a cannon-ball to the moon would establish business relations with that satellite, and it seemed to her very imprudent to risk money in such an uncertain undertaking. And, after all, perhaps Switzerland was right.

As for Spain, she could not collect more than 110 reals. The pretext given was that her railways were not completed, but the truth is that science is not much thought of in that country, which is still rather backward. Then some of the better-taught Spaniards did not exactly understand the mass of the projectile as compared with that of the moon. They feared it might damage its orbit, interfere with its action as a satellite, and, perhaps, cause its fall upon the surface of the terrestrial globe, in which case it was better to abstain; which they did, except to the extent of some few reals.

England yet remained. We have seen the contemptuous antipathy with which she received Barbicane's proposal. Englishmen have but one and the same mind for the 25 millions of inhabitants contained in Great Britain. They intimated that the

Gun Club's undertaking was contrary to the 'principle of non-intervention', and declined to subscribe a farthing.

At this news the Gun Club shrugged their shoulders, and went on with their business. When South America – that is to say Peru,

Chili, Brazil, and the provinces of La Plata and Columbia – had paid up their share of 300,000 dollars, the club found itself at the head of a very considerable capital, composed as follows: –

Subscriptions in the United States	\$4,000,000
Ditto abroad	\$1,446,675
Total	\$5,446,675

which the public had paid in to the credit of the Gun Club.

Let no one be surprised at the importance of the sum. The works of casting, boring; of masonry, and transport of workmen; the establishment of the latter in an almost uninhabited country; the construction of furnaces and buildings, the machinery for the works; the powder, the projectile, and the general expenses would, according to the estimates, fully absorb the whole amount.

During the American War some cannons are said to have cost 1,000 dollars a shot. President Barbicane's gun, unique in the history of artillery, would probably cost 5,000 times as much.

On the 28th of October an agreement was signed with the Goldspring Works near New York, which, during the war, had supplied Parrott with his best cast-iron cannons.

It was stipulated between the contracting parties that the Goldspring Works undertook to transport to Tampa Town, South Florida, the plant and machinery necessary for casting the columbiad.

This operation was to be completed, at latest, by the 15th of October next, and the gun delivered in good condition, under penalty of a fine of 100 dollars per day up to the moment when the moon should again present herself in the same conditions – that is to say, eighteen years and eleven days.

The hiring of the workmen, their payment, and all necessary arrangements, were to be at the charge of the Goldspring Works.

This agreement, executed in duplicate and in good faith, was signed by J. Barbicane, President of the Gun Club, and J. Murphison, Director of the Goldspring Works, and delivered under their respective hands and seals.

CHAPTER THIRTEEN

Stone's Hill

As soon as the choice made by the members of the Gun Club to the detriment of Texas was known to the public, everyone in America, where the ability to read is universal, applied himself to study the geography of Florida. Publishers had never sold so many copies of Bertram's *Travels in Florida*, Roman's *Natural History of East and West Florida*, Williams's *Territory of Florida*, and Clelland on the *Culture of Sugar-Cane in East Florida*. Such was the rush for these works that new editions had to be printed.

But Barbicane had no time for reading. He had to inspect and mark out the site for the columbiad. So, without loss of time, he placed the necessary funds at the disposal of the Cambridge Observatory for the construction of a monster telescope, and gave Messrs Breadwill and Co., of Albany, an order for the manufacture of the projectile in aluminum, and then left Baltimore, accompanied by J. T. Maston, Major Elphiston, and the director of the Goldspring Works.

Next day the four travellers reached New Orleans, where the Government had placed the despatch-boat *Tampico* at their disposal, and, getting up steam, the coasts of Louisiana were soon hidden from their view.

The passage was not a long one. Two days after starting the *Tampico* had steamed 490 miles, and was in sight of the coast of Florida. As they approached, Barbicane perceived a long stretch of barren, low-lying land, and after passing a series of creeks, abounding in oysters and lobsters, the *Tampico* steamed into the bay of Espiritu Santo.

This bay terminates in two narrow inlets, one leading to Tampa and the other to Hillisborough, up the former of which the steamer held its way. In a short time the batteries of Fort Brooke were seen towering above the water-line, and soon the town of Tampa appeared at the extremity of a small harbour formed by the mouth of the River Hillisborough.

Here the *Tampico* cast anchor on the 22nd of October, at 7 p.m., and the four passengers immediately went on shore.

Barbicane's heart beat with violence as he stepped on to Floridan soil, and he stamped with his foot as an architect would try the solidity of a building. J. T. Maston scratched the ground with his hook.

'Gentlemen,' said Barbicane, 'we have no time to lose; tomorrow we must be off on horseback to explore the country.'

When it was known that Barbicane had landed, the 3,000 inhabitants of Tampa Town flocked out to greet the president of the Gun Club, who had honoured them with his choice; but Barbicane escaped from the oration, and shut himself in a room of Franklin's Hotel, where he refused to receive anybody. The honours of celebrity were evidently not to his taste.

The next morning, which was the 23rd of October, they were awakened by the snorting and pawing of some small Spanish-bred horses beneath their windows; but instead of four, they found fifty, already mounted.

When Barbicane came down with his three companions, he was at first astonished to find himself in the midst of such a cavalcade, the more so that each horseman had a rifle slung over his shoulder and pistols in his holsters. A young Floridan explained the reason for this display of forces as follows.

'It is on account of the Seminoles, sir.'

'What Seminoles?'

'Wandering Indians of the prairies. We thought it more prudent to escort you.'

'Pooh!' said J. T. Maston, climbing into his saddle.

'At any rate,' said the young Floridan, 'it will be safer.'

'Gentlemen,' said Barbicane, 'I thank you for your kind attention. Let us be off.'

The little troop put itself in motion, and soon disappeared in a cloud of dust. Although only 5 a.m., the sun was shining brightly, and the thermometer registered 84°; but fresh breezes from the sea tempered the excessive heat.

After leaving Tampa Town, Barbicane travelled southwards, and followed the coast till he came to Alifia Creek. This little river flows into Hillisborough Bay about twelve miles below Tampa Town. Barbicane and his escort skirted its right bank in an easterly direction, and soon the waters of the bay disappeared behind the rising land, and the plains of Florida were alone visible.

Florida is divided into two parts. The northern part is more populous – or, rather, less deserted – and has for its capitals Tallahassee and Pensacola, one of the principal naval arsenals of the United States. The other part, which lies between the Atlantic and the Gulf of Mexico, forms a narrow peninsula worn by the action of the Gulf Stream – a slip of earth in the midst of a small archipelago, incessantly doubled by the numerous vessels of the Bahama Canal. It is the advanced guard of the Gulf of Tempests. The superficial area of the state is 38,033,267 acres, from which a site was to be chosen within the 28th parallel, for the purposes of the undertaking. So Barbicane, during his ride, examined attentively the configuration of the ground and its general distribution.

Florida was discovered in 1512, by Juan Ponce de Leon, on Palm Sunday, and was first named Pasca Florida, though its burnt and arid coast but little deserved this charming appellation; however, a few miles from the sea, the nature of the ground gradually changes, and becomes more worthy of its name. The country is cut up by a network of creeks, rios, watercourses, ponds, and small lakes, which remind one of Holland or Guiana; but the highlands spread out into cultivated plains, teeming with the vegetable productions of the north and south, immense fields rendered productive by the action of a tropical sun upon the water, retained by a clay soil, where pineapples, yams, tobacco, rice, cotton, and the sugarcane display their boundless riches with heedless prodigality.

Barbicane appeared well satisfied with the gradually increasing elevation of the ground, and when J. T. Maston spoke to him on the subject: 'My worthy friend,' he replied, 'it is very important that our columbiad should be cast in the higher ground.'

'To be nearer the moon?' asked the secretary of the Gun Club.

'No,' replied Barbicane, smiling; 'what difference can a few fathoms make? In the midst of the higher grounds our works will be carried out more easily, for we shall not have to contend against the water, and can therefore dispense with a costly system of drainage, which is an important matter when sinking a shaft 900 feet deep.'

'You are right,' said Murchison, the engineer, 'it is very important to avoid water when sinking the pit. But our pumping-engines will soon get the better of any springs we may meet with. There is no question here of an artesian well, dark and narrow, where the boring apparatus works out of sight. Our operations will be carried on in the light of day; with the aid of pickaxe, shovel, and blasting powder, we will carry the matter through in no time.'

'Nevertheless,' said Barbicane, 'if by the choice of our site we can avoid all trouble from subterranean waters our work will be done better and more rapidly, so let us look out for a spot some hundreds of fathoms above the level of the sea.'

'Very true, Mr Barbicane, and I am much mistaken or we shall find such a spot before long.'

'I should like to see the first stroke given at once,' said the president.

'And I should like to see the last,' said J. T. Maston.

'We are arrived, gentlemen,' said the engineer, 'and believe me the Goldspring Works will not have to pay you any penalty for delay.'

'So much the better for you,' said J. T. Maston. 'Are you aware that 100 dollars a day, until the moon presents herself in the same condition – that is for eighteen years and eleven days – would amount to 658,100 dollars?'

'No, I am not, sir,' replied the engineer; 'and I do not want to be.'

At about ten o'clock the little troop had got over twelve miles, and the fertile plains were succeeded by forest lands. Here they found the most varied kinds of trees in tropical profusion. These almost impenetrable forests were composed of pomegranate trees, orange trees, lemon trees, fig trees, olive trees, apricot trees, banana trees, and vines, whose fruits and flowers rivalled each other in colour and perfume. The odoriferous shade of these magnificent trees was peopled by a world of brilliantly-plumaged birds, amongst which the crab-eaters (*cancroma*) were particularly noticeable. Surely these feathered jewels must have caskets for their nests!

J. T. Maston and the major were lost in admiration of these beautiful works of nature.

But President Barbicane, who cared little for such marvels, was anxious to get on. The very fertility of the country was displeasing to him, for without being a hydroscope, he could feel the water beneath his feet, and what he was searching for was a site of incontestable dryness.

So they pushed on, fording several rivers, and not without danger, for they were infested with alligators from fifteen to eighteen feet long. J. T. Maston bravely shook his redoubtable hook at them, but he only frightened the pelicans, the seals, and the phaetons, which peopled the banks of the rivers, whilst large red flamingos stared at him in stupid wonder.

At last they left behind them this too-well irrigated country, and the size of the trees diminished. As they advanced the underwood became less dense, until nothing was left but isolated clumps scattered over immense plains, where troops of wild deer ranged in primitive freedom.

'At last,' cried Barbicane, raising himself in his stirrups, 'we are in the region of pines.'

'And of savages,' replied the major.

Just then some Seminoles appeared on the horizon, galloping their swift horses and brandishing long lances, and occasionally firing off their guns; but they confined themselves to these hostile demonstrations, and did not otherwise interfere with Barbicane and his party.

The latter had reached the centre of a vast rocky plain, inundated by the burning rays of the sun, and formed by a large extumescence of the ground, which appeared to the members of the Gun Club to combine all the conditions requisite for the manufacture of their columbiad.

'Halt!' said Barbicane, pulling up; 'has this spot a name in the country?'

'It is called Stone's Hill,' answered one of the Floridans.

Barbicane dismounted without a word, and drawing out his instruments, set himself to take the most precise observations of the spot, whilst the little troop stood around, watching him in profound silence.

At this moment the sun passed the meridian. Barbicane having completed his calculations, gave the result of his observations as follows.

'This spot is situated 300 fathoms above the level of the sea,[25] in 27° 7' latitude and 5° 7' W. longitude. It seems to me, from its rocky and arid character, to offer the most favourable conditions for our experiment. On this plain we will erect our stores, our workshops, our furnaces, and the huts for our workmen; and from this spot,' he continued, stamping his foot on the summit of Stone's Hill, 'our projectile will take its flight to the vast regions of the solar world.'

CHAPTER FOURTEEN

Spade and trowel

Barbicane and his companions returned the same evening to Tampa Town, and the engineer, Murchison, re-embarked on the *Tampico*, for New Orleans, to engage an army of workmen and bring back the greater portion of the plant. The members of the Gun Club remained at Tampa Town to organise the commencement of the works, with the aid of the people of the country.

Eight days later the *Tampico* re-entered the bay of Espiritu Santo, surrounded by a flotilla of steamers transporting 1,500 workmen.

In the bad days of slavery this number could not have been collected, but since America, the land of freedom, had none but free men for her inhabitants, workpeople crowded to every spot where their labour was likely to be required and liberally remunerated. The Gun Club did not want for money, and offered liberal pay and proportionate bonuses. Each workman engaged for Florida, could count, after completion of the work, upon a certain sum of money deposited in his name at the Bank of Baltimore; consequently Murchison could pick and choose amongst the most intelligent and most skilful of the working-classes. You may imagine that he only enrolled in his staff the *élite* of mechanicians, stokers, founders, boiler-makers, miners, brick-makers, and labourers of every kind, white or black, without distinction of colour. Many of them brought their families with them, as if for a permanent emigration.

At 10 a.m. on the 31st of October the troop landed on the quays of Tampa Town. The movement and activity in this little town, whose population was thus doubled in one day, may be better imagined than described. Tampa Town was a great gainer by this initiative of the Gun Club, not so much from the work-people, who were immediately sent on to Stone's Hill, but from the number of visitors who arrived in the Floridan peninsula from all points of the globe.

The first days were occupied with unloading the machinery, tools, and provisions brought by the flotilla, as well as some iron huts which had been packed in separate pieces, each properly numbered. At the same time Barbicane commenced marking out a line of railway, fifteen miles long, uniting Stone's Hill with Tampa Town.

We all know how American railways are constructed – with what capricious curves and steep inclines, with what disregard for railings and masonry, scaling hills and dipping into valleys without any regard for the straight line. They are not costly or troublesome, but are allowed every liberty for blowing up or running off the rails. The line from Tampa Town to Stone's Hill was a mere bagatelle, requiring neither much time nor much money.

Barbicane was the moving spirit in all this world of workmen. He imparted to them his enthusiasm and his conviction; he was everywhere at once, as though gifted with ubiquity, and J. T. Maston was constantly at his side. There was no limit to the inventions of his practical mind. For him there were no obstacles, no difficulties, no embarrassments. He was as much a miner, a mason or a mechanician, as an artillerist. He had answers to every question, and solutions for every problem. He corresponded actively with the Gun Club and Goldspring Works, and the *Tampico*, with lighted furnaces and steam up, awaited his orders, day and night, in the harbour of Hillisborough.

On the 1st of November, Barbicane left Tampa Town with a detachment of workmen, and the next day a city of iron houses had arisen on the summit of Stone's Hill. These were surrounded by palisades, and, from the movement and activity therein displayed, the whole might have been taken for one of the great cities of the Union. Perfect discipline was maintained, and the works commenced in perfect order.

The nature of the ground had been ascertained by careful borings; and, on the 4th of November, everything was ready for commencing the sinking of the principal shaft. On that day

Barbicane called a meeting of his chief foremen, and said: 'You all know, my friends, why I have brought you together in this wild part of Florida. We are to cast a cannon measuring 9 feet in diameter, 6 feet in thickness, and surrounded by 19½ feet of masonry, which will give the shaft a total width of 60 feet and a depth of 900 feet. This great work must be completed in eight months. You have 2,543,400 cubic feet of earth to extract in 255 days, which makes, in round figures, about 10,000 cubic feet per day. This would be no great task for 1,000 workmen in an open space, but in our case it will be more difficult. However, as the work must be done it will be done, and I count upon your zeal as much as upon your skill.'

At 8 a.m. the first stroke of the pickaxe was given to Floridan soil, and from that moment the tool was allowed no rest in the hands of the miners, who worked in relays of three hours each.

However colossal the undertaking might appear, it did not exceed the limits of human strength. Far from it. Many works of more real difficulty have been successfully carried out, even where it has been necessary to contend against the elements. Amongst other extraordinary works, the 'Father Joseph's Well' may be cited, which descends below the very level of the Nile, near Cairo, to a depth of 300 feet, and was constructed by Sultan Saladin at a time when machinery had not increased one hundred-fold the power of man; and another well at Coblentz, sunk by Margrave John of Baden, to a depth of 600 feet. What was required now? Merely to triple the depth and double the width – which latter rendered the work much easier; consequently not one of the foremen or workpeople had any doubt as to the success of the operation.

An important decision taken by the engineer Murchison, with the consent of President Barbicane, considerably accelerated the progress of the work. One clause in the agreement stipulated that the columbiad should be circled with rings of wrought-iron, applied when hot. This precaution was manifestly unnecessary, for the gun could evidently dispense with these rings. The clause was consequently cancelled, which proved a great economy of time, as it enabled them to adopt the new system of boring, by which the masonry is constructed at the same time as the pit is sunk. Thanks to this very simple arrangement, it is no longer necessary to shore up the earth by means of stays; the masonry keeps up the sides of the shaft, and sinks by its own weight. This work was not commenced until the pickaxe had reached the harder part of the ground.

On the 4th of November, fifty workmen sank a circular pit 60 feet wide, in the very centre of the palisaded enclosure, that is to say the upper portion of Stone's Hill. The pickaxe first met about 6 inches of black soil, which was easily removed. Below this soil were 2 feet of fine sand, which was carefully put on one side for the construction of the interior mould. Below this sand was compact white clay, like English marl, in a layer 4 feet thick. Then the iron of the pickaxe struck sparks out of a hard sort of rock, formed by petrified shells, at which time the pit was 6½ feet deep, and the works of masonry commenced.

At the bottom of this excavation, a sort of wheel or strong disc of oak was laid down and securely bolted. A hole was bored in its centre, of a diameter equal to the exterior diameter of the columbiad. Upon this wheel the masonry was erected and rendered of indubitable solidity by means of hydraulic cement. When the workmen had built from the circumference towards the centre, they were enclosed in a sort of well, 21 feet wide.

When this was completed, the miners set to work with pick and spade to dig out the rock beneath the wheel, taking care, however, to leave a sufficient number of supports. When the pit had gained 2 feet in depth, these supports were removed, and the wheel with the masonry gradually settled down, while the masons continued their work at the top of the stonework, leaving a certain number of vent-holes to allow of the escape of gas during the operation of casting.

This sort of work called for extreme skill and continuous attention on the part of the workmen. More than one, whilst excavating beneath the wheel, was dangerously and even mortally wounded by the stone splinters; but their ardour did not diminish on that account, and the work continued night and day. In the daytime the rays of the sun shed, some months later, 99° of heat over these calcined plains; at night, under the white glare of the electric light,[26] the blows of picks upon the rock, the explosions of the mines, the grinding of the machinery, and the clouds of smoke which filled the air, traced round Stone's Hill a magic circle, into which neither bisons nor Seminoles had dared to penetrate.

The works advanced regularly. Steam-cranes assisted to remove the excavated soil. No unexpected obstacles arose, but only foreseen difficulties, which were skilfully overcome.

At the end of the first month the shaft had attained the given depth of 112 feet. In December this depth was doubled, and tripled in January. During the month of February the workmen had to contend against a sheet of water which rushed in from every side. It was necessary to employ the most powerful pumps and air machines to enable the workmen to cement the orifices of the springs, as a gap is stopped on board ship. At last they conquered this difficulty, but by reason of the increased softness of the soil the wheel gave way slightly, and there was a partial collapse. You may fancy the terrible effect produced by the fall of this mass of masonry, 75 fathoms high, and will not be astonished that the accident cost the lives of several workmen.

Three weeks were spent in shoring up the stonework, repairing it below, and restoring the wheel to its original solidity. Thanks to the skill of the engineer and the power of the machinery employed, the endangered edifice was set straight, and the boring continued.

No further incident delayed the progress of the work, and on the 10th of June, twenty days before the term fixed by Barbicane, the shaft was completely lined with its facing of stone, and had attained a depth of 900 feet. At the bottom the masonry rested on a massive cube measuring 30 feet in thickness, whilst its upper portion was on a level with the ground.

President Barbicane and the members of the Gun Club warmly congratulated the engineer, Murchison, who had completed this cyclopean task with such unusual rapidity.

During these eight months Barbicane had not quitted Stone's Hill for one instant. Whilst inspecting each of the operations connected with the boring, he had given his special attention to the well-being and health of his workmen, and was so fortunate as to escape those epidemics which are common to great agglomerations of men, and specially disastrous in those regions of the globe which are exposed to tropical influences.

Of course the carelessness which is inseparable from dangerous works cost the lives of several workmen; but such misfortunes cannot be avoided, and are details to which Americans pay but little attention. They think more of humanity in general than in particular instances. Barbicane, however, professed contrary principles, and took every opportunity of putting them into practice. Thanks to his care, his intelligence, his useful intervention in difficult cases, and his prodigious and humane sagacity, the average of accidents did not exceed that of many countries which are quoted for the numerous precautionary measures they enforce, amongst others France, where there is one accident for every 200,000 francs' worth of work done.

CHAPTER FIFTEEN

The festival of the casting

During the eight months occupied in sinking the shaft, the preparatory works for the casting had been carried on simultaneously and with equal rapidity. A stranger arriving at Stone's Hill would have been much surprised at the spectacle offered to his view.

Twelve hundred smelting furnaces, each 6 feet wide and standing 3 feet apart from each other, rose in a circle round the shaft at a distance of 600 yards from the central point. The circle described by these 1,200 furnaces measured 2 miles in circumference. All were constructed on the same model, and their square, high chimneys presented a most singular spectacle. J. T. Maston considered the architectural disposition superb, and said that it recalled to his mind the monuments of Washington. To his mind there could be nothing more beautiful, not even in Greece, although, as he said himself, he had never been there.

It will be remembered that at their third meeting the committee decided to use cast-iron for their columbiad, and particularly the white description. This metal is, in fact, more tenacious, more ductile, softer, more easily bored, more applicable to all moulding operations, and when smelted with coal attains a superior quality for all articles requiring a great resisting power, such as cannons, cylinders of steam-engines, hydraulic-presses, &c.

But cast-iron which has been only once smelted is rarely sufficiently homogeneous, and requires to be smelted a second time, to be purified and refined, so as to be separated from all earthy matter.

The iron-ore, before being sent to Tampa Town, was smelted in the Goldspring furnaces, and being brought in contact with coal and silicum heated to a high temperature, became impregnated with carbon and transformed into cast-iron. After this first operation the metal was despatched to Stone's Hill. As the mass of cast-iron to be transported amounted to 36 millions of pounds, the carriage by railway would have been too expensive and would have doubled the cost of the material, so it was considered preferable to load the pigs of iron on vessels at New York. No less than sixty-eight vessels, each of 1,000 tons registered burden, were chartered for this purpose, and this fleet sailed from New York on the 3rd of May into the Atlantic Ocean, along the American coast, southwards to the Bahama Canal; doubled the Cape of Florida, and entering the Bay of Espiritu Santo on the 10th of the same month, cast anchor in the port of Tampa Town. There the cargoes were discharged into the trucks of the Stone's Hill railway, and towards the middle of January the enormous mass of metal had reached its destination.

It will readily be understood that 1,200 furnaces were not too many to liquefy at the same time the 60,000 tons of castings. Each furnace could contain about 114,000 pounds of metal. They had been constructed on the same model as those used for casting Rodman's gun; they were trapezoidal in form and extremely low-slung. The heating apparatus and the flue were at the two extremities of the furnace, so that the latter could be equally heated over its whole extent. These furnaces were constructed of fire-brick, and were composed merely of a grating for the coal, and a sole on which the pigs of iron were laid. This sole inclined at an angle of 25°, and allowed the metal to flow into the receiving drafts, from whence 1,200 converging trenches carried it to the central shaft.

The day after the works of masonry and boring were completed, Barbicane commenced the manufacture of the interior mould. It was necessary to build in the centre of the shaft, and on the same axis, a cylinder 900 feet long and 9 feet wide, which would exactly fill the space reserved for the bore of the columbiad. This cylinder was composed of a mixture of clay and sand, with some hay and straw. The interval between the mould and the masonry was to be filled with the molten metal, which would thus form the tube 6 feet thick.

To maintain this cylinder in equilibrium it was necessary to surround it with iron sheeting, and support it at certain distances by stays fixed into the stone wall; after the casting these stays would be lost in the block of metal, but this was of no importance.

This operation was completed on the 8th of July, and the casting was fixed for the next day.

'The festival of the casting will be a magnificent ceremony,' said J. T. Maston to his friend Barbicane.

'No doubt,' replied Barbicane, 'but it will not be a public festival.'

'Why, won't you allow everyone to be present?'

'Most certainly not, Maston. The casting of the columbiad is a delicate operation, not to say perilous, and I prefer to have it carried out in private. When the projectile is fired off you may have a festival if you like, but not until then.'

The president was right, the operation might give rise to unforeseen dangers which could not be averted if a large influx of spectators were allowed. It was necessary to retain complete liberty of action. No one, therefore, was admitted into the enclosure except a delegation of members of the Gun Club who had arrived from Tampa Town. There were to be seen the sprightly Bilsby, Tom Hunter, Colonel Blomsberry, Major Elphiston, General Morgan and the rest, who considered the casting of the columbiad a personal matter. J. T. Maston acted as cicerone, and did not omit a single detail; he took them everywhere – to the stores, to the workshops, through all the machinery – and forced them to visit the 1,200 furnaces in succession. At the 1,200th visit they were rather sick of furnaces.

The casting was to take place at noon precisely. On the previous day each furnace had been charged with 114,000 pounds of metal in pigs, laid in crossed piles, so that the hot air might freely circulate between them. From early morning the 1,200 chimneys vomited torrents of flame into the air, and the earth was shaken as with subterranean tremblings. For each pound of metal to be smelted, a pound of coal had to be burnt, so that 68,000 tons of coal hid the face of the sun behind a dense cloud of smoke.

The heat soon became unbearable within this circle of furnaces, whose roarings resembled the growling of distant thunder. Powerful ventilators added their continuous blast, and saturated with oxygen these incandescent fires.

The operation, to be successful, had to be executed rapidly. At a signal given by firing a cannon, each furnace was to give vent to the molten metal and empty itself completely.

When these arrangements had been made, the foremen and workpeople awaited the appointed time with an impatience not unmixed with anxiety. There was no longer anyone in the enclosure, and each foreman took his post at the aperture of the run.

Barbicane and his colleagues took their stands on a neighbouring hill to view the operation. Before them stood the cannon ready to be fired at a sign from the engineer.

A few minutes before noon the first drops of metal commenced to flow, and the receiving-troughs filled gradually. When the metal was completely liquid, it was kept in suspense for a few minutes, so as to facilitate the removal of all foreign substances.

Twelve o'clock struck. The cannon thundered and flashed its yellow flame into the air. One thousand two hundred runs were opened simultaneously, and 1,200 fiery serpents crawled towards the central shaft, unrolling their incandescent coils, and plunged with fearful noise to a depth of 900 feet. It was an exciting and magnificent spectacle. The earth quaked while these waves of molten metal, launching clouds of smoke towards the sky, evaporated at the same time the moisture in the mould, and hurled it through the wind holes of the stone lining in the shape of dense masses of vapour. These artificial clouds rolled upwards in thick spirals to a height of 500 fathoms. A savage roaming beyond the limits of the horizon, might have imagined that a new crater had been formed in Floridan soil. Yet there was neither an eruption nor a waterspout, nor a storm nor a struggle of the elements, nor any of those terrible phenomena which nature is capable of producing. Man alone had caused these ruddy vapours, these gigantic flames, worthy of a volcano; these terrific tremblings, as from the shocks of an earthquake; these roarings, which rivalled the noise of hurricanes and tempests; and it was his deed which plunged into the abyss, dug by himself, a whole Niagara of molten metal.

CHAPTER SIXTEEN

The columbiad

Had the casting been successful? This could only be matter for conjecture, although the probabilities were in favour of success, since the mould had absorbed the whole of the metal melted in the furnaces. In any case it would be some time before the result could be ascertained.

When Major Rodman cast his 160-pounder, the cooling of the metal took fifteen days. How long, then, would the monstrous columbiad, crowned with wreaths of vapour, and defended by its intense heat, remain hidden from the eyes of its admirers? This was difficult to calculate.

The patience of the members of the Gun Club was sorely tried during this time. But nothing could be done, and J. T. Maston was near being roasted for his impetuosity. Fifteen days after the casting an immense cloud of vapour still filled the sky, and the ground was burning for 200 paces round the summit of Stone's Hill.

Days and weeks passed, and yet the immense cylinder showed no signs of cooling. It was impossible to get near it. There was nothing for it but to wait, and the members of the Gun Club had to make the best of it they could.

'This is the 10th of August,' said J. T. Maston, one morning, 'and there are now hardly four months to the 1st of December. We have still to remove the centre mould, bore the tube of the columbiad, and load it. We shall not be ready in time! We cannot get near the cannon! What a cruel thing it would be if it should never cool!'

They tried to calm the impatient secretary, but without success. Barbicane said nothing, but his silence hid a growing irritation. It was hard for such doughty warriors to find themselves stopped by an obstacle which time alone could conquer, and to be at the discretion of so redoubtable an enemy.

However, daily observations showed a certain change in the state of the ground. Towards the 15th of August the vapour had notably diminished in thickness and intensity. A few days later only a few small puffs appeared occasionally above the surface of the ground, like the last breathings of the monster hidden below in its stony vault. Little by little the quaking of the earth diminished, and the circle of heat became narrower. The more impatient spectators advanced as far as possible; one day they gained two fathoms, the next day four, and on the 22nd of August Barbicane and his colleagues were able to stand upon the sheet of cast-iron which appeared upon the surface of Stone's Hill. This was certainly a most salubrious standpoint, preventing all possibility of cold feet.

'At last!' said the president of the Gun Club, heaving an immense sigh of satisfaction.

The works were recommenced next day. They began by breaking up the interior mould to clear out the bore of the gun. Pickaxes, shovels, and drilling machines worked without ceasing, and although the clay and sand had become greatly hardened by the action of the heat, they were able, with the help of their powerful machinery, to remove the burning mixture from the sides of the cannon. The excavated matter was rapidly loaded upon trucks worked by steam, and such was the ardour with which the work was carried on, so pressing was Barbicane's intervention, and such the force of his arguments, which generally took the form of dollars, that on the 3rd of September all trace of the mould had disappeared.

The boring operations commenced at once; machinery was fixed, and powerful drills were brought to bear upon the uneven parts of the cast-iron, with such effect that a few weeks later the whole inner surface of the immense tube was accurately bored and had acquired a perfect polish.

On the 22nd of September, less than one year after Barbicane's communication, the enormous gun was accurately bored and declared ready for use, after having been proved by the most delicate instruments to be pointed in an exactly vertical line. They had now only the moon to wait for, and they were quite sure she would keep her appointment.

J. T. Maston's joy knew no bounds, and he nearly had a terrific fall when looking into the tube 900 feet deep. Without Blomsberry's right arm, which the worthy colonel had fortunately retained, the secretary of the Gun Club, like a second Erostratus, would have met his death in the depths of the columbiad.

So the gun was completed and there could be no further doubt possible as to its perfect execution. On the 6th of October, therefore, Captain Nicholl was obliged to settle with President Barbicane, who credited himself in his books with a sum of 2,000 dollars. It will readily be believed that the captain's wrath was so great that he was ill for a whole week. However, there were still three bets of 3,000, 4,000, and 5,000 dollars respectively, and if he should win two the business would not be a bad one, although nothing extraordinary. But money had no share in his calculations, and his rival's success in casting a cannon which 10-fathom plates could not have resisted, was a very severe blow.

Since the 23rd of September the enclosure of Stone's Hill had been thrown open to the public, and the influx of visitors will be easily imagined. In fact they came in streams from all points of the United States. The city of Tampa had increased prodigiously during the year of the works, and now contained a population of 150,000 souls. After having swallowed up Fort Brooke in a network of streets, it now covered the narrow slip of land which divided the Bay of Espiritu Santo. New streets, new squares, and a perfect forest of houses had suddenly sprung up upon these deserted shores under the heat of the American sun. Companies had been formed for the erection of churches, schools, and private houses, and in less than a year the extent of the town had increased tenfold.

It is well known that Yankees are born traders. Wherever fate has thrown them, whether in the torrid or the frozen zone, this business instinct prevails. Thus mere idlers who had come to Florida for the sole purpose of following the operations of the Gun Club, were tempted into commercial speculations as soon as they were established in Tampa Town. The ships chartered for conveying the plant and workmen had imparted unexampled activity to the port; soon vessels of all sizes and tonnage, laden with provisions and merchandise, ploughed the waters of the bay or lay at anchor before the town. Vast offices of shipowners and brokers were built in the town, and the *Shipping Gazette* daily registered the new arrivals in the port of Tampa.

While roads were multiplying round the town, the latter, in consideration of its increased importance, was placed in railway communication with the southern states of the Union. A railway united Mobile with Pensacola, the great naval arsenal of the south, and ran from this important point to Tallahassee. Here there was already a short line of railway 21 miles long, placing Tallahassee in communication with St Marks, on the coast. This railway was extended to Tampa Town, spreading along its passage new life amongst the dead or sleeping parts of Florida. Thus Tampa, thanks to the marvels of industry, caused by an idea hatched one day in the brain of one man, was entitled to consider itself an important town. It had been surnamed Moon City, and the capital of Florida suffered a total eclipse, visible from all parts of the world.

It will now be easily understood why such rivalry existed between Florida and Texas, and why the irritation of the Texans was so great when their claims were disallowed by the decision of the Gun Club. In their sagacious foresight they had understood how much a country would gain through Barbicane's experiment, and by how much good such a cannon-shot would be accompanied. Texas lost by this choice a vast trade centre, railways, and a considerable increase of population, all which advantages had been reaped by that miserable Floridan peninsula, which had been thrown like a breakwater between the waters of the Gulf and the waves of the Atlantic Ocean. So Barbicane shared with Santa Anna the most violent Texan antipathies.

The inhabitants of Tampa Town took care not to forget the operations of the Gun Club in the midst of their commercial and industrial occupations. On the contrary, the most minute details of the undertaking, even the smallest stroke of a pickaxe, had its interest for them. There was a continual procession, or rather pilgrimage, between Stone's Hill and the town.

It was easy to foresee that, on the day of the experiment, the influx of visitors would be counted by millions, for they were already collecting, on the narrow peninsula, from all parts of the world. Europe was emigrating to America.

It is true that up to this time but little satisfaction had been given to the visitors' curiosity, and many who were counting upon the spectacle of the casting, only saw the smoke. This was not much for their hungry eyes, but Barbicane would admit no one to the operation. Hence grumblings, discontent, and murmurs. The president was blamed; he was considered autocratic; his proceeding was styled un-American. There was almost a revolt round the palisade of Stone's Hill, but, as we have seen, Barbicane remained immovable in his decision.

But when the columbiad was completely finished, this privacy could not be maintained. It would have been ungracious to keep the gates closed any longer, and might even have been dangerous in the then state of public feeling. So Barbicane threw open the enclosure to everyone; but, like a practical man, he determined to make money out of the public's curiosity.

To see the immense columbiad was worth a great deal, but to descend into its depths appeared to these Americans the *ne plus ultra* of happiness in this world, and every visitor was desirous of tasting the joys of a descent into the interior of this abyss of metal. Cages, suspended from steam pulleys, gave the spectators the means of satisfying their curiosity. There was a perfect rage. Women, children and old men, all considered it their duty to penetrate the mysteries of the colossal gun to the very bottom of the bore. The cost of each descent was fixed at 5 dollars per head, but notwithstanding this high figure the influx of visitors during the two months which preceded the experiment realised to the Gun Club nearly 500,000 dollars.

It is unnecessary to add that the first visitors to the columbiad were the members of the Gun Club, the privilege being very justly reserved to that august assembly. This solemnity took place on the 25th of September. A special cage lowered President Barbicane, J. T. Maston, Major Elphiston, General Morgan, Colonel Blomsberry, the engineer Murchison, and other distinguished members of the celebrated club to the number of ten. It was still rather

warm at the bottom of the long metal tube, and the atmosphere was somewhat stifling; but what joy! what ecstasy! There was a table laid for ten on the massive block of stone supporting the columbiad, which was lighted *à giorno* by the rays of an electric light. Numerous exquisite dishes descended as from the sky, and were placed in succession before the guests; and the best wines of France flowed in profusion during this splendid repast served 900 feet below the ground.

The feast was animated and even noisy. Numerous toasts were proposed. They drank to the terrestrial globe, to its satellite, to the Union, to the Gun Club, to the moon, to Phoebe, to Selene, to the Queen of the Night, to the 'peaceful messenger of the firmament'. The noisy cheers, borne upon the sonorous waves of the immense acoustic tube, burst from its extremity with a sound like thunder, and the crowd surrounding Stone's Hill joined their acclamations with the shouts of the ten revellers at the bottom of the gigantic columbiad.

J. T. Maston's ecstasy knew no bounds. It is difficult to decide whether he shouted more than he gesticulated, or drank more than he ate. At any rate, he would not have given his place for an empire, 'Not even if the cannon, loaded, primed, and fired on the spot, were to distribute his fragments amongst the planetary regions.'

CHAPTER SEVENTEEN

A telegram

The great work undertaken by the Gun Club was, so to speak, completed, and yet two months had to elapse ere the projectile could be despatched to the moon; two months which, to the general impatience, would appear like two years. Until now the smallest details of the operation had been each day published in the papers and greedily devoured by a million eyes; but now it was to be feared that the instalment of interest given to the public would diminish daily, and each was afraid to lose his share of diurnal emotion.

This, however, was not the case. A most unexpected, most extraordinary, most incredible, most improbable incident, again attracted public attention, and plunged the world into a new state of excitement.

One day – it was the 30th of September, at 3.47 p.m. – a telegram, sent by the submarine cable between Valentia, Newfoundland, and the American coast, arrived for President Barbicane.

President Barbicane tore open the envelope, read the despatch, and, notwithstanding his power of self-control, his lips grew pale and his eyes dim on reading the twenty words contained in this telegram.

The following is the text of the telegram, which is still in the archives of the Gun Club –

Paris, France
30th September, 4 a.m.
To BARBICANE, Tampa, Florida, United States

REPLACE SPHERICAL SHELL BY CYLINDRO-CONIC PROJECTILE. WILL START INSIDE. ARRIVE PER STEAMER *ATLANTA*.

MICHEL ARDAN[27]

CHAPTER EIGHTEEN

The passenger by the Atlanta

If this astounding news had been sent by post in a sealed cover instead of by electric wire, and if the French, Irish, Newfoundland, and American clerks had not necessarily shared the confidence of the telegraph, Barbicane would not have hesitated a single instant. He would have prudently held his tongue so as not to bring his work into disrepute. The telegram might be a hoax, especially as it emanated from a Frenchman. What probability was there that anyone could be so foolhardy as to conceive the idea of such a journey? And if such a man really existed, must he not be some madman to be confined in a madhouse rather than in a cannon-ball?

But the telegram was known, for telegraphic apparatuses are not very discreet, and Michel Ardan's proposal had already spread through the different states of the Union. So Barbicane had no reason to be silent. He assembled such of his colleagues as were present at Tampa Town, and without discussing the question as to what credence was to be given to the telegram, he calmly read out the laconic message.

'It can't be possible!' 'It's improbable!' 'It's a joke!' 'He is laughing at us!' 'It's ridiculous!' 'It's absurd!' And the whole series of expressions of doubt, incredulity, stupidity and folly, circulated through the assembly with the usual accompaniment of gesticulations.

The members smiled, laughed, shrugged their shoulders or burst into loud cachinnations, each according to his humour. J. T. Maston alone was equal to the occasion.

'It is a magnificent idea,' said he.

'Yes,' replied the major, 'but it is only permissible to have ideas like that on the condition of never even thinking of putting them into practice.'

'Why not?' replied the secretary of the Gun Club, always ready for a discussion. But the matter was not followed up.

Meanwhile the name of Michel Ardan had already reached Tampa Town. Natives and foreigners were very facetious, not about this European – who was a myth, a chimerical personage – but about J. T. Maston, who had believed in his existence. When Barbicane had proposed to send a projectile to the moon, everyone thought the undertaking natural, practical, and a mere matter of gunnery. But that any reasonable being should offer to make the journey in the projectile, and hazard this improbable voyage, was looked upon as a fantastic proposal, a joke, a hoax, and, to use a very familiar word, a piece of humbug.

These mockings lasted till the evening without ceasing, and it may be said that the whole Union held its sides with laughter, which is very unusual in a country where the most impossible undertakings find promoters and partisans.

However, Michel Ardan's proposal, like all new ideas, did not fail to disquiet some minds. It altered the course of accustomed emotions: 'We never thought of that.' The very strangeness of the proposal gave it a certain interest, and people turned it over in their minds. How many things considered impossible yesterday have become realities today! Why should this journey not be made some day or other? In any case, a man who would run the risk must be mad, and as his proposal could not be taken into serious consideration, he would have done much better to have held his tongue and not trouble a whole nation with his nonsensical hallucinations.

The first question was, did this person really exist? The name of Michel Ardan was not unknown in America. It belonged to a European often quoted for his audacious undertakings. Then there was the telegram flashed through the depths of the Atlantic, the name of the ship in which the Frenchman was said to have taken his passage, the date fixed for its arrival: all these circumstances gave a certain probability to the proposal. Something more must be known about it. Isolated individuals formed themselves into groups, the groups thickened under the action of curiosity like atoms in virtue of molecular attraction, and finally a dense crowd was formed which directed its steps towards President Barbicane's dwelling.

The latter, since the arrival of the telegram, had not made

known his opinion. He had allowed J. T. Maston's expressions to go unchallenged without manifesting either approval or blame. He was remaining quiet in the background, determined to watch the course of events, but he had not taken public impatience into account, and was but little gratified at the sight of the population of Tampa crowding beneath his window. However, the murmurs and vociferations of the crowd obliged him to make his appearance, for celebrity has its duties, and consequently its trials.

When he appeared there was a dead silence, and one of the citizens, acting as spokesman, asked him point-blank the following questions.

'Is the person mentioned in the telegram under the name of Michel Ardan on his way to America; yes or no?'

'Gentlemen,' replied Barbicane, 'I know no more than you.'

'You ought to know,' exclaimed some impatient voices.

'Time will show,' replied the president calmly.

'Time has no right to keep a whole country in suspense,' continued the speaker. 'Have you altered the plans of the projectile as the telegram requires?'

'Not yet, gentlemen; but you are quite right, we must know all about it. The telegraph which has caused all this excitement must be good enough to complete the information.'

'To the telegraph!' roared the crowd.

Barbicane came down and walked at the head of the immense assemblage to the offices of the telegraph company.

Some minutes later a telegram had been despatched to Lloyd's agent at Liverpool requesting a reply to the following questions.

'What sort of a vessel is the *Atlanta*? When did she leave Europe? Had she a Frenchman named Michel Ardan on board?'

Two hours later, Barbicane was in possession of such precise information that there was no longer any room for doubt.

'The *Atlanta*, steamer, from Liverpool, sailed on the 2nd of October, for Tampa Town, having on board a Frenchman, entered in the list of passengers under the name of Michel Ardan.'

At this confirmation of the first telegram, the president's eyes shone with a sudden fire, his hands closed violently, and he was heard to murmur: 'It *is* true, then! It *is* possible! This Frenchman exists, and will be here in a fortnight. But he must be mad! I will never consent – '

And yet that same evening he wrote to Messrs Breadwill and Co., begging them to suspend, for the present, the manufacture of the projectile.

It would be impossible to describe the excitement which spread over the whole of America; how the effect of Barbicane's communication was thrown in the shade; what the papers of the Union said on the subject, how they received the news, and how they gloried in the arrival of this hero from the Old World. It would be impossible to paint the agitation in which all lived, counting the hours, the minutes, and the seconds; to give even a small idea how minds were dominated by this one thought; to show how all occupations gave way to one single preoccupation; how works were stopped, commerce suspended; how ships on the point of sailing remained in port, so as not to miss the arrival of the *Atlanta*; how trains arrived full and returned empty; how the Bay of Espiritu Santo was incessantly ploughed by steamers, packet-boats, pleasure-yachts, and fly-boats of all dimensions. And to count the thousands of visitors who quadrupled in a fortnight the population of Tampa Town, and camped out in tents like an invading army, would be a task beyond human strength, which could not be attempted without temerity.

On the 20th of October, at 9 a.m., the semaphores of the Bahama Canal signalled a thick smoke on the horizon. Two hours later the signals were answered by a large steamer, and the name of the *Atlanta* was telegraphed to Tampa Town. At 4 o'clock the English vessel entered the Bay of Espiritu Santo, and at 6 o'clock it cast anchor in the port of Tampa.

The anchor had hardly touched the sandy bottom, when 500 embarkations surrounded the *Atlanta*, and the steamer was taken by assault. Barbicane was the first over the gunwale, and shouted with a voice, of which he vainly tried to conceal the emotion: 'Michel Ardan!'

'Here,' replied an individual, standing on the bridge.

Barbicane, with crossed arms, inquiring eye, and compressed lips, looked fixedly at the passenger of the *Atlanta*.

He was a man of about forty-two years of age, tall and slightly round-shouldered, like those caryatides which support terraces on their shoulders. His massive, lion-like head was covered with thick yellow hair, as with a mane. A short face, broad at the temples, ornamented with a stiff moustache bristling like that of a cat, small tufts of yellow hair planted in the middle of his cheeks, and round eyes with a wildish though short-sighted look, completed this eminently feline physiognomy. But the nose was well shaped, the mouth wore a kindly expression, and the forehead was high and intellectual, and furrowed like a field which is never left fallow. Lastly, a body strongly developed and firmly established on two long legs, and two muscular arms, powerful and well knit, gave this European the general appearance of a well-built fellow, 'rather wrought than cast', to borrow one of the expressions of metallurgical science.

Disciples of Lavater or Gratiolet[28] would have easily traced on the skull and physiognomy of this personage indubitable signs of combativeness – that is to say, courage in danger and a tendency to break through obstacles; also signs of benevolence and love of the marvellous, an instinct which leads certain temperaments to a passionate interest in superhuman things. On the other hand the bumps of acquisitiveness, that desire to possess and to acquire, were absolutely wanting.

To complete the description of the outward appearance of the passenger by the *Atlanta* it is necessary to mention his wide-cut dress fitting loosely to his person – his trousers and coat containing so much cloth that Michel Ardan called himself a 'cloth eater' – his loose cravat, his shirt-collar thrown widely open, fully displaying his robust neck, and his cuffs – which were invariably unbuttoned – discovering a pair of febrile hands. One felt that, even in the greatest dangers or the coldest winters, that man's blood would never run cold.

On the deck of the steamer, in the midst of the crowd, he walked up and down, and was never two minutes in the same place – 'dragging his anchor', as sailors say – gesticulating, chatting familiarly with everybody, and biting his nails with nervous eagerness. He was one of those originals which Nature invents in a moment of fancy, and of which she breaks the mould directly afterwards.

The character of Michel Ardan offered a large field to the observations of an analyst. The man lived in a state of perpetual inclination to hyperbole, and had not yet passed the age of superlatives. Objects were reflected on the retina of his eye in unusual dimensions; hence an association of gigantic ideas. Everything appeared great to him except difficulties and men.

Otherwise he was of a luxuriant nature. He was an artist by instinct and wit; not one who kept up a rolling fire of jokes, but affecting rather the dropping fire of a sharpshooter. In discussion he was heedless of logic, and a declared enemy of syllogisms; but he had his own way of coming to the point. He was fond of the *argumentum ad hominem* and of defending hopeless causes.

Amongst other manias, he called himself 'a sublime ignoramus', as did Shakespeare, and professed a great contempt for men of science: 'People,' said he, 'who mark the points while we play the game.' In one word, he was a Bohemian from the world of the marvellous – adventuresome, but not an adventurer; a breakneck; a Phaethon, driving at full gallop the chariot of the sun; an Icarus with a change of wings. He never spared his person, but threw himself with open eyes into the most dangerous undertakings. He burnt his ships with greater readiness than Agathocles; and being always ready for the worst, invariably fell upon his feet, like those little pith acrobats which children play with.

In two words his motto was 'What matter?' and the love of the impossible was his 'ruling passion' – to borrow Pope's beautiful expression.

Yet this adventuresome fellow possessed all the defects inherent to his qualities. 'Who risks nothing gains nothing,' said he. Ardan risked often and yet gained nothing. He was a thorough spendthrift; he was perfectly unselfish, and listened to his heart much more than to his head; openhanded and chivalrous, he would not have signed the death-warrant of his greatest enemy, and would have sold himself to purchase the freedom of a slave.

All over France and Europe this brilliant and noisy personage was well known to everybody. The hundred voices of renown had grown hoarse in his service. He lived in a glass house, taking the whole world into the confidence of his most intimate secrets. At the same time he possessed an imposing collection of enemies amongst those whom he had brushed against, wounded, or upset, whilst elbowing his way through the crowd.

However, he was generally liked and treated as a spoilt child. People took him as they found him, and all were interested in his audacious undertakings, which were followed with uneasy attention, for he was known to be so imprudently foolhardy. When a friend tried to stay him by prophesying a catastrophe, he replied with a jovial smile, 'The forest is burnt through its own trees,' and was not aware that he quoted the prettiest of all Arabian proverbs.

Such was the passenger of the *Atlanta*. Always agitated, always boiling under the action of an internal fire, and always in a state of excitement, not by reason of what he had come to do in America – he never gave that a thought – but by reason of his feverish organisation. If ever two persons offered a striking contrast, they were certainly the Frenchman Michel Ardan and the Yankee Barbicane, though each was enterprising, hardy, and audacious in his way.

The reflections into which Barbicane was plunged at the sight of this rival, who had come to throw him in the background, were soon interrupted by the cheers and shouts of the crowd. The shouting became so frantic, and the enthusiasm took such a personal turn, that Michel Ardan, after shaking a thousand hands till he nearly lost the use of his fingers, was obliged to escape into his cabin.

Barbicane followed him without having yet spoken.

'Are you Barbicane?' asked Michel Ardan, as soon as they were alone, and with the tone of a friend of twenty years' standing.

'Yes,' replied the president of the Gun Club.

'Well, good-day, Barbicane; how are you? Very well? So much the better; that is all right!'

'So,' said Barbicane, without further preamble, 'you have made up your mind to start?'

'Quite so.'

'Nothing would stop you?'

'Nothing. Have you altered your projectile as stated in my telegram?'

'I was awaiting your arrival. But,' continued Barbicane, 'have you well considered – '

'Considered! Have I any time to lose? I come across an opportunity of making a tour in the moon, and I take advantage of it; that is all. I don't think that requires so much reflection.'

Barbicane examined this man who spoke of his proposed journey with such light-heartedness, such complete carelessness and with such a perfect absence of all disquietude.

'But at least,' said he, 'you have arranged some plan, and some means of execution?'

'I have, my dear Barbicane; but allow me to make one remark: I prefer to tell my story to everybody at once, and to make an end of it. That avoids repetitions. So, if agreeable to you, call together your friends, your colleagues – the whole town, all Florida, all America if you like – and tomorrow I will be ready to state my means of action, and to reply to any objections. Believe me I am ready to meet them. Does that suit you?'

'It does,' replied Barbicane.

Whereupon the president left the cabin, and informed the crowd of Michel Ardan's proposal. His words were met by hand-clappings and shouts of joy, for that put an end to all difficulty. The next day everyone could see the European hero at his ease. However, certain of the more obstinate spectators refused to quit the deck of the *Atlanta*; amongst others J. T. Maston had screwed his hook into the paddle-box, and it would have been necessary to use the capstan to drag him away.

'He is a hero – a real hero!' was cried on every side, 'and we are but silly women compared with this European.'

As to the president, after having begged the visitors to withdraw, he returned to the passengers' cabin, and only left it when the ship's bells struck a quarter to twelve; at which time the two rivals in popularity shook each other warmly by the hand, and Michel Ardan was on terms of the most perfect familiarity with President Barbicane.

CHAPTER NINETEEN

A meeting

The next day the sun rose much too late for the impatient wishes of the public; much too late for the luminary which was to shine on such a festival. Barbicane, fearing that indiscreet questions would be put to Michel Ardan, would have wished to reduce the audience to a small number of adepts – his colleagues for instance. But he might as well have tried to dam Niagara; and he was obliged to give up the project and let his new friend run the chances of a public conference. The new hall of the Tampa Exchange was considered insufficient for the ceremony, notwithstanding its colossal dimensions, for the proposed assembly took the proportions of a mass meeting.

The place chosen was a vast plain just outside the town, and in a few hours a sufficient space was sheltered from the rays of the sun, for the ships in the port lent their sails, spare masts, and spars, and all the accessories necessary for the construction of a colossal tent. An immense canvas roofing spread over the scorched prairies, which it protected from the rays of the sun, and beneath this covering 300,000 persons supported for hours the stifling temperature whilst waiting for the Frenchman's arrival. Of this crowd of spectators about one-third could see and hear; another third saw and heard but little; while the remainder saw nothing and heard less, but were not on that account the less enthusiastic in their applause.

At three o'clock Michel Ardan made his appearance, accompanied by the principal members of the Gun Club, giving his right arm to President Barbicane and his left to J. T. Maston, who was as radiant as the sun and almost as glowing.

Ardan mounted a hustings from which his glances spread over an ocean of black hats. He was not embarrassed, he did not try to

show off, but was easy, jovial, familiar, and amiable. He replied by a graceful bow to the shouts which greeted his appearance, and then, claiming silence by a movement of his hand, he spoke as follows in very correct English.

'Gentlemen,' said he, 'notwithstanding the heat, I am going to occupy a few moments of your time to offer you some explanations with reference to projects in which you appear to take an interest. I am neither an orator nor a man of learning, and I had no intention of speaking in public; but my friend Barbicane tells me that you wish to hear me, and I bow to your wishes, so listen with your six hundred thousand ears and kindly excuse the mistakes of the speaker.'

This familiar address was much to the taste of the audience, who expressed their satisfaction in the usual way.

'Gentlemen,' said he, 'no sign of approval or disapproval is forbidden, with which stipulation I will begin. In the first place, do not forget that you have to do with an ignoramus, but one whose ignorance is so great that he ignores even difficulties. It has appeared to him a very simple matter, an easy thing, to take a seat in a projectile, and so start for the moon. It is a journey which, sooner or later, would have to be made; and as to the mode of locomotion, that merely follows the laws of progress. Man commenced by travelling on all-fours, then one day on two feet, then on a cart, then in a coach, then in post-chaise, then in a diligence, and at last in a railway. The projectile is the carriage of the future, and in point of fact the planets are but projectiles – mere cannon-balls thrown from the hand of the Creator. But to return to our vehicle. Some of you, gentlemen, may have thought that its rapidity is excessive. That is not the case; all the stars exceed it in velocity, and the earth itself carries us three times more rapidly in its movement round the sun. I will give you some instances; but I must ask your permission to state them in leagues, as American measures are not very familiar to me, and I am afraid of becoming confused in my calculations.'

This request appeared very reasonable, and, as no objections were raised, the speaker continued in the following terms.

'Gentlemen, these are the velocities of the different planets. I am constrained to admit that, notwithstanding my ignorance, I am well acquainted with these astronomical details; but in two minutes you will be as learned as myself. Know, then, that Neptune travels at the rate of 5,000 leagues an hour, Uranus at the rate of 7,000, Saturn at the rate of 8,858, Jupiter at the rate of

8,675, Mars at the rate of 22,011, the earth at the rate of 22,500, Venus at the rate of 32,590, Mercury at the rate of 52,520, and certain comets travel at the rate of 1,400,000 leagues in their perihelion. As to ourselves, we are mere idlers and loungers, for our velocity will not exceed 9,900 leagues, and will decrease as we continue. I put it to you whether there is anything to boast of in this, and whether it is not evident that it will be some day exceeded by greater velocities of which light or electricity will probably be the mechanical agents.'

As no one seemed to doubt this assertion, Michel Ardan continued.

'My dear hearers, if we were to believe what certain narrow-minded people maintain, humanity would be enclosed within a magic circle, and condemned to vegetate on this globe, without ever being able to reach the planetary spheres. This must not be. We shall travel to the moon, we shall travel to the planets and to the stars, as we journey today from Liverpool to New York – easily, rapidly, and with safety; and the atmospheric ocean will soon be crossed as well as the oceans of the moon. Distance is a relative term which will soon be reduced to zero.'

The meeting, though well disposed in favour of the French hero, was somewhat astounded by this audacious theory, and Michel Ardan perceived it at once.

'You do not seem convinced, my worthy hosts,' said he, with an amiable smile; 'well, let us discuss the matter. Do you know how long an express train would take to reach the moon? 300 days – not an hour more. What is, after all, a journey of 86,410 leagues? Not even nine times the circumference of the earth; and certainly the majority of sailors and travellers have been over a greater distance in their lifetime. Remember that I shall only be 97 hours on the road. Oh, you think that the moon is at an immense distance from the earth, and that one should hesitate before risking the journey! but what would you say if it were a question of going to Neptune, which gravitates 1,147 millions of leagues from the sun! There you have a journey which few people could undertake, if it cost only five cents per kilometer. Baron Rothschild himself, with his milliard of money, would not be able to pay for his ticket, and would be left on the road for want of 147 millions.'

This system of argument seemed to please the meeting immensely; besides which Michel Ardan was full of his subject, and plunged into it with great animation. Feeling that he was eagerly listened to, he continued with admirable assurance.

'Well, my friends, this distance of Neptune from the sun is nothing if compared with that of the stars. To calculate the distance of the latter, we are carried into those dazzling sums where the smallest number has nine figures and a milliard is taken as unity. I beg your pardon for being so learned on this point, but it is really a question of immense interest. Listen and judge for yourself! Alpha, of Centaurus, is distant 8,000 milliards of leagues; Wega, 50,000 milliards; Sirius, 50,000 milliards; Arcturus, 52,000 milliards; the Polar Star, 117,000 milliards; Capella, 170,000; and the other stars thousands, millions, and milliards of milliards of leagues. And after that you would talk of the distance which separates the planets from the sun! You would maintain that distance exists! Error! Falsehood! Ridiculous nonsense! Do you know what I think of the world, which commences at the orb of day and finishes with Neptune? Would you know my theory? It is very simple! To me the solar world is one solid homogeneous body; the planets which compose it are pressed together, touch each other, and adhere; and the spaces which exist between them are no more than the spaces which separate the molecules of the most compact metal, silver, iron, or platinum. I have therefore the right to assert, and I repeat it with a conviction which you all must share: "Distance is a vain word, distance does not exist." '

'Well spoken! Bravo! Hurrah!' cried the assembly with one voice, electrified by the manner and the words of the orator, and by the boldness of his conceptions.

'No,' cried J. T. Maston, more energetically than the rest; 'distance does not exist.' And carried away by the violence of his feelings, he nearly fell from the top of the hustings to the ground. Fortunately he succeeded in regaining his equilibrium, and saved himself from a fall which would have proved, somewhat brutally, that distance after all is not such a vain word.

The orator then resumed his speech.

'My friends,' said Michel Ardan, 'I think the question is now settled. If I have not convinced you, all my demonstrations and my arguments must have been too weak, and the fault must lie in my theoretic studies. However that may be, I repeat that the distance from the earth to its satellite is really very unimportant, and quite unworthy of preoccupying a serious mind. I shall not go too far, I think, in asserting that trains of projectiles[29] will soon be established, in which the journey from the earth to the moon may be comfortably made; there will be neither shock, nor shaking, nor accident to be feared, and the goal will be reached rapidly, without fatigue, in a straight line, "as the bee flies", to use the language of your trappers. Before twenty years have passed, half the earth will have visited the moon.'

'Three cheers for Michel Ardan!' cried the audience, even such as were least convinced.

'Cheers for Barbicane,' modestly replied the speaker.

This act of graceful courtesy towards the promoter of the undertaking was received with unanimous applause.

'Now, my friends,' continued Michel Ardan, 'if you have any questions to ask, you will certainly embarrass such a poor scholar as I am, but I will try to answer them.'

Up to this time the president of the Gun Club had every reason to be satisfied with the turn the discussion was taking. It was dealing with speculative theory, in which Michel Ardan, carried away by his vivid imagination, showed to great advantage. It was necessary to keep from entering into practical questions, with which no doubt he would be less able to deal. Barbicane therefore hastened to take up the discussion, and asked his new friend if he thought that the moon or the planets were inhabited.

'That is a difficult problem, my worthy president,' replied the orator with a smile; 'but unless I am mistaken men of great intelligence, Plutarch, Swedenborg, Bernardin de St Pierre, and many others, have given their opinion in the affirmative. Taking natural philosophy as the standpoint, I should feel inclined to think with them. I should say that nothing useless exists in creation; and replying to your question by another question, my friend Barbicane, I should assert that if these worlds are inhabitable, they either are, or have been, or will be inhabited.'

'Hear, hear!' cried the front ranks of the spectators, whose opinion naturally decided that of the rear.

'No one could reply more logically or more justly,' said the president of the Gun Club. 'The question, therefore, resolves itself into this: are these worlds inhabitable? For my part I think they are.'

'And I am certain of it,' replied Michel Ardan.

'However,' said one of the spectators, 'there are arguments against the inhabitableness of these worlds. It would be evidently necessary in most cases that the principles of life should be modified. Take, for instance, the planets: we should be burnt up in some and frozen in others, according as they are more or less distant from the sun.'

'I regret,' replied Michel Ardan, 'that I am not personally acquainted with my hon. contradictor, for I would try to answer him. His objection has its value, but I think it may be successfully combated as well as all such as deal with the inhabitableness of these worlds. If I were a natural philosopher, I should say that if there is less caloric put in motion in the planets nearer the sun, and more, on the contrary, in the distant planets, this simple phenomenon is sufficient to equalise the heat and render the temperature of these worlds supportable to beings organised as we are. If I were a naturalist, I would say, with many illustrious *savants*, that nature supplies us on this earth with examples of animals living under very opposite conditions; that fishes breathe in an element which is mortal to other animals; that the *amphibii* have a double existence which is very difficult to explain; that certain inhabitants of the sea live at a great depth, and support, without being crushed, pressures of 50 or 60 atmospheres; that certain aquatic insects are utterly insensible to temperature, and are found at once in springs of boiling waters and in the icy plains of the Polar Ocean; consequently, that we must acknowledge in Nature a diversity in her means of action which is often incomprehensible, but not the less real, and which almost reaches omnipotence. If I were a chemist I would tell him that the aerolites, which are bodies evidently formed outside the terrestrial world, have revealed, under analysis, indubitable traces of carbon, which substance owes its existence solely to organised beings, Reichenbach's experiments having proved that it must necessarily have been "animalised".[30] Lastly, if I were a theologian, I would say, with St Paul, that the Divine redemption seems to be applicable, not only to the earth but to all the celestial worlds. But I am neither a theologian, nor a chemist, nor a naturalist, nor a natural philosopher; so, in my complete ignorance of the grand laws which rule the universe, I confine myself to answering: I do not know if these worlds are inhabited, and as I don't know I shall go and see.'

Did the opposers of Michel Ardan's theory hazard any further arguments? It is impossible to say, for the frantic shouts of the crowd would have drowned any further expression of opinion, but when silence was restored the triumphant orator added the following observations.

'As you may well think, worthy Yankees, I have only touched superficially on so great a question. I have not come here to give a public lecture and maintain a thesis on this vast subject. There is quite a series of other arguments in favour of the habitableness of these worlds, but I will not enter into them. Allow me only to insist on one point. To people who maintain that the planets are not inhabited, we may reply: you may be right if it is proved that the earth is the best possible world; but such is not the case, Voltaire notwithstanding. It has but one satellite, while Jupiter, Uranus, Saturn, and Neptune have several at their service, which advantage is not to be disdained. But what renders our globe especially uncomfortable is the inclination of its axis towards its orbit, whence arises the inequality of days and nights; hence, also, the unpleasant diversity of seasons. On our unfortunate spheroid it is always too hot or too cold. We are frozen in winter and scorched in summer. Colds, influenzas, and bronchitis prevail on our planet, whereas on the surface of Jupiter, for instance, where the axis is but slightly inclined, the inhabitants may enjoy uniform temperatures. There is a zone of spring, a zone of summer, a zone of autumn, and a zone of perpetual winter. Each Jovite can choose the climate which he pleases, and remain protected for his lifetime from all variations of temperature. You will easily understand this superiority of Jupiter over our planet, without speaking of its cycles, which last twelve years each. Further, it is evident to me, that under such auspices, and under such marvellous conditions of existence, the inhabitants of that fortunate world must be superior beings, that their scientific men are more learned, their artists more skilful, the wicked less depraved, and the good people better in all respects. Alas! what is wanting to our spheroid? Little indeed! An axis of rotation less inclined to the plane of its orbit.'

'In that case,' cried an impetuous voice, 'let us unite our efforts; let us invent machinery and straighten the axis of the earth!'

A thunder of applause was elicited by this observation, which could only have emanated from J. T. Maston. It is probable that the impetuous secretary had been carried away by his engineering instincts to risk this bold proposal; but it must be added, in the interest of truth, that many supported it with their shouts, and doubtless, could they have found the standpoint required by Archimedes, the Americans would have constructed a lever capable of raising the world and straightening its axis. Unfortunately the standpoint was wanting to these hardy mechanicians. Nevertheless this eminently practical idea met with extraordinary success; the discussion was suspended for a good quarter of an hour, and long afterwards the proposal so energetically formulated by the perpetual secretary of the Gun Club furnished a topic of conversation to all the states of the Union.

CHAPTER TWENTY

Thrust and parry

This incident would seem to have closed the discussion. It was the last word, and better could not have been found. However, when the agitation had subsided, a clear, firm voice was heard to pronounce the following words – 'Now that the speaker has treated us to so much fiction, will he have the goodness to resume his subject, give us less theory, and discuss the practical side of his expedition?'

Everyone looked towards the man who spoke these words. He was a thin, dry man, with an energetic cast of countenance, wearing his beard, in American fashion, in a tuft beneath his chin. Profiting by the successive movements in the crowd, he had gradually made his way to the front rank of spectators. There, with crossed arms and a bright, bold glance, he stared imperturbably at the hero of the meeting. After having made his request he remained silent, and appeared in no way concerned by the thousands of glances which converged towards him, nor by the murmur of disapprobation which his words excited. As the reply did not come immediately, he repeated his question in a sharp, precise tone, and added: 'We are here to discuss the moon, and not the earth.'

'You are right, sir,' replied Michel Ardan; 'the discussion has been irregular. Let us return to the moon.'

'Sir,' continued the unknown, 'you maintain that our satellite is inhabited. Very well. But if there are any Selenites, those people most certainly live without breathing; for I must remind you, in your own interest, there is not the smallest particle of air on the surface of the moon.'

At this assertion Ardan shook his yellow mane, for he understood that a struggle was about to commence with this man upon

the main question. He stared fixedly at him, and said: 'So there is no air in the moon. And who says so, if you please?'

'Men of science.'

'Really?'

'Really.'

'Sir,' continued Michel, 'joking apart, I have a great esteem for men of science who know what they are talking about, and a great contempt for those who do not.'

'Do you know any who belong to that last category?'

'Very many. In France there is one who maintains that, mathematically, a bird cannot fly; and another whose theories prove that fishes were not made to live in the water.'

'It is no question of those, sir; and I could back up my statement by names to which even you would have to defer.'

'In that case, sir, you would cruelly embarrass a poor ignoramus – who, however, would be only too happy to learn.'

'Why, then, do you enter into scientific questions, if you have not studied them?' asked the unknown, somewhat coarsely.

'Why!' replied Ardan, 'for the reason that the man is always brave who suspects no danger. I know nothing, it is true; but it is precisely my weakness which constitutes my force.'

'Your weakness will lead you into follies,' cried the unknown in a tone of great ill-humour.

'So much the better,' replied the Frenchman, 'if my folly leads me to the moon.'

Barbicane and his colleagues examined this intruder, who thus placed himself in opposition to the undertaking. None of them knew him, and the president, somewhat uneasy as to the results of a discussion on such a basis, looked at his new friend with some apprehension. The audience were attentive, but seriously uneasy, for the result of the discussion had been to draw their attention to the dangers and even to the real impossibilities of the expedition.

'Sir,' continued Michel Ardan's adversary, 'the reasons which prove the absence of all atmosphere around the moon are numerous and indisputable. I will even say that, *a priori*, if such atmosphere has ever existed it must have been drawn from the earth. But I prefer to bring forward incontrovertible facts.'

'Bring forward as many as you please, sir,' replied Michel Ardan, with great courtesy.

'You are aware,' said the unknown, 'that when luminous rays pass through a medium such as air, they deviate from the straight line, or, in other words, undergo refraction. Well, when the stars are occulted by the moon, their rays, whilst grazing the edges of the disc, do not undergo the slightest deviation, nor give the smallest indication of refraction; the evident consequence is that the moon is not surrounded by an atmosphere.'

All looked towards the Frenchman, for if this proposition was admitted the consequences were inevitable.

'That,' replied Michel Ardan, 'is your best argument, not to say your only one, and a man of science might have some difficulty in answering; but I merely say that this argument has no absolute value, for it is based on the supposition that the angular diameter of the moon is accurately defined, which is not the case. But let that pass; and tell me, my dear sir, if you admit the existence of volcanoes on the surface of the moon?'

'Extinct volcanoes, yes; not volcanoes in activity.'

'You will admit, however, that these volcanoes have been in activity during a certain period?'

'That is positive; but as they could themselves supply the oxygen necessary for combustion, the fact of their eruption in no way proves the presence of a lunar atmosphere.'

'Let that pass, then,' replied Michel Ardan; 'and let us give up this class of arguments and come to direct observations. But I warn you that I am going to put forward names.'

'As many as you like.'

'Very well then. In 1715 the astronomers Louville and Halley, when observing the eclipse of the 3rd of May, remarked certain fulminations of an unusual nature. These flashes of light were rapid and frequently renewed, and were attributed by them to storms occurring in the atmosphere of the moon.'

'In 1715,' replied the unknown, 'the astronomers Louville and Halley mistook, for lunar phenomena, phenomena of a purely terrestrial character, such as meteoric or other bodies which are produced in our atmosphere. That is what men of science reply to the facts stated by you, and my reply is the same.'

'Let us seek further, then,' said Ardan, quite unruffled by the *riposte*. 'Herschel, in 1787, observed a large number of luminous spots on the surface of the moon. Is that not so?'

'Doubtless, but without giving any explanation as to their origin, Herschel himself did not conclude from their appearance that there must necessarily be a lunar atmosphere.'

'Well answered,' said Ardan, complimenting his adversary; 'I see you are well up in selenography.'

'I have made it my study, sir; and, I may add, that the most skilful observers, those who have best studied the orb of night, Messrs Beer and Moedler, in fact, are agreed as to the complete absence of air from its surface.'

There was a movement amongst the audience, who appeared to be growing excited by the arguments of this singular personage.

'Let us go farther still,' replied Michel Ardan with the utmost calmness, 'and let me mention an important fact. A learned French astronomer, Monsieur Laussedat, when observing the eclipse of the 18th of July, 1860, remarked that the points of the solar crescent were rounded and truncated. This phenomenon could only have been produced by a deviation of the rays of the sun through the atmosphere of the moon, and there is no other explanation possible.'

'But is this fact certain?' asked the unknown.

'Absolutely certain.'

A movement in a contrary sense brought back the audience to their favourite hero, whose adversary remained silent. Ardan continued, without appearing vain of his last advantage, and said simply: 'You see, then, my dear sir, that one must not decide absolutely against the existence of an atmosphere on the surface of the moon; probably the atmosphere is not very dense – but science today generally admits its existence.'

'Not on the mountains, with your permission,' replied the unknown, who would not give in completely.

'No, but at the bottom of the valleys, and at a height not exceeding a few hundred feet.'

'In any case you will do well to take your precautions, for the air will be terribly rarefied.'

'Oh, my good sir, there will be always enough for one man. Besides, once I am up there I will try and economise, and only breathe upon great occasions.'

A formidable shout of laughter here arose at the expense of the mysterious interlocutor, who glared defiance at the assembly.

'Therefore,' continued Michel Ardan in his easy way, 'since we are agreed as to the presence of a certain atmosphere, we are obliged to admit the presence of a certain quantity of water, which is a matter of personal satisfaction to myself. Besides, my amiable contradictor will perhaps allow me to offer one other remark; we only know one side of the moon's disc, and if there is but little air on the side which looks towards us, there may possibly be a great deal on the other side.'

'And for what reason?'

'Because the moon, under the action of terrestrial attraction, has assumed the form of an egg, of which we see the smaller end; hence the conclusion arrived at by Hansen's calculations, that its central gravity is situated in the other hemisphere. Hence also the conclusion that all the masses of air and water must have been attracted to the other face of our satellite in the first days of its creation.'

'Mere speculations,' cried the unknown.

'Not so: they are theories based upon the laws of mechanics, and they appear to me very difficult to refute. I appeal to this meeting, and I put to the vote the question, whether life, such as it exists on our earth, is possible on the surface of the moon?'

Three hundred thousand auditors applauded the proposal simultaneously. Michel Ardan's adversary still wished to speak, but could not make himself heard. Cries and threats fell upon him like hail.

'Enough, enough,' cried some.

'Turn him out,' said others.

'Turn him out,' roared the infuriated crowd.

But he clung firmly to the hustings and refused to move, notwithstanding the storm, which would have gained formidable proportions if Michel Ardan had not appeased it by a gest. He was too chivalrous to abandon his contradictor in such an extremity.

'You wished to add a few words?' he said in a most gracious tone of voice.

'Yes, a hundred,' replied the unknown angrily. 'Or, rather, no, only one! To persevere in your undertaking you must be – '

'Rash! How can you call me so? I who have asked my friend Barbicane for a cylindro-conic projectile so as not to turn like a squirrel on my journey.'

'But, unhappy man, the terrible shock will kill you at the start.'

'My dear contradictor, you have just put your finger upon the only real difficulty. However, I have too good an opinion of the industrial genius of Americans not to believe that they will be able to obviate it.'

'But the heat developed by the velocity of the projectile through the air?'

'Oh, the sides are thick, and I shall soon have got through the atmosphere.'

'But how about provisions and water?'

'I have calculated that I can take sufficient for one year, and my journey will only last four days!'

'What air will you breathe on the journey?'

'I will make it by chemical process.'

'How about your fall upon the moon, if you ever reach it?'

'It will be six times less rapid than a fall upon the earth, because the gravitation is six times less upon the surface of the moon.'

'But it will still be sufficient to smash you like glass!'

'I shall lessen the fall by means of rockets,[31] properly placed and let off when necessary.'

'But even supposing all the difficulties are overcome, and all the obstacles removed – supposing that all the chances are in your favour, and admitting that you reach the moon – how will you return?'

'I will not return.'

At this reply, which was almost sublime in its simplicity, the audience were dumfounded. But their silence was more eloquent than the loudest shouts of enthusiasm. The unknown took advantage of the pause to protest once more.

'You will infallibly be killed,' cried he, 'and your death will be but the death of an insensate, of no service whatever to science.'

'Go on, generous unknown, for truly your prophecies are most agreeable!'

'This is too much,' cried Michel Ardan's adversary. 'I don't know why I continue such a useless discussion! Carry out your mad undertaking. It is not you who are to blame!'

'Oh, don't mind me!'

'No, there is another who will bear the responsibility of your actions.'

'And who is that, if you please?' asked Michel Ardan, imperiously.

'The ignoramus who organised this impossible and ridiculous attempt.'

The attack was direct. Barbicane, since the intervention of the unknown, was making violent efforts to contain himself and 'consume his own smoke', like certain boiler furnaces; but seeing himself so outrageously insulted, he started up, and was on the point of throwing himself upon the adversary who thus defied him, when he suddenly found himself separated from him.

The platform was suddenly lifted up by a hundred vigorous arms, and the president of the Gun Club had to share with Michel Ardan the honour of being carried in triumph. The burden was heavy, but the bearers relieved each other incessantly, and each one pushed, struggled, and fought to lend the aid of his shoulders to this manifestation.

However, the unknown had not taken advantage of the tumult to escape from the spot, nor could he have done so in the midst of the compact crowd. He remained in the first rank, his arms crossed, glaring at President Barbicane.

The latter did not lose sight of him, and the glances of the two men crossed each other like the blades of two duellists.

The shouts of the immense crowd were maintained at their maximum of intensity during the triumphal march. That Michel Ardan evidently enjoyed his position was shown by his beaming face; and though the platform occasionally pitched and rolled like a ship in a storm, the two heroes of the meeting proved themselves good sailors, and held firm till their bark arrived, without damage, at the port of Tampa Town.

Michel Ardan was fortunately able to escape from the last embraces of his vigorous admirers. He rushed into Franklin's hotel, gained his bedchamber, and slipped into bed, whilst an army of 100,000 men kept watch under his window.

During this time a short but decisive scene took place between the mysterious personage and the president of the Gun Club.

Barbicane, the moment he was free, had gone straight to his adversary.

'Come with me,' said he, abruptly.

The other followed him on to the quay, and soon they were both standing alone at the entrance of a wharf opening into Jones's Fall.

There these enemies, still strangers to each other, stopped simultaneously.

'Who are you?' asked Barbicane.

'Captain Nicholl.'

'I expected as much. Until now we have never chanced to meet – '

'I came here for that purpose.'

'You have insulted me.'

'Publicly.'

'And you will give me satisfaction for this insult?'

'At once.'

'No; I wish all to pass secretly between us. There is a wood situated three miles from Tampa – Skersnaw. You know it?'

'I do.'

'Would you be good enough to enter this wood on one side, tomorrow, at 5 a.m.?'

'Yes, if you will enter by the other side at the same hour.'

'You will not forget your rifle?' said Barbicane.

'Nor will you forget yours,' replied Nicholl.

After which words, spoken with great calmness, the president of the Gun Club and the captain separated. Barbicane returned to his dwelling, but instead of taking a few hours' rest he passed the night in searching for the means to obviate the shock of the projectile, and to solve the difficult problem suggested by Michel Ardan during the discussion at the meeting.

CHAPTER TWENTY-ONE

How a Frenchman settles an affair of honour

While the president and the captain were discussing the preliminaries for the duel – (terrible and savage duel, in which each adversary becomes a man-hunter!) – Michel Ardan was resting after the fatigues of his triumph. Resting is hardly the correct expression, for American beds rival for hardness their marble or granite tables. Ardan therefore slept very badly, twisting and turning between the napkins which served for sheets, and was dreaming of establishing a more comfortable couch in his projectile, when a violent noise awoke him suddenly from his slumbers. A shower of blows was beating on his door, apparently produced by some iron instrument, whilst loud shouts mingled with this too matutinal hubbub.

'Open!' someone was crying; 'for Heaven's sake, open at once!'

Ardan had no reason for complying with this noisy request; however, he rose and opened the door, at the moment when it was on the point of giving way before the efforts of the obstinate visitor.

The secretary of the Gun Club rushed into the room. A bombshell would not have entered with less ceremony.

'Yesterday evening,' cried J. T. Maston, *ex abrupto*, 'our president was publicly insulted during the meeting. He has challenged his adversary, who is no other than Captain Nicholl, and they fight this morning in Skersnaw Wood. I learned it from Barbicane's own mouth. If he is killed our project will be annihilated. This duel must be stopped. There is but one man in the world with sufficient influence over Barbicane to stop it, and that man is Michel Ardan.'

While J. T. Maston was speaking, Michel Ardan, renouncing all idea of interrupting him, had slipped on his wide trousers, and

in less than two minutes afterwards the two friends were making their way towards the suburbs of Tampa Town. During their rapid walk, Maston told Ardan the facts of the case. He informed him of the true causes of enmity between Barbicane and Nicholl; how this enmity was of ancient date; how, until then, thanks to mutual friends, the president and the captain had never met. He added that it was nothing but a rivalry between armour-plate and cannon ball, and that the scene at the meeting had been nothing but an opportunity long sought for by Nicholl to gratify a resentment of old standing.

Nothing can be more terrible than these duels, which are special to America, and during which the two adversaries seek each other through the underwood, await each other on the edge of the clearings, and draw each other from the thickets, like wild beasts. Each of them must envy those marvellous qualities which distinguish the Indians of the prairies – their quick intelligence, their ingenious cunning, their knowledge of tracks, and their scent of an enemy; for an error, a hesitation, or a false step, may prove fatal. In these duels the Yankees are often accompanied by their dogs, and, at once hunters and hunted, they follow each other's tracks for hours together.

'What a devil of a set you are,' cried Michel Ardan, when his companion had described this scene to him with much energy.

'We are as we are made,' replied J. T. Maston, modestly; 'but let us make haste.'

It was, however, in vain that Michel Ardan and he raced across the plain, still wet with dew, taking the shortest cuts through rivulets and creeks – they could not reach Skersnaw Wood before half-past five; Barbicane had headed them by at least half an hour. An old wood-cutter was there, splitting into faggots the trees which had fallen beneath his axe. Maston ran to him, crying: 'Did you see a man go into the wood with a rifle? Barbicane, the president – my best friend?'

The worthy secretary of the Gun Club naïvely thought that his president must be known to everybody, but the wood-cutter did not appear to understand.

'A sportsman,' said Ardan.

'A sportsman! Yes,' replied the wood-cutter.

'How long since?'

'About one hour.'

'We are too late,' cried Maston.

'Have you heard any shots?' asked Michel Ardan.

'No.'

'Not one?'

'Not one. That sportsman does not appear to have much luck.'

'What's to be done?' said Maston.

'We must enter the wood, even at the risk of getting a ball which is not intended for us.'

'Oh!' cried Maston, in a tone which could not be misunderstood, 'I would rather get ten balls in my head, than one in Barbicane's.'

'Forward then,' said Ardan, wringing his companion's hand.

A few seconds later the two friends disappeared in the thicket formed of giant cypress trees, sycamores, tulip trees, olive trees, tamarinds, oaks, and magnolias. These different trees interlaced their branches in an inextricable pell-mell which made it impossible to see any distance ahead. Michel Ardan and Maston walked side by side, passing silently through the tall grass, cutting a path through the thick creepers, examining the bushes and the thick depths of foliage, and expecting to hear at each step the redoubtable crack of the rifles. As regards any traces which Barbicane might have left of his passage through the wood, they were unable to discover them, but walked blindly through the half-formed tracks, on which an Indian would have followed the march of his adversary step by step.

After one hour of vain searching, the two companions made a halt, for their uneasiness had redoubled.

'All must be over,' said Maston, in a tone of discouragement. 'A man like Barbicane would not *finesse* with his enemy, nor lay traps, nor practise any manoeuvre! He is too straightforward, too courageous. He has gone straight to the danger, and doubtless so far from the wood-cutter that the wind has carried away the sound of the rifles.'

'But we!' replied Michel Ardan, 'since our entry into the wood – we would have heard.'

'And if we had arrived too late!' cried Maston despairingly.

Michel Ardan found nothing to answer to this, and he and Maston resumed their interrupted walk. From time to time they shouted and hallooed, calling now for Barbicane, now for Nicholl, but neither of the two adversaries answered their shouts. Frightened at the noise, joyous flights of birds disappeared among the branches, and some scared deer fled precipitately into the thicket. For a whole hour the search was prolonged, and the greater portion of the wood had been explored without discovering any trace of the combatants. They began to doubt the wood-cutter's statement, and Ardan was on the point of giving up a search which he considered as hopeless, when Maston stopped suddenly.

'Hush,' said he, 'there is someone there.'

'Where?' said Michel Ardan.

'There! A man! He seems motionless. He has no rifle – what can he be doing?'

'Do you recognise him?' asked Michel Ardan, whose short-sightedness was rather against him under such circumstances.

'Yes, yes; he is turning round,' replied Maston.

'And who is it?'

'Captain Nicholl.'

'Nicholl!' cried Michel Ardan; and his heart beat rapidly.

Nicholl – unarmed! Then he could have nothing further to fear from his adversary.

'Let us go to him,' said Michel Ardan, 'we will soon know how the matter stands.'

But his companion and he had not advanced more than fifty paces when they again stopped to examine the captain more attentively. They had expected to find a bloodthirsty man gloating over his revenge. What they did see filled them with stupefaction.

A closely-spun net stretched between two gigantic tulip trees, and in the very centre of this snare a little bird with entangled wings was struggling and uttering its plaintive cries. The bird-catcher who had laid this trap was not a human being, but a venomous spider, indigenous to the country, of the size of a pigeon's egg, with eight enormous legs. At the moment when this hideous insect had been on the point of seizing its prey it had been obliged to retreat and seek safety on the high branches of the tulip tree, for it was threatened in its turn by a redoubtable enemy.

In fact Captain Nicholl, with his gun lying by his side, and quite forgetful of the danger of his situation, was engaged in delivering, as delicately as possible, the victim caught in the web of the monstrous spider. When he had finished he let the little creature go, and the bird flew joyfully away and disappeared.

Nicholl was watching its flight between the branches, when he heard the following words, pronounced in a tone full of emotion: 'You are a real good fellow, you are.'

He turned round, and Michel Ardan was before him, repeating: 'And an amiable man!'

'Michel Ardan,' cried the captain, 'what are you here for, sir?'

'To shake your hand, Nicholl, and to prevent your killing Barbicane, or being killed by him.'

'Barbicane,' cried the captain, 'I have been looking for him for the last two hours, and cannot find him. Where is he hiding?'

'Nicholl,' said Michel Ardan, 'that is not polite; a man should always respect his adversary. Do not be afraid; if Barbicane is alive we will find him, and the more easily that if he is not amusing himself like you in getting little birds out of trouble he must be on the lookout for you. But when we do find him, take Michel Ardan's word for it, there shall be no duel between you.'

'Between President Barbicane and myself,' replied Nicholl gravely, 'there is such rivalry that only the death of one of us – '

'Nonsense, nonsense,' replied Michel Ardan, 'such good fellows as you may hate each other, but you must esteem each other as well; you shall not fight.'

'I will fight, sir.'

'You will not.'

'Captain,' said J. T. Maston, with much feeling, 'I am the president's friend, his *alter ego*, his second self. If you absolutely wish to kill someone, fire at me; it will be just the same thing.'

'Sir,' said Nicholl, grasping his rifle convulsively, 'these pleasantries – '

'My friend Maston is not joking,' replied Michel Ardan, 'and I quite understand his readiness to be killed for the man he loves! But neither he nor Barbicane shall fall before Captain Nicholl's fire, for I have such a seductive proposal to make to the two rivals that they will be sure to accept it.'

'What is that?' asked Nicholl with visible incredulity.

'Be patient,' replied Ardan; 'I can only communicate it in the presence of Barbicane.'

'Let us look for him, then,' cried the captain; and the three men set off together. The captain, having uncocked his rifle, threw it over his shoulder, and stepped out in silence.

For half an hour their researches were useless. A sinister presentiment arose in Maston's mind; he watched Nicholl closely, wondering whether the captain had not already satisfied his vengeance, and whether the unfortunate Barbicane was not lying, shot through the heart, in some blood-bespattered thicket. Michel Ardan appeared to have the same suspicion, and both were observing Captain Nicholl with inquiring eyes when Maston suddenly stopped. The motionless head and shoulders of a man appeared about twenty paces off, leaning against the trunk of a gigantic catalpa, and half hidden by the grass.

'It is he,' said Maston.

Barbicane did not move. Ardan looked suspiciously at the captain, but the latter appeared unmoved. Ardan stepped forward, crying out: 'Barbicane! Barbicane!'

There was no reply. Ardan rushed towards his friend, but at the moment when he was going to seize him by the arm he stopped short and uttered a cry of surprise. Barbicane, pencil in hand, was tracing formulae and geometrical figures in his notebook, whilst his rifle lay uncocked by his side.

Absorbed in his work, Barbicane had forgotten his duel and his vengeance, and had seen and heard nothing.

But when Michel Ardan laid his hand upon him he rose, started, and looked up at him with astonishment.

'Hallo!' said he, 'you here? *Eureka*, my friend, *eureka*!'

'What is it?'

'The means!'

'What means?'

'The means to nullify the shock at the despatch of the projectile!'

'Really!' said Michel, glancing at the captain from the corner of his eye.

'Yes, with water; the water will act as a spring – Hallo, Maston, you here too?' cried Barbicane.

'*In propriâ personâ*,' replied Michel Ardan; 'and let me introduce, at the same time, worthy Captain Nicholl.'

'Nicholl!' cried Barbicane, jumping up. 'I beg your pardon, captain,' he said; 'I had forgotten – I am ready – '

But Michel Ardan interfered, without leaving the two enemies time to provoke each other.

'By Jove!' said he, 'it is fortunate that two good fellows like you did not meet sooner; we should now be mourning one or the

other; but, thank Heaven, there is nothing further to fear! Hatred that can be forgotten to work out mechanical problems, or to play tricks upon spiders, cannot be very dangerous for anyone.'

Michel Ardan related to the president how he had found the captain.

'I leave you to judge,' said he in conclusion, 'if two good fellows such as you were intended to blow each other's brains out with a rifle-bullet?'

There was something so unexpected in this rather ridiculous situation that Barbicane and Nicholl hardly knew how to face each other. Michel Ardan felt this, and resolved to hasten the reconciliation.

'My good friends,' said he, with his most fascinating smile, 'there has never been more between you than a misunderstanding – nothing else. Well, to prove that all animosity is at an end, and as you are not afraid of a little danger, accept frankly the proposal which I am going to make to you.'

'Say on,' said Nicholl.

'Our friend Barbicane believes that his projectile will fly straight to the moon?'

'Most decidedly,' replied the president.

'And our friend Nicholl is convinced that it will fall back to the earth?'

'I am certain it will,' cried the captain.

'Very good!' continued Michel Ardan. 'I have not the pretension to make you agree, but what I say is this: start with me, and see if we are stopped on our journey!'

'What?' said J. T. Maston, stupefied.

The two rivals at this sudden proposal had raised their eyes and observed each other attentively. Barbicane awaited the captain's reply, and Nicholl waited for Barbicane to speak.

'Well,' said Michel, in his most insinuating tone, 'since there is no shock to be feared!'

'Agreed,' cried Barbicane.

Notwithstanding the quickness with which he uttered the word, Nicholl had completed it at the same time as he.

'Three cheers! Bravo! Hip, hip, hurrah!' cried Michel Ardan, offering a hand to each of the two adversaries. 'And now the matter is settled, my friends, allow me to treat you *à la Française*. Let us go to breakfast.'

CHAPTER TWENTY-TWO

The new citizen of the United States

That same day all America learnt at once the meeting of Captain Nicholl and President Barbicane, and its singular termination. The part played therein by the chivalrous European, his unexpected proposal, which had settled the difficulty; the simultaneous acceptance by the two rivals; this conquest of the lunar continent, to which France and America were to march side by side – all combined to increase Michel Ardan's popularity. It is well known with what frenzy Yankees become enamoured of an individual. In a country where sedate magistrates harness themselves to a ballet-girl's carriage, and drag her in triumph through the streets, it is easy to imagine the enthusiasm provoked by the audacious Frenchman. If the horses were not taken out of his carriage it was probably because he had none; but he was overwhelmed with all the other proofs of enthusiastic regard. Every citizen had a personal affection for him: '*e pluribus unum*', according to the motto of the United States. From that day Michel Ardan had not a moment's repose. Deputations from all points of the Union harassed him without ceasing. He was obliged to receive them, whether he would or not. The hands he shook and the people he spoke with were beyond all count, and he was soon completely knocked up. His voice had become hoarse through innumerable speechifyings, only unintelligible sounds escaped from his lips, and he nearly caught a gastro-enteritis from the toasts he was obliged to drink to all the counties of the Union. So much success would have probably intoxicated any other man from the first day, but he was able to maintain himself in a charming and witty state of semi-sobriety.

Among the deputations of every kind which assailed him on all sides, that of the lunatics was careful not to forget what they owed to the future conqueror of the moon. One day some of these poor people, who are sufficiently numerous in America, begged to be allowed to return with him to their native country. Some amongst them pretended to speak 'Selenite', and wanted to teach it to Michel Ardan. The latter willingly humoured their harmless mania, and took all sorts of messages for their friends in the moon.

'What a singular hallucination,' said he to Barbicane, after having got rid of them; 'yet it is an hallucination to which the finest intelligences are subject. One of our most illustrious *savants*, M. Arago, tells me that many of the wisest people, even such as are most cautious in their conceptions, give way to great exaltation and extraordinary singularities whenever the moon is in question. Do you believe in the influence of the moon in sicknesses?'

'Not much,' replied the president of the Gun Club.

'Nor do I; yet history furnishes some astonishing facts. For instance, in 1693, during an epidemic, the greatest number of persons died on the 21st of January, during an eclipse. The celebrated Bacon fainted during eclipses of the moon, and only recovered after the complete emersion of that satellite. King Charles VI relapsed six times into idiocy during the year 1399, either at the new or at the full moon. Doctors have classed epilepsy amongst the disorders which follow the phases of the moon. All nervous disorders appear to be subject to her influence. Mead speaks of a child who fell into convulsions whenever the moon entered into opposition. Gall observed that the exaltation of weak-minded people increased twice in each month, at the time of the new and full moon. There are a thousand other observations of this sort upon vertigoes, malignant fevers, and somnambulisms, which go far to prove that the Queen of the Night has a mysterious influence on terrestrial illnesses.'

'But how? Why?' asked Barbicane.

'Why?' replied Ardan. 'By George, I'll give you the same answer which Arago repeated nineteen centuries after Plutarch: "Perhaps because it is not true." '

In the midst of his triumph Ardan could escape from none of the annoyances to which celebrities are exposed. Caterers for the public wished to exhibit him. Barnum offered him a million if he would allow himself to be carried from town to town through the United States, to be shown off like some curious animal. Michel Ardan called him 'impertinent showman', and told him to go and exhibit himself.

However, though he refused to satisfy public curiosity in this manner, his portraits were soon spread over the world, and filled the place of honour in all the albums. Copies were made in all sizes, from a full-size picture down to microscopic reductions of the size of a postage-stamp. Everyone could possess his hero in all imaginable postures – his head, his bust, his full-length figure, full face, in profile, in three-fourths, or with his back turned. More than 1,500,000 proofs were taken, and he had, further, an excellent opportunity to dispose of himself for relics, but he did not take advantage of it. He had still hairs enough left on his head to make his fortune by selling them at a dollar apiece.

In truth this popularity was not displeasing to him; on the contrary, he placed himself at the disposal of the public, and corresponded with the entire universe. His jokes were repeated and widely propagated, especially such as were not his own. Like Sheridan, more witty sayings were attributed to him than a lifetime would have sufficed to utter.

Not only had he the men on his side, but the women also. What an infinity of 'advantageous matches' he might have made, had he been desirous of 'settling'. Old maids especially, who had been withering for forty years, remained day and night in contemplation before his photograph. Most certainly he could have found wives by the hundred, even if he had stipulated that they should follow him into the air, for women are intrepid unless afraid of everything. But it was not his intention to settle on the lunar continent, and to bring up a progeny of little Franco-Americans. So he refused.

'Go up there,' said he, 'to play the part of Adam with a daughter of Eve? No, thank you; I should be afraid of serpents.'

As soon as he could escape from the too-oft-repeated joys of his triumph, he accompanied his friends on a visit to the columbiad, which he certainly owed to the monster cannon. Besides, he had become very learned in gunnery since he had lived with Barbicane, J. T. Maston, and that lot. His greatest pleasure consisted in repeating to these worthy artillerists, that they were nothing but amiable and learned murderers. He was always making jokes on this subject. On the day that he visited the columbiad he greatly admired it, and was lowered to the bottom of the bore of this gigantic mortar, which was soon to launch him to the lunar sphere.

'At least,' said he, 'that cannon will do no harm to anybody, which is rather unusual as cannons go; but as regards your machines – which destroy, and burn, and break, and kill – don't talk to me about them, and don't tell me that they are to be admired, for I do not believe it.'

We must mention here a proposal connected with J. T. Maston. When the secretary of the Gun Club heard Barbicane and Nicholl accept Michel Ardan's proposal, he resolved to join them, and make up a party of four. One day he asked to be allowed to accompany them, but Barbicane, although sorry to refuse him anything, pointed out to him that the projectile could not contain such a large number of passengers. J. T. Maston, in despair, addressed himself to Michel Ardan, who begged him to be resigned, and made use of his usual *argumenta ad hominem*.

'You see, old fellow,' said he, 'you must not be offended, but really between ourselves you are too incomplete to appear in the moon.'

'Incomplete!' cried the valiant invalid.

'Yes, my worthy friend. Think for one moment, if we were to meet inhabitants up there, would you like to give them such a sad idea of what goes on down here as to teach them what war is, and show them that we employ the best part of our time in devouring each other, and breaking legs and arms, on a globe which could maintain one hundred milliards of inhabitants, and where there are only about twelve hundred millions? Why, my worthy friend, you would have us turned out!'

'But if you arrive there in pieces,' replied J. T. Maston, 'you will be as incomplete as I am.'

'No doubt,' replied Michel Ardan; 'but we shall not arrive there in pieces.'

In fact, a preparatory experiment which was tried on the 18th of October had yielded the best results, and encouraged legitimate hopes of success. Barbicane, who was desirous of forming an opinion as to the effect of the shock at the moment of the departure of the projectile, had sent for a 32-inch mortar from the arsenal of Pensacola. It was fixed on the shore of Hillisborough Bay, so that the shell might fall into the sea, and its fall be thus broken. They wanted to ascertain the shock at the departure, and not the shock on arrival.

A hollow projectile was prepared with the greatest care for this experiment. A thick quilting, covering a network of springs made of the best steel, lined it internally. It formed a perfect nest, carefully wadded.

'What a pity not to be able to get inside,' said J. T. Maston, regretting that his size did not allow him to try the adventure.

In this charming shell, which closed by means of a screw-lid, a large cat was first placed, and then a squirrel belonging to the perpetual secretary of the Gun Club, and to which J. T. Maston was particularly attached. They wanted to find out how this little animal, which is not much subject to vertigo, would stand this experimental[32] journey.

The mortar was loaded with 160 pounds of powder, and the shell was then inserted and the gun fired.

The projectile flew upwards with great velocity, described a majestic parabola, reached a height of nearly a thousand feet, and then with a graceful curve plunged into the midst of the waves.

Without losing an instant a boat was despatched to the spot; skilful divers plunged beneath the water and fixed cables to the handles of the shell, which was immediately hauled on board. Five minutes had not elapsed between the moment when the animals were shut in and the moment when the lid of their prison was unscrewed.

Ardan, Barbicane, Maston, and Nicholl were in the boat, and assisted at the operation with a feeling of interest easily understood. Hardly was the shell opened when the cat jumped out, a little frightened, but full of life, and without any appearance of having returned from an aerial expedition. But where was the squirrel? They searched for it, but in vain, and were driven

at last to the conclusion that the cat had eaten its travelling companion.

J. T. Maston was much grieved at the loss of his poor squirrel, and resolved to inscribe its name amongst the list of martyrs to science.

After this experiment all hesitation and fear disappeared; besides, Barbicane's plans would render the projectile yet more perfect, and almost completely nullify the effects of the shock.

Nothing remained now but to start.

Two days later Michel Ardan received a message from the President of the Union, an honour of which he showed himself particularly sensible. As in the case of his chivalrous fellow-countryman, the Marquis de Lafayette, the Government conferred on him the title of Citizen of the United States of America.

CHAPTER TWENTY-THREE

The projectile-carriage

After the completion of the celebrated columbiad, public interest was immediately drawn to the projectile, the new vehicle which was to carry through space our three bold adventurers. Nobody had forgotten that Michel Ardan in his telegram of the 30th of September had asked for an alteration of the plans which had been settled by the members of the committee.

At that time President Barbicane considered with reason that the form of the projectile was of small importance, for after traversing the atmosphere in a few seconds its passage would be made in absolute vacuum. The committee had chosen the round shape, so that the shot might turn upon its axis and act as it thought fit. But from the moment that it was to become a vehicle the matter was different. Michel Ardan had no desire to travel like a squirrel, he wished to ascend with his head uppermost and his feet below, as much at his ease as in the car of a balloon – more rapidly, no doubt, but without turning a series of very undignified somersaults.

New plans were therefore sent to Messrs Breadwill and Co., of Albany, with the request to have them executed without delay. The projectile thus modified was cast on the 2nd of November, and despatched immediately to Stone's Hill by the Eastern Railway.

On the 10th, it reached its destination without accident. Michel Ardan, Barbicane, and Nicholl awaited with the greatest impatience this 'projectile-carriage' in which they were to journey to the discovery of a new world.

They were fain to admit that it was a magnificent piece of metal, and a metallurgical product which did the greatest honour

to the industrial genius of the Americans. It was the first time that aluminum had been obtained in so considerable a mass, and it might justly be considered a prodigious result. The precious projectile gleamed in the rays of the sun. To see it, with its imposing size, covered with its conical roof, it might easily have been taken for one of those turretlike pepper-boxes which the architects of the middle ages erected at the angles of their castles. It only wanted loopholes and a weathercock.

'I fully expect,' cried Michel Ardan, 'to see a man-at-arms come out of it with a partisan and steel corsolet. We shall be like feudal lords in there, and with a cannon or two we might stand a siege from a whole army of Selenites, if there be any in the moon.'

'So you like the carriage?' asked Barbicane.

'Yes, pretty well,' replied Michel Ardan, who examined it from an artist's standpoint, 'only I am sorry that the shape is not more slender and the cone more graceful. It ought to have been finished off with some ornaments in metal-work, with a griffin, for instance, or a gargoyle, or a salamander rising from the fire with spread wings and an open mouth.'

'What would be the good of that?' said Barbicane, whose matter-of-fact mind was but little sensible of the beauties of art.

'What good, friend Barbicane? Alas! since you put such a question I am afraid you would never understand.'

'Never mind that; tell me, worthy comrade.'

'Well, to my mind, one ought always to introduce art into everything that one does. Do you know an Indian piece called "The Chariot and the Child?"'

'Never heard the name,' replied Barbicane.

'I am not surprised,' continued Michel Ardan. 'Learn, then, that in this piece there is a robber who stays to consider, when on the point of breaking into a house, whether he will make his hole in the form of a lyre, of a flower, of a bird, or of a vase! Now tell me, friend Barbicane, if you had been a member of the jury, would you have brought that thief in guilty?'

'Without hesitation,' replied the president of the Gun Club, 'and with a recommendation that the full penalty might be inflicted.'

'And I would have acquitted him, friend Barbicane. That is why you will never understand me.'

'I shall not even try, most radiant artist.'

'At any rate,' continued Michel Ardan, 'since the exterior of our "projectile-carriage" is not to my taste, I must be allowed to furnish it as I like, and with all the luxury which is proper for ambassadors from the earth.'

'In that respect, my worthy Michel,' replied Barbicane, 'you shall act as you think proper. We give you full permission.'

But before going into the question of what might be agreeable, the president of the Gun Club had given his attention to what was more useful, and the means invented by him to lessen the effects of the shock were most intelligently applied.

Barbicane had said to himself, not without reason, that no spring would be sufficiently powerful to deaden the shock, and during his famous promenade in Skersnaw Wood he had arrived at an ingenious solution of this great difficulty. He intended to use water as the medium in this matter.

The projectile was to be filled to a height of three feet with a bed of water supporting a perfectly water-tight wooden disc, which worked easily against the interior walls of the projectile. Upon this raft the passengers would take their stand. As to the mass of liquid, it was divided by horizontal separations which the shock of departure would break in succession. Then each bed of water, from the lowest to the highest, escaping through service-pipes to the upper portion of the projectile, acted as a spring; and the disc, which was itself provided with extremely powerful buffers, could only reach the bottom of the projectile when the different separations had been broken through. Doubtless the travellers would still feel a violent shock after the complete escape of the liquid mass, but the first shock would be almost completely destroyed by this powerful spring.

It is true that 3 feet of water on a surface of 54 square feet would weigh nearly 11,500 pounds, but the pressure of gas accumulated in the columbiad would be sufficient, in Barbicane's opinion, to deal with this increase of weight; besides which, the shock would force out all the water in less than a second, and the projectile would promptly recover its normal weight.

This is what the president of the Gun Club had imagined, and the manner in which he considered the great question of the shock to have been solved.

In all other respects the work which had been undertaken by Messrs Breadwill's engineers had been marvellously well executed; and once the effect was produced, and the water driven out, the travellers could easily get rid of the broken partitions, and take to pieces the movable disc which supported them at the moment of their departure.

As regards the upper walls of the projectile, they had been thickly padded with leather placed over spirals of the best steel, as elastic as watch-springs; the service-pipes were hidden by this lining. Thus all imaginable precautions had been taken to deaden the first shock, and, as Michel Ardan said, 'One must have been very ill-conditioned indeed to allow oneself to be hurt.'

The projectile measured, exteriorly, 9 feet in width by 12 feet in height. In order not to exceed the given weight, the thickness of the walls had been slightly reduced and the lower portion strengthened, as the latter had to support the whole force of the gas developed by the combustion of the gun-cotton. This is the reason why, in all cylindro-conic shells, the lower portion is always the thickest. The entrance to this metal tower was by a narrow opening made in the side of the cone, and resembling the manhole of a steam boiler. It shut hermetically, by means of an aluminum plate fixed to the interior by powerful screws, so that the travellers could leave their movable prison, at will, upon arrival at the moon.

It was not sufficient, however, to make the journey, it was necessary to be able to see during the passage. Nothing could be easier! Under the padding were four lenticular glass scuttles of great thickness – two in the circular wall of the projectile, a third in its lower portion, and a fourth in the conic roof. Thus the travellers would be able to observe during their passage the earth which they were leaving, the moon which they neared, and the constellated regions of the heavens. As a precautionary measure these scuttles were protected from the shock of the departure by plates let into grooves, but which could easily be got rid of by unscrewing the bolts from within. By this means the air contained in the projectile could not escape, and observations were rendered possible.

All these mechanisms were admirably constructed and worked with the greatest ease, and the engineers had not shown themselves less intelligent in the interior arrangements of the 'projectile-carriage'.

Reservoirs, firmly fixed down, contained water and the necessary provisions for three travellers; the latter could even obtain fire and light by means of gas contained in a special reservoir, under a pressure of several atmospheres. It was only necessary to turn a tap, and during six days the gas would light and heat this comfortable vehicle. As you see, nothing was wanting of things essential to life or even to comfort. Further, thanks to the artistic instincts of Michel Ardan, taste was combined with utility, and the projectile would have become quite an artist's studio had there been sufficient space. It would be wrong to suppose that three persons would be much crowded in this metal tower. It possessed an area of 54 square feet and a height of 10 feet, which allowed the passengers a certain freedom of movement. They would not have been so much at their ease in the most comfortable railway carriage in the United States.

The question of provisions and light being thus settled, there only remained the question of air. It was evident that the air contained in the projectile would not suffice for the travellers' breathing during four days, inasmuch as each man consumes, in about one hour, all the oxygen contained in 100 litres of air. Barbicane and his two companions, with two dogs which they intended to take with them, would consume, in twenty-four hours, 2,400 litres of oxygen, or about seven pounds in weight. It was, therefore, necessary to renew the air in the projectile. But how? By a very simple process – that of Messrs Reiset and Regnault, mentioned by Michel Ardan during the discussion at the meeting.

It is known that air is composed principally of 21 parts of oxygen and 79 parts of azote (nitrogen). Now what takes place when we breathe? A very simple phenomenon. Man absorbs the oxygen of the air which is necessary to maintain life, and exhales the nitrogen intact. The air thus exhaled has lost nearly five per cent. of its oxygen, and contains then an almost equal volume of carbonic acid, produced by the combustion of the elements of blood by the inhaled oxygen. Thus, in a confined space, after a certain lapse of time, all the oxygen of the air is replaced by carbonic acid, which is a very deleterious gas.

The question was therefore reduced to this – the nitrogen remaining intact – first, how to replace the oxygen absorbed? Secondly, how to destroy the carbonic acid exhaled? Nothing could be more easy by means of chlorate of potash and caustic potash.

Chlorate of potash is a salt which presents itself in the form of white crystals; at a temperature of more than 400° it is transformed into chloride of potassium, and the oxygen which it contains is entirely liberated. Eighteen pounds of chlorate of potash produce seven pounds of oxygen, which is just the quantity required by the travellers during twenty-four hours. There you have the supply of oxygen.

Caustic potash has a great affinity for carbonic acid, and it is only necessary to wave it through the air and it will absorb all that is therein contained, and form a bi-carbonate of potash. There you have the means of getting rid of the carbonic acid.

By combining these two means, it was easy to restore all its vivifying qualities to the vitiated air – an experiment which Messrs Reiset and Regnault had successfully carried out.

It is true that the experiments, hitherto, had been made *in anima vili*, and notwithstanding the scientific precision thereby attained it was quite unknown how men would be able to bear it.

This latter remark was made at the meeting when this important question was under discussion. Michel Ardan would not admit the possibility of a doubt as to their being able to live in this artificial air, and he offered to make a trial before their departure. But the honour of making this experiment was energetically claimed by J. T. Maston.

'As I am not going with you,' said the worthy artillerist, 'at least you may allow me to pass a week in the projectile.'

It would have been ungracious to refuse him this, so his wish was granted. A sufficient quantity of chlorate of potash and caustic potash was placed at his disposal, together with provisions for eight days. Then, having shaken his friends by the hand, he let himself down into the projectile, on the 12th of November, at 6 a.m., with the express command that his prison was not to be opened before the 20th, at 6 p.m. The plate covering the aperture was hermetically closed.

What took place during these eight days? It was impossible to tell, for the thickness of the sides of the projectile prevented any sound from being heard outside.

On the 20th of November, at 6 p.m. precisely, the plate was removed. J. T. Maston's friends had not been free from some anxiety, but they were promptly reassured on hearing a loud hurrah shouted by a jovial voice. Soon the secretary of the Gun Club appeared at the summit of the cone in a triumphant attitude.

He had grown fat!

CHAPTER TWENTY-FOUR

The telescope of the Rocky Mountains

On the 20th of October of the preceding year, after the close of the subscription, the president of the Gun Club had credited the Cambridge Observatory with the amount necessary for the construction of an enormous optical instrument.

This instrument was to be either a lunette or a telescope, and sufficiently powerful to render any object, more than 9 feet in length, visible on the surface of the moon.

There is an important difference between a lunette and a telescope, which it is well to mention here. The lunette is composed of a tube, having at its upper extremity a convex lens called the object-glass, and at its lower extremity another lens called the eye-glass, to which the observer's eye is applied. The rays emanating from a luminous body pass through the first lens, and form by refraction a reversed figure in its focus. This figure is seen through the eyeglass, which magnifies it just like a magnifying-glass. So the tube of the lunette is closed at either extremity by an object-glass and an eye-glass.

The tube of the telescope, on the contrary, is open at its upper extremity. The rays of the object under observation enter freely and strike on a concave metallic mirror – that is to say, they converge. From thence the reflected rays are met by a small mirror which reflects them on to the eye-glass, by which latter the figure is magnified.

Thus in lunettes refraction plays the principal part, and reflection in telescopes. Hence the name of refractors given to the former, and that of reflectors attributed to the latter. The great difficulty of execution in these optical instruments lies in the manufacture of the object-glasses, whether lenses or metallic mirrors.

However, at the time when the Gun Club undertook its great experiment, these instruments had attained a high degree of perfection, and produced magnificent results. The time was far distant, when Galileo had observed the stars through his poor lunette which only magnified seven times. Since the sixteenth century, optical instruments had considerably increased in breadth and in length, and enabled astronomers to examine the starry firmament, to an extent hitherto unknown. Amongst the refracting instruments in existence at that time, the most notable were the lunette in the observatory of Polkowa, in Russia, of which the object-glass measured 15 inches in diameter; the lunette of the French optician Lerebours, which had an object-glass of similar dimensions; and, lastly, the lunette in the Cambridge Observatory, which was provided with an object-glass 19 inches in diameter.

Amongst the telescopes there were two of remarkable power and gigantic dimensions. The first, constructed by Herschel, was 36 feet long, and possessed a mirror 4½ feet wide; by it objects were magnified 6,000 times. The second was in Ireland, in Birr Castle, Parsonstown Park, and belonged to Lord Rosse; the length of its tube was 48 feet, the width of its mirror 6 feet, it magnified 6,400 times, and it had been found necessary to erect an immense construction in brickwork to contain the apparatus requisite for working the instrument, which weighed 28,000 pounds.

It will be seen, however, that notwithstanding these colossal dimensions, the magnifying power obtained did not exceed 6,000 times in round numbers; but an enlargement of 6,000 times would only bring the moon to a distance of 39 miles, and only render visible objects having 60 feet in diameter, unless these objects were of considerable length.

In the present instance, the projectile was only 9 feet wide by 15 feet in length; therefore the moon must be brought to 5 miles at the utmost, and, consequently, the magnifying power must be 48,000 times.

This was what the Cambridge Observatory had to execute. There were no financial difficulties in the way, so they had only to contend with the material difficulties.

In the first place they had to choose between telescopes and lunettes. The latter offered some advantages over telescopes. With equal object-glasses they possessed greater magnifying power, because the rays of light, passing through lenses, lose less by absorption than by reflection from the metallic mirror of a telescope. On the other hand, the thickness that can be given to a lens is limited, for if made too thick, it no longer allows the rays of light to pass. Further, the construction of large lenses is excessively difficult, and requires a considerable time – sometimes even years.

For this reason – although figures were to be seen with greater clearness through lunettes, which advantage would be inappreciable as regards the moon, whose light is merely reflected – it was decided to employ the telescope, which is more easily constructed and can be endowed with a greater magnifying power. However, as rays of light lose a great portion of their intensity by passing through the atmosphere, the Gun Club resolved to set up their instrument on one of the highest mountains of the Union, by which means the thickness of the stratum of air would be considerably lessened.

We have seen that in telescopes the eye-glass – that is, the magnifying-glass to which the observer places his eye – produces the enlargements; and that the object-glass, or mirror, which bears the greatest number of enlargements, is the one with the largest diameter and the greatest focal distance. To magnify 48,000 times it was necessary to greatly exceed the object-glasses constructed by Herschel and Lord Rosse. Therein lay the difficulty, for the construction of these mirrors is a very delicate operation.

Happily, some years ago, a member of the French Institute named Léon Foucault, had invented a process which greatly facilitated the polishing of object-glasses, by substituting silver-plated glasses for metallic mirrors. It was merely necessary to manufacture a sheet of glass, of the requisite size, and to give a metal back to it by means of a salt of silver. This process had given excellent results, and was adopted for the manufacture of the object-glass.

The latter was fixed in the way invented by Herschel for his telescope. In the immense instrument, constructed by the Slough astronomer, the image of the object reflected by the inclined mirror at the lower extremity of the tube, was concentrated at the other extremity where the eye-glass was situated. Thus the observer, instead of placing himself at the lower end of the tube, stationed himself at the upper end, and there looked through his magnifying-glass down into the enormous cylinder. The advantage of this arrangement was that it allowed of the suppression of the small mirror which reflected the figure on to the eye-glass. By this means the latter only received one reflection instead of two; so the stoppage of luminous rays was much less, the image was less weakened, and finally greater clearness was obtained, which was a great advantage in the observations they were about to make.

So soon as these resolutions had been taken, the work commenced. According to calculations made by the committee of the Cambridge Observatory, the tube of the new reflector was to be 280 feet long and its mirror 16 feet in diameter.

However colossal such an instrument might appear, it was not to be compared to the telescope, 10,000 feet long, which the astronomer Hook proposed to construct a few years ago. Nevertheless, such an instrument was not to be made without difficulty.

The question as to the site was quickly settled. A high mountain had to be chosen, and high mountains are not numerous in the United States.

In fact the mountain system of this great country is reduced to two chains of medium height, between which flows the magnificent Mississippi, which Americans would call 'the King of Rivers', if they admitted any sort of royalty whatever.

To the east lie the Appalachians, of which the highest point is in New Hampshire, and does not exceed the moderate height of 5,600 feet.

To the west are the Rocky Mountains, an immense chain which commences at the Straits of Magellan, follows the west coast of South America under the name of the Andes, or Cordilleras, crosses the Isthmus of Panama, and runs through North America up to the borders of the Polar Sea.

These mountains are not of any great height, and the Alps or Himalayas look down upon them with supreme contempt, for the highest point only rises to 10,701 feet, whereas Mont Blanc measures 14,439, and Kintschindjinga towers 26,776 feet above the level of the sea.

But as the Gun Club desired that the telescope, as well as the columbiad, should be established within the states of the Union, they were obliged to content themselves with the Rocky Mountains, and all the necessary apparatus was despatched to the summit of Long's Peak[33] in the Missouri territory.

Words would be powerless to describe the difficulties of all kinds which the American engineers had to conquer, and the prodigies of audacity and skill which they accomplished. They had to raise enormous stones, heavy blocks of wrought-iron, weighty corner-clamps, huge portions of the cylinder, and the object-glass (alone weighing nearly 30,000 pounds), beyond the line of perpetual snow, to a height of more than 10,000 feet, after crossing desert plains, impenetrable forests, and frightful rapids, far from the centres of population, in the midst of wild regions where every detail of existence became an almost insoluble problem. Nevertheless, American genius triumphed over these thousand obstacles, and in less than one year from the commencement of the works, in the last days of September, the gigantic reflector raised its tube, 290 feet long, towards the sky. It was suspended from an enormous framework of iron, and, by an ingenious mechanism, it could easily be turned towards all points of the firmament, and follow the movements of the stars from one horizon to the other.

It had cost more than 400,000 dollars. The first time it was directed towards the moon the observers sustained a thrill of curiosity mingled with uneasiness. What were they going to discover by means of this telescope which magnified objects 48,000 times? Populations, troops of lunar animals, cities, lakes, or oceans? No, nothing that science was not already acquainted with; but at all points of its disc the volcanic nature of the moon could be determined with absolute precision.

But before being used for the purposes of the Gun Club, the telescope of the Rocky Mountains rendered considerable service to astronomy. Thanks to its power of penetration, the depths of the heavens were scanned to their utmost limits. The apparent

diameter of a large number of stars could be accurately measured, and Mr Clarke, of the Cambridge Observatory, decomposed the Crab nebulae of Taurus, which Lord Rosse's telescope had never been able to resolve.[34]

CHAPTER TWENTY-FIVE

Last details

The 22nd of November had arrived, and the departure was to take place ten days later. Only one operation now remained, but it was delicate and perilous in the extreme, requiring infinite precautions; and Captain Nicholl had laid his third wager against its success. It was, in fact, the loading of the columbiad with 400,000 pounds of gun-cotton. Nicholl had thought, not without reason perhaps, that the manipulation of such an enormous quantity of pyroxyle would infallibly lead to some great catastrophe, and that, in any case, so explosive a substance would ignite under the pressure of the projectile.

These serious dangers were greatly increased by the carelessness of the Americans, who did not hesitate during the Federal war to smoke their cigars whilst loading bomb-shells. But Barbicane was anxious to succeed, and not fall through at the last moment, so he chose the best workmen, and made them act under his personal inspection. He did not leave them for one minute, and by his prudence and precautions managed to bring the chances of success on his side.

In the first place, he took care not to have the whole charge brought to the enclosure of Stone's Hill at once, but had it conveyed there gradually in carefully-sealed cases. The 400,000 pounds of pyroxyle had been divided into charges of 500 pounds each, so that there were 800 gigantic cartridges carefully manufactured by the most skilful artificers of Pensacola. Each case contained ten of these, and they arrived one after the other by the Tampa Town railway. In this way there were never more than 5,000 pounds of pyroxyle at one time in the enclosure. As soon as it arrived each case was unloaded by barefooted workmen, and each cartridge was carried to the orifice of the columbiad, into which it was let down by means of hand-worked cranes. Every steam-engine had been removed, and the smallest fires extinguished for two miles round. It was difficult enough to preserve this mass of gun-cotton from the heat of the sun even in November, therefore they preferred working during the night by a light produced in vacuum by means of Ruhmkorff's apparatus, which shed an artificial daylight down to the bottom of the columbiad. There the cartridges were arranged in perfect regularity, and united by means of a metallic wire which would carry the electric spark simultaneously to the centre of each. It was, in fact, by means of electricity that this mass of gun-cotton was to be ignited. All these wires, covered with an isolating substance, united at a narrow aperture, pierced at the height where the projectile would lie; there they passed through the thick wall of cast-iron, and ascended to the ground through one of the vent-holes constructed for this purpose in the stone facing. Once at the summit of Stone's Hill the wire passed on telegraph posts for a distance of two miles, and was then connected with a powerful Bunsen battery, fitted with an interruptor. Thus it was only necessary to place one's finger on the knob of the interruptor to re-establish the electric current and set fire to the 400,000 pounds of gun-cotton. It is unnecessary to add that this was only to be done at the last moment.

On the 28th of November the 800 cartridges were deposited at the bottom of the columbiad. This portion of the operation had succeeded; but what trouble, what anxieties, what struggles had not President Barbicane undergone! In vain he had forbidden admission into Stone's Hill; every day an inquisitive crowd climbed over the palisades, and some carried their imprudence to the extent of smoking amongst the bales of gun-cotton. Barbicane was in a continual state of fury. J. T. Maston assisted him as best he could, chasing the intruders and collecting the still burning cigar-ends which the Yankees scattered on all sides. This was a difficult task indeed, for more than 300,000 persons pressed round the palisades. Michel Ardan, it is true, had offered to escort the cases to the very mouth of the columbiad, but having been discovered with an immense cigar in his mouth at the very moment when hunting out the intruders to whom he was setting so bad an example, the president of the Gun Club perceived that he could not depend upon this intrepid smoker, and was obliged to place him under special guard.

However, as there is a Providence even for artillerists, no explosion occurred, and the loading was happily completed. Captain Nicholl's third wager was therefore lost, and there only remained to insert the projectile into the columbiad and place it upon the thick layer of gun-cotton.

Before commencing this operation, the articles required for the journey were placed in order in the 'projectile carriage'. They were sufficiently numerous, and if Michel Ardan had been allowed his way there would have been no space left for the travellers. You can have no idea of the extraordinary things which this amiable Frenchman wished to take with him to the moon – a veritable stock-in-trade of useless trifles. But Barbicane interfered, and he was obliged to confine himself to what was strictly necessary.

Several thermometers, barometers, and lunettes were placed in the instrument-case.

The travellers were to examine the moon during the passage, and, to facilitate their observations of this new world, they took with them an excellent map, by Beer and Moedler, entitled, *Mappa Selenographica*,[35] which is published in four sheets, and is rightly considered a masterpiece of patient observation. It reproduced with scrupulous accuracy the minutest details of that portion of the orb which is turned towards the earth. Mountains, valleys, craters, holes, and grooves are drawn according to their exact dimensions and situations, each with its proper denomination, from mounts Doerfel and Leibnitz, which raise their high summits on the eastern portion of the disc, to the *Mare frigoris*,[36] which lies in the region surrounding the North Pole.

This was a precious document for our travellers, since it enabled them to study the country before they reached it. They carried with them also three rifles and three fowling-pieces, with explosive balls, also a large quantity of powder and lead.

'We don't know what we may meet,' said Michel Ardan. 'Men or beasts may take umbrage at our visit. We must be prepared for everything.'

Besides these defensive arms, they had pickaxes, spades, hand-saws, and other indispensable tools, not to mention garments adapted to all temperatures, from the cold of the polar regions to the heat of the torrid zone.

Michel Ardan would have wished to take with him on the expedition a certain number of animals, though not a pair of each species – for he did not see the necessity of colonising the moon with serpents, tigers, alligators, and other harmful beasts.

'No,' said he to Barbicane; 'but a few beasts of burden – oxen or cows, horses or asses – would look well and be of great use to us.'

'I agree with you, my dear Ardan,' said the president of the Gun Club; 'but our "projectile-carriage" is not a Noah's ark. It is neither big enough nor in any way adapted to such a purpose, so we must remain within the limits of what is possible.'

At last, after many discussions, it was agreed that the travellers should only take with them a well-trained setter bitch belonging to Nicholl, and a vigorous Newfoundland of prodigious strength. Several boxes of the most useful seeds were added to the number of indispensable articles. If Michel Ardan had had his way he would have taken also a few sacks of earth to sow them in. However, he took a dozen shrubs, which were carefully wrapped in straw cases and placed in a corner of the projectile.

There yet remained the important question of provisions, for they had to take into account the probability of arriving at a perfectly barren part of the moon. Barbicane managed to collect enough for one year, but, it must be added, lest people should be surprised, that these provisions consisted of preserved meats and vegetables, reduced to their smallest volume under the action of the hydraulic press, and containing a large amount of nutriment. They were not very varied, but, for such an expedition, one could not be very particular. There was also a reserve of brandy, which might amount to about fifty gallons, but water for two months only; for after the last observations of astronomers, no one doubted the existence of a certain quantity of water on the surface of the moon.[37] As to the provisions, it would have been ridiculous to imagine that inhabitants of the earth could not find food up there. Michel Ardan had no doubt on this head, otherwise he could not have made up his mind to start.

'Besides,' said he, one day to his friends, 'we shall not be completely abandoned by our comrades on the earth, and they will take care not to forget us.'

'Certainly not,' replied J. T. Maston.

'How do you mean?' asked Nicholl.

'Nothing can be easier,' replied Ardan. 'Will not the columbiad be always there? Well, each time that the moon presents herself in favourable conditions as to zenith if not of perigee – that is to say about once a year – you can send us a shell laden with provisions, which we will expect on the day fixed.'

'Hear, hear!' cried Maston, with the tone of a man who had made up his mind to say something. 'Bravo! certainly, my good friends, we shall not forget you.'

'I depend upon it. So you see we shall have news from the globe very regularly, and for our part we shall be very unskilful indeed if we do not find some means of communicating with our good friends on the earth.'

These words were impregnated with such confidence that Michel Ardan, with his determined air and perfect self-possession, would have carried away the whole Gun Club in his wake. What he said appeared simple, elementary, easy, and of assured success. One must have been sordidly attached to this miserable globe not to follow the three travellers on their lunar expedition.

When the different articles had been arranged in the projectile, the water, which was to act as a spring, was introduced between the partitions, and the gas for lighting was forced into its reservoirs; as to the chlorate of potash and the caustic potash, Barbicane, fearing unforeseen delays on the road, took a sufficient quantity to renew the oxygen and absorb the carbonic acid during two months. An extremely ingenious apparatus, which acted automatically, restored to the air its vivifying qualities and purified it completely. The projectile was thus ready, and there only remained to lower it in the columbiad – an operation, however, which was full of difficulties and perils.

The enormous shell was carried to the summit of Stone's Hill, where powerful cranes seized upon it and held it suspended over the metal shaft.

The excitement of the moment was intense. If a chain had broken under this enormous weight the fall of such a mass would have certainly fired the gun-cotton.

Happily this did not occur, and, a few hours later, the 'projectile-carriage' had been slowly lowered into the bore of the cannon, and was reposing on its bed of pyroxyle. Its pressure had no other effect than to ram down more compactly the charge of the columbiad.

'I have lost,' said the captain, handing to Barbicane a sum of 3,000 dollars.

Barbicane did not wish to receive this money from his travelling companion; but he was forced to give way to Nicholl's obstinacy, for the latter made a point of paying all his debts before leaving the earth.

'In that case,' said Michel Ardan, 'I have only one thing to wish for you, my worthy captain.'

'And that is?' asked Nicholl.

'That you should lose your two other bets; in which case we shall be certain not to be stopped on our journey.'

CHAPTER TWENTY-SIX

Fire!

The momentous date of the 1st of December had arrived, and if the departure of the projectile did not take place that same evening at 46 minutes and 40 seconds past 10 p.m., more than 18 years must elapse before the moon would again be found in the same conditions of zenith and perigee.

The weather was magnificent. Notwithstanding the approach of winter, the sun shone forth in all its splendour, and bathed in its radiant light that earth which was about to be abandoned by three of its inhabitants in search of a new world. How many people found themselves unable to sleep during the night which preceded this ardently-expected day! How many bosoms were oppressed by the heavy burden of expectation! The hearts of all beat faster, except the heart of Michel Ardan. This unimpressionable personage ran backwards and forwards in his accustomed busy manner, but there were no signs apparent of any unusual preoccupation. His slumbers had been as peaceful as the sleep of Turenne, on a gun-carriage, before the battle.

From early morning an innumerable crowd covered the plains which spread around Stone's Hill. Every quarter of an hour the Tampa railway brought new visitors. The immigration soon attained fabulous proportions, and according to the statistics of the *Tampa Town Observer*, on that memorable day five millions of spectators stood upon Floridan soil.[38]

For a month past, the greater portion of this crowd bivouacked around the enclosure, and laid the foundations of a city which has since been called Ardanstown. Sheds, cabins, huts, and tents were scattered over the plain, and these ephemeral habitations

contained a population so numerous as to be envied by the greatest cities of Europe.

All the nations of the earth were represented there: all the dialects of the world were to be heard at the same time. It was like the confusion of tongues as in the biblical times of the Tower of Babel. There the several classes of American society mingled in absolute equality. Bankers, farmers, sailors, commission agents, brokers, cotton planters, merchants, watermen, and magistrates, elbowed each other with the most primitive unceremoniousness. Creoles from Louisiana fraternised with farmers from Indiana, gentlemen from Kentucky and Tennessee; elegant and haughty Virginians chatted with half-savage trappers from the lakes, and with cattle-dealers from Cincinnati. There was a varied display of broad-brimmed white beaver hats, and the inevitable panamas; trousers of blue cottonade from the manufactories of Opelousas; elegant blouses of brown holland, boots of startling colours, extravagant cambric frills; and on fingers, in ears, in shirts, in cuffs, and in cravats, an assortment of rings, pins, diamonds, chains, drops, and pendants, as costly as they were in bad taste. Women, children, and servants, in not less opulent dresses, accompanied, followed, preceded, and surrounded their husbands, fathers, and masters, who looked like chiefs of tribes in the midst of their innumerable families.

It was a sight at dinner-time to see this crowd throw themselves on the viands peculiar to the southern states, and devour, with an appetite that threatened exhaustion of all Floridan supplies, dishes most repugnant to European stomachs – such as fricasséed frogs, stewed monkeys, fish chowder, underdone opossum, or grilled raccoon.

Then what a varied series of liquors and drinks to wash down this indigestible food! What excited shouts! What engaging vociferations re-echoed in the bar-rooms and taverns, ornamented with glasses, vials, carafes, and bottles of improbable shapes, mortars for pounding sugar, and bundles of straw!

'Here is the mint-julep,' cried one of the barmen, in a loud voice.

'Claret-sangaree,' cries another.

'Gin-sling,' on one side.

'Cocktail and brandy-smash! Real mint-julep from the latest receipt!' cried the men, skilfully passing from one glass to another, as a conjuror would, the nutmeg, sugar, lemon, green mint, powdered ice, water, brandy, and fresh pineapple, of which this refreshing drink is composed.

Such, on general occasions, were the invitations addressed from every side to throats parched by the burning action of spices, producing a bewildering and deafening hubbub. But on that day, the 1st of December, such cries were unheard, as though the barmen had lost their voices by vaunting their wares. No one thought of eating or drinking, and many people in the crowd at 4 p.m. had not even taken their accustomed luncheon. A yet more significant symptom still was the fact that the national passion for games seemed quelled by a stronger excitement. The sight of the ninepins scattered through the bowling-alleys, the dice lying hid in their boxes, the packs of cards for whist, vingt-et-un, rouge-et-noir, monte, and faro, still wrapped up in their covers, proved that the event of the day absorbed every other desire, and left no room for amusement.

Until evening, a low, noiseless agitation, such as precedes great catastrophes, pervaded the anxious crowd. An indescribable uneasiness filled the minds of all; a distressing torpor, an indefinable sensation which oppressed the heart. Everyone wished that it was over.

However, about seven o'clock this heavy silence was suddenly broken. The moon appeared above the horizon, and several millions of cheers greeted her appearance. She was punctual at the rendezvous. Shouts ascended to the sky, applause burst forth from every side, whilst fair-haired Phoebe shone peacefully, in a clear sky, and caressed the excited crowd with her most affectionate rays.

At this moment, the three intrepid travellers made their appearance. At their sight, the shouts were redoubled; and unanimously, instantaneously, the national song of the United States burst from every throat, and the strains of 'Yankee Doodle', sung by five million voices, arose in a tempest of sound to the uttermost limits of the atmosphere.

Then, after this irresistible outburst, the song was hushed; the last sounds faded little by little, the noises ceased, and profound silence reigned throughout the crowd. Meanwhile the Frenchman and the two Americans had entered the reserved enclosure, round which the immense crowd was assembled. They were accompanied by the members of the Gun Club and the deputations sent by European observatories. Barbicane, calm as ever, was quietly giving his last instructions; Nicholl, with compressed lips and hands crossed behind his back, walked with a firm and measured step; Michel Ardan – always easy, dressed like a thorough traveller, with leather gaiters and a game-bag at his side, in his loosest suit of brown velvet, and a cigar between his teeth – distributed nods and smiles amongst the crowd with princely prodigality. His spirits and gaiety were inexhaustible, and he laughed, joked, and played schoolboy tricks upon the worthy J. T. Maston, remaining a true Frenchman, or, what is worse, a true Parisian, to the last second.

Ten o'clock struck. The moment was come to take seats in the projectile. The work of lowering, of securing the aperture, and removing the cranes and scaffolding which overhung the mouth of the columbiad required a certain time. Barbicane had regulated his chronometer to a tenth of a second by that of Murchison, the engineer who was entrusted with the firing of the gun-cotton by means of the electric spark. In this way the travellers, shut up in the projectile, could keep a watchful eye upon the hand which would mark the precise moment of their departure.

The moment had now arrived to say farewell. The scene was touching, and even Michel Ardan was moved, in despite of his feverish gaiety. J. T. Maston had found, beneath his withered eyelids, an ancient tear, which he doubtless reserved for this occasion, and he dropped it on the forehead of his dear and worthy president.

'Let me go too,' said he; 'there is still time.'

'It is not possible, old fellow,' replied Barbicane.

A few minutes later the three fellow-travellers were installed within the projectile, and had securely screwed down the plate which covered the entrance-hole. The mouth of the columbiad, completely freed from incumbrances, lay open towards the sky.

Nicholl, Barbicane, and Michel Ardan were definitively walled up in their metal carriage. Who could describe the general excitement which now reached its paroxysm?

The moon rose in a firmament of limpid purity, dimming along her passage the sparkling fires of the stars; she was then passing through the constellation of Gemini, and was almost half-way between the zenith and the horizon. Everyone could easily understand that they were aiming beyond the mark, as a sportsman aims ahead of the hare which he is desirous of shooting.

A fearful silence weighed upon the whole scene. Not a breath of air upon the earth – not a breath escaping from the assembled crowd! Hearts feared to beat; all eyes were fixed upon the yawning mouth of the columbiad.

Murchison watched the hands of his chronometer. There remained hardly forty seconds before the moment of departure and each second seemed a century.

At the twentieth there was a general shudder, and a sudden thought struck the crowd that the audacious travellers enclosed within the projectile were also counting the terrible seconds. Isolated cries were heard: 'Thirty-five – thirty-six – thirty-seven – thirty-eight – thirty-nine – forty – Fire!!!'

And Murchison, pressing his finger upon the interruptor, restored the electric current, and flashed a spark to the bottom of the columbiad.

The detonation which instantly followed was frightful, unheard of, superhuman; resembling nothing ever heard before – neither the bursting of a thunderbolt nor the eruption of a volcano. An immense column of flame leapt from the entrails of the earth as from a crater. The ground heaved, and but few of the spectators caught a momentary glimpse of the projectile victoriously cleaving the air in the midst of the flames and smoke.

CHAPTER TWENTY-SEVEN

Murky weather

The column of flame which rose to a prodigious height towards the sky illumined the whole of Florida, and, for the space of one moment, night was turned into day over a vast expanse of country. The immense pyramid of fire was seen to a distance of 100 miles out at sea – in the Gulf as well as in the Atlantic – and more than one ship's captain entered in his log the appearance of this gigantic meteor.

The discharge of the columbiad was accompanied by an earthquake. Florida was shaken to her very entrails. The gas from the gun-cotton, dilated by the heat, forced back the atmospheric strata with incomparable violence; and this artificial hurricane, one hundred times more rapid than the hurricane of tempests, rushed like a whirlwind through the air.

Not a single spectator remained on his feet. Men, women, and children, all lay prostrate, like ears of corn before a storm. There was an indescribable tumult; a great number of persons seriously hurt; and J. T. Maston, who had stood most imprudently to the fore, was thrown 20 fathoms back, and passed like a cannon-ball over the heads of his fellow-citizens. Three hundred thousand persons remained momentarily deaf and stupefied.

The atmospheric wave, after destroying the sheds and cabins, uprooting the trees within a radius of 20 miles, and driving the trains upon the railway back to Tampa, swept over that town and destroyed 100 buildings, amongst which were St Mary's church and the new Exchange. Some of the ships in the port were dashed against each other and sank immediately, whilst several others, anchored at a greater distance from the shore, broke their chains like threads and were driven on to the coast.

But the circle of these devastations extended farther still, beyond the limits of the United States. The effect of the shock, aided by a westerly wind, was felt upon the Atlantic to a distance of more than 300 miles from the American coast. An artificial storm, utterly unexpected, which even Admiral Fitzroy would have been unable to foresee, seized upon the ships with untold violence. Several vessels, caught by the terrific whirlwinds without time for preparation, sank with all hands on board; amongst these was the *Childe Harold*, from Liverpool, the loss of which formed the subject of bitter recriminations on the part of England. To this may be added, although the fact has no other guarantee than the statement of certain natives, that, half an hour after the departure of the projectile, the inhabitants of Gorea and Sierra Leone heard a muffled sound, produced by the last vibrations of the atmospheric wave which had crossed the Atlantic Ocean to expire on the African coast.

But to return to Florida. When the first moment of tumult had passed, the wounded, the deaf, in fact the whole crowd awoke, and frantic cries of 'Hurrah for Ardan! Hurrah for Barbicane! Hurrah for Nicholl!' rose towards the sky. Several millions of men, armed with telescopes, lunettes, and field-glasses, scanned the air, forgetful of all contusions and emotions, and thinking only of the projectile. But they sought it in vain; it could not be discovered, and they were obliged to wait for telegrams from Long's Peak. The director of the Cambridge Observatory was at his post in the Rocky Mountains, and to this learned and persevering astronomer the observations had been entrusted.

An unforeseen phenomenon, but which might have been expected, and against which it was impossible to guard, subjected public impatience to a severe trial.

The weather – so fine until then – suddenly changed, and the sky became covered with clouds. Could it be otherwise, after the terrible displacement of atmospheric strata, and the dispersion of the enormous mass of vapour arising from the combustion of 400,000 pounds of pyroxyle? The whole order of nature had been troubled. This could not be matter for astonishment, inasmuch as, in naval battles, the state of the atmosphere has been often suddenly changed by the discharges of artillery.

The next day, the sun rose upon a horizon covered with thick clouds, forming a heavy and impenetrable curtain between the earth and the sky, which unfortunately extended to the regions of the Rocky Mountains. It was a stroke of bad luck, and a concert of

expostulations arose from every part of the globe. But nature took little heed thereat; and, certainly, since men had disturbed the atmosphere by their own act, they ought not to have grumbled at the consequences.

During the first day, each one sought to pierce this opaque veil of clouds, but without success; besides which, they were all wrong in looking towards the sky, for, in consequence of the diurnal movement of the globe, the projectile was necessarily flying at that time in a straight line from the antipodes.

However that may be, when night again enveloped the earth in impenetrable darkness, when the moon had again risen above the horizon, she was completely hidden from sight, as though purposely withdrawing from the view of those rash men who had dared to fire at her. No observation was possible, and telegrams from Long's Peak confirmed this disagreeable mischance.

However, if the experiment had succeeded, the travellers, who left on the 1st of December at 46 minutes and 40 seconds past 10 p.m., would reach their destination on the 4th at midnight. Up to that time, inasmuch as it would after all have been difficult to observe a body so small as the projectile, people waited with more or less patience and without too much grumbling.

On the 4th of December, it would have been possible to follow the track of the projectile, which would then have appeared like a black spot upon the shining disc of the moon; but the weather remained cloudy, which provoked public exasperation to a fearful pitch. Insults were uttered against the moon for not showing herself, which proves the sad instability of human regard.

J. T. Maston, in despair, started for Long's Peak to make an observation for himself. He did not doubt for one instant that his friends had reached the goal of their journey. Besides, he had not heard that the projectile had fallen back upon any point of the terrestrial islands or continents, and J. T. Maston did not admit, for one instant, the possibility of its fall into the oceans which cover three-fourths of the globe.

On the 5th, the weather was the same. The large telescopes of the old world – those of Herschel, Rosse, and Foucault, were constantly directed towards the moon, for the weather in Europe was magnificent, but the comparative weakness of these instruments prevented any reliable observation.

On the 6th the weather was the same. Three-fourths of the globe were wild with impatience. The most insensate means were proposed for dispersing the clouds accumulated in the air.

On the 7th the sky changed slightly. People began to hope, but their hope did not last long, for, in the evening, thick clouds again hid the starry firmament from their eyes.

Matters were becoming serious, for on the 11th, at 9.11 a.m., the moon would enter her last quarter, after which she would daily become less, and even if the sky were to clear, the chances of an observation would be considerably diminished. In fact the moon would no longer show more than an ever-decreasing portion of her disc, and would end by becoming new – that is to say, she would set and rise with the sun, whose rays would render her almost invisible. It would consequently be necessary to wait until the 3rd of January, at 44 minutes past noon, to commence observations.

The newspapers published these objections with a thousand comments, and did not hide from the public that they would have to call all their patience to their aid.

On the 8th, nothing. On the 9th the sun appeared for a minute, as though to taunt the Americans. It was received with groans and hisses, and being no doubt offended at such conduct, withdrew almost immediately.

On the 10th, no change. J. T. Maston was nearly wild, and fears were entertained for the worthy man's brain, which had been hitherto so well preserved beneath his gutta-percha cranium.

But on the 11th one of those terrible tempests which occur in intertropical regions broke upon the atmosphere. Strong easterly winds swept away the clouds amassed for so long, and in the evening the lambent crescent of the Queen of Night floated majestically amid the limpid constellations of the heavens.

CHAPTER TWENTY-EIGHT

A new star

That same night the exciting news so impatiently awaited burst like a thunderclap upon the States of the Union, and thence through the ocean it flashed along all the telegraph wires of the globe. The projectile had been perceived by the gigantic reflector at Long's Peak.

This is the note despatched by the Director of the Cambridge Observatory; it contains the scientific conclusion as to the great experiment of the Gun Club.

Long's Peak, December 12th

To the Members of the
Committee of the Cambridge Observatory

The projectile discharged by the columbiad from Stone's Hill was perceived by Messrs Belfast and J. T. Maston on the 12th of December, at 8.47 p.m., the moon being then in her last quarter.

The projectile has not reached its goal; it has passed beside it, but near enough, however, to be retained by lunar attraction.

There, its rectilinear movement has been changed to a circular movement of extreme velocity, and it is describing an elliptic orbit round the moon, whose satellite it has become.

The elements of this new star have not yet been determined. We neither know its velocity of translation nor its velocity of rotation. The distance which separates it from the surface of the moon may be estimated at about 2,833 miles.

Two hypotheses are possible, one of which may modify this state of things.

> Either the attraction of the moon will end by dragging the travellers to their destination, or the projectile, following an immutable law, will gravitate round the lunar disc till the end of time.
>
> Future observations will decide the question, but up to the present the only result of the experiment of the Gun Club has been to endow our solar system with a new star.
>
> J. Belfast

What questions were raised by this unexpected result! What mysteries were reserved to the future investigations of science! Thanks to the courage and devotion of three men, the apparently futile undertaking of sending a cannon-ball to the moon had attained a result of incalculable importance. The travellers, imprisoned in a new satellite, even if they had not attained their purpose, at least formed part of the lunar world; they were gravitating round the orb of night, and for the first time a human eye would be able to penetrate all its mysteries. The names of Nicholl, Barbicane, and Michel Ardan will therefore be for ever celebrated in the records of astronomy, for these intrepid explorers, anxious to increase the sphere of human knowledge, had boldly rushed through space and risked their lives in the strangest experiment of modern times.

However, the note from Long's Peak elicited in the whole universe a feeling of surprise and terror. Was it possible to come to the assistance of these bold inhabitants of the earth? No, for they had placed themselves beyond the pale of humanity by crossing the limits imposed by Providence on terrestrial creatures.

They could obtain air during two months. They had provisions for a year. But after that? . . . The most unfeeling hearts beat rapidly at this terrible question.

One man alone would not admit that the situation was hopeless. One alone had confidence, and that was their devoted friend, audacious and resolute as themselves, worthy J. T. Maston.

Besides which, he did not lose sight of them. He took up his abode at Long's Peak, and his horizon was the mirror of the immense reflector. So soon as the moon rose above the horizon, he brought her within the focus of the telescope, and without losing sight of her, followed her assiduously in her journey through the starry regions. He observed with untiring patience the passage of the projectile over the disc of silver, and in reality, the worthy man remained in perpetual communication with his three friends, whom he did not despair of seeing again some day.

'We will correspond with them,' said he to whoever would listen to him, 'as soon as circumstances will permit. We shall hear from them, and they from us. Besides, I know them well! they are men of ingenuity. Amongst the three of them, they have carried into space all the resources of art, science, and industry. With that they can do almost anything, and you will see that they will get out of their difficulties.'

AROUND THE MOON

AUTOUR DE LA LUNE

CONTENTS

INTRODUCTION

Which sums up the first portion of this work as a Preface to the second

During the year 186— the whole world was greatly excited by a scientific experiment without precedent in the annals of science. The members of the Gun Club – an assembly of artillerists founded at Baltimore – had conceived the idea of placing themselves in communication with the moon – yes, with the moon! – by means of a cannon-ball. Their president, Barbicane, the originator of the idea, having consulted on the subject the astronomers of the Cambridge Observatory, took all the measures necessary for the success of the extraordinary undertaking, which had been declared feasible by the majority of competent men. After having opened a public subscription, which realised nearly 30 millions of francs (£1,200,000), he commenced his gigantic works.

In accordance with a note drawn up by the members of the observatory, the cannon which was to discharge the projectile had to be established on some spot situated between 0° and 28° of latitude, north or south, so as to aim at the moon in the zenith, and the projectile was to be endowed with an initial velocity of 12,000 yards per second. Discharged on the 1st of December at 10.48 p.m., it would strike the moon four days after its departure – on the 5th of December – at midnight precisely, at the very moment when she would be in perigee, *i.e.* at her nearest approach to the earth, being just 96,410 leagues distant.

The principal members of the Gun Club, President Barbicane, Major Elphiston, the secretary J. T. Maston, and other scientific men, held several meetings, at which were discussed the form and composition of the projectile, the disposition and nature of the cannon, and the quantity and quality of the powder to be used. It was decided: (1) That the projectile should be an aluminum shell of 108 inches in diameter, and with sides of a thickness of 12 inches, weighing 19,250 pounds. (2) That the cannon should be a cast-iron columbiad, 900 feet long, and cast direct in the ground. (3) That the charge should consist of 400,000 pounds of gun-cotton, which would produce 600 million litres of gas beneath the projectile, and would amply suffice to propel the latter to the orb of night.

These questions having been decided, President Barbicane, assisted by the engineer Murchison, made choice of a site situated in Florida at 27° 7' N. latitude by 5° 7' W. longitude. In this spot, after the execution of marvellous works, the columbiad was cast with complete success.

Matters were at this point, when an incident occurred which increased one-hundredfold the interest awakened by this great undertaking.

A Frenchman, a fantastic Parisian – an artist, as witty as he was audacious – asked permission to be enclosed in the projectile, so as to reach the moon and reconnoitre the earth's satellite. This intrepid adventurer was named Michel Ardan. He arrived in America, was received with enthusiasm, held meetings, was carried in triumph, reconciled President Barbicane with his mortal enemy Captain Nicholl, and, as a proof of reconciliation, induced them to embark with him in the projectile.

The proposal was accepted and the form of the projectile was altered from spherical to cylindro-conic. The interior of this aerial carriage was fitted up with powerful springs and partitions, which were to break and lessen the shock of the departure. It was supplied with provisions for one year, with water for some months, and with gas for several days. An automatic apparatus manufactured and supplied the air necessary for breathing purposes. At the same time the Gun Club ordered a gigantic telescope to be constructed upon one of the highest summits of the Rocky Mountains, which would enable the projectile to be observed during its passage through space. Everything was ready.

On the 1st of December, at the hour appointed, in the midst of an immense concourse of spectators, the departure took place, and, for the first time, three human beings quitted the terrestrial globe and dashed towards the planetary regions with the almost absolute certainty of reaching their goal. These audacious travellers – Michel Ardan, President Barbicane, and Captain Nicholl – were to effect their passage in 97 hours, 13 minutes, and 20 seconds. Consequently their arrival on the lunar disc could only take place on the 5th of December at midnight, at the precise moment at which the moon would be full, and not on the 4th, as some ill-informed newspapers had announced.

However, an unforeseen circumstance occurred: the explosion produced by the columbiad caused an immediate disturbance in the terrestrial atmosphere by accumulating an immense mass of vapour. This phenomenon excited general indignation, for the moon was veiled for several nights from the eyes of all observers.

Worthy J. T. Maston, the staunchest friend of the three travellers, set out for the Rocky Mountains in company with the Hon. J. Belfast, director of the Cambridge Observatory, and reached the station at Long's Peak, where the telescope was established, which brought the moon to within two leagues. The hon. secretary of the Gun Club wished to observe for himself, the vehicle of his audacious friends.

The accumulation of clouds in the atmosphere rendered impossible any observations during the 5th, 6th, 7th, 8th, 9th, and 10th of December. It was even thought that the observations would have to be postponed until the 3rd of January of the next year, inasmuch as the moon would enter her last quarter on the 11th, and would then only present a constantly decreasing portion of her disc, totally insufficient to reveal any trace of the projectile.

At last, to the general satisfaction, a violent tempest cleared the atmosphere in the night of the 11th of December, and the moon, half-illumined, stood out boldly in the midst of the black sky. That same night, a telegram was despatched from Long's Peak, by J. T. Maston and J. Belfast, to the members of the Cambridge Observatory. What did this telegram announce? It announced that on the 11th of December, at 8.47 p.m., the projectile discharged by the columbiad from Stone's Hill, had been perceived by Messrs Belfast and J. T. Maston; that the projectile, having deviated from some unknown cause, had not reached its goal, but had passed near enough to be retained by the lunar attraction; that its rectilinear movement had been changed into a circular movement, and that it had been carried away on an elliptic orbit around the orb of night, whose satellite it had become.

The telegram added that the elements of this new star had not yet been calculated; indeed, three observations, each taking the star in a different position, were necessary to determine its elements. It then pointed out that the distance separating the projectile from the lunar surface might be estimated at about 2,833 miles. It concluded by suggesting this double hypothesis – either the attraction of the moon would prove the stronger and the travellers would reach their destination, or the projectile, maintained in an immutable orbit, would gravitate round the lunar disc until the end of time.

In these two alternatives, what would be the fate of the travellers? They had provisions for a certain time, it is true; but, even supposing the success of their bold undertaking, how would they return? Would they ever be able to return? Could there be any news from them? These questions, treated by the most learned writers of the day, excited public attention to the utmost.

It is necessary to make a remark here, which should be well considered by hasty observers. When a man of science announces a purely speculative discovery to the public, he cannot be too prudent. No one is obliged to discover a comet, or a planet, or a satellite; and whoever makes an error under such circumstances becomes fair game for the laughter of the crowd. Consequently it is better to wait; and so the impatient J. T. Maston should have done, instead of publishing to the world the telegram which, in his opinion, formed the conclusion of the undertaking.

In fact, the telegram contained errors of two kinds, as was subsequently proved. First, errors of observation concerning the distance of the projectile from the surface of the moon, for, at the date of the 11th of December it was impossible to perceive it; and what J. T. Maston saw, or imagined he saw, could not have been the shot from the columbiad. Secondly, theoretical errors as to the fate reserved for the said projectile, inasmuch as to make it a satellite of the moon was to act in direct contradiction with the laws of rational mechanics.

One hypothesis only of the observers at Long's Peak might be realised, viz. that the travellers, if they still were in existence, would combine their efforts with the lunar attraction, so as to reach the surface of the moon.

Now these men, as intelligent as they were rash, had survived the terrible shock of the departure. It is their journey in the projectile-carriage which is about to be related, in its most dramatic as in its most singular details. This story will upset many theories and illusions, but it will give a true idea of the dangers inherent to such an undertaking, and will bring into bold relief the scientific knowledge of Barbicane, the resources of the industrious Nicholl, and the humorous audacity of Michel Ardan.

Further, it will prove that their worthy friend J. T. Maston was wasting his time when, leaning over the gigantic telescope, he observed the passage of the moon through the starry firmament.

CHAPTER ONE

From 10.20 p.m. to 10.47 p.m.

On the stroke of ten, Michel Ardan, Barbicane, and Nicholl took leave of the numerous friends whom they were leaving upon earth. The two dogs, destined to propagate the canine race upon the lunar continents, had already been enclosed in the projectile. The three travellers approached the orifice of the enormous cast-iron tube, and a movable crane lowered them to the conic roof of the projectile.

There an opening left for the purpose gave them access to the interior of the aluminum carriage. The tackle of the crane was hauled up, and the mouth of the columbiad was instantaneously freed from its last incumbrances.

So soon as Nicholl and his companions were inside the projectile, the former began to close up the opening by means of a strong plate, held in position by powerful screws. Other plates, firmly fixed, covered the lenticular glasses of the scuttles. The travellers, hermetically enclosed in their metal prison, were plunged into profound darkness.

'And now, dear friends,' said Michel Ardan, 'let us make ourselves at home. I am a homely man, I am, and a capital housekeeper. We must make the most of our new lodgings, and make ourselves comfortable. In the first place let us throw a little light on the subject. Devil take it! gas was not made for moles.'

So saying, the heedless fellow lit a match upon the sole of his boot, and applied it to the burner of the reservoir in which carbonised hydrogen had been stored at high pressure, in sufficient quantity to light and warm the projectile during 144 hours, or six days and six nights.

The gas ignited, and the projectile, thus lighted, appeared like a comfortable chamber with padded sides, furnished with circular divans, and having a ceiling in the shape of a dome.

The articles it contained – arms, instruments, and utensils – were firmly attached to the knobs of the padding, and would bear with impunity the shock of the departure. All humanly possible precautions had been taken to make this rash experiment a success.

Michel Ardan examined everything, and declared himself very well satisfied with the arrangements.

'It is a prison,' said he, 'but a travelling prison, and we have the right of looking out of the window. I should like to take a lease for 100 years. You smile, Barbicane. You are thinking of something. You are thinking that the prison might become our tomb! Very well! but I would not exchange with Mahomet, whose tomb floats in space but does not move.'

Whilst Ardan was speaking, Barbicane and Nicholl were making their last preparations.

Nicholl's chronometer marked 10.20 p.m. when the three travellers were definitively walled up in their projectile. The chronometer was set within a tenth of a second of that belonging to Murchison the engineer. Barbicane consulted it.

'My friends,' said he, 'it is 20 minutes past 10. At 47 minutes past 10, Murchison will flash the electric spark to the wire which communicates with the charge of the columbiad. At that moment precisely we will leave our spheroid. We have still 27 minutes to remain on earth.'

'26 minutes and 13 seconds,' replied the methodical Nicholl.

'Well!' cried Michel Ardan, in a good-humoured tone, 'much can be done in 26 minutes. We might discuss the gravest questions of morals or politics, and even solve them! 26 minutes well employed are better worth than 26 years of idleness. A few seconds of Newton or Pascal are more precious than the whole lifetime of the general run of fools.'

'And what conclusion do you draw, chatterbox?' asked President Barbicane.

'I conclude that we have 26 minutes before us,' replied Ardan.

'24 only,' said Nicholl.

'24 if you like, worthy captain; 24 minutes during which we might investigate – '

'Michel,' said Barbicane, 'during our passage we shall have all the time necessary to investigate the most arduous questions. Let us now think of our departure.'

'Are we not ready?'

'Doubtless. But there are some precautions to be taken so as to attenuate, as much as possible, the first shock.'

'Have we not layers of water between breakable partitions, whose elasticity will protect us sufficiently?'

'I hope so, Michel,' said Barbicane quietly, 'but I am not very sure.'

'This is a nice joke!' said Ardan. 'He is not sure. He hopes. And he waits for the moment when we are all locked in to make the avowal. Let me out!'

'How can we manage that?'

'That is true enough,' said Ardan; 'it would be difficult. We are in the train, and the guard's whistle will sound in 24 minutes.'

'Twenty!' said Nicholl.

For a few minutes the three travellers looked at each other. Then they examined the articles imprisoned with them.

'Everything is in its place,' said Barbicane. 'We must now decide how we can place ourselves in the best position to bear the shock of the start. The position is of great importance, and we must avoid, as much as possible, a rush of blood to the head.'

'Quite right,' said Nicholl.

'In that case,' said Michel Ardan, joining the action to the word, 'let us stand on our heads, like the clowns in the Great Circus.'

'No,' said Barbicane, 'let us lie down on our sides. In that way we shall best sustain the shock. Observe that at the moment when the shot is fired it is almost the same thing whether we are inside or in front.'

'So long as it is only *almost* the same thing I don't mind,' replied Ardan.

'Do you approve of my idea, Nicholl?' asked Barbicane.

'Fully,' replied the captain. 'Thirteen and a half minutes more!'

'That fellow Nicholl is not a man,' cried Ardan; 'he is a chronometer, with a second hand, with escapement, with eight rubies – '

But his companions paid no attention to him. They were completing their arrangements with unimaginable coolness. They looked like two travellers, in a first-class carriage, trying to make themselves as comfortable as possible. One is tempted to ask of what these American hearts are made, which beat not one pulsation faster at the approach of the most frightful dangers.

Three thick, well-made couches had been placed in the projectile. Nicholl and Barbicane deposited them in the centre of the disc, which formed the movable flooring. The three travellers were to lay themselves down a few minutes before the start.

During this time, Michel Ardan, who could not remain quiet one instant, ranged up and down his narrow prison like a wild beast in a cage; talking to his friends and to his dogs, Diana and Satellite, to which he had given, as you see, some time ago, these significant names.

'Hi, Diana! Hi, Satellite!' he cried, teasing them; 'you are going to show the Selenite dogs how well-behaved the dogs of the earth are. What an honour for the canine species! If ever I return, I shall bring back some specimens of cross-bred moon dogs, which will certainly be all the rage.'

'If there are any dogs in the moon,' said Barbicane.

'There are some,' said Michel Ardan, 'as there are horses, cows, donkeys, and hens. I bet we find hens there.'

'One hundred dollars we don't,' said Nicholl.

'Done, captain!' said Ardan, wringing Nicholl's hand. 'By-the-bye, you have already lost three bets with the president, since the funds for the undertaking were found, the casting succeeded, and the columbiad was loaded without accident. That makes 6,000 dollars.'

'Yes,' said Nicholl. 'Thirty-seven minutes and sixteen seconds past ten.'

'Quite so, captain. Well, in a quarter of an hour you will have to pay 9,000 dollars to the president – 4,000 because the columbiad will not burst, and 5,000 because the projectile will travel more than six miles in the air.'

'I have got the dollars,' said Nicholl, slapping his pocket. 'I shall be only too glad to pay.'

'Bravo, Nicholl! I see you are a man of order – which I never could be. But, after all, you have made a series of bets which are not precisely advantageous, allow me to say.'

'Why not?' asked Nicholl.

'Because, to win the first, the columbiad must burst and the projectile too, and Barbicane won't be forthcoming to repay the dollars.'

'My stake is deposited in the Bank of Baltimore,' said Barbicane simply; 'and in Nicholl's default the money will be paid to his heirs.'

'Oh! practical men,' cried Ardan; 'matter-of-fact minds. I admire you the more that I don't understand you.'

'Forty-two minutes past ten,' said Nicholl. 'Only five minutes more.'

'Yes; five short minutes!' replied Michel Ardan. 'And we are enclosed in a cannon-ball, at the bottom of a cannon 900 feet long; and beneath this projectile, are piled 400,000 pounds of gun-cotton, equal to 1,600,000 pounds of ordinary gunpowder. And friend Murchison, chronometer in hand, his eye fixed on the second hand, his finger placed on the electric apparatus, counts the seconds, and is going to launch us into the planetary spheres.'

'Enough, Michel, enough,' said Barbicane in a solemn tone. 'Let us prepare; a few instants only separate us from an awful moment. Let us shake hands, my friends.'

'Yes,' said Michel Ardan, more moved than he wished to appear. The three bold companions united in a last embrace.

'God be with us,' said the religious Barbicane.

Michel Ardan and Nicholl threw themselves on the couches placed in the centre of the disc.

'47 minutes past 10,' murmured the captain.

'20 seconds more!' Barbicane rapidly extinguished the gas and lay down beside his companions. The profound silence was only broken by the tick of the chronometer counting the seconds. Suddenly a terrific shock was felt, and the projectile was hurled into space by the force of six milliards of litres of gas developed by the combustion of the pyroxyle.

CHAPTER TWO

The first half-hour

What had passed? What effect had the terrible shock produced? Had the ingenuity of the constructors of the projectile attained the happy result? Had the shock been deadened, thanks to the springs, to the four buffers, to the layers of water, and to the breakable partitions? Had that frightful propelling strength been subdued which produced an initial velocity of 12,000 yards, sufficient to pass through Paris or New York in one second? Such certainly was the question propounded by the thousand spectators of this awful scene. They forgot the object of the journey to think only of the travellers. And if one of them – J. T. Maston for instance – could have caught a glimpse of the interior of the projectile, what would he have seen? At first, nothing. The darkness was profound in the projectile; but its cylindro-conic sides had admirably resisted. Not a crack, not a dent, not a deformation. The admirable projectile was not even damaged by the intense heat of the combustion of the gun-cotton, nor liquefied, as had been feared, into a rain of aluminum. In the interior, not much disorder after all. Some articles had been violently thrown to the roof, but the most important did not appear to have suffered from the shock; their fastenings were intact.

Upon the movable disc, which had now fallen to the bottom, since the breaking of the partitions and the escape of the water, three bodies lay without movement. Did Barbicane, Nicholl, and Michel Ardan still breathe? Was the projectile no more than a metal coffin bearing three corpses into space? A few minutes after the departure of the projectile, one of these bodies moved its arms, raised its head, and finally got upon its knees. It was Michel

Ardan. He felt himself all over, gave a sonorous 'hem', and said: 'Michel Ardan safe and sound – let us see the others!'

The courageous Frenchman tried to rise, but found himself unable to stand. His head swam round, the violently injected blood blinded him, he was like a drunken man.

'Brr!' said he; 'one would think I had drunk two bottles of Corton; but it is much less agreeable to swallow.'

Then, passing his hand several times across his forehead and rubbing his temples, he cried in a firm voice: 'Hallo! Nicholl! – Barbicane!'

He waited anxiously. No reply; not even a sigh, to prove that his companions' hearts were still beating. He repeated his call – same silence.

'The devil!' said he, 'one would think they had fallen from a fifth storey on their heads. Bah!' he added, with that imperturbable confidence which nothing could shake, 'if a Frenchman is able to get on his knees, two Americans will be certainly able to get on their feet. But first of all let's have a light.'

Ardan felt life rushing back into his veins. His blood calmed down and resumed its accustomed circulation. A few more attempts enabled him to regain his equilibrium. He succeeded in rising, drew a match from his pocket and ignited it by striking the phosphorus. Then, approaching it to the gas-burner, he lighted it. The reservoir had not suffered; the gas had not escaped. Indeed its odour would have betrayed it, and Ardan could not have lighted a match with impunity in so confined a space full of hydrogen. The gas, combined with the air, would have produced a detonating mixture, and the explosion would certainly have completed what the shock had perhaps begun. As soon as the burner was lighted, Ardan stooped over the prostrate forms of his companions. Their bodies were thrown one over the other like inert masses – Nicholl above, Barbicane below. Ardan dragged up the captain, placed him against the divan, and rubbed him vigorously. This shampooing, intelligently performed, soon brought Nicholl to himself. He instantly recovered his presence of mind, and seized Ardan by the hand; then, looking round: 'Where is Barbicane?' he asked.

'Each in his turn,' replied Michel Ardan quietly, 'I commenced with you, Nicholl, because you were uppermost. Now let us see to Barbicane.' Whereupon Ardan and Nicholl lifted the president of the Gun Club and laid him on the divan. Barbicane seemed to have suffered more than his companions. His blood had flowed; but Nicholl was reassured by discovering that it was only from a slight wound on the shoulder, a mere scratch, which was carefully dressed. Nevertheless Barbicane was a long time coming to, much to the alarm of his two friends, who did not spare their frictions.

'He breathes, at any rate,' said Nicholl, approaching his ear to the breast of the wounded man.

'Yes,' replied Ardan; 'he breathes like a man who is somewhat accustomed to that daily operation. Rub, Nicholl, rub vigorously!' And the two improvised practitioners worked so long and so well, that Barbicane recovered the use of his senses. He opened his eyes, sat up, took his two friends by the hand, and for his first word: 'Nicholl,' he asked, 'are we moving?'

Nicholl and Barbicane looked at each other. They had not yet thought about the projectile. Their first thought had been for the travellers, not for the carriage.

'Well, are we moving?' repeated Michel Ardan.

'Or are we quietly reposing on Floridan soil?' asked Nicholl.

'Or in the bottom of the Gulf of Mexico?' added Michel Ardan.

'The devil!' cried President Barbicane. And this double hypothesis, suggested by his companions, had the effect of immediately bringing him to himself.

However, they could not yet give an opinion as to the position of the projectile. Its apparent immobility, the absence of means of communication with the outside world, would not allow of the question being solved. Perhaps the projectile followed its trajectory through space! Perhaps, after a short journey, it had fallen back to earth, or even into the Gulf of Mexico, which the narrowness of the Floridan peninsula rendered possible. The question was important; the problem interesting. It must be solved as quickly as possible. Barbicane, in great excitement, and conquering physical weakness by moral strength, raised himself and listened. Outside, profound silence. But the thick padding was sufficient to intercept any noise from the earth. However, one circumstance struck Barbicane particularly. The temperature of the interior of the projectile was singularly high. The president drew a thermometer from its case and consulted it. The instrument marked 45° centigrade.

'Yes!' he cried; 'yes! we are moving. This stifling heat penetrates through the sides of the projectile. It is produced by friction with the atmospheric strata. It will decrease shortly, for already we float in a vacuum, and after being nearly suffocated we will suffer from intense cold.'

'What!' asked Michel Ardan. 'In your opinion, Barbicane, we have already passed the limits of the terrestrial atmosphere?'

'Without doubt, Michel. Listen. It is 55 minutes past 10 – we have been travelling about eight minutes, and if our initial velocity had not been diminished by friction, six seconds would have sufficed to pass through the sixteen leagues of atmosphere which surround the spheroid.'

'Very good,' replied Nicholl; 'but in what proportion do you estimate the diminution of velocity by friction?'

'About one-third, Nicholl,' replied Barbicane. 'The diminution is doubtless great, but it is proved by my calculations. If, therefore, we have had an initial velocity of 12,000 yards, on leaving the atmosphere this velocity will have been reduced to about 8,000 yards. In any case we have already passed that distance, and – '

'And,' said Michel Ardan, 'our friend Nicholl has lost his two bets; 4,000 dollars since the columbiad has not burst, and 5,000 dollars since the projectile has risen to a height greater than six miles. Nicholl, my friend, pay up.'

'Let us satisfy ourselves first,' said the captain, 'and then we will pay. It is very possible that Barbicane's arguments may be right, in which case I have lost my 9,000 dollars; but a new hypothesis occurs to my mind which would cancel the bet.'

'Which is that?' asked Barbicane.

'The hypothesis that, for some reason or another, the powder not having been ignited, we have not started.'

'Upon my word, captain!' cried Michel Ardan; 'that hypothesis is worthy of me; it cannot be serious. Were we not almost killed by the shock? Did I not bring you back to life? Does not the president's shoulder still bleed from the blow it received?'

'Agreed, Michel,' said Nicholl; 'but one question more.'

'Fire away, captain!'

'Did you hear the report, which must have been formidable?'

'No!' replied Ardan, astonished. 'You are quite right; I did not hear the report.'

'Did you, Barbicane?'

'No.'

'Well?' said Nicholl.

'True!' murmured the president. 'Why did we not hear the report?'

The three friends looked at each other somewhat crestfallen. Here was an inexplicable phenomenon! However, the projectile had started, and the report must have occurred.

'Let us find out where we are,' said Barbicane, 'and open the shutters.'

This extremely simple operation was immediately effected. The nuts which held the bolts of the exterior plates of the right-hand scuttle, gave way under the pressure of a wrench. The bolts were pushed outwards, and plugs, covered with indiarubber, stopped up the holes. At once, the exterior plate fell back upon its hinge, like a port-hole, and the lenticular glass appeared. A similar scuttle was opened, in the thickness of the wall, at the other side of the projectile, another in the dome, and a fourth in the floor. They could thus make observations in the four opposite directions. The firmament was visible through the lateral glasses, and, more directly, the earth and the moon by the upper and lower apertures in the projectile. Barbicane and his two companions had immediately rushed to the unclosed window. Not one ray of light illumined it. A profound darkness surrounded the projectile. Nevertheless President Barbicane exclaimed: 'No, my friends, we have not fallen back to earth! No, we are not submerged in the Gulf of Mexico! Yes, we are mounting through space! See the stars that shine, and the impenetrable darkness between the earth and us!'

'Hurrah! hurrah!' cried Michel Ardan and Nicholl simultaneously. In reality, this compact darkness proved that the projectile had left the earth; for if the travellers had remained on its surface, the ground would have appeared to them vividly illumined by the rays of the moon. This darkness also proved that the projectile had passed the atmospheric stratum; for the diffused light, spread through the air, would have caused some reflection on the metal walls, which reflection was wanting. This light would have illumined the glass of the scuttle, and the glass remained dark. Doubt was impossible; the travellers had quitted the earth!

'I have lost!' said Nicholl.

'I congratulate you,' replied Ardan.

'Here are 9,000 dollars,' said the captain, drawing a bundle of notes from his pocket.

'Will you take a receipt?' asked Barbicane, taking the sum.

'If not disagreeable to you,' replied Nicholl. 'It is more regular.'

And President Barbicane, gravely, phlegmatically, as if he had been at his counter, drew out his pocket-book, tore out a blank page, wrote a receipt in pencil, dated it, signed it, initialled it, and handed it to the captain, who carefully deposited it in his pocket-book. Michel Ardan, taking off his cap, bowed, without speaking, to these two companions. So much formality, under such circumstances, left him speechless. He had never seen anything so 'American'. Barbicane and Nicholl, having completed this operation, replaced themselves at the window, and studied the constellations. The stars stood out brilliantly upon the dark firmament. But from this side, they could not perceive the orb of night, which, travelling from east to west, rose gradually towards the zenith. This absence provoked a reflection from Ardan.

'What about the moon?' said he. 'Supposing she were to miss our appointment!'

'Don't be afraid,' replied Barbicane. 'Our future spheroid is at her post, but we cannot see her from this side. Let us open the other side scuttle.'

At the moment when Barbicane was about to quit the window to open the opposite scuttle, his attention was attracted by the approach of a brilliant object. It was an enormous disc, whose colossal proportions could not be estimated. One might have thought it a small moon, reflecting the light of the great one. It was travelling with prodigious swiftness, and appeared to describe an orbit round the earth, crossing the trajectory of the projectile. The movement of translation of this body was joined to a movement of rotation on its axis, as is the case in all celestial bodies abandoned in space.

'Hallo!' cried Michel Ardan, 'what is that? Another projectile?'

Barbicane did not reply. The appearance of this enormous body surprised and disquieted him. A collision was possible, which would have had disastrous results, either by forcing the projectile from its route, or breaking its flight and hurling it back to earth; or, again, by irresistibly carrying away the projectile by the power of attraction of this asteroid. President Barbicane

had rapidly grasped the consequences of these three hypotheses, which in one way or another would infallibly entail the failure of his experiment. His companions looked silently into space. The body increased prodigiously in size as it approached, and by an optical illusion it seemed as though the projectile were rushing to meet it.

'By Jove!' cried Michel Ardan, 'the two trains will collide!'

Instinctively, the travellers had started back. Their fright was great, but only lasted a few seconds. The asteroid passed at a few hundred yards from the projectile, and disappeared; not so much from the rapidity of its flight, as from the fact that its face, opposed to the moon, was soon lost in the absolute darkness of space.

'A good journey to you!' cried Michel Ardan, heaving a sigh of satisfaction. 'What! the infinite is not large enough to allow a poor little projectile to travel without danger? What is that pretentious globe which nearly ran into us?'

'I know,' said Barbicane.

'Of course, you know everything.'

'It is merely a meteorite,'[39] said Barbicane; 'but an enormous meteorite, which the attraction of the earth has maintained in the position of satellite.'

'Is it possible?' cried Michel Ardan. 'Has the earth two moons, like Neptune?'

'Yes, my friend, although she is generally supposed to have but one. But this second moon is so small, and its velocity so great, that the inhabitants of the earth cannot perceive her. It was by taking certain perturbations into account, that a French astronomer, M. Petit, was able to discover the existence of this second satellite and to calculate its elements. From two observations, it appears that this meteorite completes its revolution round the earth in 3 hours and 20 minutes, which implies a prodigious velocity.'[40]

'Do all astronomers,' asked Nicholl, 'admit the existence of this satellite?'

'No,' said Barbicane; 'but if, like us, they had met with it, they would doubt no longer. By the way, now I think of it, this meteorite, which nearly ran us down, will enable us to calculate our position in space.'

'How?' said Ardan.

'Because its distance is known, and, at the point where we met with it, we were exactly 8,140 kilometres from the surface of the terrestrial globe.'

'More than 2,000 leagues!' cried Michel Ardan. 'I should think that will take the shine out of the express trains on the miserable globe which they call the earth.'

'I should think so,' replied Nicholl, consulting his chronometer, 'it is now 11 p.m.; we left the American continent only thirteen minutes ago.'

'Only thirteen minutes?' said Barbicane.

'Yes,' replied Nicholl, 'and if our initial velocity of 12,000 yards were constant, we should travel about 10,000 leagues an hour.'

'That is all very well, my friends,' said the president; 'but the insoluble question still remains: why did we not hear the report of the columbiad?'

As no reply was forthcoming, the conversation dropped, and Barbicane, plunged in thought, began to open the second side scuttle. This operation was successful, and the moon filled the projectile with a brilliant light. Nicholl, like an economical fellow, put out the gas, which had become useless; the glare, too, prevented any observation of the planetary spheres. The lunar disc shone with incomparable purity. Her rays, which were no longer dimmed by the vaporous atmosphere of the terrestrial globe, shone through the glass, and filled the air of the interior of the projectile with its silvery reflections. The black curtain of the firmament doubled the splendour of the moon, which in this ether, unfavourable to diffusion, did not eclipse the neighbouring stars. The sky, thus seen, presented a perfectly new aspect, which the human eye could not suspect. It is easy to conceive the interest with which these audacious men contemplated the orb of night, the final goal of their journey. The satellite of the earth, in its movement of translation, insensibly neared the zenith, which mathematical point it was to reach in about 96 hours later. Its mountains and its plains were not more clearly visible to their eyes, than if they had observed them from any point of the earth; but its light through a vacuum shone with extraordinary intensity. The disc glowed like a platinum mirror. The travellers had already lost all memory of the earth which fled beneath their feet. Captain Nicholl was the first to call attention to the globe which had disappeared.

'Yes,' replied Michel Ardan; 'let us not be ungrateful to it. As we are leaving our country, let us give it our last looks. I wish to see the earth before it completely disappears from my eyes.'

Barbicane, to satisfy his friend's desire, set to work to clear away the bottom window, which would allow the earth to be seen. The disc, which the force of projection had brought to the bottom, was taken to pieces, not without difficulty. Its fragments, placed carefully against the sides, might serve again if necessary. Then appeared a circular gap 50 centimetres (21 inches) wide, cut in the bottom part of the projectile. This was closed by a glass, 15 centimetres (6 inches) thick, set in a rim of copper. Below was a plate of aluminum, fixed by bolts. The nuts having been unscrewed, and the bolt-holes plugged, the plate fell back, and visual communication was established between the interior and the exterior. Michel Ardan had knelt down to the glass. It was dark as though opaque.

'Well,' cried he, 'and the earth?'

'The earth?' said Barbicane, 'there it is.'

'What!' said Ardan, 'that thin streak? – that silvery crescent?'

'Certainly, Michel. In four days, when the moon is full at the moment when we reach it, the earth will be new, and will only appear to us in the form of a thin crescent, which will soon disappear completely, and remain for some days bathed in impenetrable darkness.'

'That the earth!' repeated Michel Ardan, looking fixedly at the thin slice of his native planet.

The explanation given by President Barbicane was correct. The earth, with reference to the projectile, was entering upon its last phasis.[41] It was in its octant, and only showed a crescent beautifully traced upon the black background of the sky. Its light, rendered bluish by the thickness of the atmospheric strata, was less intense than that of the lunar crescent. Its crescent was of considerable dimensions, like an immense bow stretched over the firmament. A few points, vividly lighted, especially in its concave portions, bespoke the presence of high mountains, which occasionally disappeared beneath thick spots, such as are never seen on the surface of the lunar disc. These were rings of cloud, lying concentrically around the terrestrial spheroid. However, thanks to a natural phenomenon – identical with that produced on the moon when in her octants – the whole contour of the terrestrial globe could be perceived. Its whole disc was rendered visible by an effect of ash-light, though less appreciably than is the case with the ash-light of the moon. And the reason of this lesser intensity may be easily understood. This reflection is caused upon the moon by the solar rays which the earth reflects on to its satellite; but the terrestrial light is about thirteen times more intense than the lunar light, which results from the difference in volume between the two bodies. Hence the result that, in the phenomenon of ash-light, the dark portion of the earth's disc is less distinctly marked out than that of the moon's disc, inasmuch as the intensity of the phenomenon is in proportion to the lighting power of the two orbs. It must also be added that the terrestrial crescent seemed to form a more extended curve than that of the disc, but this was merely the effect of irradiation. Whilst the travellers were endeavouring to pierce the profound darkness of space, a sparkling cluster of shooting-stars burst upon their eyes. Hundreds of meteorites, ignited by the contact of the atmosphere, crossed the darkness in every direction, with their luminous trains, and shed fiery spots all over the ashy portion of the disc. At this time the earth was in its perihelion; and the month of December is so prolific in these shooting-stars that astronomers have counted as many as 24,000 in an hour. But Michel Ardan, disdaining all scientific explanations, preferred to think that the earth was greeting, with its most brilliant display of fireworks, the departure of its three children. This was all that was seen of the spheroid, lost in the shadow of an inferior orb of the solar world, which, for the larger planets, rises and sets like an ordinary morning or evening star. This globe, where they had left all their affections, was nothing more than a fugitive crescent – an imperceptible point in space. The three friends, speechless but united in heart, looked long and steadfastly as the projectile flew onwards with ever-decreasing speed. Then an irresistible desire for sleep came over them. Was it fatigue of body and fatigue of mind? No doubt, for after the excitement of the last hours spent upon earth, a reaction must inevitably set in.

'Well,' said Michel Ardan, 'since we must sleep, let us do so.' And, stretching themselves upon their couches, they were soon wrapt in profound slumber. But they had not been sleeping more than a quarter of an hour, when Barbicane started up, and awakening his companions, cried with a loud voice: 'I have discovered it!'

'What have you discovered?' cried Michel Ardan, jumping from his bed.

'The reason why we did not hear the report of the columbiad.'

'What was it?' asked Nicholl.

'Because our projectile travelled quicker than sound!'

CHAPTER THREE

In which they make themselves at home

So soon as this curious but correct explanation had been given, the three friends once more relapsed into a deep sleep. Where could they have found, for slumber, a spot more calm, a centre more peaceful? Upon earth, the houses in the towns and the huts in the country feel all the shocks imparted to the earth's crust. At sea, the vessel tossed upon the waves is nothing but shocks and motion. In the air, the balloon oscillates incessantly between fluid strata of different densities. Alone this projectile, floating in an absolute vacuum, amidst absolute silence, could offer absolute repose to its inmates. Consequently, the sleep of the three adventuresome travellers would perhaps have been indefinitely prolonged, had not an unexpected noise awakened them about 7 a.m. on the 2nd of December, or nearly 8 hours after their departure. This noise was a very decided bark.

'The dogs! It's the dogs!' cried Michel Ardan, jumping up at once.

'They are hungry,' said Nicholl.

'Of course they are,' replied Michel, 'we had quite forgotten them.'

'Where are they?' asked Barbicane.

They searched, and found one of the animals hidden under the divan. Terrified and shaken by the initial shock, it had remained in this corner, until the moment when the feeling of hunger had given it tongue. It was the amiable Diana. Still somewhat frightened, she crept out of her retreat, after some enticing, and Michel Ardan encouraged her with his most gracious words.

'Come, Diana,' said he; 'come, my girl! thou whose fate will form an epoch in cynegetic annals! Thou whom pagans would have given as companion to the god Anubis, and Christians as a friend to St Roch! Thou who art worthy to be wrought in brass by the king of the infernal regions, like the puppy which Jupiter presented to Europa in exchange for a kiss! Thou whose celebrity will eclipse the heroes of Montargis and Mount St Bernard! Thou who, launched into planetary spheres, wilt perhaps become the Eve of Selenite dogs! Thou who wilt justify the words of Toussenel: "In the beginning, God created man, and, seeing how weak he was, gave him a dog" – come, Diana, come here!'

Whether Diana were flattered or not, she came out by degrees, whining plaintively.

'Good,' said Barbicane, 'I see Eve, but where is Adam?'

'Adam,' replied Michel, 'Adam cannot be far off. He is there somewhere! We must call him. Here, Satellite, here, Satellite.' But Satellite did not appear.

Diana continued to whimper. However, they discovered that she was not hurt, and an appetising mess soon stopped her whinings. As to Satellite, he appeared quite lost, but after a long search, he was discovered in one of the upper compartments of the projectile, where he had been violently thrown by the shock, in some inexplicable manner. The poor beast was sadly hurt and in a pitiable state.

'The devil!' said Michel, 'our acclimatisation is somewhat endangered.' The unfortunate animal was taken down with many precautions. His skull had been fractured against the roof, and it appeared improbable that he would recover from such a shock. Nevertheless, he was comfortably stretched out upon a cushion, and there he gave vent to a deep sigh.

'We will take care of you,' said Michel. 'We are responsible for your existence. I would rather lose my arm than a leg of my poor Satellite.' Saying which he offered the wounded dog a little water, which it drank greedily. This having been done, our three travellers observed attentively the earth and the moon. The earth was now only represented by an ashy disc, terminated by a yet narrower crescent than the day before; but its volume still remained enormous as compared with the moon, which approached nearer and nearer to a perfect circle.

'The deuce!' said Michel Ardan; 'I am dreadfully sorry we did not start at a moment of "full earth", *i.e.* when our globe was in opposition with the sun.'

'Why?' asked Nicholl.

'Because we should then have perceived our continents and seas in a new light – the former glowing under the projection of solar rays, the latter darker, as they appear upon certain maps of the world. I would have liked to see those poles upon which the eye of man has never rested.'

'No doubt,' replied Barbicane; 'but if the earth had been full, the moon would have been new, that is to say invisible amidst the irradiation of the sun. It is better for us to see the goal of our journey than the point of departure.'

'You are right, Barbicane,' replied Captain Nicholl. 'Besides, when we have reached the moon, we shall have plenty of time, during the long lunar nights, to observe leisurely the globe which our fellow-creatures do inhabit.'

'Our fellow-creatures!' cried Michel Ardan. 'They are no more our fellow-creatures now than the Selenites. We inhabit a new world, peopled only by ourselves – a projectile! I am the fellow-creature of Barbicane, and Barbicane of Nicholl. Beyond us, outside ourselves, humanity ceases and we are the only population of this microcosm, up to the moment when we shall become mere Selenites.'

'In about twenty-four hours,' said the captain.

'Which means – ?' asked Michel Ardan.

'That it is half-past eight,' replied Nicholl.

'In which case,' replied Michel Ardan, 'I can see no possible reason why we should not breakfast *instanter*.'

The inhabitants of the new star could not live without eating, and their stomachs were then undergoing the imperious laws of hunger. Michel Ardan, in virtue of his nationality, claimed to be head cook, for which important function there were no other competitors. The gas supplied the few degrees of heat necessary for the culinary preparations, and the provision chest furnished the elements of this first feast. Breakfast commenced with three plates of excellent soup, made by liquefying, in boiling water, some precious tablets of Liebig, prepared from the best parts of

the ruminants of the pampas. To the gravy soup succeeded some slices of beefsteak, compressed by the hydraulic-press, and as tender and succulent as if they had just left the kitchens of the Café Anglais. Michel, who was highly imaginative, maintained that they were red. Preserved vegetables, 'fresher than nature', as the good-humoured Michel said, succeeded to the dish of meat, and were followed by some tea and bread-and-butter, in American fashion. This beverage, which was declared exquisite, was obtained by the infusion of the most choice leaves, of which a few boxes had been presented to the travellers by the Emperor of Russia. Lastly, to crown the repast, Ardan discovered a fine bottle of Nuits, which was lying, by chance, in the provision chest. The three friends drank it to the union of the earth and its satellite. And, as if not satisfied with this generous wine which he had distilled upon the slopes of Burgundy, the sun chose to be of the party. The projectile, at this moment, emerged from the cone of shadow formed by the terrestrial globe, and the rays of the radiant orb shone full upon the lower disc of the projectile, by reason of the angle which the moon's orbit makes with that of the earth.

'The sun!' cried Michel Ardan.

'Quite so!' replied Barbicane, 'I was expecting him.'

'However,' said Michel, 'the conical shadow which the earth throws over space extends beyond the moon?'

'Far beyond, if you do not take the atmospheric refraction into account,' said Barbicane; 'but when the moon is clothed in shadow, the centres of the three orbs, the sun, the earth, and the moon, are in a straight line with each other. Then the nodes coincide with the phases of the full moon, and there is eclipse. If we had started at a moment of eclipse of the moon, our whole passage would have been made in shadow, which would have been unfortunate.'

'Why?'

'Because, although we are floating in a vacuum, our projectile, bathed by the solar rays, receives their light and their heat. Hence an economy of gas, a precious economy in every respect.'

In fact, beneath these rays, of which the brilliancy and temperature were unimpaired by any atmosphere, the projectile was heated and lighted, as though it had suddenly passed from winter to summer. The moon above and the sun below bathed it in their light.

'It is delightful here,' said Nicholl.

'I should think so,' cried Michel Ardan; 'with a little mould spread on our aluminum planet we would have new peas in 24 hours. I am only afraid lest the sides of the projectile should melt.'

'Do not be afraid, worthy friend,' replied Barbicane. 'The projectile has sustained a much higher temperature when passing through the atmospheric strata. I should not be surprised if, to the eyes of the Floridans, it took the form of a fiery meteorite.'[42]

'Then Maston must think we are roasted.'

'What surprises me,' replied Barbicane, 'is that we have not been roasted. It is a danger which we had not foreseen.'

'I was afraid of it,' replied Nicholl, simply.

'And you did not say anything about it, sublime captain!' cried Michel Ardan, wringing his companion's hand.

Meanwhile, Barbicane continued to make his arrangements in the projectile, as if he were never to leave it. It will be remembered that the basis of the aerial carriage had a superficies of 54 square feet. Twelve feet in height to the apex of the roof, skilfully arranged in the interior, not much encumbered by the instruments and travelling utensils – each of which had its special place – the projectile left, to the three guests, a certain amount of elbow-room. The thick glass, at the basis, could bear a considerable weight with impunity, and Barbicane and his companions trod upon its surface as upon a solid flooring. The rays of the sun, shining straight upon this glass, illumined the interior of the projectile, and produced the most singular effects of light and shade.

They began by examining the water reservoir and the provision chest. These had not sustained any damage, thanks to the dispositions taken to break the shock. The provisions were abundant, and sufficient to supply the wants of the three travellers during a whole year. Barbicane had taken his precautions in case the projectile should fall upon an absolutely sterile part of the moon. As to the water and reserve of 50 gallons of brandy, there would only be enough for two months. But it was shown, by the latest astronomical observations, that the moon possessed a low, dense, thick atmosphere, at least in her valleys, and there rivulets and springs could not be wanting. So, during the journey, and for one year after their arrival on the lunar continent, the adventuresome explorers would neither suffer from hunger nor thirst. There remained the question of air in the interior of the projectile. There again was perfect security. Reiset and

Regnault's apparatus, for producing oxygen, was supplied with chlorate of potash for two months. It necessarily consumed a certain quantity of gas, for it had to be maintained at a temperature above 400 degrees. Here again there was an ample supply, besides which, the apparatus required but little looking after – it worked automatically. At this high temperature, the chlorate of potash changed into chloride of potassium, giving off all the oxygen therein contained. How much would 18 pounds of chlorate of potash produce? – the 7 pounds of oxygen necessary for the daily consumption of the inmates of the projectile. But it was not sufficient to renew the oxygen – it was also requisite to absorb the carbonic acid produced by exhalation. During the last twelve hours, the atmosphere in the projectile had become charged with this deleterious gas, produced by the combustion of the elements of the blood by the inhaled oxygen. Nicholl recognised this state of the air by seeing Diana panting painfully. In fact, the carbonic acid – by a phenomenon identical with that produced in the famous 'Dogs' Grotto' – had fallen to the bottom of the projectile, by reason of its density. Poor Diana, on account of the lowness of her head, would suffer before her master from the presence of this gas. Captain Nicholl hastened to remedy this state of things. He placed, at the bottom of the projectile, several saucers containing caustic potash, which he moved about from time to time, and this substance, which has a great affinity to carbonic acid, absorbed the latter, and completely purified the air in the interior. The inventory of the instruments was then commenced. The thermometers and barometers had resisted, with the exception of a minima thermometer, of which the glass had been broken. An excellent aneroid was drawn from its wadded case and hung against one of the walls. Naturally, it only marked the pressure of air at the interior of the projectile; but it also marked the quantity of moisture which it contained. At this moment its needle oscillated between 765 and 760 millimetres. The weather was 'fair'. Barbicane had also taken several compasses, which were discovered intact. It will be understood that, under such circumstances, their needles acted wildly and without constant direction. At the distance which separated the projectile from the earth, the magnetic

pole could not have any apparent influence upon the apparatus. Perhaps, when the compasses were carried on to the lunar disc, some peculiar phenomena would be produced. In any case, it would be interesting to discover whether the earth's satellite was subject, like the earth, to magnetic influences. A hypsometer, to measure the altitude of lunar mountains; a sextant, to take the height of the sun; a theodolite, a surveyor's instrument, which is used to make plans and measure angles at the horizon; lunettes, the use of which would be much appreciated on their approach to the moon – all these instruments were carefully examined, and discovered to be in good condition, notwithstanding the violence of the initial shock.

As to the utensils – the pickaxes, the spades, the several tools which Nicholl had specially chosen – as to the different seeds and shrubs, which Michel Ardan intended to transplant into Selenite soil – they were all in their places, in the upper corners of the projectile. There was also a sort of lumber-room, filled with the articles which the prodigal Frenchman had piled up there. No one knew what they were, and the jovial fellow offered no explanation. From time to time he climbed up, by means of the cramp-irons fitted to the walls, but he reserved this inspection to himself. He arranged and rearranged, and plunged his hand rapidly into certain mysterious boxes, singing, completely out of tune, some old refrain from France, to enliven the situation.

Barbicane remarked, with interest, that the rockets and other fireworks had not been damaged. These important pieces, heavily charged, were to diminish the fall of the projectile, when the latter, entering into the sphere of lunar attraction, after passing the neutral point, would fall towards the surface of the moon, which fall, however, would be six times less rapid than on to the surface of the earth, on account of the difference in volume between the two orbs. Thus the inspection ended with general satisfaction, and each one returned to the observation of space through the lateral and bottom scuttles. The view was the same. The whole extent of the celestial spheres was alive with stars and constellations of marvellous purity, fit to drive an astronomer wild. On the one side the sun, like the mouth of a blazing furnace, a dazzling disc without a halo, stood out upon the dark background of the sky; on the other, was the moon shedding her reflected rays, motionless in the midst of the starry world. Then a large spot, like a hole in the firmament, with a silvery rim; that was the earth. Here and there nebulous masses, like large flakes of sidereal snow, and, from zenith to nadir, an immense ring formed of an impalpable cloud of stars, the 'milky way', in which the sun only counts as a star of the fourth magnitude. The spectators could not withdraw their eyes from this novel spectacle, of which no description could give an idea. How many reflections it suggested! What unknown emotions it awakened in their breasts! Barbicane wished to commence the account of his journey under the influence of these impressions, and he noted, hour by hour, all the incidents which occurred during the commencement of their undertaking. He wrote quietly, with his large square writing, and in a somewhat commercial style.

During this time Nicholl, the mathematician, was overhauling his formulae of trajectories, and used his figures with unparalleled dexterity. Michel Ardan chatted, now with Barbicane, who did not reply; now with Nicholl, who did not hear him; with Diana, who understood nothing of his theories; finally with himself, questioning and answering, going and coming, busy with a thousand details; now bent over the bottom glass, now perched in the roof of the projectile, and always singing. In this microcosm, he represented French restlessness and loquacity, and it may be believed that they were worthily represented. The day, or rather to be more correct, the space of 12 hours which forms a day upon earth, was terminated by a copious supper, well prepared. No incident had yet occurred to diminish the confidence of the travellers. So, full of hope, already certain of success, they slept peacefully, whilst the projectile, with gradually decreasing speed, held its way through the paths of the heavens.

CHAPTER FOUR

A lesson in algebra

The night passed without incident. Correctly speaking, the word 'night' is improper. The position of the projectile did not change as regards the sun. Astronomically, there was day on the lower portion of the projectile and night on the upper. When therefore, in this history, these two words are employed, they express the lapse of time which occurs between the rising and setting of the sun upon earth. The travellers' sleep was the more peaceful that the projectile, notwithstanding its excessive velocity, appeared absolutely motionless. No movement betrayed its passage through space. Motion, however rapid, cannot produce any effect upon organisms when it occurs in a vacuum, or when the mass of air follows the moving body. What inhabitant of the earth perceives its rapidity, which, however, carries him along at the rate of 90,000 kilometres (about 60,000 miles) an hour? Motion, under such conditions, is no more 'felt' than repose. Hence, all bodies are indifferent on the point. Is the body in a state of repose, it will remain so until some foreign force moves it. Is it in motion, it will continue so, and only stop when some obstacle is placed in its way. This indifference to motion or repose is inertia. Barbicane and his companions, being enclosed in the projectile, might believe themselves to be in a state of absolute immobility, and the effect would have been the same if they had placed themselves outside the projectile. Had it not been for the moon, which increased above them in size, they could have sworn that they were floating in complete stagnation.

That morning – the 3rd of December – the travellers were awakened by a joyful but unexpected sound. The crowing of a cock echoed within the carriage. Michel Ardan, the first up, climbed to the top of the projectile, and, closing a half-opened case: 'Hold your tongue!' said he, in a low tone. 'The brute is going to spoil my combination.'

However, Nicholl and Barbicane had awoke.

'A cock?' said Nicholl.

'Nothing of the kind, my friends,' replied Michel, hastily; 'I only wanted to awaken you with that rural song.' Saying which he performed a magnificent Cock-a-doodle-doo! which would have done honour to the proudest champion of the dunghill. The two Americans could not keep from laughter.

'A very pretty talent,' said Nicholl, looking somewhat suspiciously at his friend.

'Yes,' replied Michel, 'one of my country's jokes. It is very Gallic. That is how they imitate the cock in the very best society.'

Then, turning the conversation: 'Do you know, Barbicane,' said he, 'of what I have been thinking all night?'

'No,' replied the president.

'Of our friends at Cambridge. You have already remarked that I am a complete ignoramus in mathematical matters. I cannot, for the life of me, imagine how the *savants* of the Observatory were able to calculate the initial velocity which would enable the projectile to reach the moon.'

'You mean,' replied Barbicane, 'to reach the neutral point where the terrestrial and lunar attractions are equal; for from that point – which is about 7/10ths of the total distance – the projectile will fall towards the moon by force of gravitation.'

'Quite so,' replied Michel; 'but, once more, how could they calculate the initial velocity?'

'It is the simplest thing in the world,' replied Barbicane.

'Could you have made the calculation?' asked Ardan.

'Certainly. Nicholl and I would have worked it out if the note from the Observatory had not spared us the trouble.'

'Well, old Barbicane, they might have cut me into slices, from my feet upwards, before I could have worked out that problem.'

'Because you don't know algebra,' replied Barbicane quietly.

'Ah, there you are, you fellows with your *x*'s. You think algebra is an answer to everything.'

'Michel,' replied Barbicane, 'do you think one can forge without a hammer, or plough without a ploughshare?'

'With difficulty.'

'Well, algebra is a tool like the ploughshare or the hammer, and a good tool for those who know how to use it.'

'Seriously?'

'Very seriously.'

'And you could use that tool before me?'

'If it interested you.'

'And show me how the initial velocity of our carriage was calculated?'

'Yes, worthy friend. Taking into account all the elements of the problem, the distance from the centre of the earth to the centre of the moon, the earth's radius, the earth's volume, and the moon's volume, I can establish precisely what our initial velocity ought to have been, and that by means of a simple formula.'

'Let us see the formula.'

'You shall see it. However, I will not give you the curve described by the projectile between the earth and the moon, taking into account their movement of translation round the sun. I shall consider these two orbs as motionless, which will be sufficient for us.'

'Why so?'

'Because the other would be to seek the solution of the problem called "the problem of the three bodies", which integral calculi are not yet sufficiently advanced to solve.'

'How so?' said Michel Ardan, in a somewhat mocking tone of voice; 'mathematics have not said their last word yet?'

'Certainly not,' replied Barbicane.

'Good! Perhaps the Selenites have carried integral calculi farther than you. By-the-bye, what is this integral calculus?'

'It is the inverse of differential calculus,' replied Barbicane gravely.

'Much obliged.'

'In other words, it is a calculation by which you seek certain quantities, of which the differential is known.'

'At least that is clear,' said Michel, with a most satisfied air.

'Now,' said Barbicane, 'give me a slip of paper and a pencil, and in less than half-an-hour I will find out the formula required.'

Whereupon Barbicane became absorbed in his work, whilst Nicholl looked out into space, leaving the care of the breakfast to his companion. Half-an-hour had not passed when Barbicane, raising his head, showed Michel Ardan a paper covered with algebraical signs, in the centre of which was the following general formula:

$$\frac{1}{2}\left(v^2 - v_o^2\right) = gr\left\{\frac{r}{x} - 1 + \frac{m'}{m}\left(\frac{r}{d-x} - \frac{r}{d-r}\right)\right\}$$

'Which means – ?' asked Michel.[43]

'It means,' replied Nicholl, 'that one half v^2 minus v_o^2, equals *gr*, multiplied by *r* divided by *x*, minus one, plus *m'* divided by *m*, multiplied by *r* divided by *d* minus *x*, minus *r* divided by *d* minus *r* – '

'*x* upon *y* riding on *z* and mounted on *p*,' cried Michel Ardan, bursting into a laugh. 'And do you understand that, captain?'

'Nothing can be clearer.'

'Certainly not,' said Michel; 'it is as clear as daylight, and I am enlightened at once.'

'You eternal joker!' replied Barbicane; 'you wanted algebra, and you shall have your fill of it.'

'I would rather be hanged!'

'Really,' replied Nicholl, who was examining the formula as a connoisseur, 'that is very well put together, Barbicane. It is the integral of the equation of live forces, and I have no doubt it will give us the requisite result.'

'But I should like to understand,' cried Michel; 'I would give ten years of Nicholl's life to understand!'

'Listen then,' continued Barbicane, 'one half v^2 minus v_o^2 is the formula for the half variation of live force.'

'Good, and Nicholl knows what that means?'

'No doubt, Michel,' replied the captain. 'All these signs, which appear so mysterious, form the clearest and most consistent language which can be read.'

'And you pretend, Nicholl,' asked Michel, 'that by means of these hieroglyphics, more incomprehensible than the Egyptian Ibis, you can discover the initial velocity requisite to be given to the projectile?'

'Certainly,' replied Nicholl; 'and by this same formula, I could always tell you what is its velocity at a given point of its journey.'

'On your honour?'

'On my honour.'

'Then you are as clever as the president?'

'No, Michel; Barbicane had done the difficult part, which consists in establishing an equation which takes all the conditions of the problem into account. The rest is only a question of arithmetic, and only requires a knowledge of the four rules.'

'That is a good deal!' replied Michel Ardan, who had never been able to make a correct addition in his life.

However, Barbicane maintained that Nicholl would have had no difficulty in discovering the same formula.

'I don't know,' said Nicholl; 'for the more I study it, the more admirable I think it.'

'Now listen,' said Barbicane to his ignorant comrade, 'and you will see that all these letters have their signification.'

'I am listening,' said Michel with a resigned air.

'd,' said Barbicane, 'is the distance from the centre of the earth to the centre of the moon, for we must take the centres to calculate attractions.'

'I understand that.'

'r is the radius of the earth.'

'r radius – admitted!'

'm is the mass of the earth, m' the mass of the moon. It is necessary to take the masses of the two bodies into account, because the attraction is in proportion to the masses.'

'That is agreed.'

'g represents the gravity – the velocity acquired at the end of one second by a body falling to the surface of the earth. Is that clear?'

'Like spring water!' replied Michel.

'Now, I represent by x the variable distance which separates the projectile from the centre of the earth, and by v the velocity which the projectile has attained at that distance.'

'Good.'

'Lastly, the expression v_o, which figures in the equation, is the velocity of the projectile upon leaving the atmosphere.'

'Quite right,' said Nicholl; 'that is the point at which you must calculate the velocity, since we know already that the velocity at starting is exactly equal to one and a half times the velocity on leaving the atmosphere.'

'I don't understand any longer,' said Michel.

'It is simple enough,' said Barbicane.

'Not so simple as I am,' said Michel.

'It means that, when our projectile reached the limit of the terrestrial atmosphere, it had already lost one-third of its initial velocity.'

'So much as that?'

'Yes, my friend, merely by friction with the atmospheric strata. You understand that the more rapidly it travelled, the greater resistance it met with from the air.'

'I admit that,' replied Michel, 'although your *v* zero two, and your *v* zero square are rattling in my head like nails in a bag.'

'That is the first effect of algebra,' replied Barbicane. 'And now, to finish you off, we are going to establish the numeric data of these several expressions; that is, calculate their value.'

'Finish me off,' replied Michel.

'Some of these expressions,' said Barbicane, 'are known; the others have to be calculated.'

'I will undertake the latter,' said Nicholl.

'Let us see, *r*,' continued Barbicane; '*r* is the radius of the earth, which, under the latitude of Florida, our starting-point, is equal to 6,370,000 metres (say 7,000,000 yards). *d* – that is, the distance from the centre of the earth to the centre of the moon, is equal to 56 radii of the earth, say – '

Nicholl calculated rapidly. 'Say,' said he, '356,720,000 metres (about 420,000,000 yards) at the moment when the moon is in perigee – that is, at her shortest distance from the earth.'

'Good,' said Barbicane. Now, *m'/m* – that is, the relation between the mass of the earth and the mass of the moon, equals – 1/81th.'

'Hear, hear!' said Michel.

'*g*, the gravity, is, in Florida, 9 metres, 91 centimetres, whence it results that *gr* equals – '

'Sixty-two million four hundred and twenty-six thousand square metres,' replied Nicholl.

'And now?' asked Michel Ardan.

'Now that the expressions are put into figures,' replied Barbicane, 'I am going to seek the velocity, v_o – that is, the velocity which the projectile must possess on leaving the atmosphere, to reach the point of attraction, equal to an absence of velocity. Since, at that moment, the velocity will be null, I put down that it will be equal to zero, and that x, the distance where the neutral point is to be found, will be represented by 9/10ths of d – that is, the distance which separates the two centres.'

'I have a vague idea that it must be so,' said Michel.

'I shall then have: x equals 9/10ths of d, and v equals zero, and my formula will become – '

Barbicane wrote rapidly on the paper –

$$v_0^2 = 2\,gr\left\{1 - \frac{10r}{9d} - \frac{1}{81}\left(\frac{10r}{d} - \frac{r}{d-r}\right)\right\}$$

Nicholl scanned it greedily.

'That is it, that is it,' he cried.

'Is it clear?' asked Barbicane.

'It is written in letters of fire!' replied Nicholl.

'Extraordinary men!' murmured Michel.

'Have you understood at last?' asked Barbicane.

'Have I understood?' cried Michel Ardan; 'why, my head is bursting with it!'

'So,' replied Barbicane, 'v_0^2 equals 2 gr multiplied by 1 minus $10r/9d$ minus 1/81th multiplied by $10r/d$ minus $r/d-r$.

'And now,' said Nicholl, 'to obtain the velocity of the projectile on leaving the atmosphere, it is only necessary to calculate.'

The captain, like a practitioner equal to all difficulties, began to calculate with frightful rapidity. Divisions and multiplications increased under his fingers; the figures covered the white paper. Barbicane followed every line, whilst Michel Ardan repressed a growing headache with both hands.

'Well?' said Barbicane, after a few minutes' silence.

'Well,' replied Nicholl, 'v_0 – that is, the velocity of the projectile on leaving the atmosphere, to reach the point of equal attractions, ought to have been – '

'What?' said Barbicane.

'Eleven thousand and fifty-one metres (12,000 yards) in the first second.'

'Hallo!' cried Barbicane, jumping up; '11,051 metres. Damnation!' cried the president, with a gesture of despair.

'What is the matter?' asked Michel Ardan, much surprised.

'What is the matter! Why, if at that moment the velocity was already reduced by one-third from friction, the initial velocity ought to have been – '

'Sixteen thousand five hundred and seventy-three metres (18,000 yards),' replied Nicholl.

'And the Cambridge Observatory, who declared that 11,000 metres were sufficient for the departure, and our projectile, which started with only that velocity – !'

'Well?' asked Nicholl.

'Well! it will be insufficient.'

'Goodness!'

'We shall not reach the neutral point.'

'Confound it!'

'We won't even go half way.'

'God bless me!' cried Michel Ardan, jumping as though the projectile had been on the point of striking the terrestrial spheroid.

'And we shall fall back to earth.'

CHAPTER FIVE

The coldness of space

This revelation was a thunderbolt. Who would have expected such an error of calculation! Barbicane would not believe it. Nicholl went again over his figures, but they were exact. As to the formula, its correctness could not be suspected; and, after verification, it became evident that an initial velocity of 16,576 metres in the first second was necessary to reach the neutral point. The three friends looked at each other in silence. There was no further question of breakfasting. Barbicane, with compressed lips, contracted eyebrows, and hands clasped convulsively, gazed fixedly through the scuttle. Nicholl, with crossed arms, examined his figures. Michel Ardan murmured: 'There you have the men of science. They are always doing something of that sort. I would give twenty pistoles to fall upon the Cambridge Observatory and crush it, with all the dabblers in figures which it contains.'

Suddenly the captain made an observation which struck Barbicane at once.

'Hallo!' said he, 'it is 7 a.m. We have been travelling for thirty-two hours. More than half our journey is passed, and we are not falling, that I know of.'

Barbicane did not reply, but, after a rapid glance at the captain, he took a compass, which served to measure the angular distance of the terrestrial globe. Then through the lower glass he took a very exact observation, thanks to the apparent immobility of the projectile. Then rising and wiping the drops of perspiration from his forehead, he made some calculations on paper. Nicholl understood that the president was calculating from the measure of the terrestrial diameter, the distance of the projectile from the earth. He looked at him anxiously.

'No,' said Barbicane after a few minutes, 'no; we are not falling. We are already at more than 50,000 miles from the earth! We have passed the point where the projectile should have stopped, if its starting velocity was only 11,000 metres. We are still ascending.'

'That is evident,' said Nicholl; 'and we must conclude that our initial velocity under the pressure of 400,000 pounds of gun-cotton has exceeded the 11,000 metres required. I can now understand how we met, after only 13 minutes' journey, the second satellite, which revolves at a distance of 2,000 leagues from the earth.'

'This explanation is the more probable,' added Barbicane, 'that in getting rid of the water contained between the breakable partitions, the projectile suddenly found itself relieved of a considerable weight.'

'Quite right,' said Nicholl.

'Ah! worthy Nicholl,' cried Barbicane, 'we are saved.'

'Well,' said Michel Ardan quietly, 'as we are saved let us breakfast.'

In fact Nicholl was not mistaken. The initial velocity had been happily superior to the velocity fixed by the Cambridge Observatory, but the Cambridge Observatory was not the less in the wrong. The travellers, having recovered from this false alarm, took their seats and breakfasted gaily. If they ate much they talked more. The confidence was greater than after the 'algebra incident'.

'Why should we not succeed?' repeated Michel Ardan. 'Why should we not reach the moon? We have started, there are no obstacles in the way, the road is open, more open than to the ship, which fights against the waves, more open than to a balloon, which fights against the wind! If, then, a ship reaches where it will, if a balloon ascends as it pleases, why should our projectile not attain our desired goal?'

'It will,' said Barbicane.

'If it were only to honour the American people,' added Michel Ardan, 'the only nation capable of carrying out such an undertaking, the only one which could produce a President Barbicane! By-the-bye, now that I think of it, now that we have no further uneasiness, what will become of us? We shall be right royally bored!' Barbicane and Nicholl shook their heads.

'But I have provided for the case, my friends,' continued Michel Ardan. 'You have only to speak. I have at your disposal chess, draughts, cards, dominoes. There only wants a billiard-table!'

'What!' cried Barbicane, 'you have brought such trifles with you?'

'Doubtless,' said Michel; 'and not only to amuse ourselves, but with the laudable intention of endowing the Selenite public-houses with them.'

'My friends,' said Barbicane, 'if the moon is inhabited, the inhabitants must have appeared a few thousand years before those of the earth, for we cannot doubt that the orb is more ancient than ours. If, therefore, the Selenites exist for some hundreds of thousands of years, if their brain is organised like the human brain, they have already invented all that we have invented, and even what we will invent in the course of centuries. They will have nothing to learn from us, and we, on the contrary, will have everything to learn from them.'

'What!' replied Michel, 'you think they have had artists like Phidias, Michel Angelo, or Raphael?'

'Yes.'

'Poets like Homer, Virgil, Milton, Lamartine, Hugo?'

'I am certain of it.'

'Philosophers like Plato, Aristotle, Descartes, Kant?'

'I have no doubt of it.'

'Scientific men like Archimedes, Euclid, Pascal, Newton?'

'I would swear it.'

'Comics like Arnal and photographers like – Nadar?'

'I am sure they have.'

'Then, friend Barbicane, if they are as wise as we are, and even wiser – these Selenites – why have they not tried to communicate with the earth? Why have they not despatched a lunar projectile into the terrestrial regions?'

'Who says they have not?' replied Barbicane gravely.

'In point of fact,' added Nicholl, 'it would have been easier for them than for us, and for two reasons: first, because the attraction is six times less on the surface of the moon than on the surface of the earth, which would allow a projectile to ascend more easily; secondly, because it would have sufficed to send the projectile 8,000 leagues only, instead of 80,000, which only requires a force of projection ten times less.'

'Then,' continued Michel, 'I repeat, why have they not done it?'

'And I,' replied Barbicane, 'I repeat, who says they have not done it?'

'When?'

'Thousands of years ago; before the appearance of man upon earth.'

'And the projectile? Where is the projectile? I ask to see the projectile.'

'My friend,' replied Barbicane, 'the ocean covers five-sixths of our globe. Hence five good reasons for supposing that the lunar projectile, if launched, is now submerged at the bottom of the Atlantic or Pacific; unless it is buried in some crevasse, before the rind of the earth was completely formed.'

'Barbicane, old fellow,' replied Michel, 'you have an answer for everything, and I bow to your wisdom. However, there is one hypothesis which pleases me more than the others; it is that the Selenites, being more ancient than we, are also wiser, and have not invented gunpowder.'

At this moment Diana took a share in the conversation by a loud bark. She wanted her breakfast.

'Ah!' said Michel. 'In our discussion, we are forgetting Diana and Satellite.'

Immediately, a respectable mess was offered to the bitch, who devoured it with a good appetite.

'You see, Barbicane,' said Michel, 'we ought to have made a second Noah's ark of our projectile, and carried to the moon a couple of each kind of domestic animals.'

'No doubt,' replied Barbicane; 'if we had had room enough.'

'Oh,' said Michel, 'by squeezing a little!'

'The fact is,' said Nicholl, 'that oxen, cows, bulls, horses – all these ruminants would have been very useful to us on the lunar continent. Unfortunately this carriage could not contain either a stable or a pigsty.'

'At least,' said Michel Ardan, 'we might have brought an ass; one wee little ass, that courageous and patient beast which old Silenus liked so much to ride! I love the poor donkeys; they are certainly the least favoured animals in creation. Not only are they beaten during their lifetime, they are even beaten after death.'

'How so?' asked Barbicane.

'Why,' said Michel, 'don't they make drum-heads of them?'

Barbicane and Nicholl could not refrain from laughter at this ridiculous reflection; but a cry from their jovial companion stopped them. He was bent over Satellite's kennel, and arose saying, 'Good, Satellite is no longer ill.'

'Bravo!' said Nicholl.

'No,' replied Michel; 'he is dead! That is most embarrassing,' added he, in a piteous tone of voice. 'I am afraid, my poor Diana, that you will not leave any descendants in the lunar regions.'

The unfortunate Satellite had not survived his wounds. He was dead, thoroughly dead; and Michel, crestfallen, looked at his friends.

'There is one point,' said Barbicane; 'we cannot keep the carcase of this dog for another forty-eight hours.'

'Most certainly not,' replied Nicholl; 'but our scuttles work on hinges, they can be opened. We will open one of them and throw the dog into space.'

The president reflected a few minutes, and said: 'Yes, that is what we must do; but we must take the most minute precautions.'

'Why?' asked Michel.

'For two reasons, that you will readily understand,' replied Barbicane. 'The first relates to the air in the projectile, of which we must lose as little as possible.'

'But, as we renew the air?'

'Only a portion. We only renew the oxygen, good Michel; and, by the way, we must take care that the apparatus does not supply oxygen in too great quantities, for such an excess would produce very serious physiological disturbances. But in renewing the oxygen, we do not renew the nitrogen, which the lungs do not absorb, and which remains intact. Now this nitrogen would escape rapidly through the open scuttles.'

'Oh, the time to throw out poor Satellite,' said Michel.

'Very well; but let us be quick.'

'And the second reason?' asked Michel.

'The second reason is that we must not allow the exterior cold, which is intense, to penetrate into the projectile, or we should be frozen to death.'

'But the sun – '

'The sun warms our projectile, which absorbs its rays; but it does not warm the vacuum in which we float at the present moment. Where there is no air, there is no more heat than diffused light; and, as it is dark, so it is cold, where the rays of the sun do not reach directly. This temperature is therefore nothing more than the temperature produced by the starry irradiation, which is what the earth would receive if the sun were to be extinguished some day.'

'Which is not to be feared,' replied Nicholl.

'Who knows?' said Michel Ardan. 'But even admitting that the sun will not be extinguished, the earth might become more distant from it.'

'Good,' said Barbicane; 'those are Michel's notions.'

'Oh,' continued Michel, 'do we not know that the earth passed through the tail of a comet in 1861? Now, suppose a comet with an attraction greater than the solar attraction, the terrestrial orbit will incline towards the wandering star, and the earth, becoming its satellite, would be carried away to a distance where the rays of the sun would have no further action on its surface.'

'That might happen,' replied Barbicane, 'but the consequences of such a displacement might not be so redoubtable as you suppose.'

'Why not?'

'Because the heat and the cold would equalise on our globe. It was calculated that if the earth had been carried away by the comet in 1861, it would not have felt, at its greatest distance from the sun, a heat sixteen times superior to that which we receive from the moon; which heat, concentrated in the focus of the strongest burning-glasses, produces no effect.'

'Well?' said Michel.

'Wait a minute,' replied Barbicane. 'They also calculated that at its perihelium – that is, its nearest approach to the sun – the earth would have supported a heat equal to 28,000 times that of summer. But this heat, capable of vitrifying terrestrial matter and vaporising water, would have formed a dense ring of cloud, and tempered the excessive heat. Hence, compensation between the cold of the aphelium and the heat of the perihelium, and an average, probably, bearable.'

'But, at how many degrees do they estimate the temperature of the planetary spheres?' asked Nicholl.

'Formerly,' replied Barbicane, 'they thought that the temperature was excessively low. By calculating its thermometrical decrease, we reach a figure, millions of degrees below zero. Fourier, a fellow-countryman of Michel, an illustrious member of the Academy of

Sciences, reduced these figures to their closest estimates. In his opinion the temperature of space does not descend below –60°.'

'Pooh!' said Michel.

'That is about the temperature which was observed in the Polar regions,' said Barbicane, 'on Melville Island, or at Fort Reliance; about 56° below zero centigrade.'

'It remains to be proved,' said Nicholl, 'whether Fourier was not mistaken in his calculations. Unless I am mistaken, another French scientist, M. Pouillet, estimates the temperature of space at 160° below zero. We shall be able to verify.'

'Not at the present moment,' replied Barbicane, 'for the solar rays strike directly on our thermometer, and would, on the contrary, give a very high temperature. But, when we have reached the moon, during the nights, fifteen days long, which each face undergoes in turn, we shall have leisure to make our experiment, for our satellite moves in a vacuum.'

'What do you mean by a vacuum?' asked Michel. 'Is it an absolute vacuum?'

'It is a vacuum absolutely deprived of air.'

'In which nothing replaces the air?'

'Yes, ether,' replied Barbicane.

'Ah! what is ether?'

'Ether, my good friend, is an agglomeration of imponderable atoms, which, say the works on molecular physics, are, in relation to their dimensions, as far removed from each other as the celestial bodies are in space. Their distance, however, is inferior to one three-millionth part of a millimetre. These atoms, by their movement of vibration, produce light and heat by making, in each second, 430,000,000,000,000 undulations, each undulation only extending from four to six ten-millionth parts of a millimetre.'

'Milliards of milliards!' cried Michel Ardan. 'Have they measured and counted these oscillations? All those figures, my friend, are good enough for scientists. They frighten the ear and do not appeal to the mind.'

'However, one must calculate – '

'No; it is better to compare. A trillion signifies nothing. A comparison means everything. For instance, when you tell me that the volume of Uranus is 76 times greater than the Earth's, Saturn's

volume 900 times greater, Jupiter's volume 1,300 times greater, the Sun's volume 1,300,000 times greater, I am not much the wiser. I much prefer the old-fashioned comparisons of the *Double Liègeois*, which inform you simply: the Sun is a pumpkin, two feet in diameter, Jupiter an orange, Saturn a love-apple, Neptune a black cherry, Uranus a smaller cherry, the Earth a bean, Venus a pea, Mars a large pin's head, Mercury a mustard seed, and Juno, Ceres, Vesta, and Pallas mere grains of sand. One can understand that sort of thing.'

After Michel's tirade against scientists and the trillions which they cast up without winking, they proceeded to bury Satellite. It was merely necessary to throw him into space, in the same way that sailors throw a corpse into the sea. But, as President Barbicane had advised, it was necessary to operate rapidly, so as to lose as little air as possible. The bolts of the right-hand scuttle, which measured about 30 centimetres across, were carefully unscrewed, whilst Michel, in great grief, prepared to throw his dog into space. The glass, worked by a powerful lever which enabled it to overcome the pressure of the interior air against the walls of the projectile, turned rapidly on its hinge, and Satellite was thrown out. Hardly any molecules of air escaped;[44] in fact, the operation succeeded so well that later on Barbicane was not afraid to get rid, in this way, of the useless lumber which encumbered the carriage.

CHAPTER SIX

Questions and answers

On the 4th of December, the chronometers marked 5 a.m. by terrestrial time, when the travellers awoke, after 54 hours' journey. As regards time, they had only passed, by five hours, the half of the time fixed for their stay in the projectile; but, as regards distance, they had already got over 7/10ths of the passage. This singularity was owing to the regular decrease in their speed. When they observed the earth through the lower glass, it now only appeared to them like a dark spot, bathed in the solar rays. No longer any crescent, no longer any ash-light. The next day, at midnight, the earth would be new, at the precise moment when the moon would be full. Overhead, the orb of night approached nearer and nearer to the line followed by the projectile, so as to meet with it at the hour fixed. All around the dark vault was constellated with brilliant spots which appeared to move slowly, but, owing to the considerable distance at which they lay, their relative sizes did not appear to be modified. The sun and the stars appeared just as they are seen from the earth. As to the moon, she had considerably increased in size; but the travellers' telescopes not being very powerful they could not make any reliable observations, or reconnoitre her topographical or geological dispositions. Therefore, the time passed in interminable conversations, of which the moon formed the principal topic. Each one brought his contingent of special knowledge; Barbicane and Nicholl always serious, Michel Ardan always fantastic. The projectile, its situation, its direction, the incidents which might arise, and the precautions which its fall upon the moon would necessitate, supplied unlimited matter for conjecture. While they were at breakfast a question of Michel's, relating to the projectile, elicited from Barbicane a curious answer, worthy of being related. Michel, supposing that the projectile should be suddenly stopped in the midst of its terrific initial velocity, wished to know what would have been the consequences of such stoppage.

'But I don't see,' said Barbicane, 'how the projectile could have been stopped.'

'A mere supposition,' said Michel.

'An impossible supposition,' replied the practical Barbicane; 'unless the force of impulsion suddenly ceased. But in that case its velocity would have decreased gradually, and it would not have suddenly stopped. Suppose for one moment it had struck some body floating in space.'

'Which?'

'The enormous meteorite which we met with.'

'In that case,' said Nicholl, 'the projectile would have been dashed into a thousand atoms, and we also.'

'Better still,' said Barbicane, 'we should have been burnt alive.'

'Burnt!' cried Michel. 'By Jove, I am sorry the event did not occur, just to see.'

'And you would have seen,' replied Barbicane. 'We now know that heat is but a modification of motion. When we heat water – that is, when we add heat to it – it means that we set its molecules into movement.'

'By George!' said Michel, 'that is an ingenious theory.'

'And a correct one, worthy friend, for it explains all the phenomena connected with heat. Heat is only a molecular movement, a mere oscillation of the particles of a body. When the brake of a train is applied, the train stops. What becomes of the movement by which it was animated? It is transformed into heat and the brake becomes hot. Why do we grease the axles of wheels? To keep them from becoming hot, because that heat would be so much movement lost by transformation. Do you understand?'

'Do I understand!' replied Michel. 'For instance, when I have run for a long time and am in a bath of perspiration, covered with sweat, why am I obliged to stop? Simply because my movement is transformed into heat.'

Barbicane could not refrain from smiling at this repartee. Then, continuing his theory: 'Consequently,' said he, 'in the event of a shock, the same thing would have happened to our projectile as to the bullet which falls, burning, after striking a metal shield. Its movement would be changed into heat. Consequently, I maintain that if our projectile had struck the meteorite, its velocity, suddenly checked, would have created sufficient heat to volatilise it instantaneously.'

'What, then, would happen if the earth were to stop suddenly in its movement of translation?'

'The temperature would be carried to such a height,' replied Barbicane, 'that it would immediately be turned into vapour.'

'Good,' said Michel; 'there you have a way of ending the world which would simplify many things.'

'And if the earth fell upon the sun?' said Nicholl.

'According to calculation,' replied Barbicane, 'that fall would develop an amount of heat equal to the heat produced by 1,600 globes of coal each of the same volume as the terrestrial globe.'

'A nice increase of temperature for the sun,' replied Michel Ardan, 'and for which, no doubt, the inhabitants of Uranus and Neptune would be grateful, for they must be perishing from cold on their planets.

'Thus, my friends,' continued Barbicane, 'every movement suddenly checked produces heat; and this theory leads us to admit that the heat of the solar disc is maintained by a hail of meteorites incessantly falling to its surface. Calculations have been made – '

'Look out,' murmured Michel Ardan, 'here come the figures!'

'It has been calculated,' continued Barbicane, imperturbably, 'that the shock of each meteorite upon the sun would produce an amount of heat equal to that of 4,000 masses of coal of the same size.'

'And what is the solar heat?' asked Michel.

'It is equal to that produced by the combustion of a seam of coal surrounding the sun, and of a thickness of 27 kilometres.'

'And that heat – ?'

'Would be sufficient to boil, per hour, two milliards nine hundred millions of cubic myriametres of water.'

'And yet it does not roast us!' cried Michel.

'No,' replied Barbicane; 'because the terrestrial atmosphere absorbs four-tenths of the solar heat. Besides, the amount of heat intercepted by the earth, is only the two-milliardth of the total irradiation.'

'I quite see that all is for the best!' cried Michel, 'and that this atmosphere is a useful invention; for it not only allows us to breathe, but it prevents our being cooked.'

'Yes,' said Nicholl; 'but unfortunately it will not be the same in the moon.'

'Bah!' said Michel, always full of confidence; 'if there are inhabitants they must breathe; if there are no longer any they will certainly have left sufficient oxygen for three persons, if it were only at the bottom of the valleys, where its weight would have caused it to accumulate. Well, we won't climb up the mountains, that is all.' And Michel, rising, went off to observe the lunar disc, which shone with dazzling brilliancy. 'By Jove,' said he, 'it must be very hot up there.'

'Without counting,' replied Nicholl, 'that the days last 360 hours.'

'As a compensation,' said Barbicane, 'the nights are of the same duration, and as the heat arises from radiation, their temperature can only be that of the planetary spheres.'

'A nice country,' said Michel; 'but no matter – I wish I was there! By Jupiter! my friends, it will be curious to have the earth for a moon, to see it rise in the horizon, to recognise the configuration of its continents, to say, "There is America; there is Europe." Then to follow it till it loses itself in the rays of the sun. By-the-bye, Barbicane, are there any eclipses for the Selenites?'

'Yes, eclipses of the sun,' replied Barbicane; 'when the centres of the three orbs are on the same line, the earth being in the middle. But they are only partial eclipses, during which the earth is thrown like a screen upon the solar disc, allowing the greater part of it to be seen.'

'Why is there no total eclipse?' asked Michel. 'Is it because the cone of shadow, thrown by the earth, does not extend beyond the moon?'

'Yes, if you do not take into account the refraction produced by the terrestrial atmosphere; no, if you take that into account. So let ∂ be the horizontal parallax and p the half diameter visible – '

'*Ouf*!' cried Michel, 'one half of v zero square. Speak plainly, you algebraic man!'

'Well, in common parlance,' replied Barbicane, 'the mean distance from the moon to the earth being equal to 60 radii of the latter, the length of the cone of shadow is reduced by refraction to less than 42 radii. Hence it results that, in eclipses, the moon is found beyond the cone of pure shadow, and that the sun not only sends her its edge rays but also its central rays.'

'Then,' said Michel, jeeringly, 'why is there an eclipse since there should not be one?'

'Merely because the solar rays are weakened by this refraction, and the atmosphere, through which they pass, absorbs the greater number of them.'

'That reason suffices,' replied Michel. 'Besides, we shall see for ourselves when we get there. Now tell me, Barbicane, do you think that the moon is an old comet?'

'What an idea!'

'Yes,' replied Michel with inimitable foppishness, 'I occasionally have ideas like that!'

'But that is not Michel's idea,' said Nicholl.

'Good, then I am a plagiarist!'

'No doubt,' replied Nicholl. 'According to the testimony of the ancients, the Arcadians maintained that they had inhabited the earth before the moon became its satellite. Reasoning from this fact, certain learned men have considered the moon a comet, whose orbit brought it one day sufficiently near the earth to be retained by terrestrial attraction.'

'And what truth is there in that hypothesis?' asked Michel.

'None,' replied Barbicane; 'and the proof is, that the moon has not retained any trace of that gaseous surrounding which always accompanies comets.'

'But,' replied Nicholl, 'might not the moon, before having become the earth's satellite, have passed near enough to the sun in her perihelium to lose all gaseous substances by evaporation?'

'That is possible, friend Nicholl, but not probable.'

'Why not?'

'Because – By Jove! I really do not know.'

'Ah!' cried Michel, 'how many hundred volumes one might fill with what one does not know!'

'By the way, what o'clock is it?' asked Barbicane.

'Three,' replied Nicholl.

'How time flies,' said Michel, 'in the conversation of such learned men as we! Decidedly, I feel that I am becoming too learned. I feel that I am becoming a well of science!' Saying which, Michel hoisted himself to the roof of the projectile, 'to get a better look at the moon,' he said. During this time his companions gazed into space through the lower glass. There was nothing new to be seen.

When Michel Ardan had come down he approached the side scuttle, and suddenly gave vent to an exclamation of surprise.

'What now?' asked Barbicane. The president approached the glass and perceived a sort of flattened sack, which floated outside at a few metres from the projectile. This object seemed motionless, like the projectile, and was consequently animated by the same ascending motion.

'What the devil is that?' said Michel Ardan. 'Is it one of the corpuscles of space which our projectile retains within its radius of attraction, and which will accompany it to the moon?'

'What astonishes me,' replied Nicholl, 'is that the specific weight of that body, which is certainly less than the projectile's, allows it to maintain itself on our level.'

'Nicholl,' replied Barbicane, after a moment's reflection, 'I do not know what that object is, but I know perfectly well why it remains on a level with the projectile.'

'Why?'

'Because we are floating in a vacuum, my dear captain, and that in a vacuum all bodies fall or move (which is the same thing) with equal velocity whatever their weight or shape. It is air that creates, by its resistance, differences in weight. When you create a vacuum in a tube by means of an air-pump, all the articles within it, specks of dust or pellets of lead, fall with the same rapidity. Here in space, we have the same cause and the same effect.'

'Quite right,' said Nicholl; 'and all that we throw out of the projectile will accompany the latter in its journey to the moon.'

'What fools we are!' cried Michel.

'Why?' asked Barbicane.

'Because we ought to have filled the projectile with useful articles – books, instruments, tools, &c. We could have thrown them all out of window, and they would all have followed in our train. But now that I think of it, why should we not walk outside like this meteorite? Why not cast ourselves into space through the scuttle? What delight to remain suspended in ether, more favoured than the bird, who must always keep his wings moving.'

'Agreed,' said Barbicane; 'but how shall we breathe?'

'Cursed air, which fails us at such an interesting moment.'

'But if it did not fail, Michel, your density being much less than that of the projectile, you would be quickly left behind.'

'Then there is no means?'

'None whatever.'

'We must remain shut up in the carriage?'

'We must.'

'Hallo!' cried Michel in a formidable voice.

'What is it?' asked Nicholl.

'I know – I guess what that pretended meteorite is! It is not an asteroid – it is not a piece of planet!'

'What is it, then?' asked Barbicane.

'It is our unfortunate dog, Diana's husband.' In fact this deformed, unrecognisable object, reduced to nothing, was the corpse of Satellite, flattened out like an empty wind-bag, and still ascending, ascending ever!

CHAPTER SEVEN

A moment of frenzy

Thus a curious but consistent phenomenon, extraordinary, but capable of explanation, was happening under these singular conditions. Every article, thrown out of the projectile, would follow the same trajectory and only stop with it. Here was a subject of conversation sufficient for the whole evening. The excitement of the three travellers increased as they approached the end of their journey. They expected something unforeseen, some new phenomena, and nothing would have surprised them in their present frame of mind. Their excited imagination went ahead of the projectile, whose swiftness diminished notably without their being aware of it. But the moon increased before their eyes, and they already thought that they had but to stretch out their hand to grasp it. The next day, all three were on foot from 5 a.m. That day was to be the last of their journey, if their calculations were correct. That same evening, at midnight, in 18 hours, at the precise moment of the full moon, they would reach her flaming disc. This most extraordinary journey of ancient or modern times would be completed at midnight. So, from early morning, they greeted the orb of night with confident and joyous cheers through the scuttles silvered by her rays. The moon advanced majestically upon the starry firmament. Yet a few more degrees and she would reach the precise point in space, where her junction with the projectile would take place. From his own observations, Barbicane calculated that they would reach the northern hemisphere, where there are immense plains and but few mountains, which circumstance would be favourable, if the lunar atmosphere, as it was thought, was stored in the valleys only.

'Besides which,' remarked Michel Ardan, 'a plain is better adapted to disembarkments than a mountain. A Selenite who had been dropped in Europe upon the summit of Mont Blanc, or in Asia upon the top of the Himalayas, could not precisely be considered to have arrived.'

'Further,' added Captain Nicholl, 'on a flat surface, the projectile will remain motionless as soon as it has reached it; on a slope, it would roll like an avalanche. As we are not precisely squirrels, we should not get out of it alive; so, all is for the best!'

In fact, the success of the audacious experiment no longer appeared doubtful. However, one reflection preoccupied Barbicane, but, not wishing to alarm his companions, he held his peace. The direction of the projectile, towards the northern hemisphere of the moon, proved that its trajectory had been somewhat modified. The line of fire, mathematically calculated, should carry the projectile into the very centre of the lunar disc. If it did not arrive there, it was on account of some deviation. What had produced it? Barbicane could not imagine, nor determine the importance of this deviation, for all fixed points were wanting. He hoped that the only result would be, to carry them to the northern edge of the moon, which was the most propitious for landing. So Barbicane, without saying anything to his friends, contented himself with observing the moon, and trying to discover whether the direction of the projectile was not further modified; for the situation would have been terrible, if the projectile, missing its aim and carried beyond the lunar disc, were to be launched into the planetary regions. At this moment the moon, instead of appearing flat like a disc, already gave signs of convexity. If the sun had shed its rays upon her obliquely, the shadow thrown would have indicated the high mountains, and clearly defined them. The eye might have plunged into the yawning gulfs of the craters, and followed the capricious grooves which cover the extent of the plains. But all relief was levelled in one intense glow. It was even difficult to trace the large spots, which give to the moon the appearance of a human face.

'Face, if you like,' said Ardan; 'but I am sorry for the amiable sister of Apollo, it's a very worn face!'

Meanwhile our travellers, so near the end of their journey, did not cease to observe this new world; their imagination carried them through these unknown countries. They ascended the highest summits; they descended to the bottom of the deep valleys. Here and there, they thought they could perceive vast seas, hardly contained beneath a rarefied atmosphere; and watercourses pouring forth the tribute of the mountains. Leaning over the abyss, they hoped to surprise the sounds of the orb, which lies eternally mute in the solitudes of a vacuum. This last day left most exciting souvenirs. They took note of the minutest details; a vague uneasiness seized upon them as they approached the goal. This uneasiness would have redoubled had they known how much their velocity had decreased; it would have appeared to them quite insufficient to carry them to the end. At that moment the projectile had scarcely any weight. Its weight decreased continuously,[45] and would be completely null at the line where the lunar and terrestrial attractions, neutralising each other, would produce the most surprising results. However, notwithstanding his preoccupations, Michel Ardan did not forget to prepare the morning's repast with his accustomed punctuality. All ate with good appetites. Nothing could be better than the soup, liquefied by the heat of the gas, nothing better than the preserved meats; a few glasses of good French wine crowned the repast, and on this head Michel Ardan remarked, 'that the lunar vineyards, under the action of a burning sun, ought to produce the most generous wines, if there were any!' In any case, this far-seeing Frenchman had taken care not to forget a few cuttings from Medoc and Côte d'Or, from which he expected great things. Reiset and Regnault's apparatus worked with great precision, and the air was maintained in a state of perfect purity; not a particle of carbonic acid resisted the potash, and as to the oxygen, it was, as Captain Nicholl said, 'of the very best quality'. The small quantity of moisture contained in the projectile mingled with the air and tempered its dryness, so that many apartments in Paris, London, or New York, and many theatres, were not in such good sanitary condition. But to work, regularly, this apparatus had to be kept in perfect order; so each morning Michel visited the taps and regulators, and adjusted, by the pyrometer, the heat of the gas. All was going on well, and the travellers, like J. T. Maston, were getting so stout as to be unrecognisable, if their imprisonment had lasted many months. They did as the fowls do in cages – they grew fat. Looking through the scuttle, Barbicane saw the spectre of the dog and other articles thrown out of the projectile, obstinately following. Diana howled in a most melancholy manner when she saw the remains of Satellite. These remnants seemed as immovable as if they had lain upon solid ground.

'Do you know, my friends,' cried Michel Ardan, 'if one of us had died from the effects of the shock at starting, we should have had much difficulty in burying him, or, rather, in "etherising" him – since ether replaces the earth. Think how the accusing corpse would have followed us like remorse.'

'It would have been sad indeed,' said Nicholl.

'Ah,' continued Michel, 'what I regret is, not to be able to get outside! What voluptuousness to float in the midst of this radiant ether! to bathe and roll in the pure rays of the sun! If Barbicane had only thought of supplying us with a diving apparatus and an air-pump, I would have risked the experiment, and I would have assumed the posture of Chimera or a Hippogriff on the top of the projectile!'

'Well, Michel, old fellow, you would not have long played the Hippogriff, for, notwithstanding the diving-dress filled with air, you would have collapsed like a balloon which had risen too high in the air; so don't regret anything, and don't forget this: so long as we are floating in a vacuum you must dispense with all sentimental walks outside the projectile.'

Michel Ardan let himself be convinced in a certain measure. He agreed that the thing was difficult, but not impossible, which word he never pronounced. The conversation passed from this subject to another, without languishing one instant. It seemed to the three friends that, under these conditions, their ideas sprang up in their brains like leaves under the first warmth of spring, thick and fast! Amidst the questions and answers which crossed each other during this morning, Nicholl asked a certain question which did not meet with an immediate solution.

'By-the-bye,' said he, 'it's all very well to get to the moon, but how are we to return?'

His two companions looked at each other in surprise, as though that eventuality had occurred to them for the first time.

'What do you mean by that, Nicholl?' said Barbicane gravely.

'It seems to me somewhat premature,' said Ardan, 'to want to return from a country which one has not yet reached!'

'I don't say it because I wish to hang back,' replied Nicholl; 'but if you like I will withdraw my question, and substitute: how shall we return?'

'I don't know,' replied Barbicane.

'And as for me,' said Michel, 'if I had known how to return, I should not have started.'

'That is something like an answer,' cried Nicholl.

'I approve my friend Nicholl's words,' said Barbicane; 'and I will add, that the question has no present interest. Later on, when we think proper to return, we will consult on the point. If the columbiad is no longer to the fore, the projectile is.'

'That's not much good! A bullet without a gun.'

'We can manufacture the gun,' replied Barbicane; 'we can make the gunpowder. Neither metals, nor saltpetre, nor coal can be wanting in the bowels of the moon. Besides, to return, we need only conquer the lunar attraction, and it suffices to travel 8,000 leagues to fall down upon the earth by mere gravitation.'

'Enough,' cried Michel, with animation. 'Let there be no further question of returning; we have spoken too much of it already. As regards communicating with our old colleagues upon earth, that will not be difficult.'

'How so?'

'By means of meteorites cast from lunar volcanoes.'

'Bravo, Michel!' cried Barbicane, in a tone of conviction. 'Laplace has calculated that a force five times superior to that of our cannons, would suffice to send a meteorite from the moon to the earth, and there is no volcano which has not a greater force of propulsion.'

'Hurrah!' cried Michel. 'Those meteorites will make capital postmen, and cost nothing. Won't we laugh at the postal authorities! But I was thinking – '

'What?'

'A superb idea! Why did we not fasten a wire to our projectile? We might have sent telegrams to the earth.'

'The deuce we might!' said Nicholl. 'Don't you take into account the weight of a wire 86,000 leagues long!'

'That is nothing. We might have tripled the charge of the columbiad, or quadrupled it, or quintupled it!' cried Michel, the intonation of whose voice became more and more violent.

'There is only one little objection to be made to your plan,' replied Barbicane: 'that during the movement of rotation of the globe, our wire would have been wound round it, like a chain round a capstan, and it would inevitably have dragged us back to earth.'

'By the thirty-nine stars of the Union,' cried Michel, 'I have nothing but impracticable ideas today. Ideas worthy of J. T. Maston. But now that I think of it, if we don't get back to earth, J. T. Maston is capable of coming to fetch us.'

'Yes, he will come,' replied Barbicane; 'he is a worthy and courageous comrade. Besides, what can be easier? Does not the columbiad still lie open in the Floridan soil? Are cotton and azotic acid wanting for the manufacture of pyroxyle? Will not the moon again cross the zenith of Florida? In 18 years will she not again occupy the same place she occupies today?'

'Yes,' replied Michel, 'yes, Maston will come, and with him our friends Elphiston, Blomsberry, and all the members of the Gun Club; and they will be welcome! And later on, we will establish trains of projectiles between the earth and the moon. Hurrah for J. T. Maston!'

It is probable that if the Hon. J. T. Maston did not hear the hurrahs shouted in his honour, at least his ears must have tingled. What was he doing then? Doubtless, at his post, on the Rocky Mountains at Long's Peak Station, he was trying to discover the invisible projectile, gravitating in space. If he was thinking of his dear companions, it must be admitted that the latter were not behindhand with him, and that, under the influence of a peculiar exaltation, they were giving him their best thoughts. But whence did this animation arise, which was visibly increasing in the inmates of the projectile? Their sobriety could not be doubted. Was this strange excitement of the brain to be attributed to the exceptional circumstances in which they were situated? – to the proximity of the orb of night, from which they were only separated by a few hours? – to some secret influence of the moon, acting upon their nervous system? Their faces became red, as though exposed to the reflections of a furnace; their breathing became more rapid, and their lungs worked like the bellows of a forge; their eyes shone with an unaccustomed brightness; their voices resounded with terrific accents; their words escaped like champagne corks under pressure of carbonic acid; their gestures became alarming, they required so much room, and, strange to say, none of them noticed this excessive tension of their minds.

'Now,' said Nicholl sharply, 'now that I don't know whether we shall ever return from the moon, I want to know what we are going to do there?'

'What we are going to do there?' replied Barbicane, stamping with his foot as if in a fencing-school, 'I don't know!'

'You don't know?' cried Michel, with a roar which produced a sonorous echo in the projectile.

'No, I have not the slightest idea,' replied Barbicane, in the same tone as his interlocutor.

'Well, I know,' replied Michel.

'Speak, then,' cried Nicholl, who could no longer contain the growls of his voice.

'I shall speak if I like,' cried Michel, seizing violently his companion's arm.

'You will be obliged to like,' said Barbicane, with glaring eye and threatening hand. 'It is you who have brought us on this formidable journey, and we want to know why?'

'Yes,' said the captain, 'now that I don't know where I am going, I want to know why I am going there?'

'Why?' cried Michel, bounding a yard into the air. 'Why? To take possession of the moon, in the name of the United States! To add a fortieth state to the Union! To colonise the lunar regions, to cultivate them, to people them, to carry thither all the prodigies of art, of science, of industry. To civilise the Selenites, unless they are more civilised than we, and to form them into a republic if they do not already form one.'

'And if there are no Selenites?' replied Nicholl, who had become very contradictory under the influence of this extraordinary frenzy.

'Who says there are no Selenites?' cried Michel in a threatening tone.

'I!' roared Nicholl.

'Captain,' said Michel, 'don't repeat that insolence, or I will force it down your throat through your teeth!'

The two adversaries were on the point of rushing upon each other, and this incoherent discussion threatened to degenerate into a fight, when Barbicane interfered with a formidable bound. 'Stop, miserable men,' cried he, placing his two companions back to back, 'if there are no Selenites we will do without them.'

'Yes,' exclaimed Michel, who was not particularly tenacious of the point. 'We will do without them! What do we want with Selenites? Down with the Selenites!'

'The empire of the moon is ours,' said Nicholl.

'The three of us, let us form a republic; I will be the congress,' cried Michel. 'And I the senate,' replied Nicholl. 'And Barbicane president,' roared Michel. 'Not a president appointed by the nation,' replied Barbicane. 'Well, a president appointed by congress,' cried Michel; 'and as I am the congress, I appoint you unanimously.' 'Hip, hip, hurrah! for President Barbicane,' cried Nicholl. 'Hip, hip, hurrah!' screamed Michel Ardan. Then the president and the senate commenced in a terrible voice the popular 'Yankee Doodle', whilst the congress made the place re-echo with the manly notes of the 'Marseillaise'. Then commenced a frantic dance with insensate gesticulations, maniacal postures and somersaults as of boneless clowns. Diana joined in the dance, howling in her turn, and leaped to the roof of the projectile. An inexplicable flapping of wings was heard, and crowings of unusual shrillness. Five or six hens flew about beating against the walls, like lunatic bats. Then the three travelling companions, with lungs disorganised, under some incomprehensible influence, more than drunk, burnt by the air which set their respiratory apparatus on fire, fell without motion to the bottom of the projectile.

CHAPTER EIGHT

Seventy-eight thousand one hundred and fourteen leagues off

What had occurred? What was the cause of this singular frenzy, of which the consequences might be disastrous? A mere act of thoughtlessness on Michel's part; but which, happily, Nicholl was able to remedy in time. After a swoon, which lasted a few minutes, the captain, who first came back to life, recovered his intellectual faculties. Although he had breakfasted two hours previously, he felt a terrible hunger gnawing him, as if he had not eaten for several days. Every part of him, stomach and brain, were excited to the highest pitch. So he arose and called upon Michel for a new collation. Michel, completely broken-down, did not reply. Nicholl then tried to make a few cups of tea, to facilitate the deglutition of about a dozen sandwiches. He first tried to make a fire, and struck a match. What was his surprise at seeing the sulphur burn with extraordinary brilliancy, almost unbearable to the sight. He lighted the gas-burner, and a flame burst forth like the flash of an electric light. A revelation was made in Nicholl's mind. This intensity of the light, the physiological troubles which had arisen in him, the super-excitement of all his faculties moral and physical – he understood it all.

'The oxygen!' he cried; and bending over the air-apparatus he perceived that the tap was allowing this colourless gas to escape in floods – tasteless, scentless, eminently vital, it produces in a pure state the most serious disorders in the system. Michel had thoughtlessly opened the tap of the apparatus to its full extent! Nicholl hastened to stop this escape of oxygen, with which the atmosphere was saturated, and which would have caused the death of the travellers, not from suffocation, but by combustion. One hour afterwards, the air was less loaded, and their lungs

recovered their normal action. Gradually the three friends recovered from their intoxication; but they were obliged to sleep off their oxygen, as a drunkard sleeps off his wine. When Michel learnt what had been his share in this accident, he was not in the least disconcerted. This unexpected intoxication broke the monotony of the journey. Many foolish things had been uttered under its influence, but they were forgotten as soon as said.

'Besides,' said this jovial Frenchman, 'I am not sorry to have tried this heady gas. Do you know, my friends, one might set up a curious establishment with oxygen cabinets, where people, whose system is weakened, might live a more active life for a few hours. Imagine meetings where the air had been saturated with this heroic fluid! – theatres where the management kept a constant supply at high-pressure! What passion in the breasts of the spectators! What fire – what enthusiasm! And if, instead of a mere assembly, a whole nation could be saturated, what activity in its functions, what an increase of life it would receive. From a used-up nation, one might perhaps make a great and strong people, and I know more than one state in old Europe which ought to undergo a course of oxygen, for the good of its health.'

Michel spoke with an animation which might have led one to believe that the tap was still open; but with one word Barbicane put an end to his enthusiasm.

'All that is very well, friend Michel,' said he; 'but will you inform us, whence come these hens which have joined our party?'

'Hens?'

'Yes.' In fact, half-a-dozen hens and a superb cock were strutting about, fluttering and cackling.

'Oh, the fools,' cried Michel; 'the oxygen must have caused a revolution!'

'What do you want with these hens?' asked Barbicane.

'I want to acclimatise them in the moon, of course.'

'But why hide them?'

'A joke, worthy president, a mere joke, which has broken down most pitifully. I wanted to let them loose in the lunar continent, without saying anything to you. Ah! how great would not your astonishment have been, to see these terrestrial fowls pecking on the fields of the moon!'

'Oh you schoolboy, you eternal schoolboy,' replied Barbicane, 'you don't want any oxygen to excite yourself! You are always what we were under the influence of this gas! You are always mad.'

'And who says that we were not wise men then?' replied Michel Ardan.

After this philosophical reflection, the three friends repaired the disorder of the projectile. Hens and cock were returned to their coop; but, in proceeding to this operation, Barbicane and his two companions became forcibly aware of a new phenomenon. Since the moment when they had left the earth, their own weight, that of the projectile, and of the articles which it contained, had undergone a progressive diminution. If they could not ascertain this loss as regarded the projectile, the moment arrived when the effect would be very appreciable, as regarded themselves and the instruments and utensils of which they made use. It is unnecessary to add, that a pair of scales would not have indicated this loss, for, the weight with which the article was weighed would have lost precisely as much as the article itself; but a spring weighing-machine, for instance, which works without reference to attraction, would have given the exact amount of the falling off. We know that attraction, otherwise gravitation, is proportionate to the volume and in inverse ratio of the square of the distances. Hence this result: if the earth had been alone in space, if the other celestial bodies had been suddenly annihilated, the projectile, according to Newton's law, would have decreased in weight in proportion as it became more distant from the earth, without, however, ever losing its weight completely, for the terrestrial attraction would always make itself felt at no matter what distance. But in the present case, a moment must arrive in which the projectile would no longer be subject to the laws of gravitation, abstraction made of the other celestial bodies whose effect might be considered as nil. In fact, the trajectory of the projectile lay between the earth and the moon. In proportion as it left the earth, the terrestrial attraction diminished in the inverse ratio of the square of the distance, but at the same time, the lunar attraction increased in the same proportion; a point would thus be reached, where the two attractions would neutralise each other, and the projectile would have no more weight. If the volume of the earth and moon had been equal, this point would have lain at an equal distance from the two orbs. Taking into account the difference of the two masses, it was easy to calculate that the point would be situated at the 47/52nds of the journey, or, in figures, at 78,114 leagues from the earth. At this point, a body having no principle of swiftness or of displacement in itself, would remain eternally motionless, being equally attracted by the two orbs, and not being more drawn towards the one than towards the other. Now the projectile, if the force of impulsion had been exactly calculated, ought to reach this point without any velocity, having lost all indication of weight, as well as all the articles contained in it. What would then happen? Three hypotheses were possible. Either the projectile would have retained a certain velocity, and, passing the point of equal attractions, it would fall upon the moon, by reason of the excess of lunar attraction over terrestrial attraction, or, if the velocity were wanting to attain the point of equal attractions, it would fall back to earth, by reason of the excess of terrestrial attraction. Or, finally, endowed with sufficient velocity to attain the neutral point, but insufficient to pass beyond it, the projectile would remain eternally suspended in that place, like the pretended coffin of Mohamet, between zenith and nadir.

Such was the situation, and Barbicane clearly explained its consequences to his companions, which interested them in the highest degree. Now, how were they to discover that the projectile had attained this neutral point, 78,114 leagues from the earth? – at which point precisely neither they, nor the articles contained in the projectile, would be any longer under the influence of the laws of gravitation.[46] Until now, the travellers, whilst remarking that this action (gravitation) decreased more and more, had not yet discovered its total absence. But that day, Nicholl having dropped a glass from his hand, the glass, instead of falling, remained suspended in the air.

'Ah,' cried Michel, 'we shall have some amusing experiments in physics.'

Immediately various articles, arms and bottles, thrown into the air, remained stationary, as by a miracle. Diana herself, placed by Michel in space, reproduced, without any deception, the marvellous suspension performed by Caston and Robert Houdin. Further, the bitch did not seem aware that she was floating in air. They themselves, surprised and stupefied, notwithstanding their scientific reasonings, felt themselves carried into the world of the marvellous. They felt that gravitation was wanting to

their bodies. Their arms, when stretched out, no longer tended to fall back to their sides; their heads wagged upon their shoulders; their feet no longer clove to the bottom of the projectile. They were like drunken men, without stability. Imagination has created men without reflection and without shadow, but here reality, by neutralising the attractive forces, produced men in whom nothing had any weight, and who weighed nothing themselves. Suddenly Michel, taking a spring, left the bottom, and remained suspended in air, like the monk in Murillo's 'Angel's Kitchen'. In an instant, his two friends had joined him, and the three of them, in the centre of the projectile, represented a miraculous ascension.

'Is it creditable? Is it probable? Is it possible?' cried Michel. 'No! And yet it is. Ah, if Raphael could have seen us thus, what an Assumption he would have sketched upon his canvas.'

'The assumption cannot last,' replied Barbicane. 'If the projectile passes the neutral point, the lunar attraction will draw us towards the moon.'

'Then our feet will stand upon the roof of the projectile?' replied Michel.

'No,' said Barbicane, 'because the projectile, whose centre of gravity is very low, will gradually turn round.'

'Then all our arrangements will be turned topsy-turvy?'

'Don't be afraid, Michel,' replied Nicholl. 'There will be no disarrangement. Not a single article will move, for the evolution of the projectile will only take place insensibly.'

'In fact,' continued Barbicane, 'when it has passed the point of equal attractions, its lower portion, comparatively heavier, will be drawn down, along one of the moon's perpendiculars. But, in order that such a phenomenon may occur, we must necessarily have passed the neutral line.'

'Pass the neutral line!' cried Michel, 'then let us do as the sailors do when they cross the equator. Let us wet our journey.'

A slight side movement brought Michel to the padded wall. He took a bottle and some glasses, placed them in space before his companions, and, joyously clinking their glasses, they saluted the line with a triple hurrah. This influence of the attractions hardly lasted an hour. The travellers felt themselves insensibly brought towards the bottom, and Barbicane thought that he perceived the conical end of the projectile diverge slightly from its normal direction towards the moon. By an inverse movement, the bottom approached towards it. So the lunar attraction became stronger than the terrestrial attraction; it would only be 1⅓ millimetre in the first second, or 590-1000ths of a line's width. But, gradually, the attractive force would increase, the fall would be more rapid; the projectile, carried away, bottom downwards, would present its upper cone to the earth, and would fall with an increasing velocity to the surface of the Selenite continent. Thus, the goal would be reached. Now, nothing could hinder the success of the undertaking, and Nicholl and Michel Ardan shared Barbicane's joy. Then they talked of all these phenomena which had astonished them all in turn; especially the neutralisation of the laws of gravitation was an inexhaustible topic. Michel Ardan, always enthusiastic, wished to deduce purely fantastic consequences.

'Ah! my worthy friends,' cried he, 'what progress indeed if we could get rid on earth of that gravitation, which binds us to it like a chain. We should be like liberated prisoners. No more fatigues, either of legs or arms. And whereas now, to fly above the surface of the earth, to remain in air by the action of the muscles, requires a strength 150 times greater than that which we possess, if no attraction existed, a caprice, a mere effort of the will, would carry us into space.'

'True,' replied Nicholl, laughing; 'if we were able to suppress gravitation as we suppress pain, by anaesthetics, that would certainly alter the conditions of modern society.'

'Yes,' cried Michel, full of his subject, 'let us destroy gravitation, and let us have no more burdens. Therefore no more cranes, no more pulleys, no more capstans, no more handles, and other machinery; they will no longer be required.'

'Quite right,' replied Barbicane, 'but if nothing had any weight, things would not hold together. Neither your hat, worthy Michel, nor your house, whose bricks only adhere by their weight. No more ships, whose stability upon the water is but a consequence of gravitation; not even an ocean, for its waves would no longer be kept in equilibrium by terrestrial attraction. Lastly, no atmosphere, for its molecules, no longer under attraction, would disperse into space.'

'That is unfortunate,' replied Michel. 'There is nothing like matter-of-fact men to bring you brutally back to realities.'

'Console yourself, Michel,' continued Barbicane; 'if there is no orb without laws of gravitation, at least you are going to visit one where gravitation is much less than on earth.'

'The moon?'

'Yes, the moon; on whose surface things have six times less weight than on the surface of the earth – which phenomenon is easily proved.'

'And we shall be aware of it?' asked Michel.

'Certainly, for 200 kilogrammes will only weigh 30 on the surface of the moon.'

'And our muscular force will not diminish?'

'Not at all. Instead of rising one yard when you jump, you will spring to a height of 18 feet.'

'But we shall be like Hercules in the moon!' cried Michel.

'The more so,' replied Nicholl, 'that if the size of the Selenites is proportionate to the volume of their globe, they will scarcely be one foot high.'

'Lilliputians!' replied Michel. 'I shall take the part of Gulliver. We shall realise the fable of the giants. That is the advantage of leaving one's planet and travelling in the solar world!'

'One minute, Michel,' replied Barbicane; 'if you want to play at Gulliver, you must only visit the inferior planets, such as Mercury, Venus, or Mars, whose mass is less than the moon's. Don't venture on to the great planets, such as Jupiter, Saturn, Uranus, or Neptune, for there the parts would be changed, and you would become the Lilliputian.'

'And in the sun?'

'In the sun, though its density is four times less than that of the earth, its volume is 1,380,000 times greater, and gravitation is 27 times greater than at the surface of our globe. If the same proportions be maintained, the inhabitants must be at least 200 feet high.'

'The devil!' cried Michel. 'I should only be a pigmy – a myrmidon!'

'Gulliver in Brobdingnag,' said Nicholl.

'Just so,' replied Barbicane.

'And it would not be out of the way to take some artillery with one to defend oneself.'

'Good!' replied Barbicane; 'your bullets would have no effect in the sun, and would fall to earth a few yards off.'

'What do you mean?'

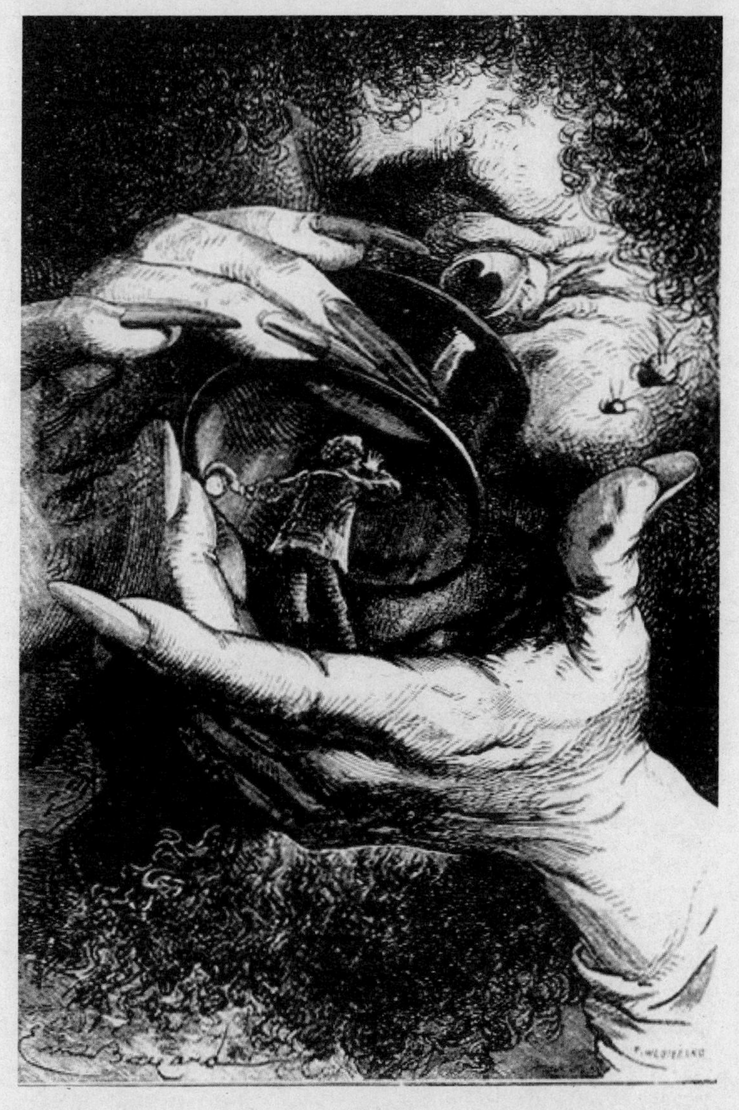

'It is quite certain,' replied Barbicane. 'The attraction is so great upon this enormous orb, that an object weighing 70 kilogrammes on the earth would weigh 1,930 on the surface of the sun; your hat, about 12 kilogrammes; your cigar, half a pound. Lastly, if you were to fall on the solar continent, your weight would be such – about 2,500 kilogrammes – that you could not get up.'

'The deuce I couldn't!' said Michel. 'In that case we must all have portable cranes! Well, my friends, let us be satisfied with the moon for today. There at least we shall make a good figure. Later on, we shall see whether we shall go to this sun, where one wants a capstan, when drinking, to haul up one's glass to one's mouth.'

CHAPTER NINE

Consequences of a deviation

Barbicane had no further uneasiness, if not as to the result of the journey, at least as to the force of impulsion of the projectile. Its velocity had carried it beyond the neutral line, so it would not return to earth, and it would not become immovable upon the point of attraction. Only one hypothesis remained to be realised – the arrival of the projectile at its goal, under the action of lunar attraction. In reality it was a fall of 8,296 leagues, upon an orb where, it is true, the gravitation was only estimated at one-sixth of the terrestrial gravitation. Nevertheless the fall was a formidable one, and all precautions possible had to be taken at once.

These precautions were of two sorts: some were to lessen the shock at the moment when the projectile touched the lunar ground, and the others were to stay its fall, and consequently render it less violent. To annul the shock, it was unfortunate that Barbicane could no longer employ the means by which he had so effectually lessened the shock of the departure, that is to say the water used as a spring, and the breakable partitions. The partitions still remained, but there was no water; for they could not make use of their reserve for that purpose, in case, during the first days, the precious element should be wanting on the lunar soil. Besides, this reserve would have been quite insufficient as a spring. The layer of water stored in the projectile at the start, and on which lay the water-tight disc, rose to a height of not less than 3 feet, over a surface of fifty-four square feet. In capacity it measured 6 cubic metres, and in weight 5,750 kilogrammes. The reservoirs did not contain 1/5th part as much, so they were obliged to give up all idea of this powerful means of lessening the shock. Happily Barbicane, not content with using water, had furnished the movable disc with strong spring buffers, for the purpose of lessening the shock against the bottom, after the breakage of the horizontal partitions. These buffers still existed; it was only necessary to readjust them and put the movable disc in place again. All these pieces were easily moved about, their weight being scarcely perceptible, and could be rapidly put together. This was done. The several parts were adjusted without difficulty; it was a mere matter of nuts and bolts. The tools were not wanting. Soon the readjusted disc stood upon its buffers like a table upon its legs. One inconvenience resulted from this replacing of the disc: the lower window became closed; hence it would be impossible for the travellers to observe the moon through that aperture when they were being perpendicularly precipitated upon her. So they were obliged to give that up. However, from the side openings they could observe the vast lunar regions, as the earth is seen from the car of a balloon. This arrangement of the disc required one hour's work, and it was past noon when the preparations were finished. Barbicane took new observations as to the inclination of the projectile, but, to his great disgust, it had not sufficiently turned for a fall; it seemed to follow a curve parallel with the lunar disc. The orb of night shone magnificently in space, while on the other side the orb of day fired it with its rays. The situation became disquieting.

'Are we arriving?' said Nicholl.

'Let us act as though we were arriving,' replied Barbicane.

'You are a timid lot,' said Michel. 'We shall arrive, and sooner than we wish for.'

This reply brought Barbicane back to his preparatory arrangements, and he began to arrange the apparatus which was to lessen the fall.

The scene at the meeting held at Tampa Town, Florida, will be remembered, when Nicholl took up an inimical position towards Barbicane and Ardan. When Captain Nicholl maintained that the projectile would be shattered like glass, Michel had replied that he would lessen its fall by means of rockets properly placed.[47] In fact, powerful rockets attached to the bottom and fired outside, might, by producing a retrograde movement, diminish to a certain extent the velocity of the projectile. These rockets would burn in a vacuum it is true: but they would not want for oxygen, for they would supply themselves, like the lunar volcanoes, whose deflagration has never been hindered by the want of atmosphere around the moon. Barbicane had therefore supplied himself with rockets contained in steel cases, which could be screwed on to the bottom of the projectile. Interiorly these cases were on a level with the bottom; exteriorly they protruded half-a-foot. There were twenty of them. An aperture in the disc allowed of the lighting of the fuse with which each was provided. All the effect was produced outside. The explosive mixture had been already rammed into each steel case, so that it was only necessary to remove the metallic plugs in the bottom of the projectile and replace them by these steel cases, which fitted the holes exactly. This new work was completed about three o'clock, and, all precautions being taken, there only remained to wait.

However, the projectile visibly neared the moon. It evidently was under her influence in a certain proportion; yet, at the same time, its own velocity carried it in an oblique line. The result of these two influences, was a line which might prove a tangent, but it was evident that the projectile was not falling to the moon in a normal manner, for its bottom, by reason of its superior weight, ought to have been turned towards her. Barbicane's uneasiness increased on seeing his projectile resist the influence of gravitation. The unknown opened before him – the unknown in the planetary spheres. He, the man of science, thought he had foreseen the three possible hypotheses – the return to earth, the return to the moon, stagnation upon the neutral line – and now a fourth hypothesis, replete with all the terror of the infinite, arose inopportunely. One must be a resolute man like Barbicane, a phlegmatic man like Nicholl, or an audacious adventurer like Michel Ardan, to look the prospect in the face without wincing. The conversation turned on this subject. Other men would have considered the question from a practical standpoint. They would have inquired whither their 'projectile-carriage' was carrying them. They, on the contrary, sought the cause which had produced the effect.

'So we have run off the rails,' said Michel; 'but why?'

'I am much afraid,' replied Nicholl, 'that notwithstanding all the precautions taken, the columbiad was not aimed correctly. An error, no matter how small, would suffice to throw us out of the lunar attraction.'

'Then they aimed badly?' asked Michel.

'I do not think so,' replied Barbicane; 'the perpendicularity of the cannon was absolute, its direction towards the zenith incontestable. The moon crossing the zenith, we must strike her in full. There is another reason, but it escapes me.'

'Won't we arrive too late?' asked Nicholl.

'Too late?' said Barbicane.

'Yes,' continued Nicholl. 'The note from the Cambridge Observatory stated that the journey should be accomplished in 97 hours 13 minutes and 20 seconds, which means that, any sooner, the moon would not yet be there, and, any later, she would be gone.'

'Agreed,' replied Barbicane; 'but we left on the 1st December, at 13 minutes and 25 seconds to 11 p.m., and we shall arrive on the 5th, at midnight, at the precise moment when the moon is full. Now this is the 5th December. It is half-past three in the afternoon, and eight and a half hours ought to be sufficient to carry us to our goal. Why do we not reach there?'

'Is it not perhaps from excess of velocity?' asked Nicholl; 'for we now know that the initial velocity was greater than we supposed.'

'No! one hundred times no!' replied Barbicane. 'An excess of velocity, if the direction of the projectile had been good, would not have hindered our reaching the moon. No; there has been deviation; we have deviated!'

'How and why?' asked Nicholl.

'I cannot say,' replied Barbicane.

'Well, Barbicane,' said Michel, 'do you want to know my opinion on the point as to whence the deviation arose?'

'Speak out.'

'I would not give half a dollar to know why we have deviated, that is the fact. It is of small importance whither we are going. We shall soon see. Confound it! since we are carried away into space we shall end by finding some centre of attraction!'

Michel Ardan's indifference could not satisfy Barbicane; not that he was preoccupied with the future, but he was desirous of learning, at any price, why his projectile had deviated. Meanwhile, the projectile continued to move laterally with the moon, and with it the string of articles which had been thrown out. Barbicane could even ascertain from the several fixed points which the moon offered, at a distance of less than 2,000 leagues, that the velocity was becoming uniform. This was a fresh proof that they were not falling. The force of impulsion was still greater than the lunar attraction; but the trajectory of the projectile was certainly nearing it to the lunar disc; and it might be hoped that, at a shorter distance from the surface, the action of gravitation would predominate, and cause a fall. The three friends, having nothing better to do, continued their observations. However, they could not yet determine the topographical dispositions of the satellite. All the excrescences were levelled, under the projection of the solar rays. They looked thus through the side windows until 8 p.m. The moon had by that time increased to such an extent that she shut out one-half the firmament. The sun on one side, the orb of night on the other, inundated the projectile with their light. At this moment, Barbicane considered that the distance still separating them from their goal might be estimated at 700 leagues only. The velocity of the projectile seemed to him about 200 metres per second, or about 170 leagues an hour. The bottom of the projectile continued to turn towards the moon, under the influence of centripetal force; but the centrifugal force having still the upper hand, it was becoming probable that the rectilinear trajectory would be changed into a curve, of which it would be impossible to determine the nature. Barbicane was still seeking the solution of his insoluble problem. Hours passed without any result. The projectile was visibly nearing the moon, but it was equally visible that it would not reach her; as to the shortest distance at which it would pass her, that would be the result of two attractive and repellent forces acting on the projectile.

'I only ask for one thing,' said Michel: 'to pass near enough to the moon to discover her secrets.'

'Accursed be the cause,' cried Nicholl, 'which has made our projectile deviate!'

'Then,' replied Barbicane, as if a thought had just struck him, 'accursed be the meteorite which we passed on our road!'

'Hallo!' said Michel Ardan.

'What do you mean?' cried Nicholl.

'I mean,' replied Barbicane, in a tone of conviction, 'I mean that our deviation is owing solely to the meeting with that wandering body.'

'But it did not even touch us,' replied Michel.

'What does that matter? Its mass was enormous compared with that of our projectile, and its attraction has sufficed to influence our direction.'

'So little?' cried Nicholl.

'Yes, Nicholl; but however little it may be,' replied Barbicane, 'upon a distance of 84,000 leagues it required no more to make us miss the moon.

CHAPTER TEN

The observers of the moon

Barbicane had evidently discovered the only plausible reason for this deviation. However small, it had sufficed to modify the trajectory of the projectile. It was a fatality. The audacious attempt fell through from a wholly fortuitous circumstance, and unless some exceptional event occurred, they could not reach the lunar disc. Would they pass near enough to solve some questions of physics or geology hitherto insoluble? This question was the only one which preoccupied the hardy adventurers. As to the fate which the future had in store for them, they would not even think of it. Meanwhile, what would become of them in the midst of these infinite solitudes, where they would soon run short of air? A few days more and they would fall suffocated to the bottom of this wandering projectile. But a few days were so many centuries to these intrepid men, and they applied each minute of their time to observe this moon which they no longer hoped to reach. The distance then separating the projectile from the satellite, was estimated at about 200 leagues. In these conditions, as regards seeing the details of the disc, the travellers were farther from the moon than are the inhabitants of the earth armed with powerful telescopes. It is well known that the instrument set up by Lord Rosse at Parsonstown, which magnifies 6,500 times, brings the moon to within 16 leagues; further, the powerful instrument established at Long's Peak magnifies the orb of night 48,000 times, and brings her to within two leagues, and objects having a diameter of 10 metres are visible with sufficient distinctness. Thus, at this distance, the topographical details of the moon, observed without a telescope, were not very visible. The eye seized the vast contour of those immense

depressions, improperly called seas, but could not recognise their nature. The prominence of the mountains disappeared in the splendid irradiation produced by the reflection of the solar rays. The eye, dazzled as though it had looked upon a mass of molten silver, turned involuntarily away.

However, the oblong form of the orb stood out clearly. It appeared like a gigantic egg, with the smaller end turned towards the earth. In fact the moon, liquid or malleable in the first days of its formation, figured then as a perfect sphere; but, entering into the attraction of the earth, it became lengthened, under the action of gravitation, losing, as a satellite, its native purity of shape. The centre of gravity was carried beyond the centre of the figure; and, from this disposition, some learned men drew the conclusion that the air and the water might have taken refuge upon the surface of the moon which is never seen from the earth. This alteration of the primitive shape of the satellite was only perceptible for a few minutes. The distance from the projectile to the moon diminished very rapidly, for its swiftness, although less than its initial velocity, was yet eight or nine times superior to that of express trains. The oblique direction of the projectile gave Michel Ardan, from its very obliquity, some hopes that they would touch at some point of the lunar disc. He could not believe that they would not reach it. No, he could not believe it; and he repeated the same continuously. But Barbicane, who was a better judge, did not cease to reply with pitiless logic: 'No, Michel, no! We cannot reach the moon except by a fall, and we are not falling. The centripetal force maintains us under lunar influence, but the centrifugal force irresistibly keeps us from the moon.'

This was said in a tone of voice which destroyed Michel Ardan's last hopes. The portion of the moon which the projectile neared, was the northern hemisphere, which selenographical maps place undermost, for these maps are generally drawn from the image supplied by lunettes, and we know that lunettes reverse objects. Such was the *Mappa Selenographica* of Beer and Moedler, which Barbicane consulted. This northern hemisphere presented vast plains broken with isolated mountains. At midnight the moon was full. At this precise moment, the travellers ought to have set foot on the moon if the unfortunate meteorite had not caused them to deviate from their direction. The orb arrived in the conditions rigorously determined by the Cambridge Observatory. It was mathematically in its perigee, and at the zenith of the 28th parallel. An observer placed at the bottom of the enormous columbiad, aimed perpendicularly with the horizon, would have seen the moon in the mouth of the cannon, as in a frame. A straight line, marking the axis of the piece, would have passed through the very centre of the orb of night.

It is unnecessary to add that, during the night of the 5th December, the travellers did not take an instant's repose. Could they have closed their eyes so near to this new world? No! All their feelings were concentrated in one thought – to see. Representatives of the earth, of humanity, past and present, it was by their eyes that the human race looked upon these lunar regions, and penetrated the secrets of the satellite. Their hearts swelled with emotion, and they went silently from one window to the other. There observations, reproduced by Barbicane, were rigorously determined. To make them they had lunettes, to verify them they had maps. Galileo was the first observer of the moon. His inadequate lunette magnified only 30 times. Nevertheless, in those spots which are scattered over the lunar disc 'as the eyes on a peacock's tail', he was the first to recognise mountains, and measured some altitudes to which he attributed an exaggerated elevation, equal to 1/20th of the diameter of the disc, or 8,800 metres. Galileo did not make any map of his observations. Some years later an astronomer of Danzig, Hevelius, by processes which were only correct twice in a month – at the first and last quadratures – reduced Galileo's observations to 1/26th of the lunar diameter, which was an exaggeration in the opposite extreme. But it is to this learned man that we are indebted for our first map of the moon. The clear round spots are given as mountains, and the darker spots as vast seas, although in reality they are only plains. To these mountains and extents of water he gave terrestrial names. We find Sinai in the midst of an Arabia; Etna in the centre of Sicily; the Alps, Apennines, Carpathians; and then the Mediterranean, the Paulo-Méotide, the Euxine, and the Caspian seas. These names were badly applied, for neither the mountains nor the seas resemble their homonyms on the globe. In the large white spot, joined at the south to yet larger continents and terminating in a point, it would be difficult to recognise the reversed image of the Indian peninsula, with the Indian Ocean and Cochin-China. Therefore these names were not retained. Another cartographer, who was better acquainted with the human heart, proposed a new nomenclature which human vanity hastened to adopt. This observer was Father Riccioli, a contemporary of Hevelius. He drew up a rough map, full of errors, but to the lunar mountains he gave the names of the great men of antiquity and of scientific men of his time, which custom has since been much in vogue. A third map of the moon was executed in the 17th century, by Dominique Cassini, and, though better drawn than that of Riccioli, it was inexact as regards measurements. Several reproductions of it were published, but its plate, which was long preserved at the royal printing establishment, has been sold by weight as lumber. La Hire, a celebrated mathematician and draughtsman, drew a map of the moon four metres high, which was never engraved. After him a German astronomer, Tobias Mayer, towards the middle of the 18th century, commenced the publication of a magnificent selenographic map, according to measurements accurately verified by him; but his death, in 1762, prevented the completion of this fine work. Next came Schroeter de Lilienthal, who sketched numerous maps of the moon; then a certain Lohrmann, of Dresden, to whom we are indebted for a plate divided into 25 sections, of which four have been engraved.

It was in 1830 that Messrs Beer and Moedler composed their celebrated *Mappa Selenographica*, in accordance with an orthographic projection. This map exactly reproduces the lunar disc such as it appears, but the configurations of the mountains and plains are only correct in the central portion; everywhere else, in the northern and southern portions, or the eastern or western, these configurations, given in reduced sizes, cannot be compared with those of the centre. This topographic map, 95 centimetres high, and divided into four sheets, is the masterpiece of lunar cartography. After these scientific men are mentioned also the selenographic scraps by the astronomer Julius Schmidt, the topographic works of Father Secchi, the magnificent proofs of the English amateur Warren De la Rue, and lastly, a map upon orthographic projection by MM. Lecouturier and Chapuis, of which a fine model was prepared in 1860, beautifully drawn and very clear in its arrangement. Such is the nomenclature of the different maps relating to the lunar world.[48] Barbicane had two in his possession, that of Beer and Moedler and that of MM. Lecouturier and Chapuis. They much facilitated his work of observation. As to the optical instruments at his disposal, they were excellent marine lunettes, specially manufactured for the journey. They magnified objects one hundred times, and would thus have brought the moon to a distance of less than 1,000 leagues from the earth. But at that moment, at a distance which towards 8 a.m. did not exceed 120 kilometres, in a medium without atmospheric disturbances, these instruments would bring the lunar surface to at least 1,500 metres.

CHAPTER ELEVEN

Imagination and reality

'Have you ever seen the moon?' asked a professor ironically of one of his pupils. 'No, sir,' replied the pupil still more ironically, 'but I must admit that I have heard her spoken of.'

In one sense the pupil's jocular reply might be echoed by the immense majority of sublunary beings. How many people have heard talk of the moon who have never seen her, at least through the eye-glass of a lunette or telescope! How many have never even examined the map of their satellite!

When looking at the selenographic map, one peculiarity strikes us first. Contrary to the disposition followed for the earth and Mars, the continents lie more particularly in the southern hemisphere of the lunar globe. These continents do not possess terminal lines so clear and so regular as South America, Africa, and the Indian peninsula. Their angular coasts are capricious, deeply indented, and rich in gulfs and peninsulas. They recall the embroglio of the islands of the Sound, where the land is excessively divided. If navigation has ever existed on the surface of the moon, it must have been singularly difficult and dangerous, and the Selenite sailors and hydrographers are to be pitied, the latter when making a survey of these tortuous coasts, and the former when navigating these dangerous parts. It was also remarked, that on the lunar spheroid, the southern pole was much more continental than the north pole. At the latter there only exists a narrow rim of land separated from the other continents by vast seas. Towards the south, the continents cover nearly the whole hemisphere. It is therefore possible that the Selenites have already planted their flag on one of their poles, whereas Franklin, Ross, Kane, Dumont d'Urville, and

Lambert have never been able to attain this unknown point of the terrestrial globe. As to the islands, they are numerous on the surface of the moon; nearly all are oblong or circular, as though traced with a compass; they form a vast archipelago, which may be compared to the charming group lying between Greece and Asia Minor, which mythology has endowed with its most charming legends. Involuntarily, the names of Naxos, Tenedos, Melos, Carpathos rise in the mind, and one looks for the vessel of Ulysses, or the clipper of the Argonauts; at least that is what Michel Ardan called for. He saw a Grecian Archipelago on the map! To his companions' less imaginative eyes, the coastlines recalled rather the broken land of New Brunswick and Nova Scotia, and there where the Frenchman found traces of the heroes of fable, these Americans pointed out the points most favourable to the establishment of factories, in the interests of lunar commerce and manufactures.

To complete the description of the continental portion of the moon, let us add a few words as to her orthographic disposition. One can easily distinguish chains of mountains, isolated mountains, circuses, and grooves. All the lunar highlands are included in this division. They are excessively varied – like an immense Switzerland, a continuous Norway, where volcanic action has done everything. This so uneven surface is the result of successive contractions of the crust at the time when the orb was in course of formation. The lunar disc is consequently favourable for the study of great geological phenomena. According to a remark of certain astronomers, her surface, although more ancient than that of the earth, has remained newer. There are no waters to deteriorate the primitive relief, and whose increasing action produces a sort of general levelling; no air, whose decomposing influence modifies the orographical profiles. There, plutonic work, unimpaired by neptunian forces, remains in its native purity – like the earth as she was before currents and swamps had coated her with sedimentary strata. After wandering over these vast continents the eye is attracted by yet vaster seas. Not only do their conformation, their situation, their aspect, recall that of the terrestrial oceans, but, as on earth, these seas occupy the greater portion of the globe. Yet they are not seas, but plains, whose nature the travellers soon hoped to determine. It must be admitted that astronomers have given these pretended seas the most extraordinary names, which however science has hitherto respected. Michel Ardan was right when he compared this map to a map of Love, got up by a Scudery or a Cyrano de

Bergerac. 'Only,' added he, 'it is not a map of Love as in the seventeenth century, it is the map of life, clearly divided into two parts, the one feminine and the other masculine. To women the right hemisphere, to men the left hemisphere.'

When he spoke thus, Michel made his prosaic companions shrug their shoulders. Barbicane and Nicholl considered the lunar map from quite another standpoint than their imaginative friend. However, their imaginative friend was to some extent right, as may be judged. In this left hemisphere extends the Sea of Clouds, where human reason drowns itself so often. Not far distant is the Sea of Rain, supplied by all the annoyances of life. Near this is the Sea of Tempests, where man unceasingly struggles against his passions – too often victorious. Then, worn out by deceptions, treasons, infidelities, and all the train of terrestrial miseries, where does he find the end of his career? – In the vast Sea of Humours, hardly sweetened by a few drops of the waters of the Gulf of Dew. Clouds, rain, tempests, humours – does man's life contain anything else? and is it not summed up in these four words? The right hemisphere, dedicated to the ladies, contains smaller seas, whose significant names suggest all the incidents of feminine existence. There is the Sea of Serenity, over which bends the young girl; and the Lake of Dreams, which reflects a happy future. There is the Sea of Nectar, with its waves of tenderness and its breezes of love; there is the Sea of Fecundity and the Sea of Crises; and then the Sea of Vapours, whose dimensions are perhaps too restricted; and finally, the vast Sea of Tranquillity, wherein all false passions, all useless dreams, all unsatisfied desires, are absorbed, and whose waters fall peacefully into the Lake of Death.

What a strange sequence of names! What a singular division of these two hemispheres of the moon, united one to the other, like man to woman, and completing a sphere of life carried into space! And was not the imaginative Michel right to interpret thus this fancy of ancient astronomers? But whilst his imagination was thus running wild, his grave companions were considering matters more geographically. They were learning this new world by heart; they measured its angles and diameter.

For Barbicane and Nicholl, the Sea of Clouds was an immense depression of ground, sprinkled with a few circular mountains, and covering the greater portion of the western portion of the southern hemisphere. It occupied 184,800 square leagues, and its centre was situated in 15° south latitude and 20° west longitude. The Ocean of Tempests, *Oceanus Procellarum*, the vastest plain on the lunar disc, covered a superficies of 380,300 square leagues, its centre being in 10° north latitude by 45° east longitude. From its bosom rose the admirable shining mountains of Kepler and Aristarchus. More to the north, and separated from the Sea of Clouds by high chains, lies the Sea of Rain, *Mare Imbrium*, having its central point at 35° north latitude and 20° east longitude. It was almost circular in form, and covered an area of 193,000 leagues. Not far the Sea of Humours, *Mare Humorum*, a small basin of only 44,200 square leagues, was situated in 25° south latitude and 40° east longitude. Lastly, three gulfs were situated on the coasts of this hemisphere: the Torrid Gulf, the Gulf of Dews, and the Gulf of Iris, small plains inclosed between high chains of mountains. The feminine hemisphere, naturally more capricious, was distinguished by smaller and more numerous seas. Towards the north, lay the Sea of Cold, *Mare Frigoris*, in 55° north latitude and 0° longitude, having an area of 76,000 square leagues, which bordered on the Lake of Death and the Lake of Dreams; the Sea of Serenity, *Mare Serenitatis*, in 25° north latitude and 20° west longitude, with an area of 86,000 square leagues; the Sea of Crises, *Mare Crisium*, well defined, very circular, covering, by 17° north latitude and 55° west longitude, a superficies of 40,000 leagues, a true Caspian Sea, surrounded by a belt of mountains. Then at the equator, by 5° north latitude and 25° west longitude, appeared the Sea of Tranquillity, *Mare Tranquillitatis*, occupying 121,509 square leagues. This sea communicated at the south with the Sea of Nectar, *Mare Nectaris*, covering 28,800 square leagues, by 15° south latitude and 35° west longitude; and at the east, with the Sea of Fecundity, *Mare Fecunditatis*, the vastest in this hemisphere, occupying 219,300 square leagues, by 3° south latitude and 50 west longitude. Lastly, quite to the north and quite to the south, two seas were yet to be seen – the Sea of Humbolt, *Mare Humboldianum*, having a superficies of 6,500 square leagues, and the Austral Sea, *Mare Australe*, covering a superficies of 26 miles. In the centre of the lunar disc,

across the equator and the zero meridian, was situated the Gulf of the Centre, *Sinus Medii*, acting as a sort of hyphen between the two hemispheres. Thus, the visible surface of the earth's satellite divided itself to the eyes of Nicholl and Barbicane. When they added together these different measures, they found that the superficies of this hemisphere was 4,738,160 square leagues, of which 3,317,600 leagues are composed of volcanoes, chains of mountains, circuses, islands – in a word, all that forms the solid portion of the moon; and 1,410,400 leagues for the seas, lakes, marshes, and all that forms the liquid portion; which, however, was a matter of perfect indifference to the worthy Michel. This hemisphere, it will be seen, is thirteen and a half times smaller than the terrestrial hemisphere. However, selenographers have already counted more than 50,000 craters! Thus it is a bloated surface, full of crevasses, a mass of scum, worthy of the unpoetical qualification which the English have given it of 'green cheese'. Michel Ardan was shocked when Barbicane pronounced this disobliging name.

'It is thus,' cried he, 'that the Anglo-Saxons of the nineteenth century treat beautiful Diana, fair-haired Phoebe, amiable Isis, charming Astarte, the Queen of the Night, daughter of Latona and Jupiter, the younger sister of the radiant Apollo!'

CHAPTER TWELVE

Orographical details

It has already been remarked that the direction followed by the projectile carried it towards the northern hemisphere of the moon. The travellers were far from the central point, which they ought to have struck, if their trajectory had not undergone an irremediable deviation. It was half-past 12, Barbicane estimated his distance at 1,400 kilometres, or rather more than a lunar radius, which distance would yet diminish as they advanced towards the north pole. The projectile was then not at the height of the equator, but across the tenth parallel, and from that latitude, which had been carefully computed on the map, Barbicane and his two companions could observe the moon in the best possible condition. In fact, by using lunettes, the distance of 1,400 kilometres was reduced to fourteen, or three and a half leagues. The telescope of the Rocky Mountains brought the moon yet nearer, but the terrestrial atmosphere greatly diminished its optical power, so Barbicane, posted in his projectile, glass in hand, already perceived certain details which were almost imperceptible to observers on the earth.

'My friends,' said the president in a grave voice, 'I know not whither we are going. I know not whether we shall ever see again the terrestrial globe. Nevertheless, let us proceed as if these works should some day be of service to our fellow-men! Let our minds be free from all preoccupation, we are astronomers, this projectile is a cabinet from the Cambridge Observatory, carried into space. Let us observe.' Whereupon the work was commenced with extreme precision, and reproduced faithfully the different aspects of the moon at the variable distances which the projectile occupied with reference to that orb. At the same time that the projectile stood at the height of the 10th parallel north, it seemed to follow rigidly the 20th degree of east longitude.

Here an important observation is to be made with reference to the map which was used for the observations. In selenographic maps, where, by reason of the reversing of the objects by the lunettes, the south is *above* and the north *below*, it would appear natural that by reason of this inversion the east should be placed to the left and the west to the right. However, this was not the case! If the map were reversed and presented to the moon such as she appears, the east would be to the left and the west to the right, contrary to what exists in terrestrial maps. This is the reason of this anomaly. The observers situated in the eastern hemisphere, in Europe for instance, perceive the moon in the south, with reference to them. When they observe her they turn their backs to the north, which is the reverse of the position they occupy when they look at a terrestrial map. Since they turn their back to the north the east is to their left, and the west to their right. For observers situated in the western hemisphere, in Patagonia, for instance, the west of the moon would be to their left, and the east to their right, as the south is behind them. Such is the reason of this apparent inversion of the two cardinal points, and they must be taken into account to follow President Barbicane's observations. Aided by the *Mappa Selenographica* of Beer and Moedler, the travellers recognised without hesitation the portion of the disc enclosed in the focus of their lunette.

'What do we see at the present moment?' asked Michel.

'The northern portion of the Sea of Clouds,' replied Barbicane. 'We are too far off to discover its nature. Are these plains composed of arid sands, as the first astronomers pretended? Are they only immense forests, according to the opinion of Mr Warren de la Rue, who allows the moon a very low atmosphere, though very dense? We shall know this later. Let us affirm nothing before we are in a position to affirm.'

This Sea of Clouds is somewhat doubtfully marked out on the maps. It is supposed that this vast plain is covered with blocks of lava thrown up by the volcanoes which are near its right portion, Ptolemaeus, Purbach, and Arzachel. But the projectile advanced and approached considerably, and soon the summits appeared which enclose the sea at its northern limits. In front rose a mountain, shining in all its beauty, whose summit seemed lost in an eruption of solar rays.

'That is – ?' asked Michel.

'Copernicus,' replied Barbicane.

'Let us see Copernicus.'

This mountain, situated by 9° latitude north and 20° longitude east, rises to a height of 3,438 metres above the level of the moon's surface. It is easily visible from the earth, and astronomers can study it perfectly, especially during the phases comprised between the first quarter and the new moon, because then the shadows are thrown from east to west, and facilitate the measurement of the heights.

This Copernicus is the most important shining point on the surface of the disc, after Tycho, which is situated in the southern hemisphere. It rises, isolated like a gigantic lighthouse, on that portion of the Sea of Clouds which borders the Sea of Tempests, and illumines with its splendid irradiation two oceans at once. The long luminous trains so dazzling in the full moon, form a spectacle without an equal, and crossing to the north the adjacent chains, they are finally extinguished in the Sea of Rain. At 1 o'clock of the terrestrial morning, the projectile, like a balloon floating in space, overhung this superb mountain.

Barbicane was able to observe exactly its principal dispositions. Copernicus is comprised in the system of annular mountains of the first order, in the divisions of the great circuses. Like Kepler and Aristarchus, which command the Ocean of Tempests, it appears sometimes like a shining spot through the ashy light, and was taken for a volcano in activity. But it is only an extinct volcano, as are all those on the surface of the moon. Its circumvallation had a diameter of about 22 leagues. The lunette discovered traces of stratifications produced by successive eruptions, and the surroundings appeared covered with volcanic remains, of which some still appeared within the crater.

'There exist,' said Barbicane, 'several kinds of circles on the surface of the moon, and it is easy to see that Copernicus belongs to the irradiating class. If we were nearer we would perceive the cones which cover its interior, and which were formerly so many fire-vomiting mouths! A curious disposition, without exception on the lunar disc, is that the interior surface of these circles is notably lower than the exterior plain, contrary to the form presented by terrestrial craters. It follows therefore that the general curve of the bottom of these circles gives a sphere of an inferior diameter to that of the moon.'

'And why this special arrangement?' asked Nicholl.

'It is not known,' replied Barbicane.

'What a magnificent irradiation!' repeated Michel; 'I could hardly imagine a more superb spectacle.'

'What would you say,' replied Barbicane, 'if the chances of our journey had carried us to the southern hemisphere?'

'I should say that it was more superb still,' replied Michel Ardan.

At this moment the projectile was floating directly over the circus. Copernicus' circumvallation formed an almost perfect circle, and its steep ramparts stood boldly out. They could even perceive a double annular fortification. All around spread a grayish plain with a wild aspect, upon which all prominences stood out in yellow. At the bottom of the circus, as though enclosed in a casket, two or three eruptive cones sparkled like enormous dazzling gems. Towards the north, the ramparts were lowered by a depression, which would probably have given access into the interior of the crater. Whilst passing over the adjacent plain, Barbicane was able to note a large number of unimportant mountains, and amongst others a small annular mountain named Gay-Lussac, which is 23 kilometres wide. Towards the south, the plain appeared very flat, without one prominent part, without one elevation of the ground. Towards the north, on the contrary, up to the spot where it bordered the Ocean of Tempests, it was like a liquid surface agitated by a storm, of which the hills and hollows figured a succession of waves suddenly congealed. Over all this extent, and in every direction, ran luminous trains which converged to the summit of Copernicus. Some of these were 30 kilometres wide and incalculably long. The travellers discussed the origin of these strange rays, but they were no more able than terrestrial observers to determine their nature.

'But why,' said Nicholl, 'should not these rays be simply spurs of mountains reflecting more vividly the light of the sun?'

'No,' replied Barbicane; 'if it were so, under certain conditions of the moon, these spurs would throw a shadow, and they do not throw any. In fact these rays only appear at the moment when the orb of day is in opposition with the moon, and they disappear so soon as the rays become oblique.'

'But how have these trains of light been explained?' asked Michel; 'for I cannot believe that men of science were ever in want of an explanation.'

'Herschel,' replied Barbicane, 'formed an opinion, but he did not insist upon it.'

'Never mind! What is that opinion?'

'He thought that these rays must be streams of cooled lava which shine when the rays of the sun fall upon them. That may be, but nothing can be less certain. However, if we pass nearer to Tycho, we shall be in a better position to judge of the cause of this radiation.'

'Do you know, my friends, what this plain resembles, seen from the height at which we are?' said Michel. 'Why, with all these pieces of lava lying about, like immense spindles, it resembles a huge game of spelikans, thrown pell-mell. There wants but the hook to take them out one by one.'

'Do be serious,' said Barbicane.

'Let us be serious,' replied Michel, quietly, 'and instead of spelikans let us say bones. The plain would then resemble an immense cemetery, where lie the mortal remains of a thousand extinct generations. Do you prefer that high-flown comparison?'

'The one is as good as the other,' replied Barbicane.

'The devil! you are hard to please!' replied Michel.

'My worthy friend,' replied the matter-of-fact Barbicane, 'it matters little what all this resembles when we don't know what it is.'

'Well answered,' cried Michel. 'That will teach me to argue with men of science.'

Meanwhile the projectile advanced with almost uniform velocity around the lunar disc. It will readily be believed that the travellers did not for one moment think of taking rest. Each minute, a new

landscape fled from beneath their eyes. Towards 1.30 a.m. they perceived the summit of another mountain. Barbicane, consulting his map, recognised Eratosthenes. It was an annular mountain, 4,500 metres high, and formed one of the numerous circles (or circuses) on the satellite. On this point, Barbicane related to his friends the singular opinion of Kepler as to the formation of these circuses. According to the celebrated mathematician, these crater-like cavities had been excavated by the hand of man.

'For what purpose?' asked Nicholl.

'For a very natural purpose,' replied Barbicane. 'The Selenites were supposed to have undertaken these immense works, and excavated these enormous holes, to take refuge in them, for protection against the solar rays, which beat upon them during 15 consecutive days.'

'The Selenites were no fools!' said Michel.

'What a singular idea!' replied Nicholl. 'But it is probable that Kepler did not know the real dimensions of these circuses, for to excavate them would have been the work of giants, quite impracticable for Selenites.'

'Why so? if gravitation on the surface of the moon is six times less than on earth?' said Michel.

'But if the Selenites are six times smaller?' replied Nicholl.

'And if there are no Selenites?' added Barbicane, which closed the discussion.

Soon Erotosthenes disappeared below the horizon, before the projectile had approached sufficiently near to admit of a precise observation. This mountain separated the Apennines and the Carpathians. In lunar orography, several chains of mountains have been remarked, which are principally distributed over the northern hemisphere; a few, however, occupy certain portions of the southern hemisphere.

This is a list of the different chains running from south to north, with their latitudes and various altitudes:

Mount Doerfel	S. latitude	84°	7,603 metres
Mount Leibnitz	S. latitude	65°	7,600 metres
Mount Rook	S. latitude	20°–30°	1,600 metres
Mount Altaï	S. latitude	17°–28°	4,047 metres
Mount Cordilleras	S. latitude	10°–20°	3,898 metres
Mount Pyrenees	S. latitude	8°–18°	3,631 metres
Mount Ural	S. latitude	5°–13°	838 metres
Mount Alembert	S. latitude	4°–10°	5,847 metres

Mount Hoemus	N. latitude	8°–21°	2,021 metres
Mount Carpathian	N. latitude	15°–19°	1,939 metres
Mount Apennine	N. latitude	14°–27°	5,501 metres
Mount Taurus	N. latitude	21°–28°	2,746 metres
Mount Riphees	N. latitude	25°–33°	4,171 metres
Mount Hercyniens	N. latitude	17°–29°	1,170 metres
Mount Caucasus	N. latitude	32°–41°	5,567 metres
Mount Alps	N. latitude	42°–49°	3,617 metres

Of these different chains, the most important is that of the Apennines, extending over 150 leagues, which is, however, much less than the extension of the great orographical elevations of the earth. The Apennines run along the east border of the Sea of Rain, and are continued at the north by the Carpathians, whose profile measures about 100 leagues. The travellers could only get a glimpse of the summit of the Apennines, which run from 10° west longitude to 16° east longitude; but the Carpathian chain extended under their eyes from the 18th to the 30th degree of east longitude, and they were able to observe its distribution. One hypothesis appeared to them well justified. On seeing the chain of the Carpathians taking here and there circular forms, and overhung by projections, they came to the conclusion that they were formerly important circuses. These mountainous rings must have been partly broken up by the vast disturbance which produced the Sea of Rain. These Carpathians would appear to have then been what Purbach, Arzachel, and Ptolemaeus would be if a convulsion threw down their left escarpments and formed them into a continuous chain. They possess an average height of 3,200 metres, which altitude is comparable with that of certain summits of the Pyrenees, such as the port of Pinedes. Their southern slopes fall abruptly towards the immense Sea of Rain. Towards 2 a.m. Barbicane found himself at the height of the 20th lunar parallel, not far from the small mountain, 1,559 metres high, which bears the name of Pythias. The distance of the projectile from the moon was not more than 1,200 kilometres, which the lunettes reduced to three leagues.

The *Mare Imbrium* spread beneath the travellers' eyes like an immense depression, of which the details were yet scarcely perceptible. Near them on the left, rose Mount Lambert, whose altitude is estimated at 1,813 metres; and farther, on the limits of the Ocean of Tempests, in 23° north latitude and 29° east longitude, shone the gleaming mountain of Euler. This mountain, which rises only 1,815 metres above the lunar surface, was the subject of an interesting work by the astronomer Schroeter. This man of science, trying to discover the origin of the mountains of the moon, had asked himself if the volume of the crater was always equal to the volume of the escarpments which formed it. This was found to be generally the case, and Schroeter concluded therefrom that a single eruption of volcanic matter had sufficed to form these escarpments, for successive eruptions would have altered the proportions. Alone Mount Euler was an exception to this general law, and had required for its formation several successive eruptions; for the volume of its cavity was double that of its escarpments. All these hypotheses were permissible for terrestrial observers, whose instruments acted but incompletely. But Barbicane would no longer be satisfied with them, and seeing that his projectile was steadily nearing the lunar disc, he did not despair, even should he not reach her, of discovering at least the secrets of her formation.

CHAPTER THIRTEEN
Lunar landscapes

At half-past two in the morning, the projectile was over the 30th lunar parallel, at an effective distance of 1,000 kilometres, reduced by instruments to 10 kilometres. It still seemed impossible that it should reach any part of the disc. Its velocity of translation, comparatively so moderate, was inexplicable to President Barbicane. At that distance from the moon, it must be considerable to make head against the force of attraction. So there was a phenomenon, the cause of which escaped them still. Besides, time was wanting to seek the cause. The lunar surface swept below the travellers' eyes, and they were desirous of not losing a single detail. So the disc, in the lunettes, appeared at a distance of two leagues and a half. What would an aeronaut perceive at that distance from the earth? It is impossible to say, for the highest ascensions have never exceeded 8,000 metres. This is, however, an exact description of what Barbicane and his companions saw from that height. Large patches of different colours appeared on the disc. Selenographers are not of the same opinion as to the nature of these colorations. They are different and vividly contrasted. Julius Schmidt asserts that if the terrestrial oceans were dried up, a Selenite lunar observer would not perceive upon the globe, between the oceans and continental plains, so great a diversity of shades as are seen on the moon by the terrestrial observer. According to him, the colour common to the vast plains, known as seas, is dark-gray mixed with green and brown. Some large craters also show this coloration. Barbicane was acquainted with this opinion of the German selenographer, shared by Messrs Beer and Moedler. He remarked that observations proved they were right, as against certain astronomers who only admit a gray coloration on the surface of the moon. In some instances, the green colour was vividly marked, as proved, according to Julius Schmidt, by the Serenity and Humours Seas. Barbicane also remarked large craters without interior cones, which shed a bluish tint, like the reflection of a steel mirror freshly polished. These colours really belong to the lunar disc, and do not arise from imperfections in the object-glass of the lunette, nor from the interposition of the terrestrial atmosphere, as some astronomers have asserted. In this respect Barbicane had no doubts whatever. He observed through a vacuum, and could commit no optical mistakes. He considered the fact of these different colours as fully established for science. Now, were these green tints owing to some tropical vegetation maintained by a dense, low atmosphere? He could not yet decide. Farther on, he noticed a reddish tint, sufficiently marked. Such a tint had already been remarked at the bottom of an isolated enclosure, known as Lichtenberg's Circus, which is situated near Mount Hercyniens, on the edge of the moon, but he could not discover its nature. He was not more fortunate concerning another peculiarity of the disc, the cause of which he could not discover. This is the peculiarity in question.

Michel Ardan was in observation near the president when he remarked some long white lines, vividly lighted by the direct rays of the sun. It was a succession of luminous furrows, very different from the radiation which Copernicus shed not long before. They lay parallel to each other. Michel, with his usual readiness, did not hesitate to exclaim: 'By Jove, cultivated fields!'

'Cultivated fields!' replied Nicholl, shrugging his shoulders.

'Ploughed at least,' retorted Michel Ardan. 'But what ploughmen these Selenites must be, and what gigantic oxen they must harness to their ploughs, to make such furrows!'

'They are not furrows,' said Barbicane, 'they are rifts.'

'As you please,' replied Ardan, with docility; 'but what do you mean by "rifts" in the scientific world?'

Barbicane imparted to his companion all he knew about lunar rifts. He knew that they were furrows, observed upon all the portions of the disc not mountainous; that these furrows, mostly isolated, measure from four to fifty leagues in length; that their

breadth varies from 1,000 to 1,500 metres, and that their edges are exactly parallel; but he knew nothing more either as to their formation or as to their nature. Barbicane, with the aid of his lunette, observed these rifts with extreme attention. He remarked that their sides were formed by extremely steep slopes. They were long parallel escarpments, and by a slight stretch of imagination, they might be considered long lines of fortifications, thrown up by Selenite engineers. Of these different rifts, some were absolutely straight, as though drawn with a tape; others were slightly curved, though still with parallel edges. The latter crossed each other, the former ran through the craters; now they furrowed ordinary cavities, like Posidonius or Petavius; and now they ran through seas, such as the Sea of Serenity. These natural accidents naturally brought into play the imaginations of terrestrial astronomers. The first observations had not discovered these rifts. Neither Hevelius, nor Cassini, nor La Hire, nor Herschel appear to have known of them. Schroeter, in 1787, was the first who drew the attention of scientific men to their existence. Others followed suit and studied them, such as Pastorff, Gruijthuijsen, Beer and Moedler. Today their number amounts to seventy. But if they have been counted, their nature has not yet been determined. They are certainly not fortifications, any more than dried-up beds of rivers; for, on the one hand, the small quantity of water on the surface of the moon could not have made such channels; and on the other hand, these furrows often cross craters placed at a great elevation. However, Michel Ardan conceived an idea which coincided with that of Julius Schmidt.

'Why,' said he, 'should not these inexplicable appearances be simply phenomena of vegetation?'

'How do you mean?' asked Barbicane hastily.

'Do not excite yourself, worthy president,' replied Michel. 'Is it not possible that the dark lines which form the bastions are rows of trees regularly planted?'

'You will have your vegetation,' said Barbicane.

'I am anxious,' retorted Michel Ardan, 'to explain what you men of science cannot explain. At least my hypothesis would have the advantage of showing why these rifts disappear, or seem to disappear, at regular periods.'

'How so?'

'Because these trees become invisible when they lose their leaves, and visible when they recover them.'

'Your explanation, dear friend, is ingenious but not admissible,' said Barbicane.

'Why not?'

'Because there is not, so to speak, any season on the surface of the moon, and consequently the phenomena of vegetation, to which you refer, could not arise. In fact, the slight obliquity of the lunar axis maintains the sun at an almost constant altitude in all latitudes. Above the equatorial regions, the radiant orb is almost invariably in the zenith, and does not pass the limits of the horizon in the polar regions, so that, in each region, there reigns perpetual winter, perpetual spring, perpetual summer, or perpetual autumn, as also in the planet Jupiter, whose axis is likewise but little inclined towards its orbit.'

'What is the origin of these rifts?'

'The question is difficult to solve. They are certainly posterior to the formation of the craters and of the circles, for several have burst into them, breaking down their circular ramparts. It is possible, therefore, that they are contemporary with the last geological periods, and are due to the expansion of natural forces.'

However, the projectile had attained the 40th degree of lunar latitude, at a distance which could not exceed 800 kilometres. Objects appeared in the focus of the lunette as only two leagues distant. At this point, beneath their feet rose Helicon, 505 metres high, and to the left stood the moderate heights which enclose a small portion of the Sea of Rain under the name of Gulf of Iris. The terrestrial atmosphere should be 170 times more transparent than it is, to allow astronomers to make complete observations at the surface of the moon; but in the vacuum, where the projectile floated, no fluid interposed between the observer's eye and the object observed. Further, Barbicane found himself at a distance to which the most powerful telescopes had never attained – neither that of Lord Rosse nor that of the Rocky Mountains. He was, therefore, in the most favourable position for solving the great question of the inhabitableness of the moon. However, this solution still escaped him. He duly perceived the deserted expanse of the immense plains, and, to the north, barren mountains. Not one work which betrayed the hand of man; not a ruin, to prove his passage. Not one agglomeration of animals, to show that life existed in the lower degrees. No movement anywhere; no trace of vegetation. Of the three kingdoms which share the

terrestrial spheroid, one only was represented on the surface of the lunar globe – the mineral kingdom.

'Hallo!' said Michel Ardan, somewhat downcast; 'is there no one at home?'

'No,' replied Nicholl, 'up to the present. Not a man, not an animal, not a tree. After all, if the atmosphere has taken refuge at the bottom of the cavities, in the interior of the circuses, or even on the opposite face of the moon, we can decide nothing.'

'Besides,' added Barbicane, 'even to the most piercing sight, a man is not visible beyond a distance of seven kilometres. So, if there are Selenites, they can see our projectile, but we cannot see them.'

Towards 4 a.m., at the height of the 50th parallel, the distance was reduced to 600 kilometres. On the left was a line of mountains of capricious shapes, standing in the full light. To the right, on the contrary, was a dark hole, like a vast pit, unfathomable and gloomy, sunk in the lunar soil. This hole was the Black Lake, or Plato – a deep circus, which can only be properly observed from the earth, between the last quarter and the new moon, when the shadows are thrown from west to east. This black colour is rarely met with on the surface of the satellite. Hitherto, it has only been noticed in the depths of Endymion, a circus to the east of the Sea of Cold, in the northern hemisphere, and at the bottom of Grimaldi on the equator, towards the eastern edge of the orb. Plato is an annular mountain, situated by 51° north latitude and 9° east longitude. Its circus is 92 kilometres long and 61 kilometres wide. Barbicane regretted that he did not pass perpendicularly over its vast aperture. There was there an abyss to fathom, perhaps some mysterious phenomenon to discover, but the direction of the projectile could not be modified; they must submit. Balloons are not to be guided, much less projectiles when you are shut in between their walls. Towards 5 a.m. the northern limit of the Sea of Rain was passed. Mounts La Condamine and Fontenelle remained, the one on the left, the other on the right. This portion of the disc, from the 60th degree became completely mountainous. The lunettes brought it to within one league, a distance less than divides the summit of Mont Blanc and the level of the sea. All this region is covered with mountains and circuses. Towards the 70th degree towered Philoläus, at a height of 3,700 metres, disclosing an elliptical crater sixteen leagues long and four wide. Then the disc, seen from this distance, offered an extremely peculiar aspect. The landscapes met the view under conditions very different from those of the earth, but also very inferior. The moon having no atmosphere, this absence of gaseous envelope entails consequences already mentioned. There is no twilight at its surface – night following day and day following night with the abruptness of a lamp which is extinguished or lighted in the midst of complete darkness. No transition from cold to heat, the temperature falling in an instant from the point of boiling water to the cold of space. Another consequence of the absence of air is this: that absolute darkness prevails wherever the rays of the sun do not penetrate. What is called diffused light upon the earth, that luminous matter which the air holds in suspension, which causes twilights and dawns, which produces shadows and half-shadows, and all that magic of the *chiaro-oscuro*, does not exist on the moon. Hence a grossness of contrasts, which only admits of two colours – black and white. If a Selenite shades his eyes from the solar rays, the sky appears perfectly dark to him, and the stars shine before his view, as in the darkest nights.

Judge of the impression produced by the strange aspect upon Barbicane and his two friends. Their eyes became confused; they could no longer judge of the respective distances of different objects. A lunar landscape, not toned down by the phenomenon of *chiaro-oscuro*, could not be represented by a landscape upon the earth – some blotches of ink upon white paper, and that was all. This aspect was not modified even when the projectile, at the height of the 80th degree, was separated from the moon by a distance of only 100 kilometres; not even when, at 5 a.m., it passed at less than 50 kilometres from Mount Gioja, which distance the lunettes reduced to a quarter of a league. It seemed that the moon could be touched with the hand. It seemed impossible that the projectile should not strike it soon, were it only at its north pole, whose brilliant arch stood vividly out from the dark background of the sky. Michel Ardan wanted to open one of the scuttles to throw himself on to the lunar surface, a fall of 12 leagues. He thought nothing of it. The attempt, however, would have been useless, for if the projectile did not reach some point of the surface of the satellite, neither would Michel, who would follow the same movement. At this moment, 6 a.m., the lunar pole appeared.

The disc no longer showed to the travellers more than one-half, brilliantly illuminated, whereas the other was plunged into darkness. Suddenly, the projectile passed the line of demarcation between intense light and absolute darkness, and was immediately enveloped in profound night.

CHAPTER FOURTEEN

The night of 354½ hours

At the moment when this phenomenon was so abruptly produced the projectile was skimming over the north pole, at a distance of less than 50 kilometres; a few seconds had sufficed to plunge it into the absolute darkness of space. The transition had occurred so rapidly, without shade, without gradation of light, without attenuation of the luminous undulations, that the orb appeared to be blown out by the action of some powerful breath.

'The moon has melted, disappeared!' cried Michel Ardan, quite aghast.

In fact there was neither reflection nor shadow. Nothing more appeared of this disc, hitherto so dazzling. The darkness was complete, and rendered more profound by the twinkling of the stars. It was the darkness of the lunar nights, which last 354½ hours for each point of the disc, which long night results from the equality of the movements of translation and of rotation of the moon – the one upon her own axis, the other round the earth. The projectile, immersed in the cone of shadow of the satellite, no longer underwent the action of the solar rays any more than any point of its invisible half.

Inside, therefore, the darkness was complete. They could not see each other – hence the necessity for dispelling the darkness. However desirous Barbicane might be to husband their limited supply of gas, he was forced to ask from it a factitious light, an expensive brilliancy which the sun then refused.

'The devil take the radiant orb!' cried Michel Ardan. 'He is going to put us to the cost of gas, instead of lighting us with his rays, gratis.'

'Do not let us accuse the sun,' said Nicholl. 'It is not his fault, but the fault of the moon, who has placed herself like a screen between us and him.'

'It is the sun!' continued Michel.

'It is the moon!' retorted Nicholl.

An unprofitable dispute, to which Barbicane put an end by saying: 'My friends, it is neither the fault of the sun nor the fault of the moon; it is the fault of the projectile, which, instead of following its proper trajectory, awkwardly left it; or, to be more correct, it is the fault of that disastrous meteorite, which caused us to deviate from our first direction.'

'Good!' replied Ardan; 'as that matter is arranged, let us breakfast. After an entire night of observation, it is necessary to repair our strength.'

This proposal met with no dissentients. In a few minutes Michel had prepared a repast. But they ate for the sake of eating; they drank without toasts – without hurrahs! The bold travellers, carried through the darkness of space without their accustomed *cortège* of rays, felt a vague uneasiness gain upon them. 'The wild shades,' so dear to Victor Hugo's pen, shut them in on every side.

However, they talked about that interminable night of 354 hours, or nearly fifteen days, which the laws of physics have imposed upon the inhabitants of the moon. Barbicane gave his friends some explanations as to the causes and consequences of this curious phenomenon. 'Most curious, indeed,' said he; 'for if each hemisphere of the moon is deprived of solar light during 15 days, that over which we float at this moment, does not even enjoy, during its long night, the view of the brilliantly-lighted earth. In one word, there is only a moon – applying this qualification to our spheroid – for one side of the disc. Now, if it were thus for the earth – if, for instance, Europe never saw the moon, and the latter were only visible at the antipodes – imagine what would be the astonishment of a European arriving in Australia!'

'People would make the journey merely to see the moon!' replied Michel.

'Well,' replied Barbicane, 'this astonishment is reserved to the Selenite who inhabits the face of the moon opposed to the earth, which face is always invisible to our fellow countrymen of the terrestrial globe.'

'And which we would have seen,' added Nicholl, 'if we had arrived here at the time when the moon was new – that is, 15 days later.'

'On the other hand,' continued Barbicane, 'I may add, the inhabitant of the visible face is singularly favoured by nature, to the detriment of his brethren of the invisible face. This last, as you see, has profound nights of 354 hours, during which no single ray breaks the obscurity. The other, on the contrary, when the sun which has lighted it during 15 days descends below the horizon, sees a magnificent orb rise on the opposite horizon. It is the earth, thirteen times larger than the moon, which we know of – the earth which develops itself at a diameter of two degrees, and which sheds a light thirteen times more intense than that tempered by the atmospheric strata – the earth, which only disappears when the sun reappears in its turn.'

'A very pretty period!' said Michel Ardan; 'somewhat academical perhaps.'

'Whence it follows,' continued Barbicane without wincing, 'that this face of the disc must be very agreeable to inhabit, as it is always looking either at the sun, when the moon is full, or at the earth, when the moon is new.'

'But,' said Nicholl, 'that advantage must be counterbalanced by the unbearable heat which this light brings with it.'

'The inconvenience, in this respect, is the same for the two faces, for the light reflected by the earth, is evidently devoid of heat. However, this invisible face is still more troubled with the heat than the visible face. I say that for you, Nicholl, because Michel would probably not understand.'

'Thank you,' said Michel.

'In fact,' continued Barbicane, 'when this invisible face receives, at the same time, the solar light and heat, the moon is new – that is, she is in conjunction, or situated between the sun and the earth. She is therefore, relatively to the situation she occupies, in opposition when she is full – nearer to the sun by double her distance from the earth. Now this distance may be estimated at the 200th part of that which separates the sun from the earth, or, in round figures, 200,000 leagues. Thus the invisible face is nearer the sun by 200,000 leagues when it receives the solar rays.'

'Quite right,' replied Nicholl.

'On the contrary – ' continued Barbicane.

'One moment,' said Michel, interrupting his grave companion.

'What do you want?'

'I want to continue the explanation.'

'Why?'

'To prove that I have understood.'

'Go on,' said Barbicane, smiling.

'On the contrary,' said Michel, imitating the tone and gestures of President Barbicane, 'on the contrary, when the visible face is lighted by the sun, the moon is full – that is to say, situated on the opposite side of the sun, relatively to the earth. The distance, which separates her from the orb of day, is therefore increased, in round figures, by 200,000 leagues, and the heat which it receives must be somewhat less.'

'Bravo!' cried Barbicane. 'Do you know, Michel, that for an artist you are intelligent?'

'Yes,' replied Michel, negligently; 'we are all like that on the Boulevard des Italiens.'

Barbicane gravely pressed his amiable companion's hand, and continued to enumerate the few advantages reserved to the inhabitants of the visible face. Amongst others, he quoted the observation, 'that the eclipses of the sun only occur for this side of the lunar disc, inasmuch as, for such to be produced, it is necessary that she should be in opposition. These eclipses, produced by the interposition of the earth between the moon and the sun, may last two hours, during which time, by reason of the rays refracted by its atmosphere, the terrestrial globe must appear like a black spot upon the sun.'

'So,' said Nicholl, 'there is one hemisphere – this invisible hemisphere – which is very badly provided for, so to speak – disgraced by nature.'

'Yes,' replied Barbicane, 'but not altogether. In fact, by a certain movement of libration, by a certain oscillation upon its centre, the moon presents to the earth rather more than half her disc. She is like a pendulum, of which the centre of gravity is carried towards the terrestrial globe, and which oscillates regularly.'

'Whence arises this oscillation?'

'From the fact that its movement of rotation upon its axis is animated with uniform velocity, whereas its movement of translation, following an elliptical orbit round the earth, is not so. In perigee, the rapidity of translation has the upper hand, and the moon shows a certain portion of her western edge; in apogee, the rapidity of rotation is the stronger, and a portion of the eastern edge appears. A strip of about 8 degrees appears now on the west, now on the east, so that out of 1,000 parts the moon shows 569.'

'Never mind,' replied Michel, 'if ever we become Selenites, we will inhabit the visible face. I like the light, I do.'

'Unless,' retorted Nicholl, 'that the atmosphere be condensed on the other side, as certain astronomers pretend.'

'That is a consideration,' replied Michel simply.

However, when the breakfast was ended, the observers were again at their post. They tried to see through the dark scuttles, by extinguishing all light in the projectile. But not a particle of light appeared in the darkness. One inexplicable fact preoccupied Barbicane. How, having passed so near to the moon, 50 kilometres about, the projectile had not fallen on to her surface. Had its velocity been enormous, one might have understood that the fall would not have occurred. But with its relatively low rate of speed, this resistance to lunar attraction could not be explained. Was the projectile subject to foreign influences? Did any other body maintain it in ether? It became evident that it would not touch any point of the moon's surface. Where was it going? Was it becoming more distant from the disc or nearer to it? Was it being carried into profound night through infinite space? How could this be discovered? How calculated amidst darkness? All these questions disquieted Barbicane, but he could not solve them. In fact, the invisible orb was there, perhaps only a few leagues, a few miles distant, but neither his companions nor he could see it. If there were any noise on its surface they could not hear it. The air, that vehicle of sound, was wanting to convey the plaints of the moon, which the Arabs call in their legends 'a man half-granite and yet palpitating'. It was enough to provoke the most patient observers, it must be admitted. It was precisely this unknown hemisphere which was hidden from their sight. That face which a fortnight sooner, or a fortnight later, would have been magnificently lighted up by the solar rays, was lost in absolute obscurity. In a fortnight, where would the projectile be? Where would the chances of attraction have carried it? Who could tell? It is generally admitted, from selenographic observations, that the invisible hemisphere of the moon is perfectly similar in composition to the visible hemisphere. In fact, about the seventh portion of it is disclosed by the movements of libration, of which Barbicane had spoken. These slips, which had been seen, were only mountains and plains, circuses and craters, analogous to those marked on the maps. The same nature and the same world, arid and dead, might be predicted. However, if the atmosphere had taken refuge on this face! If, with the air, water had given life to these regenerated continents! If vegetation were still to be found there! If animals peopled these continents and seas! If man, in these conditions of habitableness, were yet living there! What interesting questions were to be solved! What solutions might have been drawn from the contemplation of this hemisphere! What delight, to cast a glance upon this world, which the human eye had never seen!

The disgust of the travellers may be conceived, in the midst of this dark night. All observation of the lunar disc was impossible. The constellations only were open to their view, and it must be admitted that neither Faye, Chacornac, nor Secchi were ever in such favourable conditions for observing them. In fact, nothing could equal the splendour of this sidereal world, bathed in limpid ether. These diamonds, set in the celestial vault, shone with superb fire. The glance scanned the firmament from the Southern Cross to the North Star, which two constellations, in 12,000 years, by reason of the precession of the equinoxes, will cede their places as polar stars, the one to Canopus in the western hemisphere, and the other to Vega in the eastern hemisphere. The imagination lost itself in this sublime infinite, in the midst of which the projectile floated like a new star created by the hand of man. By a natural effect, these constellations shone with a softened light; they did not twinkle, for the atmosphere was wanting which produces the twinkling, by the interposition of its strata, unequally dense, and of different degrees of moisture. The stars looked like soft eyes peering in the deep night, amidst the absolute silence of space.

For some time the travellers observed in silence the constellated firmament, on which the vast screen of the moon made an enormous black hole. But a painful sensation drew them from their contemplation. It was a very severe cold, which soon covered the interior of the scuttle glasses with a thick layer of ice. In fact, the sun no longer heated the projectile with its rays, and the former gradually lost the heat stored within its walls. This heat by radiation had rapidly evaporated in space, and a considerable lowering of the temperature had resulted. The interior moisture was changed to ice on its contact with the glass, and hindered all observation. Nicholl, consulting the thermometer, saw that it had fallen to 17° centigrade below zero. So, notwithstanding all reasons for economy, Barbicane, having used the gas for light, was obliged to use it for heat. The low temperature of the projectile was no longer supportable. Its inmates would have been frozen alive.

'We will not complain,' remarked Ardan, 'of the monotony of our journey. What diversity at least of temperature! Now we are blinded with light and saturated with heat, like the Indians of the Pampas! Now we are plunged into profound darkness, in the midst of intense cold, like the Esquimaux at the north pole! Most certainly we have no right to complain, and nature is treating us handsomely.'

'But,' asked Nicholl, 'what is the exterior temperature?'

'Precisely that of the planetary regions,' replied Barbicane.

'Then,' continued Michel Ardan, 'would not this be the moment to make the experiment, which we could not try when bathed in the rays of the sun?'

'Now, or never,' replied Barbicane, 'for we are admirably placed to verify the temperature of space, and see whether the calculations of Fourier or Pouillet are exact.'

'In any case, it is cold,' replied Michel. 'See, the interior moisture condenses on the glass of the scuttles. If the fall continues, our breath will fall around us like snow.'

'Let us prepare a thermometer,' said Barbicane.

One may well believe that an ordinary thermometer would have given no results, in the conditions wherein the instrument was to be exposed. Quicksilver would have frozen in the bulb, for it does not remain liquid at 42° below zero. But Barbicane was provided with a spirit thermometer on Walferdin's system, which gives the minima of excessively low temperatures. Before commencing the experiment, the instrument was compared with an ordinary thermometer, and Barbicane prepared to use it.

'How are we going to manage?' asked Nicholl.

'Nothing can be easier,' replied Michel Ardan, who was never at a loss. 'You open the scuttle rapidly, throw out the instrument, it follows the projectile with exemplary docility, and a quarter of an hour afterwards you take it in.'

'With the hand?' asked Barbicane.

'With the hand,' replied Michel.

'Well, my friend, don't you run a risk?' replied Barbicane; 'for the hand you drew in would be nothing but a stump, frozen and deformed by this fearful cold.'

'Really!'

'You would feel the sensation of a terrible burn, as if from an iron at white heat, for whether heat leaves our flesh abruptly or enters it, the result is identically the same. Besides, I am not certain that the articles thrown out would still follow us.'

'Why?' said Nicholl.

'Because, if we are passing through an atmosphere, however little dense it may be, the articles would be delayed, and the darkness would prevent our seeing whether they were still floating around us. So, not to risk the loss of our thermometer, we will make it fast, and be better able to draw it into the interior.'

The advice of Barbicane was followed. Through the rapidly-opened scuttle, Nicholl threw the instrument, fastened to a short cord, so that it could be rapidly drawn in. The scuttle had only been open a second, but that second had sufficed to allow a violent cold to penetrate into the interior of the projectile.

'Horrible!' cried Michel Ardan; 'it is cold enough to freeze a polar bear.'

Barbicane waited until half an hour was past, which was more than sufficient to allow the instrument to fall to the level of the temperature of space, then the thermometer was rapidly drawn in.

Barbicane measured the quantity of spirits of wine which had flowed into the little receptacle fixed at the bottom of the instrument, and said: 'One hundred and forty degrees centigrade below zero.'

M. Pouillet was right and Fourier wrong. Such was the dreadful temperature of the starry regions. Such is, perhaps, that of the lunar continents, when the orb of night has lost, by radiation, all the heat absorbed during fifteen days of sunlight.

CHAPTER FIFTEEN

Hyperbola or parabola?

It may perhaps seem astonishing that Barbicane and his companions took so little care of the future reserved for them in their metal prison, which was carrying them into the infinity of space. Instead of inquiring where they were thus travelling, they passed their time in making experiments, as if they had been quietly seated in their study.

It might be answered that men of such calibre were above such cares, that they took no heed of such trifles, and that they had other things to do than to think of their future lot.

The truth is, they were not masters of their projectile; they could neither hinder its progress nor modify its direction. A sailor can alter, at will, the head of his vessel, an aeronaut can give vertical movements to his balloon, but they had no action upon their vehicle. All manoeuvres were impossible. Hence this disposition to let matters take their course. 'Let her run,' as the sailors have it.

Where were they situated at this moment, at 8 a.m. of the day called the 6th December on earth? Most certainly in the neighbourhood of the moon, and near enough for her to appear like an immense black screen spread out on the firmament. As to the distance which separated them from her, it was impossible to estimate it. The projectile, maintained by inexplicable forces, had passed within 50 kilometres of the satellite's north pole; but during the two hours since it had entered the cone of shadow, had this distance increased or diminished? Every fixed point was wanting to estimate the direction and the velocity of the projectile. Perhaps it was rapidly leaving the disc, so as to emerge shortly from the pure shadow. Perhaps, on the contrary, it was

nearing it so much as to strike some elevated portion of the invisible hemisphere, which would have ended the journey, doubtless to the detriment of the travellers.

A discussion arose on this point, and Michel Ardan, always rich in explanations, gave out this opinion: that the projectile, retained by lunar attraction, would end by falling to the surface, as an aerolite falls to the surface of the terrestrial globe.

'In the first place, comrade,' replied Barbicane, 'every aerolite does not fall to the earth, but only the smaller number. Thus, from the fact that we have passed into the state of aerolite it does not necessarily follow that we shall reach the surface of the moon.'

'However,' replied Michel, 'if we approach near enough – '

'Error,' replied Barbicane. 'Have you not seen shooting stars cross the sky by thousands at certain periods?'

'Yes.'

'Well, these stars, or rather these corpuscules, only shine on the condition of becoming heated by friction on the atmospheric strata. Now, if they pass through the atmosphere, they come within 16 leagues of the globe, and, nevertheless, they seldom fall to the surface. The same for our projectile, it may approach very near to the moon and yet not fall to the surface.'

'Then,' asked Michel, 'I shall be very curious to see how our wandering vehicle will act in space.'

'I only see two hypotheses,' replied Barbicane, after a few minutes' reflection.

'Which?'

'The projectile has the choice between two mathematical curves, and it will follow one or the other, according to the velocity with which it is endowed, and which I could not estimate at the present moment.'

'Yes,' said Nicholl, 'it will follow a parabola or a hyperbola.'

'True,' replied Barbicane. 'With a certain velocity it will take a parabola, or a hyperbola with a greater velocity.'

'I like fine words,' cried Michel Ardan; 'we all know at once what they mean. And what is your parabola, if you please?'

'My friend,' replied the captain, 'the parabola is a curve of the second order, which results from the section of a cone intersected by a plane parallel to one of its sides.'

'Ah! ah!' said Michel, in a satisfied tone. 'It is about the trajectory of a shell fired from a mortar.'

'Bravo!'

'And hyperbola?' asked Michel.

'Hyperbola, Michel, is a curve of the second order, produced by the intersection of a conic surface by a plane parallel to its axis, which constitutes two branches, separated from each other, extending indefinitely in both directions.'

'Is it possible!' cried Michel Ardan, in a most grave tone of voice, as though he had been informed of some serious matter. 'Then remember this, Captain Nicholl, what I like in your definition of the hyperbola – I was going to say hyperhumbug! – is that it is still less clear than the word which you pretend to define.'

Nicholl and Barbicane cared little for the jokes of Michel Ardan. They were in the midst of a scientific discussion. What would be the curve followed by the projectile? That was what excited their attention. The one was for the parabola, the other for the hyperbola. They gave their reasons bristling with *x*'s. Their arguments were clothed in a language which astounded Michel Ardan. The discussion was warm, and neither of the adversaries would give up his favourite curve.

This scientific dispute becoming somewhat too lengthy, ended by exhausting Michel's patience.

'Now then, gentlemen cosines,' said he, 'when will you have done throwing parabolas and hyperbolas at each other's heads? I want to know the only interesting thing in the whole matter. We shall follow one or other of your curves, but where will they bring us?'

'Nowhere,' replied Nicholl.

'Nowhere! What do you mean?'

'Certainly,' said Barbicane. 'They are open curves, which may be prolonged indefinitely.'

'Ah, men of science, I take you to my bosom,' cried Michel. 'And what matter whether we follow parabola or hyperbola, if both carry us equally into the infinity of space.'

Barbicane and Nicholl could not help smiling. They had been discussing art for art's sake. Never had a more idle question been raised at a more inopportune moment. The dreadful truth was, that the projectile, following either an hyperbola or a parabola, would never again meet either earth or moon.

Now what would happen to these bold travellers in a very proximate future? If they did not die of hunger, or of thirst, at least, in a few days, their gas would run short and they would die from want of air, if the cold had not already killed them.

Notwithstanding the importance of economising gas, the excessive fall of the temperature obliged them to consume a certain quantity. If necessary, they could dispense with light, but not with heat. Happily, the caloric, developed by the apparatus of Reiset and Regnault, somewhat raised the interior temperature of the projectile, and without great expenditure they were able to keep it at a bearable degree of warmth. However, observations had become very difficult through the scuttles. The interior moisture condensed upon the glass and immediately congealed. It was necessary to destroy this opacity of the glass by reiterated friction. However, some phenomena could be observed of the highest interest. In fact, if this invisible disc was provided with an atmosphere, ought they not to see the shooting stars cross it with their trajectories?

If the projectile itself was passing through these fluid strata, could they not catch some sound repercussed by lunar echoes – the growling of a storm, for instance, the noise of an avalanche, the detonations of a volcano in activity? And if some fire-vomiting mountain flashed forth its lightnings, would not their intense flamings be perceived? Such facts, carefully noted, would have singularly elucidated the dark question of lunar composition. So Barbicane and Nicholl, posted at their scuttle, observed with the scrupulous patience of astronomers.

But, up till then, the disc had remained mute and dark. It did not reply to the numerous interrogatories of these ardent minds, which provoked this reflection from Michel, reasonable enough in appearance: 'If ever we recommence this journey, we shall do well to choose the period when the moon is new.'

'Quite right,' replied Nicholl, 'circumstances would then be more favourable. I admit that the moon, bathed in solar rays, would not be visible during the passage, but, on the other hand, we should see the earth, which would be full. Further, if we were carried round the moon, as is now the case, we should at least have the advantage of seeing the invisible disc magnificently lighted up.'

'Well said, Nicholl,' retorted Michel Ardan. 'What do you say, Barbicane?'

'I think this,' replied the grave president: 'If ever we recommence this journey, we will start at the same period and in the same conditions. Suppose that we had attained our goal, would it not have been better to have found the continents in full light, rather than a country plunged in the darkest night? Our first settlement would have occurred under better conditions, most certainly so. As to this invisible side, we could have visited it during our reconnoitring journeys on the surface of the moon. Therefore, the period of the full moon was happily chosen, but it was necessary to reach the goal and not to deviate from the route.'

'To that, there is nothing to reply,' said Michel Ardan. 'However, we have lost a good opportunity of observing the other side of the moon. Who knows whether the inhabitants of the other planets are not more advanced than the scientific men on earth, on the subject of their satellites?'

To this remark of Michel Ardan's, the following reply might easily have been made: yes, other satellites, by their greater proximity, have rendered their study easier. The inhabitants of Saturn, Jupiter, and Uranus, if they exist, may have established easier communication with their moons. The four satellites of Jupiter gravitate at a distance of 108,260 leagues, 172,200 leagues, 274,700 leagues, and 480,130 leagues. But these distances are computed from the centre of the planet, and, on subtracting the length of the radius, which is from 17,000 to 18,000 leagues, it will be seen that the first satellite is not so distant from the surface of Jupiter as the moon is from the surface of the earth. Of the eight moons of Saturn, four are also nearer: Diana is 84,600 leagues distant, Thetys 62,966 leagues, Enceladus 48,191 leagues, and lastly Mimas is at an average distance of only 34,500 leagues. Of the eight satellites of Uranus, Ariel, the first, is only 51,520 leagues distant from the planet.

So, at the surface of these three planets, an experiment like that of President Barbicane would have presented much less difficulty. If, therefore, their inhabitants have tried the experiment, they have perhaps discovered the composition of that half of the disc which their satellite eternally hides from their eyes. But if they have never quitted their planet, they are no further advanced than the astronomers of the earth.

Meanwhile, the projectile described in shadow that incalculable trajectory which no fixed point allowed to be estimated. Had its direction been modified, either under the influence of lunar attractions or under the action of some unknown orb? Barbicane could not tell. But a change had taken place in the relative position of the vehicle, and Barbicane remarked it towards four o'clock in the morning. The alteration consisted in this, that the bottom of the projectile was turned towards the surface of the moon,[49] and maintained itself in a perpendicular drawn through its axis. Attraction, that is to say gravitation, had occasioned this alteration. The heaviest part of the projectile inclined towards the invisible disc, exactly as though it were falling towards it.

Was it, then, falling? Were the travellers at last going to reach the much-desired goal? No! And an observation, from a somewhat inexplicable fixed point, proved to Barbicane that his projectile was not nearing the moon, and that it was moving on an almost concentric curve.

This point of mark was a luminous flash, which Nicholl suddenly perceived, on the limit of the horizon formed by the black disc. This flash could not be mistaken for a star. It was a reddish incandescence which increased by degrees, which was incontestable proof that the projectile was moving towards it, and was not falling towards the surface of the orb.

'A volcano! It is a volcano in activity! An outburst of the internal fires of the moon!' cried Nicholl. 'So that world is not yet completely extinct.'

'Yes, an eruption,' replied Barbicane, who was carefully examining the phenomenon through his night-glass. 'What could it be if not a volcano?'[50]

'But then,' said Michel Ardan, 'there must be air to allow of combustion. So there is an atmosphere on this part of the moon.'

'Perhaps,' replied Barbicane, 'but not necessarily. The volcano, by the decomposition of certain substances, can supply its own oxygen, and thus vomit flames in a vacuum. It even appears to me, that yonder deflagration has the intensity and brilliancy of a combustion in pure oxygen. Do not let us too hastily assert the existence of a lunar atmosphere.'

The fire-vomiting mountain must have been situated at about the 45th degree of south latitude of the invisible portion of the disc, but, to Barbicane's great displeasure, the curve described by the projectile was carrying the latter far from the point marked by the eruption; thus, he could not determine its nature more exactly. Half an hour after being perceived, this luminous spot disappeared behind the horizon. However, the noting of this phenomenon was an important fact in selenographic studies. It proved that all heat had not yet disappeared from the bowels of this globe; and, where heat exists, who can assert that the vegetable kingdom, and even the animal kingdom, have not hitherto resisted destructive influences? The existence of this volcano in eruption, indisputably acknowledged by men of science on earth, would doubtless have given rise to many theories favourable to this great question of the inhabitableness of the moon.

Barbicane allowed himself to be carried away by his reflections. He forgot himself in a mute reverie, wherein were agitated the mysterious destinies of the lunar world. He tried to unite the facts hitherto observed, when a new incident brought him abruptly back to reality.

This incident was more than a cosmical phenomenon, it was a danger menacing the most disastrous consequences. Suddenly, in the midst of the ether, in this profound darkness, an enormous mass had appeared. It was like a moon, but a burning moon, of a brilliancy the more dazzling, that it contrasted with the deep darkness of space. This mass, of a circular form, shed so much light that the projectile was filled with it. The faces of Barbicane, Nicholl, and Michel Ardan, bathed in these white rays, took that spectral, livid, haggard appearance, which is produced by the flames of spirits mixed with salt.

'A thousand devils!' cried Michel Ardan, 'we are hideous. What is that ill-behaved moon?'

'A meteorite,' replied Barbicane.

'A burning meteorite in a vacuum?'

'Yes.'

This globe of fire was, in fact, a meteorite. Barbicane was not mistaken. But if these cosmical meteors, when observed from the earth, generally present a light only little inferior to the moon, seen in the dark ether, they are resplendent. These wandering bodies carry with them the principles of their incandescence. Circumambient air is not necessary to their combustion; and, in

fact, if certain of these meteorites pass through the atmospheric strata at two or three leagues from the earth, others, on the contrary, describe their trajectories at a distance to which the atmosphere could not extend. Such were the meteors which appeared, the one on the 27th October, 1844, at a height of 128 leagues; the other on the 18th August, 1841, which disappeared at a distance of 182 leagues. Some of these meteors are three and four kilometres wide, and possess a velocity which may amount to 75 kilometres per second, following an inverse direction to the movement of the earth.

This shooting globe which suddenly appeared in the darkness, at a distance of 100 leagues at least, must have measured, according to Barbicane's estimate, about 2,000 metres in diameter. It advanced with a velocity of about two kilometres per second, or 30 leagues a minute. It crossed the line of the projectile, and must reach it in a few minutes. As it approached it increased to enormous proportions.

Let the position of our travellers be imagined if possible. It is quite impossible to describe it. Notwithstanding their courage, their presence of mind, their heedlessness of danger, they remained mute, immovable, with stiffened limbs, a prey to the wildest terror. Their projectile, over whose course they could have no control, was flying straight towards that fiery mass, more intense than the open mouth of a furnace. It seemed to rush towards an abyss of fire.

Barbicane had seized the hands of his two companions, and all three looked, through half-closed eyelids, towards this asteroid at a white heat. If thought was not destroyed within them, if their brains still worked in the midst of their terror, they must have thought themselves lost.

Two minutes after the abrupt appearance of the meteor – two centuries of anguish! – the projectile seemed on the point of colliding, when the globe of fire blew up like a shell, but without any noise, in the midst of this vacuum where sound, which is but the agitation of the strata of air, could not be produced.

Nicholl had uttered a cry. His companions and he had rushed to the glass of the scuttles. What a sight! What pen could describe it, what palette could be rich enough in colours to reproduce its magnificence!

It was like the outburst of a crater, like the scattering of an immense conflagration. Thousands of luminous fragments lit up and irradiated space with their fires. All sizes, all colours were mingled. There were yellow irradiations, yellowish-red, green-gray – a crown of fireworks of a thousand colours. Of

the enormous, redoubtable globe, there remained nothing but these fragments, borne in all directions, become asteroids in their turn, some flaming like a sword, some surrounded with a whitish cloud, others leaving in their wake brilliant trains of cosmical dust.

These incandescent masses crossed each other, collided, broke into smaller fragments, some of which struck the projectile. Its left window was even cracked by a violent blow. It seemed to float amidst a hail of bombshells, the smallest of which could annihilate it in an instant. The light, which saturated the ether, developed itself with incomparable intensity, for these asteroids dispersed it in every direction. At a certain moment, it was so vivid that Michel, drawing Barbicane and Nicholl to his scuttle, cried: 'The invisible moon visible at last!' and all three, through a luminous effluvium of a few seconds, perceived the mysterious disc which the eye of man saw for the first time.

What did they distinguish at this distance which they could not estimate? A few long bands upon the disc, clouds formed in a very limited atmospheric medium, from which emerged not only all the mountains but also all the less important prominences, the circuses, the yawning craters, capriciously arranged as on the visible surface. Then immense spaces, no longer arid plains, but real oceans, which reflected on their liquid mirror all the dazzling magic of the fires of space. Lastly, on the surface of the continents, vast dark masses, such as immense forests would appear under the rapid illumination of a flash of lightning.

Was it an illusion, an error of sight, an optical deception? Could they give a scientific affirmation to an observation so superficially made? Would they dare to give an opinion on the question of its habitableness after such a transient glimpse of the invisible disc?

Meanwhile, the lightnings of space diminished by degrees, their accidental brilliancy grew less; the asteroids dispersed on different trajectories and disappeared in the distance; the ether recovered its accustomed darkness; the stars, eclipsed for one moment, glowed in the firmament, and the disc, scarcely perceived, was again lost in impenetrable night.

CHAPTER SIXTEEN

The southern hemisphere

The projectile had just escaped a terrible danger and an unforeseen one. Who would have imagined such a meeting of meteors? These wandering bodies might place the travellers in serious peril. For them, they were so many rocks, upon this sea of ether, which, less happy than the mariners, they could not avoid. But did those adventurers of space complain? No, for nature had given them this splendid spectacle of a cosmical meteor, bursting by formidable expansion; for this incomparable firework, which no Ruggieri could hope to imitate, had illumined, for a few seconds, the invisible nimbus of the moon. In this rapid flash, continents, seas, forests had appeared to them. So an atmosphere did bring to this unknown face its vivifying molecules. Questions still insoluble – eternally open to human curiosity.

It was then 3.30 p.m. The projectile was following its curvilinear direction round the moon. Had its trajectory been again altered by the meteor? It was to be feared. However, the projectile must follow a curve unalterably determined by the laws of rational mechanics.

Barbicane was inclined to think that the curve would be rather a parabola than an hyperbola. However, the parabola admitted, the projectile must soon leave the cone of shadow thrown upon space opposed to the sun. In fact, this cone is very narrow, for the angular diameter of the moon is small if compared with the diameter of the orb of day. Up to the present, the projectile floated in this deep shadow. Whatever might be its velocity – and it could not have been small – its period of occupation continued. That was an evident fact. But perhaps, ought that not to have been in the supposed case of a strictly parabolic trajectory? This was a new problem which tormented Barbicane's brain, completely imprisoned in a circle of unknown quantities, from which it could not escape.

None of the travellers thought about taking a moment's repose. Each was on the alert for some unexpected event which should throw a new light upon uranographical studies. Towards 5 o'clock, Michel Ardan distributed, under the name of dinner, a few pieces of bread and cold meat, which were rapidly disposed of, without anyone having abandoned his scuttle, the glass of which was continually becoming encrusted by the condensation of vapour.

Towards 5.45 p.m. Nicholl, with the aid of his lunette, discovered towards the southern edge of the moon, and in the direction followed by the projectile, some brilliant spots which stood out from the dark screen of the sky. They were like a succession of pointed peaks, looking in profile like a jagged line. They shone very brightly. Such appears the terminal line of the moon, when she appears in one of her octants.

They could not be mistaken. It was no longer a question of a simple meteor, for this luminous ridge had neither its colour nor its mobility, nor yet a volcano in eruption. So Barbicane did not hesitate to give his opinion.

'The sun!' cried he.

'What! the sun?' replied Nicholl and Michel Ardan.

'Yes, my friends, it is the radiant orb itself which illumines the summits of those mountains, situated on the southern edge of the moon. We are evidently nearing the south pole.'

'After having passed by the north pole,' replied Michel. 'We have taken a turn round our satellite!'

'Yes, worthy Michel.'

'Then no more hyperbolas, no more parabolas, no more open curves to fear.'

'No, but a closed curve.'

'Which means?'

'An ellipse. Instead of being lost in the planetary regions it is probable that the projectile will describe an elliptical orbit around the moon.'

'In truth!'

'And that it will become her satellite.'

'Moon of moons!' cried Michel Ardan.

'Nevertheless I would have you remark, worthy friend,' retorted Barbicane, 'that we are not the less lost on that account.'

'Yes; but in another manner, and a much more pleasant one,' replied the heedless Frenchman, with his most amiable smile.

President Barbicane was right. In describing this elliptical orbit, the projectile would doubtless gravitate eternally around the moon, like a sub-satellite. It was a new star added to the solar world; a microcosm peopled by three inhabitants, whom want of air would soon destroy. Barbicane could not rejoice at the definitive situation imposed upon the projectile by the double influences of centripetal and centrifugal forces. His companions and he would see again the lighted face of the lunar disc; perhaps their existence would be prolonged, until they could again see the full earth superbly lighted by the solar rays. Perhaps they might send a last adieu to the globe which they would never see again. Then their projectile would be nothing but an extinguished dead mass, like those inert asteroids which circulate in ether. One consolation for them was, to quit at last these unfathomable darknesses, to return to light, to reenter the zones bathed by the solar irradiation. However, the mountains recognised by Barbicane stood out more and more distinctly from the dark mass. They were mounts Doerfel and Leibnitz, which rise to the south in the circumpolar region of the moon.

All these mountains of the visible hemisphere have been measured with absolute exactness. This exactness may excite astonishment, and yet the hypsometric methods are precise. It may even be asserted that the altitude of the mountains of the moon is not less exactly determined, than that of the mountains of the earth.

The method most generally employed, is to measure the shadow cast by the mountains, taking into account the altitude of the sun at the time of the observation. This measurement is easily obtained, by means of a lunette, supplied with a reticule having two parallel threads – it being admitted that the real diameter of the lunar disc is accurately known. This method also allows of calculating the depths of craters and cavities of the moon. Galileo made use of it, and since then Messrs Beer and Moedler have used it with the greatest success.

Another method, called by tangent rays, can also be applied to the measurement of lunar projections. It is applied at the moment when the mountains form luminous spots removed from the line of separation of shadow from light, which shine on the dark portion of the disc. These luminous spots are produced by solar rays, higher than those which determine the limit of the phasis. Thus, the measure of the dark interval which remains between the luminous spot and the luminous portion of the nearest phasis, gives the exact altitude of this spot. But it will be seen that this method only applies to mountains in the neighbourhood of the line of separation of light and shade.

A third method consists in measuring the profiles of lunar mountains, which are seen upon the background by means of a micrometer. But this is only applicable to mountains near the edge of the orb.

In any case, it will be seen that this measurement of shadows, of intervals, or of profiles, can only be executed when the solar rays strike the moon obliquely as regards the observer. When they fall full upon her – in one word, when she is full – all shadow is banished from her disc, and observations are no longer possible.

Galileo first – after having recognised the existence of lunar mountains – used the method of shadows to calculate their height. He attributed to them, as has already been stated, an average of 4,500 fathoms. Hevelius diminished these figures considerably, but Riccioli on the contrary doubled them. These measures were exaggerated on the one side and the other. Herschel, by the aid of perfected instruments, came much nearer the hypsometric truth. But it must be sought for finally in the reports of modern observers. Messrs Beer and Moedler, the most perfect selenographers of the whole world, have measured 1,095 lunar mountains. From their calculations it results that six of these mountains rise above 5,800 metres, and 22 above 4,800 metres. The highest summit of the moon measures 7,603 metres; thus it is inferior to those of the earth, some of which exceed 5,000 or 6,000 fathoms. But one remark must be made. If they are compared to the respective volumes of the two orbs, the lunar mountains are relatively higher than the terrestrial mountains. The former form the 470th portion of the diameter of the moon, and the latter only the 1,440th part of the diameter of the earth. A terrestrial mountain to attain the relative proportions of a lunar mountain, would have to measure a perpendicular altitude of six leagues and a half. But the highest has not a height of nine kilometres.

So then, to proceed by comparison, the chain of the Himalayas counts three summits higher than lunar summits: Mount Everest 8,837 metres, Kimchinjuga 8,588 metres, and Dwalagiri 8,187 metres high. Mounts Doerfel and Leibnitz in the moon have an altitude equal to that of Yewahir of the same chain, say 7,603 metres. Newton, Casatus, Curtius, Short, Tycho, Clavius, Blancanus, Endymion, the principal summits of the Caucasus and of the Apennines, are higher than Mont Blanc, which measures 4,810 metres. Are equal to Mont Blanc: Moret, Theophyles, Catharnia; to Mont Rose, or 4,636 metres: Piccolomini, Werner, Harpalus; to Mont Cervin, 4,522 metres: Macrobus, Eratosthenes, Albatecus, Delambre; to the peak of Teneriffe, which rises to 3,710 metres: Bacon, Cysatus, Philolaus and the summits of the Alps; to Mont Perdu, of the Pyrenees, 3,351 metres: Roemer and Boguslawski; to Etna, 3,237 metres: Hercules, Atlas, Furnerius.

Such are the points of comparison which permit us to appreciate the altitudes of lunar mountains.

Precisely the trajectory followed by the projectile carried it towards the mountainous region of the southern hemisphere, where rise the finest specimens of lunar orography.

CHAPTER SEVENTEEN

Tycho

At 6 p.m. the projectile passed the south pole, at less than 60 kilometres, or the same distance to which it had approached the north pole. The elliptic curve was being rigidly described.

At this moment, the travellers re-entered the beneficent effluvium of solar rays. They saw again the stars moving slowly from east to west. The radiant orb was greeted with a triple hurrah. With its light came heat, which soon pierced through the metal walls. The glasses recovered their accustomed transparency. Their layer of ice melted as by magic. Immediately, for economy's sake, the gas was put out. Alone, the air apparatus consumed its accustomed quantity.

'Ah!' said Nicholl, 'how delightful are these rays of heat. With what impatience, after so long a night, the Selenites must await the reappearance of the orb of day.'

'Yes,' replied Michel Ardan, imbibing as it were this brilliant ether; 'light and heat – all life is there.'

At this moment, the bottom of the projectile had a tendency to diverge slightly from the lunar surface, so as to follow an elliptic orbit somewhat drawn out. From this point, if the earth had been full, Barbicane and his companions might have seen it; but drowned in the radiation of the sun, it remained absolutely invisible. Another sight attracted their attention, viz. that which the southern portion of the moon presents when brought by lunettes to within half a quarter of a league. They did not quit the scuttles, but noted all the details of this strange continent.

Mounts Doerfel and Leibnitz form two separate groups which extend almost to the south pole. The former group extends from the pole to the 84th parallel on the eastern portion of the orb;

the second, rising on the eastern edge, extends from the 65th degree of latitude to the pole.

On their fantastically formed ridge, appeared dazzling sheets such as Father Secchi has described. With greater certainty than the illustrious Roman astronomer, Barbicane could recognise their nature.

'It is snow,' cried he.

'Snow?' repeated Nicholl.

'Yes, Nicholl, snow, which is deeply frozen on the surface. See how it reflects the luminous rays: cooled lava would not give so intense a reflection. So there is water and there is air on the surface of the moon. As little as you like, but the fact cannot be contested.'

No, it could not be contested! and if ever Barbicane returns to earth his notes will witness to this important fact in selenographic observations.

Mounts Doerfel and Leibnitz rose in the midst of plains of medium extent, bordered by an infinite succession of circuses and annular ramparts. These two chains are the only ones which meet in the region of circuses. Comparatively but slightly marked, they throw out here and there some sharp-pointed peaks, of which the highest summit measures 7,603 metres. But the projectile overhung all this mass, and the projections disappeared in the intense dazzling brilliancy of the disc. To the eyes of the travellers, the archaic aspect of the lunar landscapes reappeared with raw tones, without gradation of colours, without degrees of shadow, coarsely white or black, as diffused light is wanting. However, the view of this desolate world did not fail to captivate them by its very strangeness. They were passing over that chaotic region as if they had been borne on the blast of a storm, seeing summits fly beneath their feet – plunging their glances into cavities, examining rifts, scaling escarpments, fathoming mysterious holes, levelling all fissures. But there was no trace of vegetation; no appearance of cities – nothing but stratifications, floods of lava overflowings, polished like immense mirrors, reflecting the rays of the sun with unbearable brilliancy. Nothing of a living world, all of a dead world, where avalanches rolling from the summits of mountains plunged, without noise, to the bottom of abysses. They retained the movement, but the noise was still wanting. Barbicane discovered, by repeated observations, that the projections on the borders of the disc, although they had evidently been submitted to different forces than those of the central regions, presented a uniform conformation. There were the same circular aggregation, the same projections of the ground. However, it might be thought that their disposition would not be analogous. In the centre, the malleable crust of the moon had been submitted to the double attraction of the moon and the earth acting in inverse direction, according to a prolonged radius of the one to the other. On the contrary, on the edges of the disc, the lunar attraction has been, so to speak, perpendicular to the terrestrial attraction. It seems as though the projections of the ground, produced under these two conditions, must have taken different forms. But such has not been the case. So the moon had found in herself the principle of her formation and of her constitution. She owed nothing to foreign action, which justifies that remarkable proposition of Arago: 'No action outside the moon has contributed to the formation of its projections.'

Whatever the facts may have been, this world in its present state was the image of death; and it was impossible to say whether life had ever animated it.

Nevertheless, Michel Ardan thought that he perceived an agglomeration of ruins, which he pointed out to Barbicane. They were near the 80th parallel, in 30' of longitude. This heap of stones, arranged with sufficient regularity, represented a vast fortress overhanging one of those long rifts which were formerly the beds of prehistoric rivers. Not far off, arose to a height of 5,646 metres, the annular mountain of Short, equal to the Asiatic Caucasus.

Michel Ardan, with his accustomed ardour, maintained the evidence of his fortress. Below, he perceived the dismantled ramparts of a town; here, the still intact arch of a portico; there, three or four columns lying below their bases; farther on a succession of pillars which must have supported an aqueduct; elsewhere, the shattered piers of a gigantic bridge, half hidden in the depths of the rift. All this he saw, but there was so much imagination in his glance through so fanciful a lunette that his observations are to be mistrusted. And yet, who could assert, who would dare to say, that the amiable Frenchman had not really seen what his two companions refused to perceive?

The moments were too precious to be sacrificed to a useless discussion. The Selenite city, pretended or not, had already

disappeared in the distance. The distance of the projectile from the lunar disc was increasing, and the details of the surface became lost in a confused mixture. Alone the projections, the circuses, the craters, the plains, resisted and sharply defined their terminal lines.

At this moment, there arose towards the left one of the finest circuses of lunar orography, one of the curiosities of this continent. It was Newton, which Barbicane had no difficulty in recognising with the aid of his *Mappa Selenographica*. Newton is exactly situated in 77° south latitude, and 16° east longitude. It forms an annular crater, with apparently insurmountable ramparts, 7,264 metres high. Barbicane remarked to his companions that the height of this mountain, above the plain, was far from equal to the depth of its crater. This enormous hole escaped all measurement, and formed a dark abyss, to the bottom of which the solar rays could never penetrate. There, according to Humboldt's remark, reigns absolute darkness, which the light of the sun and earth can never break. Mythologists would have made it, and with reason, the mouth of the infernal regions.

'Newton,' said Barbicane, 'is the most perfect type of these annular mountains, of which the earth possesses no sample. They prove that the formation of the moon by cooling is due to violent causes, for whilst, under the action of internal fires, the projections were thrown out to considerable heights, the bottom contracted and withdrew to much below the lunar level.'

'I did not say it didn't,' replied Michel Ardan.

A few minutes after passing Newton, the projectile overhung the annular Mount Moret. It passed at some distance from Blancanus, and towards 7.30 p.m. it reached Circus Clavius.

This circus is one of the most remarkable of the disc, and is situated in 58° south latitude and 15° degrees east longitude. Its altitude is estimated at 7,091 metres. The travellers, 400 kilometres distant, reduced to four by the lunettes, could admire every point of this vast crater.

'The terrestrial volcanoes,' said Barbicane, 'are only molehills compared with the volcanoes of the moon. On measuring the former craters, caused by the first eruptions of Vesuvius and Etna, they have been found to be only 6,000 metres wide. In France, the Cantal circus measures 10 kilometres; in Ceylon, the circus of the Isle 70 kilometres, which is considered the largest on the globe. What are these diameters compared with Clavius, which we overlook at this moment?'

'What is its width?' asked Nicholl.

'It is 227 kilometres,' replied Barbicane. 'This circus, it is true, is the most important on the moon, but many others measure 200, 150, and 100 kilometres.'

'Ah! my friends,' cried Michel, 'think what this peaceful orb of night must have been when these craters, full of thunderbolts, vomited at once torrents of lava, showers of stones, clouds of smoke, and sheets of flame. What a prodigious sight then! – and now what a falling off! The moon is nothing but the case of a piece of firework, in which the crackers, squibs, serpents, and suns, after a magnificent explosion, have left but the remnants of burst pasteboard. Who could tell the cause, the reason, the justification of these cataclysms?'

Barbicane did not listen to Michel Ardan. He was contemplating these escarpments of Clavius, formed of wide mountains several leagues thick. At the bottom of the immense cavity, were a hundred smaller extinct craters, piercing the ground like a sieve, and overhung by a mountain 5,000 metres high.

All around, the plain had a desolate aspect. Nothing could be more barren than these projections, nothing more sad than these ruins of mountains, and, if one can make use of the expression, these fragments of peaks and mounds which strewed the ground! The satellite seemed to have burst at that spot.

The projectile still continued and this chaos was not changed. The circuses, the craters, the shattered mountains, succeeded each other without ceasing. No more plains, no more seas! An interminable Switzerland or Norway. At last in the centre of this region of fissures, at its culminating point appeared the most splendid mountain of the lunar disc, the dazzling Tycho, with which posterity will always connect the name of the illustrious Danish astronomer.

When observing the full moon in a cloudless sky, everyone must have seen this brilliant spot in the southern hemisphere. Michel Ardan employed in its description all the metaphors which his vivid imagination could supply. For him, Tycho was a burning focus of light, a centre of radiation, a crater vomiting rays! It was the tire of a sparkling wheel, an immense flaming eye, a nimbus for the head of Pluto! It was like a star hurled from the Creator's hand and flattened against the lunar surface.

Tycho forms such a luminous concentration that the inhabitants of the earth can perceive it without glasses, though they are at a distance of 100,000 leagues. Imagine, then, what must have been its intensity to the eyes of observers placed only 150 leagues distant. Through the pure ether its glare was so unbearable that

Barbicane and his friends had to blacken the eye-glass of their lunettes with the gas smoke, to be able to support its brilliancy. Then mute, only giving vent to a few expressions of admiration, they gazed and contemplated. All their sentiments, all their impressions, were concentrated in their glance; like life, which, under violent emotion, concentrates entirely in the heart.

Tycho belongs to the class of radiating mountains, like Aristarchus and Copernicus. The most complete, the most decided of all, it proves indubitably the frightful volcanic action to which the formation of the moon is due.

Tycho is situated in 43° south latitude and 12° east longitude. Its centre is formed by a crater 87 kilometres wide; it has somewhat of an elliptical form, and is enclosed by annular ramparts, which overhang the exterior plain to the east and to the west, to a height of 5,000 metres. It is an aggregation of Mont Blancs placed round a common centre, and crowned with a radiating crest.

What this incomparable mountain is, the projections converging towards it, and the interior excrescences of its crater, photography has never been able to depict.

In fact, it is during the full moon that Tycho shows in all its splendour. But then, shadows are wanting, the foreshortenings of perspective have disappeared, and the proofs are blanks. This is an unfortunate circumstance, for it would be curious to reproduce this strange region with photographic accuracy. It is but an agglomeration of holes, craters, circuses, a vertiginous network of crests; then, as far as eye can reach, a volcanic network cast upon this encrusted soil. It will be thus understood that the bubbles of the central eruption have retained their primitive shape. Crystallised by cooling, they have become stereotyped, the aspect presented formerly by the moon under the influence of Plutonian forces.

The distance, which separated the travellers from the annular summits of Tycho, was not so great but that they could perceive the principal details. On the embankment which formed the circumvallation of Tycho, the mountains, rising from the sides of the inside and outside slopes, formed gigantic terraces. They appeared 300 or 400 feet higher to the west than to the east. No system of terrestrial encampment could be compared with this natural fortification. A city built at the bottom of this circular cavity would have been absolutely impregnable.

Inaccessible, and marvellously spread over this ground covered with picturesque projections, nature had not left the bottom of this crater flat and hollow. It possessed its special orography – a mountainous system which made it like a separate world. The travellers clearly distinguished caves, central hills, remarkable movements of ground naturally adapted to receive the masterpieces of Selenite architecture. There was the site for a temple, here, the place for a forum; in this spot, the foundations for a palace, in that other, the plan of a citadel. The whole was overlooked by a central mountain 1,500 feet high – a vast enclosure which would have contained ancient Rome ten times over.

'Ah!' cried Michel Ardan, full of enthusiasm at the sight, 'what a magnificent town might be built in that circle of mountains! – A tranquil city, a peaceful place of refuge, outside all human misery. How calm and isolated all misanthropes could live there – all haters of humanity – all who are disgusted with social life!'

'All! It would be too small for them,' replied Barbicane simply.

CHAPTER EIGHTEEN

Important questions

Meanwhile, the projectile had passed over Tycho's enclosure, and Barbicane and his two friends were observing, with scrupulous attention, the brilliant rays which the celebrated mountain disperses so curiously to all the horizons.

What was this radiant aureola? What geological phenomenon had formed this fiery crest? This question naturally preoccupied Barbicane. Under his eyes, ran in all directions luminous furrows, with raised edges and concave hollows, some 20 kilometres wide, some 50. These shining trains proceeded in some places as far as 300 leagues from Tycho, and seemed to cover, especially to the east, north-east, and north, half the southern hemisphere. One of its jets extended to the circus Neandre, situated on the 40th meridian. Another, following a curve, furrowed the Sea of Nectar and broke against the chain of the Pyrenees, after a circuit of 400 leagues. Others, towards the west, covered the Sea of Clouds and the Sea of Humours with a luminous network.

What was the origin of these shining rays which appeared equally on plains and projections, no matter how high? All started from a common centre, the crater of Tycho. They emanated from it. Herschel attributed their brilliant aspect to former currents of lava congealed by cold, which opinion has not been adopted. Other astronomers have seen in these inexplicable rays a sort of *moraines*, rows of erratic blocks, thrown up at the period of Tycho's formation.

'And why not?' asked Nicholl of Barbicane, who related these different opinions and discarded them.

'Because the regularity of these luminous lines, and the violence necessary to carry volcanic matter to such a distance, are incompatible.'

'By Jupiter!' replied Michel Ardan, 'it seems easy enough to me to explain the origin of these rays.'

'Indeed!' said Barbicane.

'Certainly,' continued Michel; 'it is sufficient to call it a vast star, like that produced upon a window-pane by the shock of a ball or a stone.'

'Good!' replied Barbicane smiling; 'and whose hand could have been powerful enough to cast the stone to produce such a shock?'

'The hand is not necessary,' replied Michel, who was not to be put down. 'And as to the stone, let us suppose it to be a comet.'

'Ah! comets indeed,' cried Barbicane, 'how they are abused. My worthy Michel, your explanation is not a bad one, but your comet is useless. The shock which has produced this breakage may have come from the interior of the orb. A violent contraction of the lunar crust, under the action of cooling, may have sufficed to make this gigantic star.'

'A contraction, by all means, something like a lunar stomach-ache,' replied Michel Ardan.

'Besides,' added Barbicane, 'this opinion is shared by an English *savant*, Nasmyth, and it seems to me to explain sufficiently the radiation of these mountains.'

'That fellow Nasmyth was no fool,' replied Michel.

For a long time, the travellers, who could not tire of such a sight, admired the splendour of Tycho. Their projectile, impregnated with luminous effluvia in the double irradiation of the sun and the moon, must have appeared like an incandescent globe. They had suddenly passed from severe cold to intense heat. Nature was preparing them for becoming Selenites.

Becoming Selenites! This idea again brought up the question as to the inhabitableness of the moon. After what they had seen could the travellers decide this question? Could they conclude for or against? Michel Ardan called upon his two friends to give their opinions, and asked them, straightforwardly, whether they thought that animal and human life were represented in the lunar world.

'I think that we can reply,' said Barbicane; 'but to my mind the question should not be put in that form. I ask to alter it.'

'Fire away,' cried Michel.

'The problem,' replied Barbicane, 'is double, and requires a double solution. Is the moon inhabitable? Has she been inhabited?'

'Good!' said Nicholl; 'first let us inquire if the moon is inhabitable.'

'In good truth, I don't know,' retorted Michel.

'And I reply negatively,' continued Barbicane. In the state in which she is at present – with an atmospheric envelope certainly very limited, the seas mostly dried up, the water insufficient, the vegetation restricted, the abrupt alternations of heat and cold, the days and nights of 354 hours – the moon does not appear to me habitable, and does not seem adapted to the development of the animal kingdom, nor sufficient for the necessities of existence such as we understand them.'

'Agreed!' replied Nicholl; 'but is the moon not habitable for beings otherwise organised than we?'

'To that question,' retorted Barbicane, 'it is difficult to reply. I will try however. But I will ask Nicholl if *movement* appears to him to be the necessary result of life, whatever be its organisation?'

'Without a doubt,' replied Nicholl.

'Well,' worthy comrade, 'I will answer that we have observed the lunar continents at a distance not greater than 500 metres, and that nothing has been seen to move on the surface of the moon. The presence of any kind of human life would have been betrayed by its appropriations, by divers constructions, or even by ruins. Now, what have we seen? Everywhere and always the geological work of nature, never the work of man. If representatives of the animal kingdom existed on the moon, they must be hidden in cavities which the eye cannot fathom; which I cannot admit, for they would have left traces of their passage on the plains, covered by an atmospheric stratum, however thin. Now, such traces are nowhere visible. There only remains the hypothesis of a race of living beings without motion, which is life.'

'You might as well say living creatures which do not live,' retorted Michel.

'Precisely,' replied Barbicane; 'which for us has no sense.'

'Then we can form our opinion,' said Michel.

'Yes,' replied Nicholl.

'Well,' continued Michel Ardan, 'the scientific commission assembled in the projectile of the Gun Club, after having based their arguments upon facts recently observed, have decided unanimously upon the question of the inhabitableness of the moon. No! the moon is not habitable.'

This decision was entered by President Barbicane in his note-book, wherein appear the minutes of the meeting of the 6th December.

'Now,' said Nicholl, 'let us attack the second question, which is the necessary corollary of the first. I therefore ask the honourable commission: if the moon is not habitable, has she ever been inhabited?'

'Citizen Barbicane to speak,' said Michel Ardan.

'My friends, replied Barbicane, 'it did not require this journey to form my opinion upon the past habitableness of our satellite. I will add that our personal observations have but confirmed my view. I believe, I can even assert that the moon has been inhabited by a human race organised as ours, that she has produced animals anatomically formed like terrestrial animals; but I will add that these human races and animals have had their time and are for ever extinct.'

'Then,' asked Michel, 'the moon is an older world than the earth?'

'No,' replied Barbicane with conviction, 'but a world which has aged more rapidly, where formation and deformation have been more sudden. Comparatively, the organising forces of matter have been much more violent in the interior of the moon than in the interior of the terrestrial globe. The present state of this fissured, distorted, and uneven disc proves it superabundantly. The earth and the moon were only gaseous masses in their origin. These gases passed to a liquid state under certain influences, and the solid mass was formed subsequently. But certainly our spheroid was gaseous or liquid still, when the moon was already solidified by cooling, and had become inhabitable.'

'I believe it,' said Nicholl.

'Then,' continued Barbicane, 'an atmosphere surrounded it. The water contained by this gaseous envelope could not evaporate. Under the influence of air, water, light, solar heat, central heat, vegetation seized upon continents prepared to receive it; and certainly life appeared towards this period, for nature does not expend her forces uselessly, and a world so marvellously habitable must necessarily have been inhabited.'

'However,' replied Nicholl, 'many of the phenomena inherent

to the movements of our satellite, must have hindered the expansion of the vegetable and animal kingdoms. For instance, the days and nights of 354 hours.'

'At the terrestrial poles,' said Michel, 'they last six months.'

'Which argument has little value, since the poles are not inhabited.'

'Observe, my friends,' continued Barbicane, 'that if, in the present state of the moon, these long nights and days create differences of temperature insupportable to human organisms, it was not thus at the period of prehistoric times. The atmosphere enveloped the disc as with a fluid mantle. Vapours lay there under the form of clouds. This natural screen tempered the ardour of the solar rays and hindered nocturnal radiation. Light and heat were diffused in the air. Hence an equilibrium between these influences, which no longer exist, now that the atmosphere has almost entirely disappeared. Besides, I shall much astonish you – '

'Pray do so,' said Michel Ardan.

'But I am inclined to think that at the period when the moon was inhabited the nights and days did not last 354 hours.'

'Why?' asked Nicholl, hastily.

'Because, most probably at that time the movement of rotation of the moon upon its axis was not equal to her movement of revolution, which equality presents each point of the disc, during fifteen days, to the action of the solar rays.'

'Agreed,' replied Nicholl; 'but why should these two movements not have been equal, as they are so now?'

'Because this equality has only been determined by the terrestrial attraction. Now, what tells us that this attraction was sufficiently powerful to modify the movements of the moon at a time when the earth was only fluid?'

'True,' replied Nicholl. 'And what proves that the moon has always been a satellite of the earth?'

Imagination was carrying them away into the infinite field of conjecture. Barbicane wished to restrain them.

'These are,' said he, 'too great speculations, and truly insoluble problems. Do not let us enter into them. Let us only admit the insufficiency of primordial attraction, and then, by the inequality of the two movements of rotation and revolution, days and nights may have succeeded each other on the moon, as they succeed each other on earth. Besides, even without that condition life was possible.'

'So,' asked Michel Ardan, 'you suppose that humanity has disappeared from the moon?'

'Yes,' replied Barbicane, 'after having doubtless existed during thousands of centuries. Then, gradually the atmosphere became rarefied, the disc became uninhabitable, as the terrestrial globe will become some day, by cooling.'

'By cooling?'

'Doubtless!' replied Barbicane. 'In proportion as the internal fires were extinguished, the incandescent matter became concentrated, and the lunar crust cooled. Gradually, the consequences of this phenomenon appeared, viz. disappearance of organised beings, disappearance of vegetation. Soon, the atmosphere became rarefied, probably drawn away by terrestrial attraction; disappearance of breathable air; disappearance of water, by means of evaporation. At this period, the moon having become uninhabitable, was no longer inhabited. It was a dead world, such as we see it today.'

'And you say that such a fate is reserved to the earth?'

'Very probably.'

'But when?'

'When the cooling of its crust has rendered it uninhabitable.'[51]

'And has the time been calculated which our unfortunate spheroid will require to cool?'

'Doubtless.'

'And you know the calculation?'

'Perfectly.'

'Say on then, you tedious man,' cried Michel Ardan; 'you make me boil with impatience.'

'Well, worthy Michel,' replied Barbicane quietly, 'it is well known what diminution the temperature of the earth undergoes in the lapse of one century. According to certain calculations this mean temperature will be reduced to zero in a period of 400,000 years.'

'400,000 years!' cried Michel; 'I breathe again. Really I was afraid. To hear you speak, one would have thought that we had not more than 50,000 years to live.'

Barbicane and Nicholl could not refrain from laughter at their comrade's fears. Then Nicholl, who wished to conclude, again asked the second question which had just been treated: 'Has the moon been inhabited?' asked he.

The reply was affirmative and unanimous.

But during this discussion, fertile in hazardous theories though summarising the general ideas of science on the point, the projectile had rapidly neared the lunar equator whilst moving at a greater distance from the disc. It had passed circus Willem and the 40th parallel, at a distance of 800 kilometres. Then, having Pitatus to the right on the 30th degree, it passed over the south of that Sea of Clouds, the northern portion of which it had already surveyed. Sundry circuses appeared confusedly in the shining whiteness of the full moon: Bouilland, Purbach almost square-shaped with a central crater, then Arzachel, the interior mountain of which shines with an indescribable brilliancy.

At last, as the projectile increased its distance, the lineaments faded from the travellers' eyes, the mountains melted into one another, and, of all those marvellous fantastic strange forms of the earth's satellite, nothing remained but an imperishable souvenir.

CHAPTER NINETEEN

A struggle against the impossible

For a long time, Barbicane and his companions, mute and pensive, contemplated this world which they had only seen from a distance, as Moses had seen the land of Canaan, and from which they were retreating without hope of return. The position of the projectile as regards the moon was altered, and now its bottom was turned towards the earth.

This alteration, discovered by Barbicane, did not fail to surprise him. If the projectile was to gravitate around the satellite, upon an elliptical orbit, why did it not turn the heaviest portion towards it as the moon does to the earth? That was an obscure point.

By observing the advance of the projectile, they could see that it followed, when leaving the moon, a curve similar to that traced when approaching her; therefore it described a lengthened ellipse, which probably would extend to the point of equal attractions, where the influences of the earth and its satellite were neutralised.

Such was the conclusion which Barbicane justly deduced from the facts observed, and his conviction was shared by his two friends.

And questions followed each other in quick succession.

'And when at this point what will become of us?' asked Michel Ardan.

'That is the unknown,' replied Barbicane.

'But we may make conjectures, I suppose?'

'Two,' replied Barbicane. 'Either the velocity will be insufficient, and the projectile will remain eternally motionless on this line of double attraction – '

'I prefer the other hypothesis whatever it may be,' replied Michel.

'Or its velocity will be sufficient,' said Barbicane; 'and it will resume its elliptic route, to gravitate eternally round the orb of night.'

'Not a very consoling revolution,' said Michel, 'to become the humble servitors of the moon, which we are accustomed to consider a servant! And is that the future in store for us?'

Neither Barbicane nor Nicholl replied.

'You are silent,' continued the impatient Michel.

'There is nothing to reply,' said Nicholl.

'Is there nothing to be tried?'

'No!' replied Barbicane. 'Would you struggle against the impossible?'

'Why not? Shall a Frenchman and two Americans retire before such a word?'

'But what would you do?'

'Conquer the movement which is carrying us away.'

'Conquer it?'

'Yes,' continued Michel with animation; 'destroy it, or alter it, use it, in fact, for accomplishing our projects.'

'And how?'

'That is your business. If artillerists are not masters of their shot, they are not artillerists. If the projectile has command over the gunner, the gunner should be shoved into the cannon. Fine *savants*, in sooth! There they are, not knowing what to do after having induced me – '

'Induced!' cried Barbicane and Nicholl. 'Induced! What do you mean by that?'

'No recriminations,' said Michel. 'I do not complain. The journey pleases me. I like the projectile. But let us do what is humanly possible to fall back somewhere, if not on to the moon.'

'That is all we ask for, worthy Michel,' replied Barbicane; 'but the means are wanting.'

'Can we not modify the movement of the projectile?'

'No!'

'Nor diminish its velocity?'

'No!'

'Not even by lightening it, as you lighten a ship too heavily laden?'

'What would you throw out?' replied Nicholl. 'We have no ballast on board. And besides, it seems to me that the lightened projectile would travel faster.'

'Not so fast,' said Michel.

'Faster,' retorted Nicholl.

'Neither faster nor slower,' said Barbicane, to put his two friends in humour; 'for we are floating in a vacuum, where the specific weight is of no account.'

'Well,' cried Michel Ardan in a determined tone, 'there is only one thing to be done.'

'What is that?' asked Nicholl.

'Breakfast!' replied the audacious Frenchman imperturbably. An infallible solution in the most difficult conjunctures. In fact, if that operation had no influence upon the direction of the projectile, at least it could be tried without inconvenience and even with success, as regarded the stomach. Most certainly, Michel's ideas were good for something.

So they breakfasted at 2 a.m., but the hour was of little importance. Michel served up his accustomed bill of fare, crowned by a bottle drawn from his secret cellaret. If ideas did not flow to their brains, Chambertin of 1863 must be despaired of.

The repast terminated, observations recommenced.

Around the projectile, the articles which had been thrown out maintained themselves at the same invariable distance. Evidently the projectile in its movement of translation round the moon, had not passed through any atmosphere, or the specific weight of these several articles would have modified their respective progress.

On the side of the terrestrial spheroid, nothing was to be seen. The earth only counted one day, having become new the previous day at midnight, and two more days must pass ere its crescent would emerge from the solar rays, to act as a timepiece to the Selenites; since, in its movement of rotation, each of its points pass always 24 hours later through the same meridian of the moon.

On the side of the moon, the spectacle was different. The orb shone in all its splendour, in the midst of innumerable constellations, whose purity could not be troubled by her rays. On her disc, the plains were already recovering the dark shade which is seen from the earth. The remainder of the nimbus continued

bright, and in the midst of the general resplendence, Tycho stood out like a sun.

Barbicane could not in any way calculate the velocity of the projectile, but reason showed him that the velocity must gradually diminish, according to the laws of rational mechanics.

In fact, it being admitted that the projectile would describe an orbit round the moon, this orbit would necessarily be elliptic. Science proves that it must be so. No movable body, circulating round another body, escapes this law. All orbits described in space are elliptical; those of the satellites round planets, those of planets round the sun, that of the sun round the unknown orb which serves as a central pivot. Why should the projectile of the Gun Club escape this general law? Now, in elliptical orbits the attracting body occupies always one of the foci of the ellipse. The satellite therefore finds itself at one moment nearer, and at another moment more distant from the orb round which it gravitates. When the earth is nearest to the sun, it is in its perihelium, and in its aphelium when at its most distant point. As regards the moon, she is nearest to the earth in her perigee and farthest in her apogee. To use analogous expressions, which will enrich astronomical language, if the projectile remained as a satellite to the moon, it must be said that, at its farthest point, it is in its aposelenium, and, at its nearest point, in its periselenium.

In this last instance, the projectile would attain its maximum of velocity, in the former case its minimum. Now it was evidently travelling towards its aposelenitic point, and Barbicane was right in thinking that its velocity was decreasing up to that point, to recover gradually as it approached the moon. This velocity would even be completely annulled, if that point coincided with the point of equal attractions.

Barbicane studied the consequences of these different situations, and he was seeking what advantage might be drawn from them, when he was suddenly interrupted by a cry from Michel Ardan.

'By Jove!' cried Michel, 'it must be admitted that we are regular fools.'

'I don't deny it,' replied Barbicane; 'but why?'

'Because we have a very simple means of lessening the velocity which is bearing us from the moon, and we do not use it.'

'And what is this means?'

'It is to utilise the force contained in our rockets.'

'Bravo!' said Nicholl.

'We have not yet utilised this force,' replied Barbicane, 'but we will utilise it.'

'When?' asked Michel.

'When the moment has come! Observe, my friends, that in the position occupied by the projectile, which position is yet oblique as regards the lunar disc, our rockets, by modifying its direction, might turn it aside instead of forcing it nearer to the moon. Now it is the moon that you want to reach, is it not?'

'Certainly,' replied Michel.

'Wait then. By an inexplicable influence, the projectile is gradually turning its base towards the earth. It is probable that at the point of equal attractions, its conic roof will point directly towards the moon. At that moment, we may hope that its velocity will be *nil*. That will be the moment to act, and by the force of our rockets, we may perhaps occasion a direct fall to the surface of the lunar disc – '

'Bravo!' said Michel.

'Which we did not do, which we could not do at our first passage through the dead point, because our projectile was still endowed with too great velocity.'

'Well argued,' said Nicholl.

'Let us wait patiently,' continued Barbicane; 'let us put every chance on our side, and after despairing so long I find myself believing that we shall yet reach our goal.'

This conclusion was a signal for 'hip, hip, hurrahs' from Michel Ardan. Not one of these audacious madmen recollected the question which they had just decided in the negative: 'No, the moon is not inhabited. No, the moon is probably not inhabitable;' and yet they were about to try to reach her.

One single question remained to be solved: At what precise moment would the projectile attain the point of equal attractions, where the travellers were to play their last card?

To calculate this moment within a few seconds, Barbicane had only to consult the notes of his journey, and calculate the different altitudes taken on the lunar parallels. Thus the time employed in travelling the distance separating the dead point and the south pole must be equal to the distance between the north pole and the dead point. The hours representing the time of travelling were carefully noted, and the calculation became easy.

Barbicane found that this point would be reached by the projectile at 1 a.m. in the night of the 7th of December – at this moment it was 3 a.m. in the night of the 6th of December – so that, if nothing impeded its progress, the projectile would reach the required point in 22 hours.

The rockets had been originally arranged to lessen the fall of the projectile on to the moon, and now these bold men intended to use them to produce an absolutely contrary effect. In any case they were ready, whenever the moment arrived, to set light to them.

'As there is nothing to be done,' said Nicholl, 'I make a proposal.'

'What is that?' asked Barbicane.

'I propose to take some sleep.'

'Nonsense!' exclaimed Michel Ardan.

'We have not closed our eyes for forty hours,' said Nicholl; 'a few hours' sleep will restore all our strength.'

'Never!' replied Michel.

'Very well,' continued Nicholl, 'let each one do as he likes. I shall sleep.'

And stretching himself on the divan, Nicholl was soon snoring like the ball from a 48-pounder.

'Nicholl is a sensible man,' said Barbicane presently. 'I shall imitate him.'

A few minutes afterwards his continued bass supported the captain's baritone.

'Decidedly,' said Michel Ardan, 'these practical people have sometimes opportune ideas.'

And stretching his long legs, and folding his great arms beneath his head, Michel slept in his turn.

But this sleep could neither be lasting nor peaceful. The minds of those three men were too full of preoccupation, and, a few hours later, towards 7 a.m., all three were on foot at the same moment. The projectile was still leaving the moon, inclining more and more towards her its conic portion – a phenomenon hitherto inexplicable, but which happily assisted Barbicane's designs. Seventeen hours more, and the moment for acting would have come.

This day appeared long. However audacious they might be, the travellers were deeply impressed by the approach of that moment which was to decide all – either their fall towards the moon or their eternal enchainment in an immutable orbit. They counted the hours, which passed too slowly for their wishes – Barbicane and Nicholl obstinately buried in calculations, Michel going and coming between the narrow walls and observing the impassive moon with a longing eye.

Occasionally recollections of earth rapidly crossed their minds. They again saw their friends of the Gun Club, and the dearest of all, J. T. Maston. At that moment, the honourable secretary must have been at his post in the Rocky Mountains. If he perceived the projectile upon the mirror of his gigantic telescope, what would he think? After seeing it disappear behind the south pole of the moon, he saw it reappear above the north pole! It was thus a satellite of a satellite! Had J. T. Maston spread this unexpected news over the world? Was this then the result of the great undertaking?

However, the day passed without incident. Terrestrial midnight arrived. The 8th of December was about to commence. One hour more, and the point of equal attraction would be reached. What was the velocity of the projectile? It could not be estimated. But no error could have been made in Barbicane's calculation; at 1 a.m. the velocity should be, and would be, *nil*.

Besides which, another phenomenon would mark the arrival of the projectile upon the neutral line. At this spot, the two terrestrial and lunar attractions would be annulled. Bodies would then have no weight. This singular fact, which had so greatly surprised Barbicane and his companions on the journey hither, would be reproduced on the return under identical conditions. It was at this precise moment that they must act. Already the conic roof of the projectile was turned towards the lunar disc. The projectile presented itself in such a manner, as would utilise all the recoil produced by the force of the rockets. The chances were therefore in favour of the travellers. If the velocity of the projectile was absolutely *nil* at the dead points, a determined movement towards the moon would suffice, however light it might be, to produce its fall.

'Five minutes past one,' said Nicholl.

'All is ready,' replied Michel Ardan, approaching a prepared fuse to the gas flame.

'Wait,' said Barbicane, chronometer in hand.

At this moment, gravitation had no more effect. The travellers felt in themselves its complete absence; they were very near the neutral point, if they did not touch it.

'One o'clock,' said Barbicane.

Michel Ardan approached the lighted fuse to a train which communicated with all the rockets.[52] No detonation was heard in the interior, for air was wanting. But through the scuttles Barbicane perceived a prolonged flash, which then expired.

The shock to the projectile was very perceptible inside.

The three friends gazed, listened without speaking, almost without breathing – their hearts might have been heard beating in the midst of the profound silence.

'Are we falling?' asked Michel Ardan at last.

'No,' replied Nicholl, 'for the bottom of the projectile is not turned towards the lunar disc.'

At this moment Barbicane, leaving the glass at the scuttle, turned towards his two companions. He was fearfully pale, his forehead wrinkled, and lips contracted.

'We are falling,' he said.

'Ah!' cried Michel Ardan, 'towards the moon?'

'Towards the earth,' replied Barbicane.

'The devil!' cried Michel Ardan. 'Ah!' he added philosophically, 'when we got into this projectile, we suspected there would be some difficulty in getting out of it.'

In fact this dreadful fall commenced. The velocity retained by the projectile had carried it beyond the dead point, and the explosion of the rockets had not been able to stop it. This velocity, which on the outward journey had carried the projectile past the neutral line, still carried it on the return. The laws of physics required that, in its elliptical orbit, it should again pass through all the points by which it had already passed.

It was a terrible fall, from a height of 78,000 leagues, which no spring could lessen. According to the laws of gunnery the projectile would strike the earth with a velocity equal to that with which it left the columbiad, a velocity of 16,000 metres in the last second.

And, to give a figure of comparison, it has been calculated that an object thrown from the top of the tower of Notre Dame, which is only 200 feet high, would reach the pavement with the velocity of 120 leagues an hour. Here, the projectile would strike the earth with a velocity of 57,600 leagues an hour.[53]

'We are lost,' said Nicholl calmly.

'Well, if we die,' said Barbicane, with a sort of religious enthusiasm, 'the scope of our journey will be magnificently extended. It is his own secret that God will tell us. In the next life, the soul will not require, for knowledge, either machinery or engines. It will be identified with eternal wisdom.'

'Quite right,' replied Michel Ardan, 'the whole of the next world may well console us for the loss of the miserable orb which is called the moon.'

Barbicane crossed his arms on his breast with a movement of sublime resignation. 'The will of Heaven be done!' said he.

CHAPTER TWENTY

The soundings of the Susquehanna

'Well, lieutenant, how about that sounding?'

'I think, sir, that the operation is almost completed,' replied Lieutenant Bronsfield. 'But who would have expected to find such a depth so near the land – only a hundred leagues from the American coast?'

'You are right, Bronsfield; it is a very great depression,' said Captain Blomsberry. 'There exists in this spot a submarine valley made by Humboldt's current, which skirts the American coast, down to the straits of Magellan.'

'These great depths,' continued the lieutenant, 'are not very favourable for laying telegraphic cables. It is better to have a level bottom, like that which bears the American cable between Valencia and Newfoundland.'

'I agree with you, Bronsfield. And by the way, lieutenant, where are we now?'

'Sir,' replied Bronsfield, 'we have at this moment 21,500 feet of line payed out, and the shot at the end has not yet touched the bottom, for it would have come up by itself.'

'An ingenious apparatus, that of Brookes,' said Captain Blomsberry; 'it enables us to obtain very correct soundings.'

'Touched!' cried at this moment one of the men at the fore-wheel, who was superintending the operation.

The captain and lieutenant went forward to the quarterdeck.

'What is the depth?' asked the captain.

'Twenty-one thousand seven hundred and sixty-two feet,' replied the lieutenant, entering the figures in his note-book.

'Good, Bronsfield,' said the captain. 'I shall make a note of the result on my chart. Now haul in the sounding-line. It will be a work of several hours, during which time the engineer can light up his furnaces, and we shall be ready to start as soon as you have finished. By the way, lieutenant, it is 10 o'clock. I shall turn in.'

'Aye, aye, sir,' replied Lieutenant Bronsfield, obligingly.

The captain of the *Susquehanna*, one of the best of men, and very humble servant of his officers, returned to his cabin, took a brandy grog, which earned many expressions of satisfaction for the steward, got into bed, not without complimenting his servant upon the manner of making it, and relapsed into peaceful slumber.

It was then 10 p.m. The 11th day of the month of December was terminating in a magnificent night.

The *Susquehanna*, a corvette of 500 horse-power, of the national navy of the United States, was engaged in making soundings in the Pacific about 100 leagues from the American coast, on a level with that long peninsula which stretches down the coast of New Mexico.

The wind had gradually fallen. Not the slightest agitation moved the strata of air. The pennant of the corvette hung motionless and inert from the main-topgallant mast.

Captain Jonathan Blomsberry – first cousin of Colonel Blomsberry, one of the most ardent members of the Gun Club, who had married a Miss Horschbidden, aunt of the captain and daughter of an honourable Kentucky merchant – Captain Blomsberry could not have wished for better weather for carrying out the delicate operations of sounding. His corvette had not even experienced any portion of that vast tempest which swept away the clouds from the Rocky Mountains, and allowed the course of the famous projectile to be observed. All was going to his wish, and he did not fail to thank heaven with all the fervour of a Presbyterian.

The series of soundings executed by the *Susquehanna* had for their object to discover the most favourable bottom for laying a submarine cable from the American coast to the Hawaiian Islands.

This was a great undertaking, due to the initiative of a powerful company. Its intelligent director, Cyrus Field, proposed to unite all the islands of Oceania in a vast electric network; an immense undertaking, worthy of American genius.

The first soundings had been entrusted to the corvette *Susquehanna*. During the night of the 11th of December, she lay exactly in 27° 7' north latitude and 41° 37' longitude west of the meridian at Washington.

The moon, then in her last quarter, began to show above the horizon.

After the departure of Captain Blomsberry, Lieutenant Bronsfield and some officers were together on the quarterdeck. At the appearance of the moon, their thoughts were carried towards that orb, which the eyes of a whole hemisphere were then contemplating. The best marine glasses could not have discovered the projectile circling round its globe, and yet all were pointed towards its flaming disc, which millions of eyes were observing at the same moment.

'They have been gone ten days,' said Lieutenant Bronsfield; 'what has become of them?'

'They have arrived, lieutenant,' exclaimed a young midshipman, 'and they are doing what every traveller does when he reaches a new country – they are walking about.'

'Of course they are, as you say so, young shaver,' replied Lieutenant Bronsfield, smiling.

'However,' continued another officer, 'their arrival cannot be a matter of doubt. The projectile must have reached the moon at the moment when she was full, on the 5th, at midnight. It is now the 11th of December, which makes six days. In six times 24 hours, without darkness, one has time to make one's arrangements comfortably. I think I see them, our brave fellow-countrymen, encamped at the bottom of a valley on the banks of a Selenite rivulet, near the projectile, half broken by its fall, in the midst of volcanic fragments – Captain Nicholl commencing his surveys, President Barbicane copying out his travelling notes, Michel Ardan scenting the lunar solitudes with the perfume of a Londres.'

'Yes that must be so, that is so,' cried the young midshipman, filled with enthusiasm by the ideal description of his superior.

'I should like to believe it,' replied Lieutenant Bronsfield, who was not easily carried away. 'Unhappily, direct news from the lunar world is always wanting.'

'I beg your pardon, lieutenant,' said the midshipman; 'but cannot President Barbicane write?'

This question was met with a roar of laughter.

'Not letters,' continued the young man hastily. 'It is not a question of the postal administration.'

'It is perhaps an affair for the administration of telegraphic lines?' asked one of the officers ironically.

'Certainly not,' replied the midshipman, who was not to be put down; 'but it would be very easy to establish writing communications with the earth.'

'And how?'

'By means of the telescope at Long's Peak. You know that it brings the moon within two leagues of the Rocky Mountains, and that objects having a diameter of nine feet can be seen on the lunar surface. Well, our industrious friends could construct a gigantic alphabet; they could write words 100 fathoms long and sentences a league in length, and they could send us news in this manner.'

The imaginative young midshipman was noisily applauded. Even Lieutenant Bronsfield admitted that the idea was feasible. He added that by sending luminous rays, grouped in bundles by means of parabolic mirrors, direct communication could also be established; in fact these rays would be as visible on the surface of Venus or Mars, as the planet Neptune is on the earth. He ended by remarking, that the brilliant spots observed on the nearer planets, might possibly be signals made to the earth. But he remarked, if by this means we can have news from the lunar world, we could not send news from the terrestrial world, unless the Selenites had instruments at their disposal proper for making distant observations.

'Evidently,' replied one of the officers. 'But what has become of the travellers? What they have done, what they have seen, that is what would be specially interesting. Besides, if the experiment has succeeded, which I do not doubt, it will be tried again. The columbiad is still encased in Floridan soil. It is only a question of a projectile and powder, and each time the moon crosses the zenith we can send her a cargo of visitors.'

'It is evident,' replied Lieutenant Bronsfield, 'that J. T. Maston will one day go to join his friends.'

'If he will take me,' said the young midshipman, 'I am ready to accompany him.'

'Oh, there will be no lack of volunteers,' replied Bronsfield; 'and if they were allowed, one half of the inhabitants of the earth would soon have emigrated to the moon.'

This conversation between the officers of the *Susquehanna* was continued till about 1 a.m. It would be impossible to relate what astounding theories, what extraordinary systems were broached by these bold spirits. Since Barbicane's trial nothing seemed impossible to the Americans. They already proposed to send, not a commission of *savants*, but a whole colony to the Selenite regions, and a whole army, with infantry, artillery, and cavalry, to conquer the lunar world.

At 1 a.m. the hauling in of the sounding-line was not yet completed. Ten thousand feet were still out, which required several hours' work. According to the captain's orders, the fires had been lighted, and steam was getting up. The *Susquehanna* might have started at that very moment.

At this instant – it was 17 minutes past 1 a.m. – Lieutenant Bronsfield was preparing to leave the deck to regain his cabin, when his attention was attracted by a distant and quite unexpected whistling.

His comrades and he thought at first that this whistling was produced by an escape of steam, but, lifting their heads, they could observe that the noise came from the most distant strata of the air.

They had no time for questions; but this whistling attained a frightful intensity, and suddenly, to their dazzled eyes, appeared an enormous meteor, enflamed by the rapidity of its course, and friction on the atmospheric strata.

This fiery mass increased before their eyes, dashed with the noise of thunder against the bowsprit of the corvette, which it smashed to the stem, and plunged into the waves with a deafening noise. A few feet nearer, and the *Susquehanna* had gone down, all hands on board.

At this moment, Captain Blomsberry appeared half dressed, and rushing to the poop where the officers were assembled: 'By your leave, gentlemen, what has happened?'

And the midshipman, acting as spokesman for all, cried: 'Captain, it is "they" come back again!'

CHAPTER TWENTY-ONE

J. T. Maston recalled

The excitement was great on board the *Susquehanna*. Officers and men, forgetting the terrible danger which they had just escaped – the possibility of being crushed and sunk – thought only of the catastrophe which terminated this voyage. So then the most audacious undertaking of ancient or modern times had cost the lives of the hardy adventurers who had attempted it.

'It is "they" come back again,' had said the young midshipman, and all had understood. No one doubted that this meteor was the Gun Club's projectile. As to the fate of the travellers contained therein, opinions differed.

'They are dead,' said one.

'They are alive,' replied another. 'The stratum of water is deep, and the shock has been deadened.'

'But they want air,' continued the first, 'and have died of suffocation.'

'Burnt,' replied another. 'The projectile was but a burning mass rushing through the atmosphere.'

'What matter!' was the unanimous cry; 'alive or dead they must be got out of there.'

Meanwhile, Captain Blomsberry had assembled his officers, and, with their permission, he held a council. It was necessary to take a decision at once. The most important was to fish out the projectile – a difficult but not an impossible operation. But the corvette had not the necessary machinery, which must be at the same time powerful and accurate. It was resolved to steam to the nearest port and inform the Gun Club of the fall of the projectile.

This determination was taken unanimously. The choice of the port had to be discussed. The neighbouring coast gave no anchorage on the 27th degree of latitude. Higher, above the Monterey peninsula, lay the important town which gives it its name. But, situated on the confines of a perfect desert, it was not united with the interior by means of telegraphic lines, and this important news could only be spread with sufficient rapidity by electricity.

A few degrees higher up was the bay of San Francisco. From the capital of the gold country communication would be easy with the centre of the Union. In less than two days the *Susquehanna*, under high pressure, could reach the port of San Francisco. It must therefore start at once.

The fires were lighted, they could start immediately. Two thousand feet of line yet lay in the water. Captain Blomsberry, not wishing to lose precious time by hauling them in, resolved to cut the line.

'We will fasten a buoy to the end,' said he, 'and the buoy will show us where the projectile went down.'

'Besides,' replied Lieutenant Bronsfield, 'we have our exact situation – 27° 7' north latitude and 41° 37' west longitude.'

'Good, Mr Bronsfield,' replied the captain; 'and with your permission, have the line cut.'

A large buoy, strengthened by a couple of spars, was thrown upon the surface of the ocean. The end of the line was firmly attached, and being only subject to the rise and fall of the swell, the buoy would not much shift its place.

At this moment, the engineer informed the captain that steam was up and they could start at once. The captain thanked him for this excellent communication, and gave the course, north-north-east. The corvette, wearing round, steered at high pressure direct for the bay of San Francisco. It was 3 a.m. Two hundred and twenty leagues to travel was little enough for such a fast sailer as the *Susquehanna*. In 36 hours she had covered the distance, and on the 14th December, at 1.27 p.m. she entered the bay of San Francisco.

At the sight of this vessel of the national fleet arriving full steam, with shorn bowsprit and stayed foremast, public curiosity was much excited. A dense crowd filled the quays, awaiting the arrival.

Having cast anchor, Captain Blomsberry and Lieutenant Bronsfield were lowered into an eight-oared boat, which rapidly carried them to the shore.

They jumped upon the quay.

'The telegraph?' asked they, without answering the thousand questions put to them.

The captain of the port himself conducted them to the telegraph office, in the midst of an immense concourse of eager spectators.

Blomsberry and Bronsfield entered the telegraph office whilst the crowd crushed against the doors.

A few minutes later four copies of a telegram were sent to – 1st, the Secretary of the Admiralty at Washington; 2nd, to the Vice-President of the Gun Club, Baltimore; 3rd, to the Hon. J. T. Maston, Long's Peak, Rocky Mountains; 4th, to the Sub-Director of the Cambridge Observatory, Mass. It was worded as follows.

> IN 20° 7' NORTH LATITUDE AND 41° 37' WEST LONGITUDE, ON THE 12TH DECEMBER, AT 1.17 A.M., PROJECTILE OF COLUMBIAD FALLEN IN PACIFIC; SEND INSTRUCTIONS.
>
> BLOMSBERRY, COMMANDER *SUSQUEHANNA*

Five minutes afterwards, all the town of San Francisco had heard the news. Before 6 p.m. the different states of the Union learnt the supreme catastrophe. After midnight, by submarine cable, all Europe knew the result of the great American attempt.

It is useless to try to describe the effect produced over the entire world by this unexpected *dénouement*.

On receipt of the despatch the Secretary to the Admiralty telegraphed to the *Susquehanna* orders to remain in the bay of San Francisco, without extinguishing her fires. Day and night she was to be ready to put to sea.

The Cambridge Observatory held an extraordinary meeting, and with that serenity which distinguishes learned bodies, they calmly discussed the scientific bearings of the question.

At the Gun Club there was an explosion. All the artillerists were assembled. The Vice-President, the Hon. Mr Wilcome, was reading that premature despatch by which J. T. Maston and Belfast announced that the projectile had just been perceived in the gigantic reflector at Long's Peak. This communication also stated that the projectile, retained by lunar attraction, had become a sub-satellite in the solar world.

The truth on this point is known. However, on the arrival of Blomsberry's telegram, which so formally contradicted J. T. Maston's telegram, two parties were formed in the bosom of the Gun Club. On the one hand were those who admitted the fall of the projectile, and consequently the return of the travellers; on the other, those who, confident in the observations at Long's Peak, concluded that there was some mistake on the part of the captain of the *Susquehanna*. For these latter, the pretended projectile was nothing but a meteor, a shooting globe, which in its fall had broken the bowsprit of the corvette. It was difficult to meet their arguments, for the velocity with which it was endowed must have rendered any observation of the moving body very difficult. The commander of the *Susquehanna* and his officers might certainly have been mistaken, in all good faith. One argument, nevertheless, militated in their favour: it was, that if the projectile had fallen upon the earth, its juncture with the terrestrial spheroid could only have occurred on the 27th degree of north latitude, and taking count of the time past, and of the earth's movement of rotation, between the 41st and 42nd degree of west longitude.

However, it was unanimously decided in the Gun Club that Blomsberry's brother, Bilsby, and Major Elphiston, should immediately start for San Francisco, and consult as to the best means of drawing the projectile from the depths of the ocean.

These worthy men set off without loss of time, and the railroad which will soon cross the whole of Central America carried them to St Louis, where rapid mail-coaches awaited them.

Almost at the same instant that the Secretary to the Admiralty, the Vice-President to the Gun Club, and the Sub-Director of the Observatory, received the telegram from San Francisco, the Hon. J. T. Maston experienced the most violent emotion in his whole existence – an emotion which even the bursting of his celebrated cannon had not caused him, and which, for a second time, nearly cost him his life.

It will be remembered that the secretary of the Gun Club had left some moments after the projectile, and almost as quickly as the latter, for his post at Long's Peak in the Rocky Mountains. The learned J. Belfast, director of the Cambridge Observatory, accompanied him. Arrived at the station, the two friends had immediately taken up their position, and had not since left the summit of their enormous telescope. We know that this gigantic instrument had been constructed under conditions as to reflectors called 'front view'. This disposition gave only one reflection to the objects, and consequently rendered the vision clearer. Also, when J. T. Maston and Belfast were observing, they were placed at the upper portion of the instrument and not below. They reached it by a spiral staircase, a masterpiece of lightness, and below them yawned the metal pit, terminated by a metallic mirror, and measuring 280 feet in depth.

Upon this narrow platform, above the telescope, the two *savants* passed their existence, cursing the day which hid the moon from their sight, and the clouds which obstinately veiled her from their view by night.

What was then their joy when, after a few days' waiting, on the night of the 5th December, they perceived the vehicle which carried their friends into space! To this joy succeeded a deep disappointment when, confiding in incomplete observations, they had sent, with their first telegram, through the world that erroneous assertion which made the projectile a satellite of the moon, revolving in an immutable orbit.

Since that instant, the projectile had not been perceived, which disappearance was the more explicable that it was then passing behind the invisible disc of the moon. But when it ought to have reappeared upon the visible disc, judge of the impatience of the impetuous J. T. Maston, and of his companion not less impatient than he. At each minute of the night they thought they could perceive the projectile, and they did not perceive it. Hence, incessant discussions between them and violent disputes; Belfast asserting that the projectile was not visible, and J. T. Maston maintaining that it was staring him in the face.

'It is the projectile,' repeated J. T. Maston.

'No,' replied Belfast; 'it is an avalanche from a lunar mountain.'

'Well, we will see it tomorrow.'

'No, we shall not see it; it is carried into space.'

'We shall.'

'No.'

And in these moments, when interjections fell like hail, the well-known irritability of the secretary of the Gun Club constituted a permanent danger to the Honourable Mr Belfast.

The existence of these two together would soon have become impossible, but an unexpected event cut short these interminable discussions.

During the night of the 14th December the two irreconcilable friends were occupied observing the lunar disc. J. T. Maston was abusing, according to his custom, the learned Belfast, who was getting angry on his side. The secretary of the Gun Club maintained, for the thousandth time, that he had just perceived the projectile, adding even that Michel Ardan's face had been visible through one of the scuttles. He gave further weight to his assertions by a series of gesticulations, which his redoubtable hook rendered very disquieting.

At this moment Belfast's servant appeared on the platform – it was 10 p.m. – and handed him a despatch. It was the telegram of the commander of the *Susquehanna*.

Belfast tore open the envelope, read, and uttered a cry.

'Hallo!' said J. T. Maston.

'The projectile!'

'Well?'

'Has fallen back to the earth.'

A second cry – a roar – this time answered him. He turned towards J. T. Maston. The unfortunate man, imprudently leaning over the metal tube, had disappeared into the immense telescope, a fall of 280 feet!

Belfast, horrified, rushed to the orifice of the reflector.

He breathed. J. T. Maston, caught by his metal hook, was hanging to one of the stays which propped up the telescope. He was howling terribly.

Belfast called out. His assistants improvised a pulley, and, not without difficulty, hauled out the imprudent secretary of the Gun Club. He appeared, unhurt, at the upper orifice.

'By George,' said he, 'if I had broken the mirror!'

'You would have paid for it,' replied Belfast severely.

'And this infernal projectile has fallen?' asked J. T. Maston.

'Into the Pacific.'

'Let us be off.'

A quarter of an hour afterwards, the two *savants* were descending the slopes of the Rocky Mountains, and two days later, at the same time as their friends from the Gun Club, they reached San Francisco, having killed five horses on the road.

Elphiston, Blomsberry's brother, and Bilsby rushed towards them on their arrival.

'What is to be done?' cried they.

'Fish out the projectile,' replied J. T. Maston, 'as soon as possible.'

CHAPTER TWENTY-TWO

Saved

The very spot where the projectile had plunged beneath the waves was known exactly. The instruments to grapple it and bring it to the surface of the ocean were still wanting. They had to be invented, and then manufactured. But American engineers could not be embarrassed by so little. Grappling irons once obtained, and with the aid of steam, they were certain to raise the projectile, notwithstanding its weight; which latter was diminished by the density of the liquid in which it lay.

But it would not suffice to recover the projectile, it was necessary to act properly in the interest of the travellers. Nobody doubted their still being alive.

'Yes,' repeated J. T. Maston unceasingly, and his confidence gained upon the others, 'our friends are clever men, and cannot have fallen like fools. They are alive, thoroughly alive; but we must make haste and get them out. I am not afraid about provisions or water, they have enough for some time; but air! that is what they'll soon be wanting, so let us make haste.'

And they did make haste. They prepared the *Susquehanna* for her new destination. Her powerful machinery was regulated so as to work the hauling chains. The aluminum projectile only weighed 19,250 pounds, which was much less than the weight of the transatlantic cable which was raised under similar conditions. The only difficulty was to haul up the cylindro-conic projectile, the smooth surface of which was difficult to grapple.

For this end Murchison, the engineer, who had hastened to San Francisco, had enormous grappling irons constructed upon an automatic system, which would not let the projectile go if once they seized it in their powerful claws. He also had diving dresses prepared, which, beneath their impervious and resisting cover, enabled divers to reconnoitre the bottom of the sea. He also embarked on board the *Susquehanna* an ingeniously-contrived apparatus of compressed air. These were perfect chambers pierced with scuttles, and which water, introduced into certain compartments, could drag down to great depths. This apparatus was in use at San Francisco, where it had served for the construction of a submarine breakwater. This was fortunate, for the time was wanting to construct one.

However, notwithstanding the perfection of these apparatus, notwithstanding the ingenuity of the men who were going to use them, the success of the operation was certainly not assured. What could be more uncertain than a question of raising a projectile from 20,000 feet below the waters? Then, even if the projectile should be brought to the surface, how would the travellers have borne the terrible shock which 20,000 feet of water had perhaps not sufficiently broken?

However, it was necessary to act as quickly as possible. J. T. Maston pressed on the workmen day and night. He was quite ready either to put on a diver's dress, or to try the air apparatus to reconnoitre the situation of his courageous friends.

Notwithstanding all the diligence used in the manufacture of the different machinery, notwithstanding the considerable sums which were placed at the disposal of the Gun Club by the Government of the Union, five long days – five centuries – had passed before these preparations were completed. During this time, public opinion was excited to the highest degree. Telegrams were incessantly passing over the entire world by the wires and electric cables. The saving of Barbicane, Nicholl, and Michel Ardan was an international matter. All the nations who had subscribed to the Gun Club's loan took a direct interest in the travellers' safety.

At last the hauling chains, the air chambers, the automatic grappling irons were embarked on board the *Susquehanna*. J. T. Maston, Murchison, the engineer, the delegates of the Gun Club, already occupied their cabins. It only remained to start.

On the 21st December, at 8 p.m., the corvette put to sea in

fine weather, and a fresh breeze from the north-east. The whole population of San Francisco crowded the quays, excited but mute, reserving their hurrahs for the return.

The steam was raised to its highest pressure, and the screw of the *Susquehanna* carried them rapidly from the bay.

It would be useless to relate the conversations on board between the officers, men, and passengers. All these men had but one thought. All hearts beat with the same emotion whilst they were rushing to their assistance. What were Barbicane and his companions doing? What had become of them? Were they in a position to attempt some audacious manoeuvre to regain their liberty? None could tell. The truth is that all means would have failed. Submerged about two leagues below the ocean, the metal prison defied all the efforts of the prisoners.

On the 23rd December, at 8 a.m., after a rapid passage, the *Susquehanna* had reached the fatal spot. It was necessary to wait for noon to obtain a correct observation. The buoy to which the line was attached had not yet been discovered.

At noon, Captain Blomsberry, aided by his officers, who checked the observation, took the reckoning in the presence of the members of the Gun Club. There was then an instant of anxiety. Her position determined, the *Susquehanna* was found to be a few points to the west of the very spot where the projectile had plunged beneath the waves.

The course of the corvette was given so as to reach this precise spot.

At 47 minutes past noon the buoy was sighted. It was in good condition, and had not much drifted.

'At last!' cried J. T. Maston.

'Shall we commence?' asked Captain Blomsberry.

'Without losing a second,' replied J. T. Maston.

All precautions were taken to maintain the corvette in almost complete immobility.

Before trying to seize the projectile, Murchison, the engineer, first tried to recognise the position on the bottom of the ocean. The submarine apparatus required for this search received their provision of air. The working of these engines is not without danger, for at 20,000 feet below the surface of the water, and under such considerable pressure, they are exposed to breakages, of which the consequences would be terrible.

J. T. Maston, Blomsberry, Crother, and the engineer, Murchison, without heeding these dangers, took their place in the air-chamber.[54] The captain, stationed on the bridge, superintended the operation, ready to stop or haul in the chains on the slightest signal. The screw had been shipped, and all the force of the machinery brought to bear on the capstan, so that the apparatus would have been rapidly hauled on board.

The descent commenced at 25 minutes past 1 p.m., and the chamber, borne down by the reservoirs full of water, disappeared below the surface of the water.

The emotion of the officers and sailors on board was now shared between the prisoners in the projectile and the prisoners in the submarine apparatus. As to the latter, they forgot their own danger, and, stationed at the windows of the scuttles, they observed attentively the liquid masses through which they passed.

The descent was rapid. At 2.17 p.m. J. T. Maston and his companions had reached the bottom of the Pacific. But they saw nothing but the barren desert which neither marine fauna nor flora animated. By the light of their lamps, provided with powerful reflectors, they could observe the dark layers of water, within an extended radius, but the projectile remained invisible to their eyes.

The impatience of these hardy divers could not be described. Their apparatus being in electric communication with the corvette, they made the agreed signal, and the *Susquehanna*, for the space of a mile, moved their chamber, suspended some yards from the bottom.

They thus explored all the submarine plain, deceived each moment by optical illusions which broke their hearts. Here a rock, there an excrescence, seemed like the sought-for projectile; then they perceived their error and despaired.

'Where are they? Where are they?' cried J. T. Maston. And the poor fellow cried out: 'Nicholl! Barbicane! Michel Ardan!' as if their unfortunate friends could have heard or replied through this impenetrable medium.

The search continued under these conditions up to the moment when the vitiated air in the apparatus obliged them to ascend.

The hauling commenced at 6 p.m., and was only completed at midnight.

'Till tomorrow,' said J. T. Maston, setting foot on the deck of the corvette.

'Yes,' replied Captain Blomsberry; 'in another spot.'

'Yes!'

J. T. Maston did not doubt of success; but already his companions, no longer intoxicated with the animation of the first hours, understood all the difficulties of the undertaking.

What appeared so easy at San Francisco, appeared almost impossible here in the open ocean. The chances of success decreased in a great proportion, and it was to chance alone that they must look to discover the projectile.

The next day, on the 24th December, notwithstanding the fatigues of the preceding day, the operation was recommenced. The corvette moved a few points to the west, and the apparatus, provided with air, carried once more the same explorers to the depths of the ocean.

All the day was passed in fruitless researches. The bed of the sea was a desert. The 25th brought no result; nor yet the 26th.

It was disheartening! They thought of those unfortunate fellows shut up in the projectile for 26 days. Perhaps at this moment they were feeling the first sensations of asphyxia, if even they had escaped the dangers of their fall. The air was being exhausted, and with air, courage and energy.

'Air, perhaps,' replied J. T. Maston invariably; 'but energy never.'

On the 28th, after two more days' searching, all hope was abandoned. The projectile was an atom in the immensity of the sea. They must give up all hope of finding it. However, J. T. Maston would not hear of leaving. He would not quit the spot, without having at least sighted his friends' tomb. But Captain Blomsberry could not remain longer, and notwithstanding the complaints of the worthy secretary, he was forced to give orders to sail.

On the 29th December at 9 a.m., the *Susquehanna*, with her head to the north-east, resumed her course towards the bay of San Francisco.

It was 10 a.m. The corvette was moving off at half-steam, and as if with regret from the place of the catastrophe, when a sailor from the mast-head cried suddenly: 'A buoy on the lee bow!'

The officers looked in the direction indicated, and perceived that the object signalled had in reality the appearance of those buoys which serve to mark the passes of bays or rivers. But, curious detail, a flag floating in the wind surmounted its cone, which rose five or six feet out of the water. This buoy shone in the rays of the sun, as if its sides had been of silver.

Captain Blomsberry, J. T. Maston, the delegates of the Gun Club, were standing on the bridge, and examining this object wandering haphazard on the waves.

All looked with feverish anxiety, but in silence. None dared give utterance to the thought which arose in the minds of all.

The corvette approached within two cable-lengths of the object. A shudder ran through the crew. The flag was the American flag. At this moment a perfect roar was heard. It was worthy J. T. Maston who had fallen in a heap. Forgetting on the one hand that his right arm had been replaced by an iron hook, and that, on the other hand, his brain was only covered by a gutta-percha cap, he had given himself a terrific blow.

They rushed towards him, raised him, and brought him back to life. What were his first words?

'Brutes! idiots! boobies that we are!'

'What is the matter?' was cried from every side.

'What is it?'

'Speak, then.'

'Fools,' roared the terrible secretary, 'the projectile only weighs 19,250 pounds.'

'Well!'

'And displaces 28 tons, otherwise 56,000 pounds, and consequently *it will float*.'

Ah! how the worthy man emphasised this word 'float'. And it was the truth. All, yes, all the *savants* had forgotten this fundamental law; by reason of its specific lightness the projectile, after having been carried in its fall to the lowest depths of the ocean, had naturally returned to the surface, and was floating quietly at the mercy of the waves.

The boats were lowered, J. T. Maston and his friends jumped into them; the excitement attained its highest pitch; all hearts beat rapidly as the boats neared the projectile. What did it

contain? Living men or dead? Living men; yes, living men, unless death had carried off Barbicane and his friends since they hoisted the flag.

A profound silence reigned in the boats; all were breathless; eyes grew dim; one of the scuttles of the projectile was open; a few pieces of glass remained in the frame, showing that it had been broken. This scuttle was about five feet above the waves.

One of the boats came alongside. It was J. T. Maston's. J. T. Maston rushed to the broken glass. At this moment a joyous voice was heard – the voice of Michel Ardan crying with the accents of victory: 'Blank all, Barbicane. Blank all.'

Barbicane, Michel Ardan, and Nicholl, were playing dominoes!

CHAPTER TWENTY-THREE

To conclude

It will be remembered what immense sympathy had accompanied the three travellers at their departure. If at the outset of their undertaking they had excited so much emotion in the old and new worlds, what enthusiasm would greet their return! Would not those millions of spectators who had invaded the Floridan peninsula rush to meet these sublime adventurers? Would the legions of foreigners drawn to American shores from all parts of the globe, leave the territory of the Union without again seeing Barbicane, Nicholl, and Michel Ardan? No! And the ardent passion of the public would worthily meet the grandeur of the undertaking. Human creatures who had left the terrestrial spheroid and returned from this strange journey in celestial regions, could not fail to be received like the prophet Elias, when he shall return to earth. To see them first, and then hear them; such was the general desire.

This desire would be promptly realised by almost all the inhabitants of the Union.

Barbicane, Michel Ardan, Nicholl, and the delegates of the Gun Club returned without delay to Baltimore, where they were received with indescribable enthusiasm. The notes of President Barbicane's journey were ready for publication. The *New York Herald* purchased the manuscript for a price which is not yet known, but cannot fail to have been considerable. In fact, during the publication of *A Journey to the Moon*, the daily sale of the paper amounted to 5,000,000 copies. Three days after the return of the travellers to earth, the minutest details of their expedition were known. It only remained to see the heroes of this superhuman undertaking.

The exploration of Barbicane and his friends round the moon had permitted them to verify certain theories admitted on the subject of the terrestrial satellite. These *savants* had observed *de visu* and in very particular conditions. People now knew what systems to reject and what to admit, as to the formation of this orb, its origin and its inhabitableness. Its past, its present, its future, had given up their last secrets. What could be objected to these conscientious observers, who had sighted at less than forty kilometres that curious mountain Tycho, the strangest system of lunar orology. What could be replied to these *savants* who had plunged their glances into the abyss of Plato's circus? How could these audacious men be contradicted, whom the chances of their undertaking had carried over that invisible face of the disc which no human eye had hitherto seen?

It was now their right to impose limits to that selenographic science which had recomposed the lunar world, as Cuvier did the skeleton of a fossil, and to say: the moon *was* an inhabitable world, and inhabited before the earth; the moon *is* an uninhabitable world and now uninhabited.

To celebrate the return of the most illustrious of its members and of his two companions, the Gun Club thought of giving them a banquet, but a banquet worthy of these conquerors and of the American nation, and under such conditions that all the inhabitants of the Union could share in it. All the termini of the States were united by flying rails. Then in all the stations, decorated with the same flags and ornaments, tables were laid and served alike.

At fixed hours, calculated successively and marked upon electric clocks which beat the seconds at the same instant, the populations were invited to take their seats at the banqueting tables.

During four days, from the fifth to the ninth of January, the trains were suspended, as on Sunday, on all the railways of the Union, and all the lines remained open. One express locomotive, drawing a car of state, had alone the right to travel during these four days over the American railways. The locomotive, manned by a driver and a stoker, bore, by special favour, J. T. Maston, the secretary of the Gun Club.

The car was reserved for President Barbicane, Captain Nicholl, and Michel Ardan.

At the whistle of the engine, after the hurrahs, and shouts, and all the onomatopoeia of admiration contained in the American language, the train left the station of Baltimore. It travelled with a velocity of 80 leagues an hour; but what was that speed compared with the velocity when the three heroes had left the columbiad!

Thus they went from town to town, finding the populations at table along their passage, saluting them with the same acclamations, lavishing the same bravos. Thus they travelled through the east of the Union – Pennsylvania, Connecticut, Massachusetts, Vermont, Maine, and New Brunswick; they passed through the north and west by New York, Ohio, Michigan, and Wisconsin; they passed to the south by Illinois, Missouri, Arkansas, Texas, and Louisiana; they ran to the south-east by Alabama and Florida; they reascended by Georgia and the Carolinas; they visited the centre by Tennessee, Kentucky, Virginia, Indiana; then, after a halt at Washington, they re-entered Baltimore, and during four days they might say that the United States of America, seated at one immense banquet, saluted them simultaneously with the same hurrahs.

The apotheosis was worthy of the three heroes, whom mythology would have ranked amongst demigods.

And now, will this attempt, without precedent in the annals of travel, produce any practical results? Will direct communication with the moon ever be established? Will a service of navigation through space be established to open up the solar world? Will we go from one planet to another – from Jupiter to Mercury; and later on from one star to another – from the Pole Star to Sirius? Will any mode of locomotion allow of visiting these suns which swarm in the firmament?

To these questions no answer can be given; but knowing the audacious ingenuity of the Anglo-Saxon race, no one will be astonished that the Americans should try to make some use of President Barbicane's experiment.

So, some time after the return of the travellers, the public will receive, with marked favour, the prospectus of a company (limited), with a capital of 100,000,000 dollars, divided into 100,000 shares of 1,000 dollars each, under the style of the 'National Company of Interstellary Communication'. President, Barbicane; Vice-President, Captain Nicholl; Secretary, J. T. Maston; Director of Movements, Michel Ardan.

And, as it is in the American character to foresee every eventuality in business, even failure, the Hon. Harry Trollope, Judge Commissary, and Francis Drayton, Liquidator, are appointed beforehand.

THE END

NOTES

1 *American War of Secession* The American Civil War.

2 *Gun Club* Verne's satirical description of the Gun Club and its origins closely reflects the real situation in America at the time of the Civil War.

3 *Barbicane* This name evokes the French word *barbacane* and the English *barbican*, typically a fortified double watch tower over a castle or city entrance.

4 *Thirty-six states* The number of States in the Union when Verne was writing. Barbicane's rhetorical notion of the moon as the next American state anticipates the American vision of space as an extension of the Western frontier, as in *Star Trek*'s 'Space: the final frontier'.

5 *Selenographic maps* Selenography is the description of the moon's surface, typically in maps. Selene is the Greek word for moon.

6 *Poe* Verne has just provided a history of stories of imaginary voyages to the moon, ending with Edgar Allan Poe's 'The Unparalleled Adventure of One Hans Pfaall,' (1835). This story is argued in the Introduction to this volume to be the model for Verne's two moon novels.

7 *Knock-me-down* Verne explains it as 'an appalling drink of the lower classes'.

8 *248,447 miles per second* Verne's scientific sources erroneously thought that electricity travelled through wires at the speed of light, measured at this rate in Verne's time.

9 *United States, ten times as large as France* Verne only counted the area of the legally constituted states of his time in his comparison with France.

10 *Bond and Clark* 'The Cambridge Observatory' is Verne's way of referring to the real Harvard College Obsevatory. Verne's first

names are those of real historical individuals. William Cranch Bond (1789–1859) had been the first director of the Harvard College Observatory – Verne's Cambridge Observatory – and had indeed seen stars within the Andromeda nebula. Alvan Clarke (1804–1887) had indeed discovered that Sirius has a dim companion. Verne then moved on to the fictional Observatory Director, J. M. Belfast, who in this way is made to seem to be a real person as well.

11 *Apogee* and *perigee.* When moon is furthest from the Earth it is in apogee. When it is nearest to the Earth it is in perigee.

12 *Zenith* When the moon is directly overhead.

13 *Satellites of the planets* Many more planetary moons have been found since Verne's time.

14 *The moon's volcanic nature* Verne's historically organised account of what was known about the moon is mostly acceptable today. The main change is that we no longer regard the moon's craters as volcanic.

15 *Selenites* – supposed inhabitants of the moon.

16 *Aluminum* This variant spelling of *aluminium* conintues to be used in America. In Verne's France, aluminium was a newly prepared metallic element, seen as opening up all sorts of exciting possibilities.

17 *Forty miles* The Earth's atmosphere extends upwards for much more than forty miles, ever thinning. Falling meteors begin to glow between 40 and 70 miles up, depending on their initial speed. Even so, Verne's figure is a good approximation for his purposes.

18 *Insignificant resistance of the atmosphere* Barbicane's insistence that because atmospheric resistance will only be slowing the projectile for five seconds it is insignificant is, as Verne knows, a major problem in the whole project. Many shooting stars burn out in the upper atmosphere in less than that time.

19 *Milliard* the term for one thousand million, now known throughout the English-speaking world as a billion.

20 *Gun-cotton* Verne publicised the potential of this material early in its development. Initially dangerous to prepare, it turned out to be of limited use as it exploded too rapidly for use in firearms. (A rapid explosion is just what is needed to fire a projectile as high as

the moon.) A range of products were later developed from gun-cotton, many liable to catch fire or explode prematurely. As nitro-cellulose, it was successfully developed into smokeless powder, but also into the celluloid of billiard balls that exploded when hit hard and into nitrate film stock, famous in the early 20th century for spontaneously catching fire.

21 *The shell would fall back in boiling rain* Nicholl is correct with some of these objections. The last has attracted subsequent discussion. The projectile must push out the air in front of it in the barrel of the cannon as it speeds up to its full 12,000 yards per second. The pressure of the explosion behind and the resistance of the air in front would work against one another to crush and melt it. (Perhaps most of the air in the cannon could be sucked out and the mouth of the cannon made flimsily air-tight until the projectile broke through. Or would the initial explosion itself still be enough to crush the projectile?)

22 *Vomito negro* is yellow fever when identified by the symptoms of its final stages (black vomit).

23 *Tampa, Florida* is not far from Cape Kennedy, from where NASA fired its moon rockets.

24 *Urbi et orbi* This title alludes to the Pope's traditional papal blessing – to the city of Rome and the world. In this chapter, the world gives its blessing to the moon project by contributing to its finance.

25 *300 fathoms above sea level* Nowhere in Florida is so high as 300 fathoms (1800 feet). The highest point is actually Britton Hill, in North-West Florida, at 345 feet.

26 *Electric light* Verne was an early enthusiast for electricity. In 1865, arc lamps were the main form of electric lighting.

27 *Ardan* is thought to be an anagram of Nadar, the pseudonym of Gaspard-Felix Tournachon, now remembered as a pioneering photographer. A friend of Verne, his ballooning enterprises (which included the first aerial photography and the construction of a giant balloon) inspired Verne's *Five Weeks in a Balloon*. Verne's character profile of Ardan reflects his admiration of Nadar.

28 *Lavater or Gratiolet* Johann Caspar Lavater (1741–1801) pioneered physiognomy, the notion that a person's character can be read from their outer appearances, especially the face. Louis Pierre

Gratiolet (1815-1865) was an anatomist and zoologist who looked for a better scientific basis for such ideas. Verne's description of Ardan in this paragraph also draws upon the ideas of phrenology – that the shape of the skull, reflecting the shape of the brain inside it, reveals a person's character. Such ideas were immensely popular in the early and mid-nineteenth century.

29 *Trains of projectiles.* In arguing for the future ease of space travel, Ardan develops the metaphor of the space train. As the dream of the simplicity and frequency of future space travel caught on in later space fiction, the engraving which accompanied this chapter became iconic.

30 *Animalised.* The notion that the carbon present in some meteorites has a living origin was a scientific speculation of Verne's time.

31 *Rockets.* This notion of using rockets turned out to be inspirational for later space science. Here Ardan proposes to use them to slow the projectile's descent onto the moon. They are eventually put to a slightly different use in *Around the Moon.* However, Verne does not seem to have believed that they could ever be powerful enough to do much more.

32 *Experimental animals* It was as well that Barbicane used animals to test the survivability of being fired from a cannon in a hollow projectile, but what would have happened at such a late stage in the project if the animals had been crushed? The experiment looks like Verne's afterthought.

33 *Long's Peak* (Longs Peak) is in what is now Colorado.

34 *Three new telescopic discoveries* None of Verne's three new discoveries has turned out to be straightforwardly true: – proving the volcanic nature of the moon, being able to measure the diameters of some stars, and resolving the Crab Nebula in Taurus (that is, finding that the nebula was made up of stars).

35 *Mappa Selenographica* Beer and Mädler's *Mappa Selenographica* (1834) was large scale and precise moon map and the most influential lunar publication of the 19th century. It is on a scale of 38 inches to the moon's diameter and is crammed with detail.

36 *Mare Frigoris* Sea of Cold. The darker smoother regions of the moon, once thought to be seas (maria), have kept the oceanic reference in their names. They are actually basaltic plains formed long ago.

37 *Water on the moon* The general run of evidence in Verne's day (and ours) was that the moon's surface is dry.

38 *Five millions of spectators* That compares well with the million people who turned up around the Cape Kennedy Space Centre to watch the takeoff for the first moon visit in 1969.

39 *Meteorite* In modern usage, a meteorite is a meteor that has fallen to Earth. In this book it is used as another word for meteor.

40 *Petit's satellite.* In 1846, Frédéric Petit announced that he had found a second moon of Earth, in a very low elliptical orbit. He made further claims about a second moon in 1861, but died in 1865. His claims were not confirmed by other astronomers. Verne adjusted the claim to suit his fictional purposes.

41 *Phasis* Any one of the phases of the moon.

42 *Fiery meteorite* The projectile would indeed get hot in the full sun of outer space, although the aluminium casing would conduct heat from the warm to the shady side. Meteors are seen to be fiery only when they hit the Earth's atmosphere.

43 *Which means – ?* Was Verne trying to teach his readers how to make complex calculations? Probably not. Barbicane and Nicholl explain to Ardan how to apply the formula, but not how to derive it. All that matters for the plot is their conclusion: that to reach the moon, the initial speed of the projectile should have been greater to make allowance for air resistance. It seems such an elementary mistake. Somebody should have been checking. Fortunately, this time there were other compensating mistakes. Modern readers may be reminded that in 1998, the Mars climate orbiter crashed on arrival in Mars because two teams involved in its programming unwittingly failed to reconcile the two systems of units they were using.

44 *Hardly any molecules of air escaped* Well, who was to know otherwise in 1870?

45 *Its weight decreased continually* In free fall, the projectile is weightless. It is, however, slowing as it moves away from the Earth.

46 *No longer under the influence of the laws of gravitation* Verne's account of weightlessness, which he wrongly supposed would only be experienced at the neutral point between the Earth and the moon, is in modern hindsight, a fascinating mixture of insight and error.

47 *Rockets properly placed* In historical hindsight, Verne's account of how rockets are used to slow his projectile has considerable interest.

48 *The different maps relating to the lunar world* Verne's historical survey of lunar maps gives the reader the sense that this is not a purely imaginary journey but a well informed account of what might be seen in a flight around the moon. It is also clear that Verne based this part of the voyage on his own close study of the maps.

49 *The bottom of the projectile was turned towards the surface of the moon* Verne's notion that the projectile keeps its heaviest part pointing down towards the local source of gravity structures his narrative and enables him to avoid such problems as how the crew would cope if their projectile was tumbling.

50 *A volcano* Verne expected that there would be volcanoes on the moon, building dramatic events around them where he could.

51 *Earth uninhabitable* Barbicane tells us that when the Earth's crust has cooled, our planet will, like the moon, become uninhabitable. The time table he offers for this apparently alarming end state has lengthened since the discovery of radioactivity.

52 *Rockets* The rockets are finally used. The modest effects they produce helps us understand why Verne didn't appreciate their potential for space travel.

53 *57,600 leagues an hour* This figure, about 40 miles per second, appears to be exaggerated or miscalculated. It makes the projectile's eventual survival all the more amazing.

54 *Air-chamber* The device the rescuers use to search for the lumar projectile is capable of diving 21,000 feet, carrying its own air supply and is in electrical communication with the surface. Verne was doubtless thinking about deep sea diving, as he was working up his next book, *Twenty Thousand Leagues Under the Sea* (1870) The air-chamber is said to have inspired the bathysphere, first used in 1934 by William Beebe and Otis Barton.